THE ENEMIES OF WOMEN

THE ENEMIES OF WOMEN

VICENTE BLASCO IBÁÑEZ

TRANSLATED FROM THE SPANISH

BY IRVING BROWN

AN IBÁÑEZ BOOK

AN IBÁÑEZ BOOK

Published by Wildside Press, LLC
www.wildsidebooks.com

INTRODUCTION

Vicente Blasco Ibáñez (29 January 1867 – 28 January 1928) was a Spanish realist novelist writing in Spanish, a screenwriter, and occasional film director.

Born in Valencia, today he is best known in the English-speaking world for his World War I novel *Los cuatro jinetes del apocalipsis.* Filmed in 1921 as *The Four Horsemen of the Apocalypse*, it was filmed again in 1962, reset in World War II. However, in his time he was a best-selling author inside and outside of Spain, and also known for his controversial political activities. While *Sangre y arena* (*Blood and Sand*) and *Los cuatro jinetes del apocalipsis* are his most popular novels, particularly outside of Spain, his Valencian novels such as *La barraca* and *Cañas y barro* are the ones most valued by scholars.

He finished studying law, but hardly practiced. He divided his time between politics, literature, and dalliances with women, of whom he was a deep admirer. He wrote with uncanny speed and energy. He was a fan of Miguel de Cervantes.

His life, it can be said, tells a more interesting story than his novels. He was a militant Republican partisan in his youth and founded a newspaper, *El Pueblo* (translated as either *The Town* or *The People*) in his hometown. The newspaper aroused so much controversy that it was brought to court many times and censored. He made many enemies and was shot and almost killed in one dispute. The bullet was caught in the clasp of his belt. He had several stormy love affairs.

He volunteered as the proofreader for the novel *Noli Me Tangere*, in which the Filipino patriot José Rizal expressed his contempt of the Spanish colonization of the Philippines. He travelled to Argentina in 1909 where two new cities, Nueva Valencia and Cervantes, were created. He gave conferences on historical events and Spanish literature. Tired and disgusted with government failures and inaction, Vicente Blasco Ibáñez moved to Paris at the beginning of World War I. (He was a supporter of the Allies in World War I.)

He died in Menton, France in 1928, the day before his 61st birthday, in the residence of Fontana Rosa (also named the House of Writers, dedicated to Miguel de Cervantes, Charles Dickens and William Shakespeare) that he built.

CHAPTER I

THE Prince repeated his statement:

"Man's greatest wisdom consists in getting along without women."

He intended to go on but was interrupted. There was a slight stir of the heavy window curtains. Through their parting was seen below, as in a frame, the intense azure of the Mediterranean. A dull roar reached the dining-room. It seemed to come from the side of the house facing the Alps. It was a faint vibration, deadened by the walls, the curtains, and the carpets, distant, like the working of some underground monster; but there rose above the sound of revolving steel and the puffing of steam a clamor of human beings, a sudden burst of shouts and whistling.

"A train full of soldiers!" exclaimed Don Marcos Toledo, leaving his chair.

"The Colonel is at it again, always the hero, always enthusiastic about everything that has to do with his profession," said Atilio Castro, with a smile of amusement.

In spite of his years, the man whom they called the Colonel sprang to the nearest window. Above the foliage of the sloping garden, he could see a small section of the Corniche railroad, swallowed up in the smoky entrance of a tunnel, and reappearing farther on, beyond the hill, among the groves and rose colored villas of Cap-Martin. Under the mid-day sun the rails quivered like rills of molten steel. Although the train had not yet reached this side of the tunnel, the whole country-side was filled with the ever-increasing roar. The windows, terraces, and gardens of the villas were dotted black with people who were leaving their luncheon tables to see the train pass. From the mountain slope to the seashore, from walls and buildings on both sides of the track, flags of all colors began to wave.

Don Marcos ran to the opposite window overlooking the city. All he could see was an expanse of roofs with no trace of Nature's touch save here and there the feathery green of the gardens against the red of the tiles. It was like a stage setting broken into a succession of wings: in the foreground, amid trees, isolated villas with green balustrades and flower-strewn walls; next, the mass of Monte Carlo, its huge hotels bristling with pointed turrets and cupolas; and hazy in the background, as though floating in golden dust, the rocky cliffs of Monaco, with its promenades; the enormous pile of the Oceanographic Museum; the New Cathedral, a glaring white; and the square crested tower of the palace of the Prince. Buildings stretched from the edge of the sea halfway up the mountains. It was a country without fields, with no open land, covered completely with houses, from one frontier to the other.

But Don Marcos had known the view for years, and at once detected the unfamiliar detail. A long, interminable train was moving slowly along the hillside. He counted aloud more than forty cars, without coming to the rear coaches still hidden in a hollow.

"It must be a battalion ... a whole battalion on a war footing. More than a thousand soldiers," he said in an authoritative manner, pleased at showing off his keen professional judgment before his fellow guests, who, for that matter, were not listening.

The train was filled with men, tiny yellowish gray figures, that gathered at the car windows, doors, and on the running-boards with their feet hanging over the track. Others were crowded in cattle pens or stood on the open flat-cars, among the tanks and crated machine guns. A great many had climbed to the roofs and were greeting the crowds with arms and legs extended in the shape of a letter X. Almost all of them had their shirt sleeves rolled up to the elbows, like sailors preparing to maneuver.

"They are English!" exclaimed Don Marcos. "English soldiers on their way to Italy!"

But this information seemed to irritate the Prince, who always spoke to him in familiar language, in spite of the difference in their ages. "Don't be absurd, Colonel. Anybody would know that. They are the only ones who whistle."

The men still seated at the table nodded. Military trains passed every day, and from a distance it was possible to guess the nationality of the passengers. "The French," said Castro, "go past silently. They have had a little over three years of fighting on their own soil. They are as silent and gloomy as their duty is monotonous and endless. The Italians coming from the French front sing, and decorate their trains with green branches. The English shout like a lot of boys, just out of school, and in their enthusiasm, whistle all the time. They are the real children in this war; they go with a sort of boyish glee to their death."

The whistling sound drew nearer, shrill as the howling of a witches' Sabbath. It passed between the mountains and the gardens of Villa Sirena; and then went on in the other direction, toward Italy, gradually growing fainter as it disappeared in the tunnel. Toledo, who was the only one in the room to watch the train pass, noticed how the houses, gardens, and *potagers* on both sides of the track were alive with people, waving handkerchiefs and flags in reply to the whistling of the English. Even along the seashore the fishermen stood up on the seats of their boats and waved their caps at a distant train. The quick ear of Don Marcos distinguished a sound of footsteps on the floor above. The servants doubtless were opening the windows to join with silent enthusiasm in that farewell.

When only a few coaches were still visible at the mouth of the tunnel, the Colonel came back to his place at the table.

"More meat for the slaughter house!" exclaimed Atilio Castro, looking at the Prince. "The racket is over. Go on, Michael."

Under Toledo's watchful eye, two beardless Italian boys, unprepossessing in appearance, were serving the dessert at the luncheon.

The Colonel kept glancing over the table and at the faces of his three guests, as though he were afraid of suddenly noticing something that would show the lunch had been hastily arranged. It was the first that had been given at Villa Sirena for two years.

The master of the house, Prince Michael Fedor Lubimoff, who sat at the head of the table, had arrived from Paris the evening before.

The Prince was a man still in his youth, fresh with the well controlled vigor that is furnished by a life of physical exercise. He was tall, robust, and supple, of dark complexion, with large gray eyes, and a massive face, clean shaven. The scattered gray hairs at his temples seemed even more numerous in contrast with the blue-black of the rest. A number of premature wrinkles around the eyes, and two deep furrows running from his wide nostrils to the corners of his mouth, were the first indication of weariness in a powerful organism that seemed to have lived too intensely, in the mistaken confidence that its reserve of strength was endless.

The Colonel called him "Your Highness," as if Michael Fedor were a member of a ruling house, instead of a mere Russian prince. But this was when some one was present. It was a habit Don Marcos had adopted in the days of the late Princess Lubimoff, to maintain the prestige of the son, whom he had known since the latter was a child. In their intimate relations, when they were alone, he preferred to call him "Marquis," Marquis de Villablanca, and the Prince was never successful in disturbing, by his witticisms on the subject, the precedence thus established by Don Marcos in his terms of respect. The title of Russian Prince was for those who are dazzled by the lofty sound of titles, without being able to appreciate their respective merits, and origins; as for himself, the Colonel preferred something nobler, the title of Spanish Marquis, in spite of the fact that that title for Lubimoff was quite unknown in Spain, and lacked official recognition.

Toledo was well acquainted with Prince Michael's three guests.

Atilio Castro was a fellow countryman, a Spaniard who had spent the greater part of his life outside his own country. He affected great intimacy with the Prince and, on the grounds of a distant blood relationship between them, even spoke to him with some familiarity. Don Marcos had a vague idea that the young Spaniard had been a consul somewhere for a short time. Atilio was continually poking fun at him without his being always immediately aware of it. But the Colonel, seeing that it pleased "His Highness" greatly, felt no ill-will on that account.

"A fine fellow, good hearted!" the Colonel often said, in speaking of Castro. "He hasn't led a model life, he's a terrible gambler—but a gentleman. Yes, sir, a real gentleman!"

Michael Fedor defined his relative in other terms.

"He has all the vices, and no defects."

Don Marcos could never quite understand what that meant, but nevertheless it increased his esteem for Castro.

The Prince was only two or three years older than Atilio, and yet their ages seemed much farther apart. Castro was over thirty-five, and some people thought him twenty-four. His face had an ingenuous, rather child-like expression, and it acquired a certain character of manliness, thanks solely to a dark red mustache, closely cropped. This tiny mustache, and his glossy hair parted squarely in the middle, were the most prominent details of his features, except when he became excited. If his humor changed—which happened very rarely—the luster in his eyes, the contraction of his mouth, and the premature wrinkles in his forehead gave him an almost ominous expression, and suddenly he seemed to age by ten years.

"A bad man to have for an enemy!" affirmed the Colonel. "It wouldn't do to get in his way."

And not out of fear, but rather out of sincere admiration did the Colonel speak admiringly of Castro's talents. He wrote poetry, painted in water color, improvised songs at the piano, gave advice in matters of furniture and clothes, and was well versed in antiquities, and matters of taste. Don Marcos knew no limits to that intelligence.

"He knows everything," he would say. "If he would only stick to one thing! If he would only work!"

Castro was always elegantly dressed, and lived in expensive hotels; but he had no regular income so far as was known. The Colonel suspected a series of friendly little loans from the Prince. But the latter had remained away from Monte Carlo almost since the beginning of the war, and Don Marcos used to meet Castro every winter living at the Hôtel de Paris, playing at the Casino, and associating with people of wealth. From time to time, on encountering the Colonel in the gaming rooms, Castro had asked him for a loan of "ten louis," an absolute necessity for a gambler who had just lost his last stake and was anxious to recoup. But with more or less delay he had always returned the money. There was something mysterious about his life, according to Don Marcos.

The two other guests seemed to him to live much less complex lives. The one who had frequented the house for the longest period, was a dark young man, with a skin that was almost copper colored, a slight build, and long, straight hair. He was Teofilo Spadoni, a famous pianist. Spadoni's parents were Italian—this much was sure. No one could quite make out where he had been born. At times he mentioned his birthplace as Cairo, at other times, as Athens, or Constantinople, all the places where his father, a poor Neapolitan tailor, had lived. No one was astonished by such vagaries and absent-minded discrepancies on the part of the extraordinary virtuoso, who, the moment he left the piano, seemed to move in a world of dreams and to be quite incapable of adapting himself to any regular mode of life. After giving concerts in the large capitals of Europe and South America, he had settled down at Monte Carlo, explaining his residence there by the war, while Don Marcos imputed it to his love of gambling. The Prince knew him through having engaged him as a member of the orchestra on board his large yacht, the Gaviota II, for a voyage around the world.

Sitting beside the host was the last guest, the latest to frequent the house, a pale young man, tall, thin, and nearsighted, who was always looking timidly around as though ill at ease. He was a professor from Spain, a Doctor of Science, Carlos Novoa, who received a subsidy from the Spanish government to make certain studies in ocean fauna at the Oceanographic Museum. The Colonel who had spent many years at Monte Carlo without running across any of his compatriots, other than those whom he saw around the roulette tables, had expressed a certain patriotic pride in meeting this professor two months previously.

"A man of learning! A famous scientist!" he exclaimed in speaking of his new friend. "They can say all they want now about us Spaniards being ignoramuses."

He had only the vaguest notion of the nature of his fellow countryman's learning. What is more: from his earliest conversations he had guessed that the professor's ideas were directly opposed to his own. "One of those heretics with no other God than matter," he said to himself. But he added by way of consolation: "All those learned men are like that: liberals and free-thinkers. What of it...." As for the professor's fame, in the opinion of Don Marcos it was unquestionable. Otherwise why would they have sent him to the Oceanographic Museum, large and white as a temple, whose halls he had visited only once, with a feeling of awe that had prevented him from ever going back again.

On the occasional evenings when the professor would go to Monte Carlo and chance to meet Don Marcos, the latter would present him to his friends as a national celebrity. In this fashion Novoa had made the acquaintance of Castro and Spadoni, who never asked him more than how his luck was going.

When the coming of the Prince was announced, Toledo insisted that his illustrious friend the Professor should accompany him to the station in order to lose no time in introducing him to "His Highness."

"One of our country's prides.... Your Highness is so fond of everything Spanish."

Michael Fedor had spent a considerable portion of his life on the sea, and felt a certain sympathy for the modest young man, on learning of the studies in which he specialized.

They talked for a long time about oceanography, and the following day Prince Michael, who was in the habit of entertaining elaborately at his table the most divergent kinds of guests, said to his "chamberlain":

"Your scholar is a very fine fellow. Invite him to luncheon."

The guests all spoke Spanish. Spadoni was able to follow the conversation, with the little he had picked up while giving piano recitals in Buenos Ayres, Santiago, and other South American capitals. He had been there with an impresario, who finally got tired of backing him, and struggling with his childish irresponsibility.

As they were sitting down at the table, the Colonel noticed that the Prince seemed preoccupied with some absorbing meditation. He made a point of talking with Professor Novoa, expressing his surprise at the slight compensation the scientist received for his studies.

Castro and Spadoni gave their whole attention to their food. The days of the famous chef, to whom Prince Michael gave a salary worthy of a Prime Minister, were over. The "master" had been mobilized and at that moment was cooking for a general on the French front. However, Toledo had managed to discover a woman of some fifty years, whose combinations were less varied, perhaps, than those of the artist whom the war had snatched away, but more "classical," more solid and substantial—and the two men ate with the delight of people who, forever obliged to eat in restaurants and hotels, at last find themselves at a table where no economy or falsifications are practised.

About dessert time the conversation, becoming general, turned, as always happens when men are dining alone, to the subject of women. Toledo had a feeling that the Prince had gently steered the guests' talk in this direction. Suddenly Michael summed up his whole argument by declaring a second time:

"Man's greatest wisdom consists in getting along without women."

And then had followed the long interruption as the train of English soldiers, in a whirl of shouts, whistling and hissing, had gone by.

Atilio Castro waited until the last car had disappeared in the tunnel, and said with a subtle and somewhat ironical smile:

"The shouting and whistling sound like a mixture of applause and scorn for your profound remark. However, please don't bother with such inexpert opinion. What you said interests me. You abominate women, you who have had thousands of them!... Go on, Michael!"

But the Prince changed the conversation. He spoke of his impressions on returning to Villa Sirena after a long absence. Nothing remained to recall the former days, before the war, save the building and the gardens. All the men servants were mobilized: some in the

French army, others in the Italian. The day after his arrival he had asked, as a matter of course, for an auto to go to Monte Carlo. There was no lack of machines. Three, of the best make, were lying as though forgotten, in the garage. But the chauffeurs too were at the front; and moreover there was no gasoline; and a permit was necessary to use the roads.... In short, he had been obliged to stand at the iron gate of the garden and wait for the Manton electric. It was a novelty for him, an interesting means of locomotion. It seemed as if he had suddenly been transported into a world he had forgotten, as he found himself among the common people on the car. The general curiosity annoyed him. Everyone was whispering his name: and even the conductor showed a certain emotion on seeing the owner of Villa Sirena among his passengers.

"And the worst of it all, my friends, is that I'm ruined!"

Spadoni stared with wide opened eyes as though hearing something extraordinary and absurd. Castro smiled incredulously.

"You ruined?... I'd be satisfied with a tenth of the remains."

The Prince nodded. He reminded one of those great transatlantic liners which, when they are wrecked, make the fortune of a whole population of poverty stricken people along the shore. Wealth was of course a relative thing. He might still have more than many people; but ruin it was for him, nevertheless.

"In view of what I am going to say later, I must not conceal from you the situation I am in. A few weeks ago I sold my Paris residence which my mother built. It was bought by a 'newly rich.' With this war, I'm going to become a 'newly poor.' You know, Atilio, how things have gone with me, since this row among the nations started. From the time they fired the first cannon they sent me from Russia only an eighth of what I received in times of peace; later much less. The revolution came and cut down my income still more. And, now under Comrade Lenin and the red flag, there is nothing coming through at all, absolutely nothing. I have no idea whatsoever of the fate of my houses, my fields, my mines ... I don't know even what has become of those who were looking after my fortune there. They have probably all been killed."

The Colonel raised his eyes to the ceiling: "The revolution!... What they need is a master."

"But a rich man like you with reserve funds in the bank all the time, can always find some one to make him a loan until times are better."

"Perhaps; but it means practically poverty for me. My administrator told me when I was leaving Paris, that I ought to limit my expenses, live according to my present income. How much have I?... I don't know. He doesn't even know himself. He is balancing my accounts, collecting from some people and paying others—I had a lot of debts, it seems. Millionaires are never asked to pay their bills promptly.... In short, I shall have to live, like a ruined prince, on some sixty thousand dollars a year; perhaps more, perhaps less. I really don't know."

Castro and Spadoni seemed to be stirred with longing at the mention of such a sum. Novoa looked with an air of respect at this man who called himself his friend and thought himself poor with sixty thousand dollars a year.

"My administrator spoke to me of selling Villa Sirena as well as the Paris residence. It seems that the newly rich would like to get everything I have. A complete liquidation.... But I wouldn't listen to it. This is my own little nook; I made it what it is myself. Besides, life is impossible out in the world. The war has filled it with bitterness. Living in Paris is very gloomy. There is no one there. The streets are dark. The 'Gothas' make the people of our class worried and nervous. It is much better to leave. I thought I would settle down here and wait till this world madness is over."

"It is going to be a long wait," remarked Castro.

"I'm afraid so. However, this is an agreeable spot, a pleasant refuge, all the more delightful because of the selfish feeling that at this very moment millions of men are suffering every sort of hardship, and thousands are dying every day.... But after all, it isn't the same as it used to be. Even the Mediterranean is different. The minute the sun goes down, my good Colonel has to mask with black curtains the windows and doors looking out on the sea, so that the German submarines cannot guide themselves by our lights.... Dear me! Where are those wonderful days we spent here in time of peace, the festivals we used to have, those nights on the Gaviotta II when she anchored in the harbor of Monaco?"

A far away look came into Castro's eyes, as though he were in a dream. In his imaginings he saw the gardens of Villa Sirena, softly lighted, wrapped in a milky haze that settled on the invisible waves like rays of reflected moonlight.

The window curtains were crimson, and from them, drifting through the warm darkness of the night, came the sound of laughter, cries, the sighing of violins, amorous love songs, that told of women's throats, white and voluptuous, swelling with desire and the rapture of the music. The stars, specks of light lost in the infinite, twinkled in answer to the electric stars, hidden in the dark foliage. Walking slowly, couples arm in arm disappeared amid the deep shadows of the garden. All the women of the day had turned up there sooner or later: famous actresses from Paris, London, and Vienna; beauties of the smart cliques of two hemispheres, women of high society, smiling the smile of slaves before the potentate who could banish their debts with the stroke of a pen. Oh, the Pompeian nights of Villa Sirena!...

Spadoni saw, rather, the Gaviotta II, a palace with propellers, which, when anchored in the small harbor of La Condamine, seemed to fill it completely and to make the yachts of the American millionaires and the Prince of Monaco look like tiny things indeed. It was an alcazar, a palace of the Arabian Nights, topped off with two smoke stacks, and parading over every sea of the planet, its private parlors adorned with fountains and statues, its enormous library, its ball room with a raised platform, from which fifty musicians, many of them celebrated, gave concerts for a single visible auditor, Prince Michael, who half reclined on a divan, while the tropical breeze came through the high windows, caressing the heads of the officers and chief functionaries of the steamer crowding about the openings. The pianist could see once more the lonely harbors of dead historic countries, with flights of seagulls wheeling against the quiet azure vault; the mighty bays, filled with the smoke and bustle of North America; the coasts of the Antilles with groves of cocoanut palms, black at sunset against the reddish sky; the islands of the Pacific, of hard coral, forming a ring about an inner lake.... And that omnipotent magician confessed the loss of his wealth!...

The Prince, as though he guessed their thoughts, added:

"It's the end of all that: I don't know whether forever or for many years.... And even if things should be the same some day as they were before the war, what a long time we shall have to wait!... I may die before then.... That is why I am going to make a proposal to you."

He paused a moment, to enjoy the curiosity he read in the eyes of his auditors.

Then he asked Castro:

"Are you satisfied with your present life?"

In spite of Castro's good natured, smiling placidity, he started in surprise as if indignant at such a question. His life was unbearable. The war had upset his habits and pleasures, scattering his friendships to the four winds. He did not know the fate of hundreds of persons of various nationalities, who had filled his life before the war, and without whom he would then have thought it impossible to live.

"Besides, I have less money than ever. I am staying at Monte Carlo just for the gambling; and even if I always lose in the end, like everyone else, I always keep a tight grip on a little something to live on!... But what a life!"

He glanced at Novoa as though the recency of his acquaintance inspired a certain suspicion, but immediately he went on, with an air of assurance:

"There is no reason why I should not speak quite plainly. A little while ago the Professor told us how much he earned: some hundred dollars a month; less than any employee at the Casino. I am going to be as frank as he. I live in the Hôtel de Paris: Atilio Castro cannot afford to live anywhere else; he must keep up his connections. But there are many weeks when I have the greatest difficulty in paying for my room, and I eat in cheap restaurants and Italian wine shops, when no one invites me out to dine. I pay three or four times as much for my bed as I do for my board. Evenings when luck is against me, and I lose everything to the last chip, I get along with a ham sandwich at the Casino bar. I belong to the same school as the Madrid gambler we nicknamed the 'Master,' and who used to say to us: 'Boys, money was made for gambling; and what's left, for eating.'"

"And in spite of that, you like good food," said the Prince.

Castro's laments took on a comical seriousness. With the war the good old customs had been forgotten. No one kept house; everyone lived in hotels, and the proprietors of the luxurious palaces took the scarcity of food as a pretext to serve the sort of meals one gets in third rate restaurants, scanty and poor. An invitation merely gave one a chance to fool one's hunger.

"It has been months, maybe years, since I've eaten as I have to-day, and I've sat at the tables of all the big hotels on the Riviera.

I had ceased to believe that such chicken as you have just served existed in the world any longer. I imagined they were dream birds, mythological fowl."

The Colonel smiled, bowing as if that were a tribute to him.

"And you, Spadoni?" the Prince went on inquiringly. "How are you enjoying life?"

"Your Highness—I—I," stammered the musician, at the sudden question.

Castro intervened, coming to his rescue.

"Our friend Spadoni can always get a free meal at the villas of a number of invalid ladies, who live at Cap-Martin and who are mad about music. Besides some English people at Nice often invite him. He doesn't need to bother about paying hotel bills either. He has at his disposal a whole big villa, large and well-furnished: it goes with his job, as watchman over a corpse."

Novoa started with surprise at the news.

"Don't be astonished," continued Atilio. "He has the benefit of a magnificent house in exchange for looking after a tomb."

"Oh, Professor!... Don't mind him," groaned the musician with the air of a martyr.

"But with all these advantages," Castro went on saying, "there is one terrible drawback: he is a worse gambler than I. He has a nickname in the Casino 'the number five gentleman.' He never plays any other number. Anything he can get hold of he puts on five, and loses it. I am the 'number seventeen gentleman' and it turns out as badly with me as with him.... Besides, he has his English friends. Queer ducks! They come from Nice every day in a two horse landau, and just as if they didn't get enough gambling with the Casino, they set up a green table on their knees and take out a deck of cards. They play poker with the Corniche landscape, that people come from all over the world to see, right before their eyes. And our artist, when he takes a fourth hand with the two Englishmen and an old maid, there within the sight of the Mediterranean, golden in the setting sun, loses everything he took in at some concert at Cannes or Monte Carlo."

Spadoni started to say something, but stopped, seeing that the Prince turned to Novoa:

"I shan't ask you," said the Prince; "I know your situation. You live in the old part of Monaco, in the house of an employee of the

Museum; and his lodgings can't be much. Besides, as Atilio was saying, you receive much less than a croupier at the Casino."

And looking at his guests he added:

"What I want to propose to you is that you live with me. The invitation is a selfish one on my part; I'm not denying that. I intend to stay here until the world quiets down, and life is pleasant once more. If my Colonel and I were here alone we would end by hating each other. You will keep me company in my retreat."

All three remained dumbfounded at such an unexpected proposal. Novoa was the first to regain the use of his tongue.

"Prince, you scarcely know me. We saw each other for the first time three days ago.... I don't know whether I ought...."

The Prince interrupted him with the sharp tone and imperious manner of a man who is not accustomed to considering objections.

"We have known each other for many years; we have known each other all our lives." Then he added soothingly:

"It isn't much that I'm offering you. Servants are scarce. There are no men except my old valet and those two Italian monkeys that the Colonel managed to recruit somewhere. The rest of the service is done by women.... But even so, our life will be pleasant. We shall isolate ourselves from a world gone crazy. We will not mention this war. We shall lead a comfortable existence, as the monks did in the monasteries of the Middle Ages, which were refreshing oases of tranquillity in the midst of violence and massacres. We shall eat well; the Colonel guarantees me that. The Library from the yacht is here. When I sold the boat, I had Don Marcos install all my books on the top floor. Our friend Novoa will find some volumes there which perhaps he does not know. Everyone will do what he pleases; free monks all of us, with no other obligation than to repair to the refectory at the proper hour. And if the 'number five gentleman' and the 'number seventeen gentleman' want to drop in at the Casino, they can do so, and someone will see to it that their pockets are kept filled. We must give something to vice, what the devil! Without vices, life wouldn't be worth living."

A silent approbation greeted these words of the master of Villa Sirena.

"The one thing I insist on," continued the Prince after a long pause, "is that we live alone, as men among men. No women! Women must be excluded from our life in common."

The pianist opened his eyes in astonishment; Castro stirred in his chair; Novoa removed his glasses with a mechanical gesture of surprise, immediately adjusting them once more to his nose.

There was another silence.

"What you propose," said Atilio, at last, with a smile, "reminds me of a comedy of Shakespeare. No women! And the hero in the end gets married."

"I know that play," replied the Prince, "but I am not in the habit of governing my life according to comedies, and I don't believe in their teachings. You can rest assured that I shan't marry, even if it gives the lie to Shakespeare and the French king from whose chronicle he got the material for his work."

"But what you're attempting is absurd," Castro went on: "I don't know what the rest think, but prevent me from...!"

With a gesture he ended his protest.

Then seeing that the Prince had remained thoughtful, he added:

"It is quite evident that you have had your fill!... You have gotten all you wanted, and now you want to force on us...."

The Prince, although absorbed in his own train of thought, he had not heard him, interrupted.

"Seeing that you can't get along without it.... All right! I have no fixed intention of making a martyr of you. Go on being a slave to a necessity that is a result more of the imagination than of desire. Now that I really know life, I am astonished that men do so many foolish things for the sake of a passing pleasure. While you are here you may satisfy your whims whenever you like ... but no women."

The three listeners looked at one another in astonishment; and even the Colonel, who never betrayed his feeling when his "lord" was speaking, showed a certain surprise on his countenance. What did the Prince mean?

"You are not ignorant, Atilio, of what a woman is. In the great majority of peoples on this earth there are only females. There are young females and old females; but there are no 'women.' Woman, as we understand the word, is the artificial product of civilizations which, somewhat like hot-house flowers, have reached their maturity with a complex perverse beauty. Only in the large cities that have come to be decadent because they have reached their limits, do you find 'women.' Not being mothers like the poor females, they give up all their time to love, prolong their youth marvelously, and scheme to inspire passions at an age when the others live like grandmothers. There you have the creatures that, personally, I am afraid of! If they come in here, it's the end of our society, our tranquil, even life."

The Prince arose from the table, and they all followed suit. Lunch being over they all passed into the great hall adjoining, where coffee was served. The Colonel looked about anxiously, examining the boxes of Havanas, and the large liquor chest with its varied cut glass and colored flasks, placed in a row.

While cutting the tip of his cigar, the Prince continued, speaking all the while to Castro:

"When you want ... anything like that, all you need do is to choose in the vicinity of the Casino. A hundred or two francs; and then, good-by!... But the other ones! The women! They work their way into our lives, and finally dominate us, and want to mold our ways to suit their own. Their love for us after all is merely vanity, like that of the conqueror who loves the land that he has conquered with violence. They have all read books—nearly always stupidly and without understanding, to be sure, but they have read books—and such reading leaves them determined to satisfy all sorts of vague desires, and absurd whims, that succeed only in making slaves of us, and in moving us to act on impulses we have acquired in our own early romantic readings.... I know them. I have met too many of them in my life. If women from our social sphere mingle with us here, it means an end to peace. They will seek me out through curiosity on remembering my past life, or greed in thinking of my wealth; as for you men, they will come between you, making you jealous of one another and the life that I desire here will be impossible.... Besides, we are poor."

Atilio protested, smilingly: "Oh! poor!"

"Poor when it comes to the follies of the old days," continued the Prince, "and for love one needs money. All that talk about love being a disinterested thing was made up by poor people, who are satis-fied with imitations. There is a glitter of gold at the bottom of every passion. At first we don't think of such things; desire blinds us. All we see is the immediate domination of the person so sweetly our adversary. But love invariably ends by giving or taking money."

"Take money from a woman!... Never!" said Castro, losing his ironic smile.

"You will end by taking it, if you are poor, and frequent the society of women. Those of our times think of nothing but money. When their love is a rich man, they ask him for it, even if they have a large fortune of their own. They feel less worthy if they don't ask. When they are fond of a poor man, they force him to receive gifts from them. They dominate him better by degrading him. Besides, in doing so they feel the selfish satisfaction of the person who gives alms. Woman, having always been forced to beg from man, has the greatest sensation of pride, and thinks she in turn can give money to some one of the sex that has always supported her."

Novoa, cup in hand, listened attentively to the Prince. Lubimoff was speaking of a world quite unknown to him. Spadoni, as he sipped his coffee, with a vague look in his eyes, was thinking of something far away.

"Now you know the worst, Atilio," the Prince went on. "No women!... That way we will lead a great life. All the morning, free! We shan't see one another until lunch time. Down below is the cove, there are still a number of boats. We can fish, while it's sunny; we can go rowing. In the afternoon you will go to the Casino; occasionally I shall go, too, to hear some concert. Spring is drawing near. At night, sitting on the terrace, watching the stars, our friend Novoa, the man of learning of our monastery, will expound the music of the spheres; and Spadoni, our musician, will sit down at the piano, and delight us with terrestrial music."

"Splendid!" exclaimed Castro. "You are almost a poet in describing our future life, and you have persuaded me. We are going to be happy. But don't forget your permission for the 'female,' and your prohibition of 'women.' No skirts in Villa Sirena! Nothing but men; monks in trousers, selfish and tolerant, coming together to live a pleasant life, while the world is aflame."

Atilio remained thoughtful a few moments, and continued:

"We need a name; our community must have a title. We shall call ourselves 'the enemies of women'."

The Prince smiled.

"The name mustn't go any farther than ourselves. If people outside learned of it, they might think it meant something else."

Novoa, feeling honored by his new intimacy with men so different from those with whom he had previously associated, accepted the name with enthusiasm.

"I confess, gentlemen, that according to the distinction made by the Prince, I have never known a 'woman'. Females ... poor ones, to be sure, a very few perhaps! But I like the name, and agree to join the 'enemies of women' even though a woman is never to enter my life."

Spadoni, as though suddenly awakening, turned to Castro, and continued his thought aloud.

"It's a system of stakes invented by an English lord, now dead, who won millions by it. They explained it to me yesterday. First you place...."

"No, no, you satanic pianist!" exclaimed Atilio. "You can explain it to me in the Casino, providing I have the curiosity to listen. You've made me lose a lot, with all your systems. I had better go on playing your 'number five.'"

The Colonel, who had listened in silence to the conversation in regard to women, seemed to recall something when Castro mentioned gambling.

"Last evening," he said to the Prince, in a mysterious voice, "I met the Duchess in the Casino"....

A look of silent questioning halted his words.

"What Duchess is that?"

"The question is quite in point, Michael," said Atilio. "Your 'chamberlain' is better acquainted in society than any man on the Riviera. He knows princesses and duchesses by the dozen. I have seen him dining in the Hôtel de Paris with all the ancient French nobility, who come here to console themselves for the long time it takes to bring back their former kings. In the private rooms in the Casino, he is always kissing wrinkled hands and bowing to some group of disgusting mummies loaded down with the oldest and most famous names. Some of them call him simply 'Colonel'; others introduce him with the title of 'aide de camp of Prince Lubimoff'."

Don Marcos stiffened, offended by the waggish tone in which his high estate was being mentioned, and said haughtily:

"Señor de Castro, I am a soldier grown old in defense of Legitimacy; I shed my blood for the sacred tradition, and there is nothing remarkable about my association with...."

The Prince knowing by experience that the Colonel did not know what time was, when once he began to talk about "legitimacy" and the blood he had shed, hastened to interrupt him.

"All right; we know that very well already. But who was this Duchess you met?"

"The Duchess de Delille. She often asks about your Highness, and upon hearing that you had just arrived, she gave me to understand that she intended paying you a call."

The Prince replied with a simple exclamation, and then remained silent.

"We are starting well," said Castro, laughing. "'No women!' And immediately the Colonel announces a visit from one of them, one of the most dangerous.... For you will admit that a Duchess like that is one of the 'women' you described to us."

"I won't receive her," said the Prince resolutely.

"I have an idea that this Duchess is a cousin of yours."

"There is no such relationship. Her father was the brother of my mother's second husband. But we have known each other since childhood, and we each have a most unpleasant memory of one another. When I was living in Russia she married a French Duke. She had the same desire as the majority of wealthy American girls: a great title of nobility in order to make her friends among the fair sex jealous and to shine in European circles. A few months later she left the Duke, assigning him a certain income, which is just what her noble husband wanted perhaps. This woman Alicia never appealed to me particularly.... Besides, she has lived life just as she pleased.... She has seen almost as much of it as I have. She has as much of a reputation as I. They even accuse her, just as they do me, of love affairs with people she has never seen.... They tell me that in recent years she has been parading around with a young lad, almost a child ... dear me! We are getting old!"

"I saw her with him in Paris," said Castro. "It was before the war. Later in Monte Carlo I met her, all by herself, without being able to find a trace of her young chap anywhere. He must have been a passing fancy of hers.... She has been here three years now. When summer comes she moves to Aix-les-Bains, or to Biarritz, but as soon as the Casino is gay and fashionable again, she is one of the first to return."

"Does she play?"

"Desperately. She plays high stakes and plays them badly, although we who think we play well always lose just the same, in the end. I mean, she puts her money on the table without thinking, in several places at a time, and then even forgets where she placed it. The 'leveurs des morts' are always hanging around to pick up the pieces that no one claims and when she wins, they always manage to get something of it. She gambled for two years with nothing less than chips of five hundred and a thousand francs. At present her chips are never for more than a hundred. It won't be long before she is using the red ones, the twenties, the favorites of your humble servant."

"I shall refuse to receive her," affirmed the Prince.

And doubtless in order not to talk any more about the Duchess de Delille, he suddenly left his friends, and walked out of the room.

Atilio, in a conversational mood, turned and asked a question of Don Marcos, who was speaking with Novoa, while Spadoni went on dreaming, with eyes wide open, of the English lord's system.

"Have you seen Doña Enriqueta lately?"

"Are you asking me about the Infanta?" replied the Colonel gravely. "Yes, I met her yesterday, in the courtyards of the Casino. Poor lady! If it isn't a shame! The daughter of a king.... She told me that her sons haven't anything to wear. She owes two hundred francs for cigarettes, at the bar of the private play rooms. She can't find anyone who will lend her money. Besides, she has frightful bad luck; she loses everything. These are fatal days for people of royal blood. I almost wept when I heard all her poverty and troubles, and felt that I couldn't give her anything more. The daughter of a king?"

"But her father disowned her, when she eloped with some unknown artist," said Atilio. "And besides, Don Carlos wasn't a king anywhere."

"Señor de Castro," replied the Colonel, drawing himself up, like a rooster, "let's not spoil the party. You know my ideas: I have shed my blood in the cause of Legitimacy, and the respect that I have for you should not...."

Novoa, wishing to calm Don Marcos, intervened in the conversation.

"Monte Carlo here is like a beach, where all sorts of wreckage, living and dead, is washed up sooner or later. In the Hôtel de Paris there is another member of the family, but of the successful branch, the one that is ruling and taking in the money."

"I know him," said Atilio, laughing. "He's a young man of calipigous exuberance and wherever he goes his handsome gentleman secretary goes with him. He always meets some venerable old lady who, dazzled by his royal kinship, takes it upon herself to keep up his extravagant mode of living.... Don't know what the devil he can possibly give her in return! As for the secretary, he gives him a slap from time to time just to assert his ancient rights."

Don Marcos remained silent. He was not interested in the members of that branch, not he.

"Also," Castro continued mischievously, "in the Casino before the war, I met Don Jaime, your own king at present. A great fellow for gambling! He risked thousand franc chips by the handful. He had a lot of money coming from somewhere. In the Casino they all used to say that it was sent him from Madrid, on condition that he should have no children and allow his claims to the throne to die out with him."

"And just to think," murmured Novoa, without realizing that he was speaking aloud, "that for both of these families, back there, so many men have killed one another. To think, that for a question of inheritance among people like that we have gone back a century in European life!"

"You too!" exclaimed the Colonel, provoked again. "A scholar, saying a thing like that! I can hardly believe my ears!"

CHAPTER II

AT the end of the second Carlist war a Spanish officer, Don Miguel Saldaña, had found himself, as a result of the defeat, banished forever from his own country and condemned to a life of poverty and obscurity. The Madrid papers, without prefixing his name with any slanderous adjectives, called him simply "the rebel chief Saldaña." This courtesy, doubtless, was intended to distinguish him from the other party chiefs who in Aragon, Catalonia, and Valencia, had waged a campaign of pillage and executions for five years. Among his own people he was known as General Miguel Saldaña, Marquis of Villablanca. The pretender, Don Carlos, had given him that title because Villablanca was the name of the town where Saldaña had practically annihilated a column of the Liberal army. The topographical information of Saldaña's Chief of Staff—a local priest who had spent his whole life in doing nothing except saying mass on Sundays and spending the rest of the week hunting in the mountains with his dog and gun—gave him an opportunity to take the enemy by surprise, and he won a notorious victory.

When he crossed the frontier as a fugitive, through refusing to recognize the Bourbons as the constitutional rulers, "the rebel chief Saldaña" was twenty-nine years of age. A second son in a proud and ruined family, he had been obliged to resist the traditions of his house which presented for him an ecclesiastical career. When his studies at the Military School at Toledo were just finishing, the Revolution of 1868 caused him to renounce a commission to escape being under orders from certain generals who had participated in overthrowing royalty. When Don Carlos took up arms, Saldaña was one of the first to volunteer his services; and having gone through a military school, and received a good education, he at once became conspicuous among the guerrillas of the so-called Army of the Center, made up, for the most part, of country squires, village clerks, and mountain priests.

Besides, Saldaña distinguished himself for a reckless though rather unfortunate bravery. He always led the attack at the head of his men and consequently was wounded in the majority of his fights. But his wounds were "lucky wounds" as the soldiers say. They left marks of glory on his body without destroying his vigorous health.

Finding himself alone in Paris, where his only resource was the admiration of a few elderly "legitimist" ladies of the aristocratic Faubourg Saint Germain, he left for Vienna. There his king had friends and relatives. His youth and his exploits gained him admission as a hero of the old monarchy to the circle of archdukes. The war between Russia and Turkey tore him away from his pleasant life as an interesting hanger-on. Being a fighting man and a Catholic, he felt it his duty to wage war against the Turks; and with recommendations as a protégé of some influential Austrians, he went to the Court at Saint Petersburg. General Saldaña became a mere Commander of a Squadron in the Russian Cavalry. The officers conversed with him in French. His horsemen understood him well enough when he placed himself in front of his division, and, unsheathing his sword, galloped ahead of them against the enemy.

Various successful charges and two more "lucky wounds" won him a certain celebrity. At the end of the war he had gained numerous friends among officers of the nobility, and was presented in the most aristocratic drawing rooms. One evening at a ball given by a Grand Duchess, he saw close at hand the most fashionable and most talked of young woman of the season: the Princess Lubimoff.

She was twenty-two, an orphan, with a fortune said to be one of the largest in Russia. The first to bear the title of Prince Lubimoff, a poor but handsome Cossack, unable to read or write, succeeded in winning the attention of the Great Catherine, who made him the favorite among her lovers of second rank. During the years that her imperial caprice lasted, the new Prince was forced to seek his fortune far from the Court, since the favorites before him had gained possession of all that was near at hand. The Czarina allowed him to make his selection on the map of her immense Empire; distant territories beyond the Urals, which the new proprietor was, like the majority of his successors, never to see. With the introduction of the railroad, enormous riches came to light in these lands chosen by the Cossack; in some, veins of platinum were discovered; in others, quarries of malachite, deposits of lapis lazuli, and rich oil wells. Besides, tens of thousands of serfs, recently freed by the Czar, continued to work the land for the Lubimoff heirs, just as they had before the emancipation. And all this immense fortune, which nearly doubled each year with new discoveries, belonged entirely to one woman, the young Princess, who considered herself as one of the Imperial family owing to the relationship of her ancestor, and had more than once given the sovereign cause for worry through the eccentricities of her character.

She was an aggressive young woman, capricious and inconsistent in both words and deeds, a puzzle to everyone through the sharp contradictions in her conduct. She mingled with the officers of the Guard, treating them as comrades, smoking and drinking with them and taking a hand in their exercises in horsemanship; and then suddenly she would shut herself up in her palace for whole weeks, on her knees most of the time, before the holy ikons, absorbed in mystic fervor, and loudly imploring the forgiveness of her sins. She looked on the Emperor with veneration, as the representative of God. At the same time she was known to sympathize with the Nihilists.

The courtiers were scandalized whenever they told how she had accompanied a girl, whom the police were watching to a wretched house on the outskirts of the capital, and had there mingled with the revolutionary rabble composed of workmen and students. With them she had entered a narrow room, and joined the line passing before a coffin that was constantly in danger of being upset by the pushing of the gloomy curious crowd. The dead man's name was Fedor Dostoiewsky. The princess had scattered a bouquet of the most costly roses on the protruding forehead and monkish beard of the novelist.

And in her moments of anger this same Nadina Lubimoff beat the servants in her Palace, as though they were still serfs, and forced her maids to grovel at her feet. Her irritability and fiery temper turned everything upside down, to such an extent that a certain elderly Prince, who by Imperial order had been chosen as her guardian, desired, in spite of the fact that it would mean to him loss of the management of an immense fortune, to see her married as soon as possible.

Nadina Lubimoff inspired a feeling of dread in her suitors. They were all afraid that she would answer their request for her hand with a cruel jest. Twice she had announced her engagement to gentlemen of the Court, and at the last moment she herself had begged the Czar to refuse his consent. By this time no one dared propose, for fear of laughter and comment. Yet in spite of the freedom and unconventionality of her conduct, no one doubted the uprightness of her character.

On seeing her, Saldaña thought of a naiad of the North, rising from an emerald river, in which cakes of ice were floating. She was tall and majestic, with a somewhat massive figure, like the divinities painted in frescos for ceilings. Her skin was of radiant whiteness. The pupils of her gray eyes gave out a greenish light, and her silky hair was a faded washed-out red. Owing to the marvelous whiteness of her complexion, her flesh appeared somewhat soft, but a fresh fragrance emanated from it, "the fragrance of running brooks," to use the words of her admirers. Her nostrils were rather wide, and in the stress of emotion they quivered, like those of a horse, thus recalling her glorious ancestor, the virile Cossack of the Czarina.

The ball was nearly over before she noticed the Spaniard. There were so many officers constantly at her heels, greeting her cruel jokes and vulgar expressions with a smile of gratitude!—Suddenly Saldaña, who was standing between two doorways, was startled by a clear but commanding female voice.

"Your arm, Marquis."

And before he could offer it to her the young Princess took it, and led him off to the buffet in the drawing room.

Nadina drank a good sized glass of vodka, preferring this liquor of the people to the champagne which the servants were pouring out in large quantities. Then smiling at her companion she drew him into the embrasure of a window where they were almost hidden by the curtains.

"Your wounds!... I want to see your wounds!"

Saldaña was dumfounded at the command of this great lady accustomed to carrying out her most whimsical ideas. Blushing like a soldier, who had lived all his life among men, he finally drew up the left sleeve of his uniform, revealing a brown, hairy forearm, with large tendons, and deeply furrowed by the scar of a bullet wound received back in Spain.

The Princess admired his athletic arm, with its dark skin, cut by the jagged white of the new tissue.

"The other—the others! I want to see the rest of them!" she commanded, gazing at him fiercely, as though she were ready to bite, while her lips, moist and shining, curved sharply downward.

She had seized his arm with a hand that trembled, while with the other she tried to undo the gold cords on the officer's breast.

Saldaña drew back, stammering. "Oh! Princess!" What she desired was impossible. It was impossible to show the other wounds to a lady....

He felt on the one visible scar the contact of two lips. Nadina, bowing her proud head, was kissing his arm.

"Hero!... Oh! my hero!"

Immediately afterward she drew herself up again, cold and distant, with no other sign of emotion than a slight quivering of her nostrils. No longer was she tormented by the desire to see immediately those frightful scars of which she had heard from some of the comrades of the brave adventurer. She was sure of being able to see them to her heart's content whenever she pleased.

In a few days the rumor began to circulate that the Princess Lubimoff was to be married to the Spaniard. She herself had started the news going, without bothering to ascertain beforehand the inclination of her future husband.

The arguments with which she justified her decision could not have been more weighty. She was blond and Saldaña was dark. They had both been born at outermost limits of Europe. These considerations were sufficient to make a happy marriage. Besides, the Princess was convinced that she had always been fond of Spain, although she would not have been able to place it accurately on the map. She recalled certain verses of Heine mentioning Toledo, and others by Musset addressing Andalusian Marquises of Barcelona; and she used to hum a love song about the oranges of Seville.... Her hero must surely be from Toledo, or, better yet, an Andalusian from Barcelona.

In vain certain people of the court spoke of the Czar's not allowing the match. A great heiress marrying a foreign soldier banished from his country!... But the Princess by her very conduct, gave the sovereign to understand her will.

"Either I marry him, or I start out as a dancer in a Paris theater."

It was rumored that Saldaña was about to be deported.

"So much the better: I will go and join him, and be his sweetheart."

The old Prince, her guardian, lamented this obstinacy on the part of the Court. If it had not been for this opposition, Nadina's caprice for Saldaña, like so many of her whims, would have lasted only a few days. It was said that perhaps the Emperor, in order to break her will, would dispossess her of her vast estates in Siberia. The grandchild of the Cossack shrieked in reply that she would kill herself rather than obey.

At last the ruler prudently allowed her to fulfil her desire. In getting married she would give up her eccentricities perhaps, and the Russian court, so rich in scandals, would have one less.

The wedding journey of the Princess Lubimoff lasted all her life. Only twice, for reasons relating to her great fortune, did she return to Russia. Western Europe was more favorable than the court of an autocrat to her love of freedom. In the first year of her marriage, while in London, she had a son, who was to be the only child. She allowed him to be called Michael, like his father, but insisted that he should have a second name, Fedor, perhaps in memory of Dostoiewsky, her favorite novelist, whose character inspired in her a feeling of sympathy, through a certain resemblance to herself.

No one succeeded in ascertaining with certainty whether or not Don Miguel Saldaña felt happy in his new position as Prince Consort, which permitted him to enjoy all the pleasure and magnificence of immense wealth. According to Spanish customs, he started out to impose his will as a husband and a man of character, to curb the eccentricities of his wife. Vain determination! The very woman who at times could be sentimental and moan at the thought of social inequalities and the suffering of the poor, could, by her fiery impetuosity, reduce the stoutest and most firmly steeled will.

In the end Saldaña relapsed into silence, fearing the aggressiveness of the daughter of the Cossack. To keep his prestige as a great noble, anxious for the respect of the servants and for the consideration of his guests, he feared violent scenes that filled the drawing rooms and even the stairways of his luxurious residence with feminine shrieks. He did not care more than once to see the Princess with one kick send the oaken table flying against the dining room wall, while all the porcelain and crystal service smashed into bits with one catastrophic crash.

When the Paris architects had carried out the orders of the Princess, the family left the castle they were occupying in the vicinity of London. A group of rich Parisians, Jewish bankers for the most part, were covering the level grounds around the new Park Monçeau, with large private dwellings. The Princess Lubimoff had an enormous palace, with a garden of extraordinary size for a city, built in this quarter. She even set up a tiny dairy behind a grove of trees, and without leaving her place she could enjoy the rôle of a country woman, whipping cream and churning butter, in imitation of Marie

Antoinette, who likewise played at being a shepherdess in the Petit Trianon.

At times a wave of tenderness swept over her, and she adored and obeyed her husband, pushing her humility to extremes that were alarming. She told her visitors about the General's campaigns, and his daring exploits back in Spain, a land which inspired in her a romantic interest, and which for that very reason she did not care ever to see. Suddenly she would cut her eulogies short with a command:

"Marquis, show them your wounds."

As proof of her tenderness, she refrained from getting angry when her husband refused.

She always called him "Marquis," perhaps in order to keep the princely title for herself alone, perhaps because she felt that he should not be deprived of a rank he had gained with his blood. The Marquis never paid any attention to this breach of etiquette. His wife had already committed so many!

A year after their marriage, when the news reached London that Alexander II had been killed by the explosion of a Nihilist bomb, the Princess ran about her apartments like a mad woman, and took to her bed after an extraordinary fit of anger.

"The wretches! He was so good!... They've killed their own father."

And thereafter when Saldaña entered the luxurious dwelling in Paris, he often came across strange visitors, at whom the lackeys in breeches stared in amazement. They were uncouth girls with spectacles, and cropped hair, carrying portfolios under their arms; men with long hair and tangled beards, whose eyes contained the startled expression of visionaries; Russians from the Latin Quarter under police surveillance, terrorists, who appealed not in vain to the generosity of the Princess, and used her money perhaps to make infernal machines which they sent back to their country and hers.

When the Prince Michael Fedor recalled his childhood memories, he could see his father holding him on his knees and caressing him with his firm hands. The child would gaze up at the dark face and large mustache that joined Saldaña's closely cropped mutton chop whiskers. He could not be sure whether the moisture in those black, commanding eyes came from tears; but after he learned Spanish he was sure that the Marquis had often murmured, as he smoothed the tiny brow:

"My poor little boy!... Your mother is mad!"

When Michael reached the age of eight, the problem of his education caused the Princess to show her motherly concern for a few weeks. One of those visitors, who so greatly worried the servants, brought his books and his frayed garments from a narrow street near the Pantheon, and took up his abode in the lordly dwelling of the Lubimoffs. He was a silent young man, given to the study of chemistry, and forbidden to return to his country. The very day of his arrival, a secret service agent came and questioned the porter of the palace.

"I want my son to know Russian," said the Princess. "Besides, he will learn a great deal from Sergueff. Sergueff is a real man of learning, and worthy of a better fate."

Saldaña insisted that he should likewise have a Spanish teacher, and she raised no objections. All the members of her family had possessed to an unusual degree the talent of the Slavs for learning languages easily.

"Prince Michael Fedor," said his mother, "is the Marquis of Villablanca, and ought to know the language of his second country."

On this account the General once again sought out his former companions in arms who were still scattered in various parts of Paris. The fame of his enormous wealth had brought him many requests, even from persons of whom he had formerly stood in awe. But although the Princess, who was generous to a fault, allowed him the management of her fortune, Saldaña, with chivalrous unyielding integrity, felt that he had no right to her money, and gradually came to avoid the insistent suppliants. Besides, a great change had come over this silent man during his travels through Europe. The former soldier of the absolute monarchy was now an admirer of England and her constitutional history.

"You see things differently when you travel about," was all he said. "If all my fellow countrymen had only seen the world."

One day the new teacher presented himself at the palace. He was twelve years younger than Saldaña. He had been under the latter's command toward the end of the war, and instead of calling him by his title of Marquis or Prince he addressed him proudly, at every opportunity, as "my General."

The General had not the slightest recollection of him; but the fact that he could give exact details of the last campaign, and had been recommended by various friends, did not permit of any doubt as to his veracity. He must have been one of those lads who had run away from home and joined the Carlist bands, making up those forces of irregulars whom Saldaña, unable to tolerate their frequent atrocities, more than once threatened with execution en masse. The teacher claimed that the General himself had given him a subordinate's commission in the last months of the war, owing to his having a better education than his ragged comrades.

Thus Marcos Toledo entered the palace of the Lubimoffs.

The solemn husband of the Princess laughed with boyish glee upon hearing the story of Toledo's first experiences as an *emigré* in Paris.

During the first few months, since he did not know French, he used to stop the priests in the street, to talk with them in Latin. He eked out a miserable existence, giving lessons on the guitar, and lecturing in a Polyglot Institute, where the auditors did not pay the slightest attention to the subjects discussed, but tried simply to accustom their ears to his Spanish pronunciation.

Seven francs and a half, for talking an hour and a half! But Toledo made up for the smallness of the compensation in the pleasure it gave him to orate about the happy days of Philip II, so much superior to "these days of liberalism."

"At present, I have only one ambition, General," he ended by saying, "and that is to dress well."

The passion for luxurious display came from his youthful days as a guerrilla, when he would steal red and yellow petticoats from peasant women in order to make uniforms for himself. In Paris, he did not feel so keenly the lack of nutritious food, as he did the fact that he was obliged to wear clothes that did not belong to any known fashion.

When he was given quarters on the top floor of the palace, like the Russian teacher, and the General had selected various garments for him from his large wardrobe, Toledo felt he had realized all the dreams that he had elaborated while running about Paris as a persistent agent for a thousand unsaleable things.

His fellow countrymen, former comrades in poverty, admired him on seeing him all dressed up like a rich man, and often riding in the carriage of a Prince. It scarcely seemed honorable that he, a former fighter, should occupy a position as a teacher, and he used to say in an apologetic manner:

"I am now General Saldaña's *aide-de-camp*. I don't think it will be long before we take to the mountains again."

Young Prince Michael admired his Russian teacher, because his mother affirmed that he was a great scholar. The boy felt a certain fear in the presence of this melancholy sage. On the other hand, Michael Fedor treated the Spaniard with an air of friendly and patronizing superiority. Toledo made his father laugh, and that was enough to cause the son to consider him an inferior being, but one worthy of esteem nevertheless, because of his docility and patience.

"Say: is it true that you were going to be a priest?" Michael Fedor used to ask Toledo. "Is it true that after you left the seminary you were a druggist's clerk?"

"Prince," the teacher replied with dignity, "I am Don Marcos de Toledo. My name tells my nobility, in spite of everything that envious people may say, and I have a right to use the 'Don' since I am an officer and your father, the Marquis, gave me my commission."

In a short time the pupil was speaking Spanish correctly. It seemed that he had learned it as rapidly as possible in order to be better able to poke fun at his *hidalgo* teacher.

The father also contributed to the education of the heir of the Lubimoffs the one thing he was able to teach. Every morning, after the lessons given by the Russian, which left the little fellow with a solemn face, Saldaña would wait for him in a large room on the ground floor.

"Prince, on guard!"

And he, who had been the best blade in the Carlist army, and had on his conscience the slashing of a skull to the jawbone in a duel during the Turkish campaign, smiled proudly when he saw how this eleven year old boy stood his ground during the fencing lesson, parrying the hard blows and returning them successfully at the least unguardedness on his father's part. Michael Fedor was going to be a splendid fighting man, a worthy descendant of the Cossack of Russia, and of the guerrilla of the Spanish mountains.

But Saldaña was not to enjoy this satisfaction for long. Among his various "lucky wounds," which only bothered him slightly with the changing of the seasons, there was one which from time to time inflicted periods of acute pain. For many years he had carried in his body a Spanish bullet which the sawbones of his guerrilla band had been unable to extract. When the surgeons of London and Paris attempted the operation it was too late.

One morning the General's valet, on entering the room, found him dead.

Michael Fedor never forgot the sorrow he had felt on that occasion, nor the sumptuous funeral which the Princess had ordered, equal to that of a king deceased in exile. But what he remembered most clearly was the extraordinary grief of his mother. She too wanted to die. Her Russian maids were once obliged to snatch from her hands a phial of laudanum, receiving for their pains a few more blows than usual. Then, with her hair streaming down her back, she ran about wailing like a madwoman in front of all the portraits of the General. Oh! Her hero! Now she really knew how much she loved him....

For several months she received her visitors in a drawing room with black furnishings and curtains. Wearing loose mourning garments, she half reclined on a sofa in front of a full length portrait of Saldaña. His swords, his uniforms, and even a Russian saddle were on exhibition in the drawing room, which had been converted into a sort of museum of the deceased.

"He died like the man he was!" moaned the widow. "He was killed by his wounds."

At this period began the ultimate stage in the rise of Don Marcos Toledo. The Russian scholar receded into the background. A part of the dead man's glory passed to his humble fellow countryman who had witnessed his great exploits. One evening, the Princess, while engaged in conversation in the drawing room museum with some noble relatives who had arrived from Russia, wept so copiously at the memory of her husband, that she decided to leave the room for a moment.

"Colonel, your arm."

Toledo was present in company with his pupil, and looked around with an expression of bewilderment. The Princess had to repeat her command in a more imperious voice. "Colonel, your arm!" She was speaking to him! For some time Don Marcos thought that the new title was a whim of the Princess and that some day when he was least expecting it his commission as "Colonel" would be withdrawn.

But when the first months of mourning had passed and the widow, tiring of solitude, started to resume her social calls, she insisted on being accompanied by Toledo, and on introducing him to her acquaintances in the aristocratic world.

"He is the aide-de-camp of the dead Marquis," she explained.

The very title he had invented to give himself an air of importance in the eyes of his half-starved companions in poverty! Toledo no longer questioned the validity of his promotion. Now that the Princess was presenting him as her husband's aide-de-camp, he might well be a Colonel. And a Colonel he was, even for the young Prince, who at first had given him the title to make fun of him, but finally came to call him "Colonel" by force of habit.

Toledo's dreams of splendid and showy toggery were now realized magnificently. With the Princess he did not need to fear the scruples sometimes shown by Saldaña, who hated extravagance and mismanagement. The great lady even felt disdain for those who were niggardly in availing themselves of her generosity. Don Marcos was enabled to change his attire several times a day, and held long conferences with famous tailors. He sought personal elegance. He wished to dress like a gentleman of distinction, but at the same time to wear clothes of a cut that would plainly show that he was accustomed to uniforms: He had in mind something like a Napoleonic Marshal obliged to wear a dress suit. Through his barber, likewise, he effected a great transformation. He imitated the manner in which the General had worn his hair, with a part that started at his forehead and ended at the back of his neck, and with stray locks hanging down at the temples. His mustache was taught to mingle with his side whiskers, in the Russian fashion. In accompanying the Princess, he learned to kiss ladies' hands with the grace and ease of an old courtier. He also learned to carry on long conversations without saying anything, to keep himself in the background, practically unseen, while his superiors were talking.

When the Princess, after the first year of mourning, resolutely returned to her box at the Opera, Don Marcos attended her, remaining discreetly in the rear, like the Chamberlain of a Queen. One evening, during an intermission, on passing to the front of her box, the Princess heard the Colonel telling an old French general, a friend of the house, about the battle of Villablanca.

"And the Marquis said to me: 'Now it's your chance, Toledo: Let's see how you can make out with a bayonet charge.' So I bared my sword, and at the head of my regiment...."

"He's a true soldier," interrupted the Princess, "a worthy companion of my hero.... The Marquis often talked to me about him."

And at that moment she was really sure she had heard the silent Saldaña relate the gallant deeds of his aide-de-camp.

The Russian teacher, regarded by Toledo as an unpleasant person who would bear watching, soon left the Lubimoff palace. Perhaps he was jealous of the Colonel's growing influence; perhaps mysterious reasons needed his attention far from Paris. The Princess did not mind in the least the disappearance of the scholar. She had forgotten her rebellious looking Russians; she stopped giving them money. At present she had other interests.

She suddenly evinced a desire to live for some time in London, and for this reason, she granted her son's request to be allowed to travel alone throughout Europe.

"You're a man now; you will soon be fourteen. Travel, and don't stop at expense; always remember that you are Prince Lubimoff.... The Colonel will go with you. He will be your aide, as he was for the heroic Marquis."

His first trip was to Spain. Michael Fedor wanted to see his father's native land. Toledo thought it in point for the young Prince to show great admiration for Spain. Michael must remember they were in the enemy's country. Toledo was a Carlist Colonel who had refused amnesty, and had declined to recognize the reigning dynasty! But they traveled for three months in Spain, without being noticed except for the largeness of their tips. It is quite true that Toledo avoided coming in contact with any of his former comrades. He felt that he now belonged to a different world. Inwardly he felt the same change the General had.

As soon as Michael Fedor had recovered from his first enthusiasm for bull fighting, they continued their travels across the continent as far as Russia, arriving considerably later than the numerous letters of introduction sent by the Princess Lubimoff to her relatives. The Prince remained there a year, visiting his less distant estates, and making the acquaintance of all the great families in his mother's circle of friends. The Colonel talked grandiloquently about everything related to war with various generals who received him as an equal. Was he not the aide and companion in heroic deeds of Saldaña, whom they had known in the war against Turkey, when they were mere subalterns?

The former friends of the Princess Lubimoff told her son some unexpected news. His mother had announced her forthcoming marriage to an English gentleman. She had written to the Czar asking his authorization. This news startled no one save Michael Fedor. The times of the wild Nadina had long since passed. Her actions aroused no further interest. Other young Princesses had effaced her memory with adventures that caused even greater commotion. No one save a few of the ladies of the old court, when they forgot their cares and interests as mothers, would bring to mind the Princess Lubimoff, recalling days of vanished youth, which for old people are always more interesting than the present.

When the young man returned to the Paris palace, he found his mother as much of a Princess as ever, but married to a Scotch gentleman, Sir Edwin Macdonald.

"Some day you will leave me," she said with a tragic note in her voice she used on great occasions. "A Prince Lubimoff should live at the court, serve his Emperor, be an officer in the Guard; and I need a companion, some one to lean on. Sir Edwin is the personification of distinction; but don't ever think that I shall forget your father. Never!... My hero!"

Michael Fedor saw a gentleman who, indeed, was "the personification of distinction"; attentive to everyone, very precise in his bearing, a man of few words, who shut himself up for long hours—studying, according to the Princess. English politics was his preoccupation, and his one great dream was to return to Parliament, which he had been forced to leave by defeat at election.

This cold man, with a pale smile and extreme insistence on good form even in the most trivial actions, neither displeased Michael as a step-father nor appealed to him as a friend. He was an inoffensive, somewhat stuffy person, whom Michael grew accustomed to seeing every day in his father's former place, and whom he had expected to see sooner or later anyhow.

This marriage brought other people to the Lubimoff palace, with all the intimacy inspired by relationship.

One of Sir Edwin's brothers had been obliged, like all the second sons in wealthy British families, to go out in the world and earn his living. After a life of adventure, he had finally settled down in the United States, near the Mexican border, and had soon found himself, through a marriage with an heiress of the country, much richer than his elder brother.

His wife was a Mexican. She owned famous silver mines in the interior and vast ranches on the border. She had only one daughter; and the latter was in her eighth year when Arthur Macdonald died as a result of a fall from his horse. The widow, with her little Alicia, moved to Europe. She wanted to live in London, to be near her brother-in-law, Sir Edwin, then a member of Parliament, and much admired by the Mexican woman as one of the directors of the world's affairs. Later she established herself in Paris, as the capital most to her taste, and as the place where she could meet many people from Mexico.

The Princess Lubimoff treated her relative well, although her friendship suffered sudden changes, often going from extreme affection to sudden coldness.

She and Doña Mercedes could talk about mines and vast estates, although neither of them had any accurate knowledge of their respective fortunes. They estimated their wealth only by the enormous quantities of money—millions of francs a year—which their distant business agents sent them, and which they spent without knowing just how. There was another thing which attracted the Princess, in her moments of good will, to Doña Mercedes: she herself was blond, while the Spanish Creole still kept traces of Hispanic-Aztec beauty, with a dark, somewhat olive complexion, large, wide-open, almond eyes, and hair astonishing for its blackness, brilliancy, and length.

But an instinctive rivalry frequently embittered the relations of the two multi-millionaires. The Princess was sure that her own wealth was far the greater. When Doña Mercedes talked about Mexican silver, she mentioned Russian platinum! "What is silver worth compared to platinum!" And in order completely to floor her opponent, the Princess would bring out her family history. Beginning with the remote Cossack ancestor, who almost became the legitimate husband of Catherine the Great, she paraded before her Mexican rival generals, marshals of the Emperor's household, hetmans, followed by their retinues of half savage horsemen, princes and ambassadors. Sir Edwin's wife talked as though she belonged to the reigning house, letting it be understood that her famous ancestor had played a part in the establishing of one of the Czars. For this reason she had always been shown special consideration at court.

Doña Mercedes, inwardly jealous of so much greatness, nevertheless smiled a sweet enigmatic smile, as though she were to say, "That is all very far away—and perhaps a lie."

Then immediately she would begin talking in her rapid whimsical French, a French which she had never been able to free from numerous Spanish locutions that still clung tenaciously.

"Mama was an intimate friend of Eugenie.... Don't you know who Eugenie is? The Empress, the wife of Napoleon III. When Madame Barrios—that was my mother's name—was announced at the Tuileries, the doors were opened wide. Papa was one of the men who made Maximilian emperor."

Over against the aristocratic grandeur of the Saint Petersburg court she set the image of the Mexican court, of the brief Empire which had ended in the execution of the Archduke Maximilian, and the madness of his bride, Carlotta. The Emperor endeavored to establish the musty old etiquette of the Austrian Court, but the Mexican matrons, when they called on the young Empress, said in the frank maternal fashion of the colonies: "How is everything, Carlotta?... How do you like the country, my dear?"

Moved by a similar frankness, Doña Mercedes would end her discourse by saying carelessly:

"Papa, seeing that the Empire was going badly, recognized Juarez as the head of the government, and joined the side of the Republic. He did it to save our mines."

Then she would talk on for a long time about the Barrios, who, according to her, were descendants of the most ancient aristocracy of Spain. All the nobles of Madrid were therefore relatives of hers. Everybody knew that! As a child she had seen at home a lot of papers which proved her right to the title of Marchioness; but owing to the revolutions in her country, and her travels, she no longer knew where to find them.

If the Princess referred to the splendor of her palace, the Creole would immediately mention her elegant private mansion in the Champs Élysées. The arrival of Colonel Toledo, as a valorous adornment giving the princely residence military prestige, did not intimidate Doña Mercedes. She too had a Spaniard, an Aragonese cleric, who acted as a sort of royal private chaplain, and whom she considered a man of science, because, bored by his sinecure in her employ, he had taken up elementary astronomy, and had set up a telescope on the roof of her house.

Whenever the Mexican lady dared to imitate her entertainments, her carriages or her clothes, the Princess Lubimoff would audibly lament the fact that Paris was not in Russia, where she might call on the chief of police to force this low-bred Creole to show the respect due to her superiors. But after these bursts of anger she would feel a sudden wave of tenderness for Doña Mercedes. "In spite of your illiteracy," she would say, "you are a woman of natural talent and the only one with whom I can talk for an hour at a stretch."

Between these two declining beauties, who had seen themselves the center of attraction and adoration in former years, there was a common bond, something which moved them both like far off lovely music, like the cherished memory of youth: It was the daughter of Doña Mercedes, the vivacious Alicia Macdonald.

Doña Mercedes seemed to see her own beauty, renewed with fresh vigor, in her child. But in this she was mistaken. Alicia added to her dark southern splendor the slenderness and slightly boyish freedom of movement of her father's race. The Princess, observing the girl's independent character, thought she saw herself back once more in the days when she was beginning to shock the Imperial Court. This too was a mistake. She herself had been able to follow all her most wilful impulses, without fear of gossip. She possessed everything. Besides her immense wealth, she had the advantages of birth, enabling her to elevate any man whatsoever to her own level, no matter how far beneath her he might be. Alicia had one ambition; to unite her fortune with a great title of the old aristocracy in order to be presented at court. Since her fifteenth year this desire had been fixed, calculating design, dissimulated under apparent recklessness. From her fairy-story days, her mother had talked to her about wonderful marriages, and of princes who in former times used to marry shepherdesses, but who were in search nowadays of millionaires' daughters.

Michael Fedor felt somewhat embarrassed at meeting this girl in his palace. She looked at him so boldly, with such a dominating expression, as though everything and everyone should bow before her!

She had beauty of a type more fascinating than conventional. Her complexion, slightly tinged with a strange golden orange color, her large eyes a trifle slanting, her luxuriant hair, which, fleeing its bondage of hairpins, seemed alive and coiling like a cluster of snakes, gave her an exotic charm. The rest of her body revealed a modern physical education. Her limbs were firm and agile from continued exercise and play.

Doña Mercedes seemed to urge Alicia and Michael toward each other from the first meeting.

"Don't stand on formality," she said in a motherly way. "You are cousins."

Although Michael didn't succeed in making out this relationship, he endeavored to treat the young girl in a friendly manner, while the Creole mother smiled as she already pictured Alicia with the coronet of a princess, bowing before the Czar. Princess Lubimoff was in one of her kindly moods; for the moment she did not believe in caste and privileges, to the extent that she would again have given money to the long-haired individuals who used to visit her. She accepted her friend's ambitious projects tolerantly and without comment.

The Prince, meanwhile, was telling the Colonel his impressions.

"Too much of a young lady! I like the others better."

Don Marcos, having been Michael's companion in wide and joyous travels, knew whom the boy meant by "the others"; for Prince Lubimoff had begun very young to nibble at the grapes of life.

On other occasions it irritated him that, with her unabashed demeanor of a foolish virgin, she should seem so much like "the others."

"She's worse than a boy. If you only knew, Colonel, the things she says to me!"

As for Alicia she was not wholly satisfied with the young Prince. She was accustomed to seeing other men make an effort to be gracious and show her flattering attentions, while Michael manifested a haughty character, like her own, arguing with her, and even daring to contradict her.

Occasionally, accompanied by Toledo, they went out together for a gallop in the Bois de Boulogne. All this was torture for Don Marcos, who had been a mountain warrior! But his present position called for certain duties. So he rode along as well as could be expected from a colonel of infantry.

Alicia was a tireless rider. At the residence in the Champs-Élysées, Doña Mercedes had frequently been obliged to look for her in the stables, where she made herself at home among the hostlers and coachmen, and talked with professional authority as she supervised the grooming of the horses. Afterwards, when she came back into the drawing room her hair would have a decidedly horsey odor. Back in her native land she had mounted a horse and clung to it before she knew how to walk. In Paris she boldly made her way among the vehicles, knocked down the passersby occasionally, and often found her mad gallops intercepted by the police.

The Colonel endeavored to keep up with her. He never said anything, but his heart was heavy. The Prince protested against her racing in this fashion, which might have been all very well on her native plains. The girl's retorts widened the breach between them, with feelings of hostility. "No one is going to talk to me like that, not even my mother," she said. "I'm old enough to know what I ought to do." She was fifteen.

One morning in the Bois, coming to a cross road that happened to catch her fancy, Alicia started her horse for the Avenue without consulting her companion.

"No, this way," Michael called in a commanding voice.

"I don't like that; this is the way!" she answered aggressively.

The Prince made an effort to cut her off by crossing ahead of her, and she spurred her horse against Michael's with a shock that brought the two animals to their knees. The Colonel, who was behind them, caught an exchange of angry glances, and harsh words. Alicia raised her whip, and struck the Prince across the shoulders.

"You do that to *me*!" shouted Michael furiously.

The face of this scion of the old Cossack Lubimoff underwent a rapid series of expressions, finally taking an aspect of extreme ugliness and savagery. His nostrils seemed to dilate even more than usual. He raised his whip and struck, but Toledo had put his horse between the two, receiving the tip of the lash on his cheek, which began to bleed. The sight of blood and the thought that the blow was intended for her, drove the young woman mad with rage.

"Brute! Savage!... Russian!"

This seemed too mild, and she stopped for a moment, to think up a greater insult. Her childhood memories helped her; the legend she had heard from the half-breeds back in her own land inspired her with a new affront, as if Michael Fedor were Fernan Cortes.

"Spaniard!... Murderer of Indians!"

And fearing a new lashing after that supreme insult, she fled at a mad pace without stopping until she reached the Arch of Triumph.

After this incident Doña Mercedes lost all hope of her daughter's becoming a Lubimoff.

"A Russian Princess!" she said scornfully. "Why, everyone is a Prince in Russia!... A mere English baron is better, or a French or Spanish count."

Michael was in a mood no more conciliatory when the Colonel lectured him.

"I don't want to hear anything more about that wench!" said he.

And the Princess, in one of her petulant moments averred that she considered this word the proper one. These relatives of Sir Edwin had always seemed to her very ordinary people. Likewise it seemed to her very natural that her son should think of going back to Russia to fill his station as a Prince. The life of caste and privilege there was more suitable to his rank than the democratic ways of Paris, where certain American Indians, because they had millions, could imagine they were the equals of the Lubimoffs.

Prince Michael remained in Russia until he was twenty-three. His military studies were passed brilliantly, according to Toledo, and the boy succeeded in distinguishing himself among the most famous cavalry officers of the Guard. He took prizes in exhibitions of horsemanship. With his revolver he could pot coins held up at fifty paces by his comrades. He wielded the sabre with a skill that his Cossack ancestor and General Saldaña would have admired. Every morning in the courtyard of his Petersburg palace he found awaiting him a life-sized dummy made of the firm sticky clay used by sculptors. He would stay for half an hour in front of it, going through his exercises. It was not enough to be able to strike one's enemy. The important thing was to strike well, with the greatest possible depth and force. And the head and limbs of the dummy went flying, severed by the steel blade. The study of military science was all well enough for those in the infantry or the artillery—sons of clerks and merchants!

At first the Colonel was astonished at the magnificence and extravagance of Russian life. Finally he came to take it all quite naturally, as though he had been accustomed to something similar from his earliest boyhood. "My son, remember the name you bear," the Princess used to write to the Prince. "Do not disgrace it. Spend according to what you are." And the son, without asking her for anything, followed her advice faithfully by coming to a direct understanding with the Russian administrators. Don Marcos figured that the Lieutenant in the Guard was spending something over three millions a year. His racing stables were the most celebrated in the capital. Many famous beauties of the court and the theaters were on good terms with Prince Michael Fedor. His supper parties in the Lubimoff palace or in the fashionable restaurants were sought after by all the young men of the aristocracy. To be invited to one of them was an extraordinary honor, something like being a member of an academy of supermen. It often happened that toward morning on nights of such parties celebrated women finished by dancing naked on the tables, so that the host "might not be displeased."

Sometimes these celebrations ended in drunken brawls, where wine mingled with blood. The Colonel had seen one of these suppers result in a duel between two of the guests. It took place in the palace garden, just before dawn. One of the men was killed. His best friends carried the corpse to the quay of the Neva, and placed a revolver in his hand to make it look like a case of suicide.

No: Don Marcos did not care much for those nocturnal feasts. He considered them dangerous. On one occasion, a youthful Grand Duke, absolutely drunk, amused himself by daubing the Colonel's whiskers with caviar, until, tired of such brazen familiarity, the Spaniard in turn put his hand in the dish and smeared the other man's august face with green. The duke hesitated for a moment whether or not to kill him, but finally embraced him, covering him with kisses and shouting aloud, "This is my father."

Toledo preferred his own honorable and quiet friendships with General Saldaña's former companions in arms; solemn personages who talked to him about world politics and future wars. Besides, the Prince's generosity permitted the Colonel secret pleasures, less noisy, and agreeably unostentatious.

One night, returning to the Lubimoff palace after two o'clock, he saw there was a supper party in the great dining hall used on gala occasions. Some fifty guests had assembled, and in the course of the night many more had arrived. It seemed that the news had spread throughout all the pleasure resorts of the capital, attracting all the youthful libertines.

Opposite the Prince was seated a Cossack officer, short, lithe as a panther, dark skinned, with Asiatic eyes. His wrinkled uniform showed signs of recent traveling. Michael Fedor showed him the greatest attention, as though he were the only guest. Toledo, being acquainted with all the friends of the house, was unable to place this uncouth Cossack, who looked as though he had come from some remote garrison in Siberia. Some one offered to relieve his uncertainty. He was startled on learning that it was the brother of a court lady who just at that moment was being much talked about on account of her extreme familiarity with Michael Fedor. The two men looked at each other with keen interest, exchanging silent toasts in huge glasses of champagne. At the other end of the hall arose the ceaseless wail of gypsy violins. Several dark skinned girls with striped aprons of many colors were dancing about the tables. But in spite of that, Don Marcos, glancing about, felt instinctively a note of gloom.

"Leon, the sabres!"

The Prince, after looking at his watch, had arisen and given this order to his body servant, who was standing behind him. All the guests rushed for the doors forming a jam, like a crowd, pushing and shoving, at the entrance to a theater. There was no reason now to conceal their real feelings. They were eager for the promised spectacle. The Colonel finally found some one who could talk intelligibly.

"He came last night, to ask the Prince to marry his sister. A thirty-eight day trip.... The Prince refuses.... It isn't often you'll see a match like this.... He's the best swordsman in Siberia."

The garden was covered with snow. It was night, and the uncertain moon illumined it with slanting rays, lengthening immeasurably the shadows of the trees. More than a hundred men formed in two black masses on the borders of the walk. The Colonel noticed the arrival of several servants. One was bringing swords; the rest were carrying large trays with bottles and glasses.

Michael Fedor bowed to his enemy, his eyes shining with kindliness and drink.

"Would you like another glass of something?"

The Cossack thanked him with a gesture, and immediately Toledo saw him remove his long coat, the breast of which was adorned with cartridge pouches. Then he took off his shirt, and finally remained in nothing save his trousers and high boots. Then he stooped, and seizing two handfuls of snow, began to rub his wiry body and muscular arms.

The Prince, like many of the spectators, shivered slightly with surprise and cold; but nevertheless that the condition of the combat might be equal, Lubimoff felt it imperative that he should follow the example of his hardy adversary. While he was removing the upper part of his uniform several torches were lighted and began to blaze like red stars in the semi-darkness of the moonlit garden.

Don Marcos could see the two men face to face. They were bare from the waist up. Their breasts shone from the moisture of the recent massage. In their hands quivered sabres as sharp as razors.

"Ready!"

Some one was directing the fight.

"Why this is barbarous!" thought the Spaniard. "These men are savages."

He did not dare say it aloud because he was a soldier, and more than that, a Colonel; but during the rest of his life he never could forget that scene.

They crossed swords, parried, attacked, the Prince with firm poise, the other with catlike agility. Toledo could see that their bodies were blood red, but at the moment he thought it an effect of the torchlight. As they drew near him, circling about in their deadly play, he realized that they were actually red with blood. Their bodies seemed covered with a purple vestment that was torn to shreds and the shreds quivered at the ends as the blood dripped off. Standing out against that warm moist garment rose their white arms. The Prince was getting the worst of it. Toledo suddenly saw a deep gash appear in his brow; a moment later he thought he saw one of his ears hang half severed from the skull. But that wild cat from the steppes always sprang free from every sabre thrust. No one dared intervene; it was a duel without quarter, without rest, with no condition save the death of one or the other combatant. At times they came together, forming a single body bristling with white flashes in the shadow of the trees; a moment later they appeared apart, seeking each other in the fiery circle of the torches.

Suddenly Toledo heard a wild cry of pain, the howl of a poor animal caught unawares. The Prince was the only one still standing. A straight thrust had slashed his adversary's jugular. Lubimoff stood there a moment motionless. Then his superhuman strength, which had sustained him until then, left him. With the loss of blood, all the weariness of the struggle came over him like a shot. He too tottered and fell, but into the arms of friends. There was not a single doctor among the spectators. No one had thought of that. They considered the presence of one unnecessary in an encounter that could end only in death.

All the curiosity seekers left the garden, following the unconscious Prince. A few servants stayed behind, gathered about the body of the Cossack. He was lying face downward. With respectful awe they watched as his legs quivered for the last time, as the blood slowly emptied itself from the neck, and spread out across the snow, in a black stain that was beginning to take on a bluish tinge in the livid light of dawn.

At the court, which had already shown frequent alarm over the Prince's notorious adventures, this event caused a great stir. Lubimoff's duels, his love affairs, his scandalous entertainments, annoyed the young Emperor, who had taken it upon himself to improve the morals of his associates.

In aristocratic gatherings, the freakish whims of the almost forgotten Nadina Lubimoff were brought to memory and discussed again. The young Cossack was related to people of influence, and his death contributed to the complete disgrace of his sister.

Michael Fedor had not yet entirely recovered from his wounds, when he received the order to leave Russia. The Czar was banishing him, and for an indefinite period. He might live in Paris with his mother.

"That's all right; so long as they respect his income," was the Colonel's only comment.

Arriving in Paris, the Prince was convinced of his mother's insanity. That was something he had suspected for some time, from her letters. Sir Edwin had died, rather suddenly, three years before, in England, following defeat in an election. The palace in the Monçeau quarter had suffered an interior transformation that represented a cost of several millions. The Princess was devoting all her time to it. The Arabic, Persian, Greek, or Chinese drawing rooms, the construction and decoration of which had made the fortune of two architects and several dealers in doubtful antiques, had just disappeared; while furnishings acquired years before as extremely rare pieces had been scattered to the four winds as though they were mere rubbish of no value. The palace remained the same as before on the outside; but the interior, beginning with the stairway, was rebuilt in imitation of a medieval castle. Not a single window remained without its stained glass, not a room but was shrouded in the vague half light of a cellar. All the conventional Gothic known to modern contractors was employed by order of the Princess in the restoration of the house. Three stories and one entire wing had been torn down to form the nave of a cathedral.

Michael saw advancing toward him a tall austere woman, with long transparent fingers, and large, staring, uncanny eyes. She was dressed in black, with loose sleeves that almost touched the ground, and with a white bonnet fitting close to the head beneath her mourning veils. In spite of the fact that she had a rosary at her wrist and talked with the air of a martyr, her son imagined that he was looking at an opera singer.

The expulsion of the Prince from Russia had caused her neither surprise nor sorrow.

"Those Romanoffs have always disliked us. They cannot forget that your illustrious ancestor, so they say, used to beat Catherine when he caught her with anyone else."

Her thoughts rose above all such worldly considerations. She had never, as a matter of fact, taken any stock in religion; but now she declared herself a Catholic. She had made no public declaration of conversion, to be sure, but she felt she must adopt the belief. Her new and final personality demanded it.

"Your father approves of my new stand. Often in the night I have talked with my hero. He is glad to see me in the path of truth."

No sooner had Michael Fedor and the Colonel arrived, than they noticed the strange visitors who were frequenting the palace. The long haired terrorists had been succeeded by numerous fortune tellers, soothsayers, clairvoyants, and solemn professors of occult sciences. A plain old lamp-stand, which looked as though it might have walked upstairs by itself from the concierge's quarters, was jumping about and rapping, at all hours, in the bedroom of the Princess.

One day she decided to tell her son the great secret of her life. At last she knew who she was; the spirits had revealed to her the knowledge of her true personality. In one of her many previous existences she had been the most unfortunate and beautiful, the most "romantic", of queens. The soul of the Russian princess, Nadina Lubimoff, centuries ago had dwelt in the body of Mary Stuart.

"That is why I always had a special liking for the story of the unhappy queen. And now I know why, when I saw Sir Edwin in London, I fell in love with him on the spot, in the most irresistible fashion. His ancestors were Scottish."

Such reasons were to her as unanswerable as all the others which had guided her actions. And to pay homage to the queenly soul which was, according to all her mystic attendants, reincarnated in her, she was going to live like the beheaded sovereign of Scotland, copying the Queen's clothes as she had seen them in pictures, converting her palace into a mediæval castle, and eating from antique plates nothing but Renaissance delicacies, the recipes for which she had employed a history professor to discover in ancient chronicles.

Carriages now rarely entered the Court of Honor of the palace. The grand stairway was growing mossy between its steps. Not so the delivery entrance. There, each day, the professionals of "the beyond" appeared, poorly dressed and suspicious looking men and women, who were exploiting the Princess, generous as a queen—and was she not one?—under the guise of aiding her in the manipulation of the lamp table, and conjuring up historic phantoms which, to prove their presence, moved the carpets, made the pictures fall from the walls, changed the positions of the chairs, and committed other childish deviltries.

Doña Mercedes avoided visiting the Princess. Her simple faith caused her to be frightened at queens that last for centuries, and at those halls with old furniture that seemed to palpitate with mysterious life. She preferred the quiet wholesome conversation of the priests whom she was supporting for herself. The Aragonese vicar had allowed himself to be snatched away in triumph by another devout millionaire. He had grown tired, no doubt, of the excessive ease and idleness afforded him by his penitent, and was bored with astronomical observations on the roof of the dwelling in the Champs-Élysées.

At present she was offering her hospitality to a Monsignor, a Bishop *in partibus*, who directed the widow's money into various pious charities of his own invention.

Alicia had married a French Duke, twenty years her senior, and after a few months of marriage was causing herself to be very much talked about. Doña Mercedes, offended, was punishing her by seeing her very seldom, in hopes that such coldness would cause the Duchess de Delille to follow the example of her mother. In the meantime, the latter was concentrating all her family affection on the Monsignor, a saint, and a man of the world, who in the evening, to avoid a discordant note, took off his cassock and sat down at table in a tuxedo, while a flock of mechanical birds sang and flapped their wings in the large gilded cage in the Creole's dining room.

Michael Fedor saw Alicia twice in the Lubimoff palace. She did not feel there the uneasiness her mother experienced, and even declared the manias of the Princess very original and interesting. Afternoons when she was bored, and paid the Princess a visit, she too seemed to believe in the lamp table and in the "Queen's" protégés with the mystic gestures.

She too consulted them to find out whether she would be happy, and especially whether she would be greatly loved, although she never told who it was that was supposed to love her. On other occasions she asked the oracle, with a note of jealous anxiety in her voice, what a certain unknown person was doing at that particular time. The name of the person was kept secret, but some months he would be dark and at other times he would be blond. She and the lamp table understood each other perfectly.

"I always said that girl was cleverer than her mother," the Princess affirmed.

When Alicia first met the Prince, on his return home, she burst out laughing, and almost embraced him.

"Do you remember how we used to hate each other? Do you remember that day in the Bois when we whipped each other?"

She looked at him with an air of interest, scrutinizing him from head to heel without detecting anything of the displeasing youth of former times. She knew of his adventures in Russia, his loves, his duels, his expulsion. An interesting man! A Byronic fellow! Besides, she had heard that he was a bit of a brute with women.

"Come and see me. We must be friends. Remember we are relatives."

Michael scrutinized her also, but with a certain seriousness. He had heard a great deal about her since arriving in Paris. During her three years of married life the Duke had tried twice to divorce her. It weighed on his mind to think that he should be enjoying immense wealth just in return for allowing her to bear his name. When he shook hands with a friend, he was never sure of the latter's relations with his wife. But Alicia had married the Duke in order to be a Duchess, and in the end the couple came to a practical agreement. Half of her income was to go to the Duke, who was to travel, or, if he wished, reside in Paris with a former mistress. Alicia might live as she pleased in her splendid white mansion in the Avenue du Bois de Boulogne, and display a ducal coronet on her underwear, on her silver, and on the doors of her motor cars.

The little horsewoman of the Mexican plains, trained to morning gallops, had been transformed into a woman of proud and arrogant beauty. To Michael she looked like a California orange, golden, gleaming, wafting a strong sweet fragrance.

Inwardly he winced at the gaze of those dark eyes, so enticing and fascinating, so provoking and commanding, in full consciousness of power.

But no. He remembered that various men whom he disliked, had, according to common gossip, already preceded him in falling under Alicia's spell. And for the time being he was interested in a French actress, whom he had met on the train returning from Russia.

Besides, he suddenly beheld her again in his imagination as she was years before. Perhaps she had not changed. She was used to managing men with a firm hand, to changing from one to another, as though they were post horses. He and Alicia would quarrel at their second meeting. They might easily end by coming to blows.

He saw no more of her. New preoccupations changed the direction of his thoughts. One day in the street he met a Russian who seemed old and ill. It was Sergueff, his former teacher. Sergueff must now have been some forty years of age. He looked as though he were in his seventies, with a dirty white beard, grayish skin, and a wrinkled almost motheaten face, with no sign of life save in the two green holes that marked his eyes. From Saint Petersburg they had sent him to a prison in Siberia. He had escaped, crossed half of Asia on foot and alone, as far as a Chinese seaport, and there he had taken ship for the United States. The story of this tour of the world was told in a few words, as though it were a single walk on the boulevards.

Michael Fedor took him to the palace. The Colonel seemed dismayed by Sergueff's presence, and drew back into his shell. He must remember his own connections with nobles of the Russian court! Some of them were former generals of police!

The son of Princess Lubimoff talked for several days with the fugitive. The memory of his own expulsion from the court caused Michael vaguely to sympathize with this man who was likewise an exile. Besides, in the depths of his mind something of his mother's character was stirring, with all its inconsistencies and hazy vague desires. The officer of the Guard listened as attentively as a scholar to the doctrines of the revolutionist.

"Why, those men are right!" he exclaimed with the passionate enthusiasm that the Princess herself expressed for every novelty.

For the first few days he felt a yearning for martyrdom, a deep desire for renunciation, the mystic abnegation of the man of his race. He thought of many princes like himself, educated at court, with high social positions, who had given away their wealth to live among the poor and dedicate their lives to the triumph of truth and justice. He would do the same. He would reawaken to true life, and he was sure that his mother would approve. General Saldaña had given his blood to rehabilitate the past; he would give his to overcome all obstacles in the pathway of the future. Times change. The past consists of a certain number of centuries; the future is infinite.

But Lubimoff was not a true Russian. No sooner had he decided to carry out his mystic determination, than the Latin love of pleasure reawakened in him. Life is good, and offers many pleasant things! For him the tree of life was still overflowing with sap; there still remained for him so many leafy springs, so many fruitful summers! Later, perhaps, when only the dry wood remained....

The one positive and immediate result of this resurrection was Michael's sense of his own ignorance and of the emptiness of his life. There was something in the world besides knowing languages, wielding rapiers, and riding horses. Man should seek the realization of his greatness in more serious enterprises than love making, duels and betting. Fate, in giving him wealth, had exempted him from the harsh necessity of work. But that was no reason why he should renounce making his mark in the world, as he passed through it, just as thousands of his predecessors had done, and as millions of men to come would continue to do.

For the first time in his life Michael sought the comradeship of books, and this initial reading stirred him with a new desire. He made up his mind to know the world, to see strange countries, to struggle with the blind forces, which form the pulsing of the planet, and to live the coarse rough adventures of men who go from port to port. His father had told him of remote ancestors of the Saldaña family, who had gained titles and fortunes by setting sail from humble Spanish harbors, swooping out like sea gulls across the gloomy Ocean, in the track of Columbus and the Pinzons, in search of new lands of mystery. An ancestor of his, disembarking with the aged Ponce de Leon in Florida, in search of the famous "Fountain of Youth," had been one of the discoverers of the present United States. The first Saldaña to be a noble had obtained his title of "don" by founding a city in the neighborhood of Panama. Why should he not be a navigator like his forebears, a wanderer of the seas, enjoying exotic pleasures, and perhaps succeeding in wresting some secret from the blue deep?

Life in that palace which his mother's mania had rendered ugly, was becoming uncomfortable and distasteful, and was impelling him to flee. The Princess did not make the slightest objection, when informed that her son desired to buy a yacht to navigate the seven seas. Let him do so, by all means! It was a princely pastime, quite worthy of a Prince Lubimoff. They were constantly growing richer. The oil, the platinum, all the precious ores of their properties and the products of their lands, as large as nations, made up an enormous income. The preceding year it had reached the sum of seventeen million francs: a million a month! For a single private family it meant unbelievable wealth, and the Princess Lubimoff, who had temporarily regained her sanity, modestly added:

"But for a queen it isn't much."

In England Michael purchased a sailing yacht, with a sharp bow, bold masts, and an auxiliary engine, and gave it the Spanish name for the sea gull, the "Gaviota."

His idea was to continue on the ocean the life he had led on land, selecting, however, only its most interesting phases. For that reason he decided to take Sergueff along. The teacher seemed melancholy, as though the comforts and the liberal sums of money which the Prince bestowed on him weighed on his conscience like remorse. He had something more urgent to do in the world than voyage idly hither and thither in a luxurious boat. He disappeared one day, to return to Russia, as though the gallows had a fascination for him. Or was it that he preferred, in case of better luck than that, to travel once again around the world, but in his own manner?

The Colonel, as the aide de camp of the Prince, felt obliged to embark. He had never yet left "his boy's" side! But, oh, he was not blessed with sea legs, and, much less, with a sea stomach! He was a hero of the mountains! They were obliged to send him back to Paris from a port in Brazil.

The voyage of the *Gaviota* lasted for five years. In the second year Michael Fedor thought his career as a navigator was about to be interrupted. The war between Russia and Japan had just broken out and he cabled from a Pacific port, asking for his former place in the Guard. The reply was a long time in coming. The Czar was still angry with him and kept him in exile.

"So much the better!" Michael finally said to himself in a voice choked with anger. He guessed what was going to happen; what was to be the final fate of those brave Russians of the sharp sabers, when they came to face the astute little yellow men who had silently gone on appropriating the most scientific occidental arts of killing.

His adventures in the various ports, his relations with women of every race and color, were sufficient to fill his life.

"I am studying geography," he wrote Don Marcos, after inquiring about his mother's health. "I am studying the geography of love."

It was not long before he was obliged to interrupt his cruise to return to the Princess. The physicians had ordered her away from the Paris palace, with its gloomy decorations so stimulating to her obsessions. They were sending her to the Riviera to drink sunlight and open air.

And poor Maria Stuart, absolutely *incognito*, went from one large hotel to another, occupying entire floors with her retinue of much beaten Russian servants and much adored soothsayers and witch doctors. She was the despair of the hotel keepers, who were always glad to see her depart, though she alone paid more than all the other guests put together.

Her son found her looking like a specter in her flowing mourning garb. She was weaker and thinner, and her eyes had taken on an alarming, fixed stare, which gave one the creeps. Her complexion had lost its former whiteness, gradually growing darker as though burned by an inner fire. For the moment her sole preoccupation was the construction of a palace on the Blue Coast. On French territory, in sight of Monte Carlo, she had bought a small promontory, a spur of land and rocks jutting out into the sea, a ridge covered with century-old olive trees and gnarled pines. She was kept busy quarreling with a stubborn old couple, an aged peasant and his wife, who were refusing to sell her the extreme point of the headland. She had already spent many thousands of francs on the plans of the future palace. Architects, painters, and landscape gardeners were constantly working for her, making studies of the historic past, in the endeavor to view of the Mediterranean an enormous Scottish castle express her imaginings. Her idea was to erect in full as Scotch as could possibly be imagined; in short, according to the Princess, it was to be "a novel of Walter Scott, done in stone."

Michael was frightened. The sumptuous dungeon in Paris was to be repeated in the face of that luminous sea, in one of the most smiling landscapes of the earth. Behind his mother's back he talked with all the men who were working on the future Villa Sirena, the "Villa of the Sirens." The Princess had selected this name, in the conviction that on moonlight nights the daughters of the briny deep would come and visit her, singing on the reefs beneath her window. That was the least they could do for her!

Each day the veil of mystery was opening more widely before her eyes, allowing her to see things which for others were invisible.

Don Marcos, who, deserted by his former pupil, had gone back to the Princess, likewise received instructions from Lubimoff. He was to prevent the unhappy lady from perpetrating such a sacrilege on the Mediterranean. But what could the poor Colonel do with that madwoman who spent whole weeks without speaking to him, as though she did not know who he was!

The Prince returned to his yacht, and a year later being by chance in upper Norway on his return from an expedition to the Arctic Ocean, he received the sad but expected news. His mother had died, just as she saw rising from among the olive trees and pines of the rosy promontory, the beginning of huge stone walls artificially blackened like the painted panels in the antique shops, and which looked as though they were about to fall in ruins from mere age, as soon as they had risen from the ground.

CHAPTER III

MICHAEL arrived in time to receive the body of the Princess in Paris. Before her death her mind had been illuminated by the sudden flare of reason which is the signal of the end in cases of serious mental disturbances. She had left various papers on which she had noted loans made to certain persons, and judicious suggestions for her son in regard to the management of the enormous fortune. She wanted to be buried beside her husband, her first husband, "the hero," in the Père Lachaise cemetery. During the last years she had stayed in Paris, she had been seized once more by the craze for building, and had busied herself with the preparation of her final dwelling place. Beside the mausoleum of the Marquis of Villablanca, whose image, frowning and indomitable, held in one hand a broken sword, she had set up another monument no less ostentatious with a statue which was supposed to be her exact likeness and was nothing less than the semblance of the unhappy Queen of Scots, as it appears in the engraving of the Romanticist period.

During the funeral ceremonies, Michael Fedor met again many persons who formerly visited the Lubimoff palace, and whom he had thought were dead. Doña Mercedes in tears embraced him. She had become extraordinarily stout, and the coppery complexion inherited from her Aztec ancestors had taken on an unhealthy ascetic pallor. She looked like the Mother Superior of a noble convent of nuns. At her side, Monsignor, in his silk cassock and with an air of compunction, was moving his lips to save the dead woman's soul. "My son! We have all our sorrows." And as she said this, the poor lady looked at another woman elegantly dressed in mourning who stood there somewhat aloof, in the cemetery, and seemed utterly incapacitated by the ceremony which had obliged her to rise before noon.

The Duchess de Delille also came forward to meet him, taking both his hands and giving him a strange glance.

"Your mother loved me ... really loved me. During these last years we saw each other very often."

Michael nodded assent. He knew that already. The Princess Lubimoff had been the one loyal friend of this passionate unscrupulous woman, who was gradually losing every one's respect. She had defended Alicia when other high society women declared open war and closed their doors to her, fearing for their husbands' fidelity. As she used to play every winter at Monte Carlo, she had been in the company of the Princess up to the last moments.

"She loved me more than my mother ever did.... Perhaps she remembered that I might have been her daughter."

The Prince walked away, as though annoyed by this allusion. He had heard such things about her!... But all during the ceremony he kept seeing her in his mind's eye. She was still beautiful, but so strangely beautiful. Her skin had lost the golden tinge of ripened fruit, and now was pale, the dull white of Japanese paper. Her large eyes, which gave off green and yellow glints, stared with disturbing fixity and seemed at the same time to have a blank expression, as though covered by an invisible spider web. Her least bitter enemies accused her of a certain propensity for spirits. She drank all sorts of American mixed drinks like an habitué of the bars. Other people attributed her pallor and the continual darkly bewildered look in her eyes to morphine, opium and all the various liquids and perfumes producing lethargy and creating "artificial paradise." The little Alicia of former years was drinking, draining it to the last drop from the cup of life in deep draughts.

Michael Fedor thought that he had seen the last of her, but a few days later he began to receive letters. He was alone, and must be feeling sad, so she was inviting him to come and eat with her, informally, of course, as was natural among close relatives. His evasions brought fresh invitations by telephone. The Prince, like a person fulfulling a tiresome social obligation, finally went one evening to her little palace in the Avenue du Bois, one of the numerous imitations of the Petit Trianon, which are to be found in various parts of the world.

The Duchess de Delille was proud of this edifice and the tiny garden with its sharp, gilded grating, in front of which all fashionable Paris passed. Michael was acquainted with the drawing rooms without ever having been inside them. The illustrated journals, which cover the styles of wealthy social life, had published photographs, in Europe and America, of the interior of her residence. Gossip had kept him informed of Alicia's strange life. She had suddenly been taken with the mad desire of seeing people, of being admired, and of astonishing every one by her prodigality. She gave a series of great fêtes, and publicly protested because the municipality of Paris would not allow her to illuminate the entire Champs Élysées and the Arch of Triumph so that her guests might ride up to her very door in a fiery apotheosis. She had given a garden party in the Bois de Boulogne, with water sports, and dances of sacred dancers, brought from Asia. The buffet supper had been prepared for three thousand guests. On another occasion, for a single costume ball, she spent a hundred thousand francs, to transform part of her residence into an interior of Persian style and the next day she began to have the rooms restored to their original state.

Suddenly she would disappear, and people would wink and make malicious comments because she left no address. Some new love affair! Hers were nearly always wandering fancies, that called for long trips and new horizons! Perhaps she was in Constantinople or in Egypt; perhaps she was in hiding in one of the large New York hotels. At times such guesses were right; and then again the most intimate friends of the Duchess could affirm that she had not left Paris. Was not her automobile standing in front of the door?

This was another of Alicia's eccentricities. At all hours of the day and night, one of her various expensive cars was kept in readiness in front of the stairway. Three chauffeurs divided the service between them. They stayed in the porter's quarters; and as soon as the bell was heard, they had only to put on their gloves, run to the machine, and start the motor. She often chose the most extraordinary hours for going out. Sometimes it would be just after returning from a ball, then again she would get up for a ride after she had gone to bed. Frequently she would select the early morning hours which were usually her time of soundest sleep.

At times the chauffeurs would succeed each other, week after week, without leaving the gate of the mansion. The Duchess did not care to go out. She no longer felt her sudden impulses to ride aimlessly about Paris, while the city slept, pay unseasonable calls, or glide through the woods on the outskirts of the capital at the height of some violent storm. Meantime, the autos seemed to age, as they stood there motionless, now with their wheels deep in the snow of the courtyard, and again with the glass of the wind shield flecked with the tear drops of the slanting rain, that swept under the glass covered porte-cochère. During all such periods, Alicia, in spite of her restless impulsive nature, would be spending whole days in bed, telling her intimate friends that to keep one's beauty one must take a "rest cure" from time to time. She would entertain her friends at dinner without getting out of bed. The table would be spread in luxurious fashion in her large bedroom, and lying between the sheets, with the dishes within reach on a tiny table, she would laugh and chat for hours with her guests. Months would go by without her seeing the outside of her house, while the costly objects in her rooms, amassed to indulge her whims, were quite forgotten. Her vanity was satisfied, at such times, by the mere fact of having constructed a costly jewel case to harbor her idleness.

The Prince met her in a little reception room on the ground floor. She was in truth receiving him with absolute lack of ceremony. She was dressed in a black tunic of her own invention, a combination of the Greek peplum and the Japanese kimono. Her bare arms floated free from the soft silk that almost seemed to live, it clung so closely to her body. Underneath it, half revealed, were the contours and perfumed warmth of her flesh, hidden by no inner veils. Michael glanced at his tuxedo and gleaming shirt-front as though his own costume were quite out of place.

As she took him to the elevator, which was white and quilted like a glove box, he caught a rapid glimpse of the drawing rooms of the lower floor, ostentatious, but left in a shadow almost as dark as night; of the large dining-hall, deserted, with the furniture covered; of the little dining-room in which there were no signs whatsoever of preparations.... Where was she taking him?... Was the table set in her bedroom?

The elevator passed the second floor without stopping? "We are going to my study," said Alicia. "I eat there when I am alone."

The Prince was amazed at the so-called "study," a large room which occupied a major portion of the third floor, and in which only one or two books in a small book-rack were to be seen. The place was decorated in imitation "Far East" style: plain black lacquer furniture, silk either of pale shades or of an intense dark purple, and an array of frightful idols. A diffused bluish light, like that used in night scenes on the stage, descended from the ceiling. A screen, embroidered with a design in gold, formed a sort of second more intimate room, the floor of which was covered with white rugs of fur, with long, silky hair. Heaped about were dozens of pillows of various colors adorned with winged reptiles and unheard of flowers.

An exotic, penetrating odor made Lubimoff wince. He knew that perfume. And there was a look of severity in his eyes as he glanced sharply at the Duchess.

"Sit down," she said. "They are going to serve us."

As the Prince looked about, without seeing any sort of a chair, Alicia set him an example, dropping on a heap of cushions. Michael sat down in the same fashion, beside a tiny mother of pearl table no bigger than a tabouret. On it a lamp with a dark shade let fall a circle of soft light. Inwardly the Prince began to feel a boiling of suppressed anger as he thought of his evening wasted.

"You must have eaten this way often," she continued, "you have traveled more than I. The style of decoration must be familiar to you."

Yes; he knew the style, the original and authentic style, and for that very reason he did not care to see it again in imitation. Besides obliging him to eat on the floor, there in a house on the Avenue de Bois.... What an affectation!

But in a short time his opinion began to change. A poseur she undoubtedly was, but affectation had already become a more or less natural trait in her, a sort of second nature. He guessed that even in its slightest details none of this had been prepared especially for him. Alicia lived and ate there when she was alone just as she was doing then. She was prey to a desire to be different from other people even when no one was noticing her.

The servant in charge of the meal was a copper-colored man with a long down-curling mustache. He was dressed in a black tuxedo, with a white cloth wrapped around his legs like a skirt. He had long hair, done up on his head like a woman's and held in place by a tortoiseshell comb. The Asiatic was placing the huge trays containing the food on the floor: Some of the dishes were of ancient hammered silver, others of many colored lacquer, or of semi-transparent materials made in imitation of emerald, topaz, and red sealing wax.

For Michael the meal looked like something a great chef might have prepared if he had suddenly gone mad and made up the dishes in the midst of his ravings. There was not a single item that suggested the harmonious course of an ordinary dinner. The palate acted on the imagination, awakening memories of distant travels, visions of far off lands. Exotic preserves alternated with hot dishes. Pastry flavored with penetrating perfumes was served along with sharp, biting, or intensely bitter sauces.

Alicia, half reclining on the cushions, looking at the dishes without appetite, extended her hand carelessly toward the most unusual delicacies, and those with the most pungent and racy savors. Clearly the perversion of her palate was profound. She herself saw to it that Michael's glass was always filled. It was a drink of her own invention, having a champagne base. It burned and rasped his mouth, paralyzing all other sensation with its stinging coolness. It penetrated his nostrils with a lingering scent of the rarest flowers and of Asiatic spices.

Speaking of the dead Princess, Alicia came to mention her own mother. They were now on terms of open hostility. Her eyes began to gleam with defiance as she was reminded of Doña Mercedes, confined in the Champs-Élysée residence with her court of clericals, and showing herself in public only for the organizing of pious works. She was trying to starve her only daughter to death!... And as Michael smiled at this explosion of anger, she explained her grievances.

"She gives me hardly anything; a mere nothing: half a million francs. And I have to hand two hundred and fifty thousand a year over to my husband: a rather expensive lover, whom I avoid seeing. You are really rich, my dear, and don't understand such things.... Since the fortune is all in her name, she tries to starve me out and keeps her money to squander it with the priests.... Poor Señora! She can't find any admirers now except that *Monsignor* and other sponges like him.... And I, her own daughter, have to implore her like a beggar for the crumbs she gives me, seasoned with sermons.... Oh, if it hadn't been for your mother! She really was a great lady: I never lamented my poverty to her in vain; she gave me even more than I asked for. You know of course that I owe you some money. A little.... I don't know how much. Didn't you really know that?... I shall pay you back when I get my inheritance."

And with brutal frankness she expounded her full thought.

"When will that bigot leave me in peace?... Old people ought to make way for the young. What fun do they get out of going on living?"

They had finished eating. She went on filling both their glasses with her special drink. At first Michael had found it repugnant, but in the end he was attracted to its refreshing fragrance which gently troubled the senses, like an intoxication with perfumes.

"Of course you use the pipe," said Alicia simply.

He shook his head and thought of the odor which struck him on entering. He knew what sort of a "pipe" it was, and gazed about the study. The smoking den must be in some hidden corner!

"A man like you!" she went on. "A sailor! And I fooled myself into thinking we'd smoke together!"

She even gave him to understand that the hope of being able to give him that forbidden pleasure was the principal reason for her invitation. She became resigned when she learned that the Prince, vigorous as he was, suffered nausea every time he attempted to experiment with that Asiatic vice. And while he lighted a havana, Alicia took from a silver case the cigarettes which she smoked in the presence of the "uninitiated": Oriental tobacco, but heavily dosed with opium. Suddenly Michael was convinced of something of which he had a presentiment the moment he entered the place, or even earlier, the moment their glances had met in the cemetery. He saw her half rising from the cushions, with a panther-like contraction of her muscles, as though she were ready to spring at him. It was the concentrated impulse of the beast, beautiful and sure of its power, unable to wait, and not knowing how to feign.

Alicia had forgotten the demi-tasse she held in her hand, as she sat there, looking at him fixedly. The tiny blue electric spark dancing in her eyes was something well known to Michael.

It was the offering glance of female silence, inviting violence, and mastery. He had encountered that glance often along his path of triumph as a conquering millionaire.... He felt he must say something at once to break the silent charm of the beautiful witch, who, sure of her final victory, was smiling and blowing puffs of cigarette smoke toward him. So Michael alluded to her amorous fame, to the great number of lovers she was supposed to have had. That might widen the distance between them.

"Ah! You too?" said Alicia laughing, with masculine frankness. "I don't suppose your morals are the same as Mamma's! You are not going to read me a sermon on my behavior. Although, after all, Mamma doesn't blame me for what I do. What makes her angry is the fact that I am not afraid of what people say, and that sometimes I am attracted to unknown men of low birth. Poor Señora! If I were to have an affair with a king or a crown prince, perhaps she'd even let us see each other in her house, and have her *Monsignor* mount guard into the bargain."

She remained silent for a moment. That disturbing glance was still fixed on Michael.

"It is true; I have had a lot of men. And how about you? Do you think I don't know about your wanderings all over the planet in quest of types of women unknown to the novels and capable of giving new sensations?... We have both done the same: only it wasn't necessary for me to travel around so much to learn just what you have learned.... And you are not so absurd as to imagine, as certain men do, that our cases are not to be compared because we are of different sexes."

The Prince listened silently as she expounded her ideas. She was deeply in love with life, and in return she demanded all that life could give her.... The minds of other women were occupied with questions of a material nature: desire for wealth, longings for luxury, domestic cares.... As for her, she possessed everything; to-morrow held no worries for her; not even in regard to her beauty, sustained as it was by wonderful health, and seeming to increase in spite of age and her prodigal waste of energies.

In her life, made up of caprices, always completely satisfied, even to the point of satiety, only one thing interested her, from its infinite variety and from its many phases, which might seem to vulgar people a monotonous repetition of one another, but which in reality were distinct for a mind attuned, as hers was, to exquisite sensations. That thing was love.

"Oh please understand me, Michael; don't sit there laughing to yourself. You know me too well ever to imagine that I believe in love as the majority of women do. I know that a certain amount of illusion is necessary to color the material aspect of love; we all lie about it a little, and we enjoy the lie even though we know it as such; but way down deep, I laugh at love as the world understands it, just as I laugh at so many things which people venerate.... I don't want lovers, I want admirers. I am not looking for love; I care more for adoration."

She was proud of her beauty. She spoke of Venus as though the goddess were a real person. She admired the Olympic serenity with which the Deity of Passion gave herself to gods and men, never surrendering her superiority even at the moment when she was submitting to the domination of the stronger sex. Alicia considered herself a super-beauty, belonging to a sphere outside the ordinary limits of vice and virtue. She thought herself a living work of art;

and art is neither moral nor immoral; its mission is fulfilled when it is beautiful.

"Poets, painters, and musicians seek to abandon themselves to the greatest number of admirers. They do their utmost to enlarge their circle of public worshipers and with feminine coquetry they try to attract new suitors. I am like them. I do not need to create beauty, for as they say, I have it in myself. I am my own work, but I love glory; I need admiration; and for that reason I give myself generously, content with the happiness which I apportion, but keeping my public at my feet, without allowing myself to be dominated by those whom I seek."

Michael was sure that many artists must have left their imprint on that woman's life. It was evident in the words and imagery with which she endeavored to express her enthusiasm for her own body. Her pride in her beauty was boundless. What were the ambitions of men, compared to the satisfaction of being lovely and desired? Only the glory of warriors, of blood-stained conquerors, whose names are known even in the remotest wilds of the earth, equals the glory that a woman feels in the sense of universal power over men.

"To me," continued Alicia, "the truest and most beautiful thing ever written is 'the old men on the wall.'"

The Prince looked at her questioningly; so she went on to explain. She referred to the old Trojan men in the *Iliad*, who were protesting against the long siege of their city, against the blood sacrifice of thousands of heroes, against poverty and hardship, all due to the fault of a woman.... But Helen, majestic in her beauty, passed before the old men, trailing her golden tunic; and they all lapsed into silent contemplation, rapt in wonder, as though divine Aphrodite had descended upon earth; and they murmured like a prayer: "It is indeed fitting that we should suffer thus for her. So lovely she is!"

"I like to see men suffer on my account. How glorious if I might be the cause of a great slaughter, like that ancient immortal woman!... I have an exultant feeling of pride when I notice that envy and spite are whispering behind my back, starting all that gossip that makes my mother so furious. Only extraordinary people stir up torrents of abuse.... And afterwards, in the drawing rooms, the very same austere gentlemen who have seconded all that their wives and daughters have to say against me, look at me with sly admiring glances, as I pass; and some of them blush in confusion and others turn pale. It is easy to guess that I have only to beckon and their silent admiration would.... I too have my 'old men on the wall.'"

Michael suddenly realized that while she was talking she had been coming gradually closer, from cushion to cushion as she lay resting on her elbows. She was almost at his feet, with head held high, endeavoring to envelop him in a wave of magnetism from her fixed and dominating eyes. She seemed like a black and white snake, twisting forward little by little among the cushions as though they were rocks of various colors.

"The only man of whom I have ever thought the least bit, the only one I ever considered at all different from other men," she continued in a half whisper, "is you.... Don't be alarmed: it isn't love. I am not going to invert rôles, and propose to you. Perhaps it is because, as children, we used to hate each other; because you never wanted me. That is such an unheard of thing in my life, that it alone is enough to interest me."

She put her hands on his knees, as though she were about to rise.

"When I saw you in the cemetery, after so many years, I remembered all that I had heard about you. Many women whom I know have been sweethearts of yours, and I said to myself: Why not I, too? Then I thought of all the men who have come into my life, and I added: Why not he?" ...

And now Alicia's elbows were resting on his knees, and as the Prince was seated on but two pillows, their lips and eyes were almost on a level. As she talked he could feel her breath on his face. It was like the breeze in an Asiatic forest, whispering beneath the moon. The spices and flowers with which the wine was saturated seemed to float in that volatile caress.

Michael tried to avoid her advance, but one of Alicia's hands was already on his shoulder. He merely shook his head.

"Don't be afraid," she added, exaggerating the caressing quality of her sigh. "There are no embarrassing obligations with me. You may leave me when you wish; perhaps I shall be the one to leave you first. I have wanted you for the last few days. You must surely desire me as the others do.... Let us live this moment, like people who know the secret of life and all it can give.... Then if we tire of each other, good-by, with no hard feeling and no pining!"

When from time to time in after years the Prince recalled that scene, he always felt a certain dissatisfaction with himself. He was sure he had seemed brutal as well as ridiculous. In his travels he had approached women frequently in the most matter of fact way, often remembering them afterwards with some repugnance; yet here he was, rebelling with a feeling of offended modesty at the advances of the Duchess. No! With her, never! Rising within him he felt the same displeasure that had once made him raise his whip in his youth.

He found himself on his feet in the middle of the study, looking anxiously toward the door and muttering stupid excuses. "No, I must go: it is late. Some friends are waiting for me...." She had gained control of herself. She too was standing looking at him with astonishment and wrath.

"You are the only one who could do a thing like this," she said, in a cutting tone, as they parted. "I see it all clearly now. I hate you as you hate me. My whim was a stupid one. You have permitted yourself a liberty which no one in the world will ever be able to take again. If I were younger than I am I would thrash you again as I did in the Bois; but instead, just consider that I am repeating everything I said then."

They did not see each other again.

When the Prince had set in order everything concerning the inheritance from his mother, he thought of resuming his voyages, but on a more magnificent scale. It was no longer necessary for him to ask the Princess for money. He was one of the great millionaires of the world. Those who were in charge of the administration of his affairs—an office with numerous clerks, almost equalling the government bureau of a small state—made the announcement that the fifteen million francs which the Princess had received annually would soon be twenty, through the development of Russian railways, which allowed more intensive working of his mines.

The Colonel was commissioned to have the heavy medieval walls of Villa Sirena torn down, and the place replanned according to the Prince's tastes. The latter hated architectural resuscitations. He could not bear modern buildings patterned to flatter the pride of the rich proprietors, after the Alhambra, the palaces of Florence, or the solemn and orderly constructions of Versailles.

"The furniture ought to correspond to the period," said Michael, "and people ought to live in such houses as they lived in in the century which produced that particular style. People living in an ancient house ought to dress and eat as in former times.... What an absurdity to reconstruct those historic shells, with the interior arranged to suit the needs of modern men who are forced to commit an anachronism at every step!"

He recalled the project of a millionaire friend of his, a member of the Institute, who had built a Roman house on the Riviera, Roman in all the exactness of its details. At the house-warming the guests were obliged to sleep on corded beds and to eat reclining on couches; and even more intimate conveniences were modeled on the principle of hygiene known to the ancient Cæsars. Within twenty-four hours they all pretended they had received urgent telegrams calling them to Paris, and the owner himself after a few months, left his house in charge of a keeper to show to tourists as a museum.

Michael was fond of modern architecture, whose cathedrals are machine shops and large railway stations. Applied to dwellings it pleased him for its lack of style: white walls, a few moldings, rounded corners, with no angles whatsoever, so that the dust might be pursued to its remotest hiding places, wide openings letting in the breeze and the sunlight, double walls between which hot or cold air, and water at various temperatures, could circulate.

"Up to the present time," the Prince asserted, "man has lived in magnificent jewel cases of art and filth. Modern architects have done more in the last thirty years to make life pleasant than the artist-builders, so much admired by history, did in three thousand. They have declared running water and the bath-room as indispensable, things which were unknown to kings themselves half a century ago. They have invented the furnace and the water closet. Don't talk to me about the magnificent palaces of Versailles, where there was not a single toilet, and where every morning the lackeys were obliged to empty two hundred vessels for the king and his courtiers. Often to be through quicker, they threw their contents out of the majestic windows, and sometimes it would fall on the sedan chair and the retinue of a Dauphine or an ambassador."

Toledo applied himself to supervising the construction of Villa Sirena in accordance with the desires of the Prince, making it a plain white building, and without any definite style of architecture. Lubimoff himself, at the proper time, would take charge of the artistic touches, placing famous pictures, statues, tapestries, or rugs, just where they would be most pleasing to the eye. The house was to be a harmony of simple, pure lines. The walls were to have heating and cooling systems for the different seasons, and running water was to be available in abundance everywhere. Each room was to have its electric lights and its electric fan.

The Prince found it a much easier task to make over his wandering ocean residence. He simply sold the Gaviota, which reminded him of his youthful dependence on his family, and went to the United States to look into an advertisement. Three years before a certain multimillionaire had begun the construction of a yacht, designed to be more luxurious and of greater tonnage than that of any European sovereign. As the American was about to witness the consummation of this triumph of the democratic kings of industry over the historic kings of the Old World, he was killed in an automobile accident, and his heirs did not know what to do with the leviathan which would only be of use to an immensely rich, and, in their opinion, somewhat crazy traveler. They were thinking of selling it at a loss to the Kaiser, William II, having decided finally to endure his demands as a sharp business man, when Prince Lubimoff appeared. A week later on the white stern and bows of the yacht a new name in gold letters was displayed, a name that was repeated in addition on the life preservers and on the various tenders, the dingies, the steam launches, and the motor boats. The American yacht had become the *Gaviota II*.

It had the tonnage of a small trans-Atlantic liner and the speed of a torpedo boat. Each day the wealth of an ordinary man went up in smoke through the *Gaviota II's* double funnels. During a trip to some distant island, the supply of coal gave out. Immediately a collier chartered by the Prince, came to meet the *Gaviota II* in the farthest seas to fill the bunkers with fuel.

Quiet harbors came to be illuminated at night, as though the sun had risen. When the Prince gave a *fête*, the ship would be a blaze of glory from the water to the mastheads, its outline marked by electric bulbs of various colors, while powerful searchlights shot out movable streams of radiance and drew the waves, the shores, and rows of city houses from the depths of the darkness. At other times, the white fire of the *Gaviota II's* monstrous eyes would flash on walls of ice towering to the clouds, and seals, penguins, and polar bears would waken from sleep frightened by the strange luminous, puffing monster that darted off like lightning into the mystery of night.

To be the owner of a floating palace which, when anchoring off large cities, drew such crowds of sightseers as rare spectacles only attract, was not enough for Michael Fedor. So he created something more interesting even than the luxurious salons, and the refinements of comfort of the *Gaviota II*: he built up an orchestra.

Sensuous delight in music was for him the most exquisite of emotions. When his ears were satiated with the sweetness and melody of traditional music, he sought unknown and often bizarre composers, who aroused his curiosity; but he always came back to demanding as the *pièces de résistance* of his harmonic feasts, the masters who had been his first love, and above all, Beethoven.

Treated as though they were officers, paid to their liking, and with the added inducement of being able to see a great deal of the world, musicians from every country offered their services to the yacht's orchestra. Famous concert players and young composers came in as mere instrumentalists. Some were ill, and sought to regain their health in a voyage around the world in real luxury and without expense; others embarked through love of adventure, to see new lands in this floating castle, in which everything seemed organized for an eternal holiday. There were never less than fifty of them.

"My orchestra is the finest in the world," the Prince would proudly say when his guests complimented him after one of the concerts his musicians gave at rare intervals on land.

In tropical nights, beneath the enormous honey-colored moon changing the sea to a vast plain of quick-silver, the musicians, seated in evening clothes before the rows of music racks illuminated by tiny electric lights, would weave on the quiet air, which seemed to have retained the first faint cries of the planet at its birth, the most original melodies, the most subtle combination of sounds that the sublime rapture of artists in god-like inspiration ever created. The music floated out behind the boat in the mystery of the ocean, like a scarf unfolding, breaking and scattering in fragments, with the smoke of the funnels. When the orchestra paused one could hear the distant subdued beat of the propellers, churning the foam with a humming sound; and then from time to time the slow tolling of the bell calling the men on watch, or the cry of the lookout snuggled into the crow's nest on the mainmast, reporting his vigilance with the rhythmic into-nation of a muezzin from a minaret. And the monotonous music of the sea gave an impression of night, and of immensity, to the music of man.

At the foot of the companionways, or on the outjutting parts of the lower decks, the various officers and officials of the Prince gathered to hear the concert in the night. On the prow the sailors squatted, listening to the music in religious silence, as is often the case with simple men when confronted with something they do not understand, but which inspires awe. Aft, the only listener would be Michael Fedor, standing at a distance from the music, and with his back toward the musicians, watching at his feet, the divided, foaming waters which rushed by like a double river far out and away from the boat. As occasionally he raised his cigar to his lips, his pensive features would appear for a moment in the darkness, lighted by the red glow.

The yacht held another more silent group. Those who succeeded in getting on board in the ports always obtained a distant glimpse of a woman or two with white shoes, blue skirts, jackets with rows of gold buttons, masculine collars and neckties, and officers' caps. No one knew for certain how many such women there may have been. The men of the crew were forbidden access to the central quarters of the boat, and to the upper deck. Some of them, chancing to break the rule through oversight, had met the Prince's companions attired in elegant naval uniforms, or more lightly clad, like dancers, in elaborate and exotic costumes. At the large ports, steam launches landed these mysterious and beautiful travelers for a few hours on shore. It was remarked that they dressed with modest elegance and that they would speak various languages.

When the *Gaviota II* returned and anchored in the same harbor she had visited the preceding year, those whose curiosity had been aroused found that the personnel of the wandering harem had been completely renewed. They might occasionally recognize one or two of the former ladies, but now their faces wore the placid expression of the odalisque who has been supplanted, but is nevertheless contented with luxury and oblivion.

Some years Michael Fedor suspended his travels, during the summer, to take up his abode at fashionable beaches. The women who accompanied him on his long voyages remained on board, with all the lavish comforts to which they were accustomed. At other times he parted with them, as one dismisses a crew when a ship goes out of commission, at the end of a trip.

Immediately he became interested in women living stay-at-home lives, in shore society, and in summer flirtations at famous watering places. He would take up his abode in a hotel on the coast, while his yacht was to be seen rising from the azure waters, motionless, like a palace of mystery and magnificence, the center of all feminine imaginings.

Living in Biarritz he came to know Atilio Castro intimately through learning that they were related on his father's side. The Spaniard admired the fascination exercised by the Prince, often without wishing to do so, on all women.

Never at any period had women been more strongly attracted by luxury or felt less scruples in the means of obtaining it than at present. This was the opinion of Castro. Lavish display, which in other centuries had been within reach of only the very few families, was now possible for every one. All one needed to indulge in it was money. Besides, it was necessary to take into account present-day progress in material things, which has made life easier, but at the same time has increased our needs.

"The motor car and the pearl necklace have made more victims than the wars of Napoleon," said Atilio.

"These two things are like the gala uniform of women, and those who are forced to go without them consider themselves unfortunate and ill treated by fate. This twin image has shattered the illusions of maidens and the fidelity of wives. Mothers in middle class society, with melancholy dejection written on their faces as though they had made stupid failures of their lives, advise their daughters: 'If you are going to get married, make sure you will get an auto and a pearl necklace.' And long after the modest marriage this desire still remains, strengthened by maternal advice. Luxury is the one thought, luxury at whatever cost. Luxury has been democratized. It is within reach of all, obtainable through money, which has no taint, no odor, no sign of its origin."

"You are the great provider of the expensive motor car of fashionable make and of the rope of pearls," continued Castro. "You are the great Sultan of magnificence. Your signature to a check is enough to sweep a woman off her feet in a torrent of gold. Make the most of your opportunity! The period in which you were born has left you an open field for your talents."

And the Prince, who was not at all in need of such advice, went his way as conqueror through a world in which the best accredited virtues collapsed before his attack. Even sincere resistance finally appeared to him to be a clever device for postponing surrender and increasing the market value of desire. The millions from Russia were scattered broadcast in smaller and smaller subdivisions, maintaining the well being and display of many homes, indulging the taste for luxury of numerous ladies, and keeping numberless factories busy producing elegant novelties of female luxury. A few women felt a sincere interest in Michael Fedor for his own sake, because of the mysterious prestige of his voyages in a boat which was talked about as though it were an enchanted palace; and also because of his adventures with celebrated actresses and women of high society, which made him more attractive. But once their vanity and curiosity were satisfied, they allowed their own self-interest to have a word. "Why should I be any more altruistic than the rest?"

They were not obliged to use cunning or round-about phrases in formulating their requests. Some at the second meeting, took on a melancholy air, and spoke of the sad realities of life. But the generous Prince anticipated their desires. He preferred to pay his mistresses and dazzle them with splendid gifts. Thus he could regard them as favored slaves covered with jewels. In this way also, it was easier to break with them: He could go away from them whenever he so desired, satisfied with his own behavior, and quite unmoved by their tears and laments. From his semi-oriental Russian ancestors he had inherited a great sensual capacity, which caused him to be attracted to women, and at the same time to feel an inalterable scorn for them. He indulged them but could not love them; he adored them, but was stirred to indignation when they presumed to be on terms of equality with him. He was capable of ruining himself, of braving death for them, but he was ready to thrust them aside with his foot if they tried in the least to govern his life. The ambitious ones who feigned deep, passionate love for him in the hope of marriage, the sentimental ones who tried to interest him with psychological subtleties, and those who kept their maternal enthusiasm even in adultery, and murmured in his ear how happy they would be to have a child who might resemble him, waited for him in vain the following day. "Neither deep passion, nor children!" ... Two trails of smoke were soon rising from the yacht, carrying its owner to another port or perhaps to another continent: or if he wished to flee from a city in the interior, he gave orders that his private car should be coupled to the first train that was leaving.

These flights were never undertaken without a generous remembrance. Michael Fedor's munificence continued for those whom he had abandoned. Each year new names were added to his budget, like that of a reigning house which allots pensions to its forgotten servants. But the pensions of Prince Lubimoff were for the maintenance of luxury and not of life. The most modest were over thirty thousand francs a year. The average was double that amount.

"Your Excellency: there will have to be a revision," his administrator would say.

Michael would examine the list of names, hesitating at a few. He could not recall clearly the persons who bore them. Then suddenly he would smile, as certain visions were suddenly and attractively awakened in his mind. He was immensely wealthy: why not keep up the luxury which was the one dream of all of them?... He was not disturbed by the jealous thought that his successors would be reaping the benefit of that luxury.

He felt a certain god-like pride in making his generosity felt at all times, without letting himself be seen. In Paris a jewelry shop managed by a Jew of Spanish origin limited its entire business to the production of the Prince's gifts. His gems of high intrinsic value, with no false artifices, had a certain family resemblance, a sort of imaginary perfume which enabled the women who displayed them to recognize each other. When it was least expected, at tea time, in the dining-room of a hotel, at an elegant watering place at a dance, two women who had just met would gaze at each other's ears and breast in silence, until the boldest, blushing imperceptibly under her rouge, would ask simply: "You knew Prince Lubimoff too?..."

Atilio Castro felt a deep admiration for his relative, less on account of his triumphs than of the iron constitution required to sustain them.

"What a Cossack! A regular Cossack!... He is a true descendant of that lover of the Great Catherine!"

Nevertheless, frequently the yacht would hurriedly put out to sea on long voyages, without its master being forced to flee from any dangerous or entangling passion. He was running away from himself, from his perverse imagination and curiosity, which made him seek and allure different women, upsetting his peace of mind, without rousing in him any real desire. He undertook the most extraordinary voyages, for the sake of the bracing air and the sense of restfulness the sea brings. The orchestra accompanied him; but the "harem" remained on shore. He had gone completely around the globe, following the shortest route; then he had repeated this circumnavigation, but over a zig-zag course, to become acquainted with all the coasts of the earth. At present he was on going on whimsical trips; he was sailing from one hemisphere to another for the pleasure of visiting one or another of the small islands which seem lost in the Pacific, and are so tiny that on the maps they look like mere dots placed after long names traced on the blue colored surface.

Returning from one of these excursions on which he went around the world as though it were his personal property, he received by wireless the news that Germany had declared war against Russia and France.

He felt no great surprise. He knew William II personally. It was because of him that Prince Lubimoff avoided cruising off the coast of Norway in summer.

The year following his acquisition of the *Gaviota II* he had come across the Imperial yacht in those parts. The Kaiser, like an officious, all-knowing neighbor, came to see him in order to look over the yacht, examining it in all its details, giving advice, reviewing the men and materials, making a dissertation on the engines and interrupting himself to advise certain changes in the uniform of the crew. After a breakfast on his own yacht, and luncheon on the Emperor's, Prince Michael had had enough of this unexpected friendship. Lohengrin, with his winged helmet, white mantle, and both hands on the hilt of his sword, was less unbearable than this gentleman with turned up mustache, and wolfish teeth, dressed like a sailor, who laughed a false and brutal laugh, and (whenever he met on the seas a multimillionaire from America or Europe) played the rôle of a man of great simplicity and of an unconventional sovereign. Money inspired deep veneration in this story-book hero, this mystic with a mind fed on grandeur. Michael had never shared the enthusiasm of various snobs for the German Emperor. He smiled at the Hohenzollern's theatrical tastes, his war-like bravadoes, and his intellectual ambitions which pretended to embrace the whole knowable universe.

"He is a comedian," Michael said on receiving the news of the war, "a comedian who for a long time is going to make the whole world weep.... And to think that the fate of mankind should depend on such a man!..."

Michael Fedor considered himself as a being set apart from the rest of mankind. He lamented the war as something terrible for the rest, but which could not influence his own particular fate. Since a madness for blood had descended upon Europe, he would go on sailing distant seas. Thanks to his wealth he could keep beyond the margins of the struggle.

But times changed rapidly; life was not the same: all old values had lost their significance. In spite of her Russian flag, the *Gaviota II* found herself halted by some English torpedo boats and was forced to submit to a minute inspection. They could not believe that any one should be cruising for pleasure when all the seas had been converted into a battlefield. In the latitude of the Azores it became necessary to force the yacht's engines to escape from a German corsair.

Besides, fuel was getting scarce. The various coaling stations located here and there on the coast were reserved exclusively for the warships. Important news kept coming by wireless from far-off Paris, where the chief agent of the Prince was located. Communication had been broken off between the Paris office and the administrators of the Lubimoff fortune in Russia. No money was coming from there, and the French banks, with their vaults closed by the *moratorium*, were willing secretly to lend money to a millionaire like the Prince, but not in quantities sufficient to meet his current needs.

The yacht came to anchor in the port of Monaco, and Michael Fedor, on arriving in Paris, almost laughed, as though witnessing some preposterous change in the laws of nature. The heir of the Lubimoffs in need of money, and compelled to make an effort to obtain it—something he had never done in all his life! Here he was having to ask for loans at frightfully usurious rates, on the security of his distant and famous wealth, which for the first time was regarded somewhat contemptuously!...

When communications were reëstablished in an intermittent fashion between Western Europe and Russia—which was practically isolated—the administrator of the Prince gave a look of despair. The collections had been reduced eighty per cent.

"According to that, I am going to be poor?" asked Lubimoff, laughing, the news seemed so unbelievable and absurd.

It was very difficult to send money as far as Paris. Besides the rouble was decreasing in value at a dizzy rate. Millions on reaching France became mere hundred thousands. Mobilization had left the mines without workmen; there was no outlet for the produce; the peasants, seeing their sons in the army, refused to pay any money, and even to work. The Russian government, to keep as much money as possible at home, limited to small amounts the money sent to citizens residing abroad.

"The Czar putting me on a pension!" said the Prince in amazement. "A thousand or two thousand francs a month!... How absurd!"

But he did not laugh long. His anger against the Russian court, which had gradually been growing in his subconsciousness ever since his expulsion so long ago from Petersburg, now moved by a selfish impulse suddenly flared up. The Czar and his counselors, desirous of Russianizing all Eastern Europe, were responsible for the war. They certainly might have kept peace with Germany. Why disturb the peace of the world, for the sake of a little race of people in the Balkans?

He coolly made fun of certain of his friends who, by devious routes across Europe and the icy Northern seas, returned to Russia to regain their former commissions in the army. As for him, he had no desire to die for the Czar. It made little difference to him whether his country were governed by Germans. There were times when he even thought that would be preferable, so long as peace were restored rapidly, allowing him once more to reap the benefit of his wealth, and resume the life he had been leading a few months before, or, as it now seemed, a half century before.

The next two years went by for Lubimoff like a nightmare. What sort of a world was he living in?... His former friends were disappearing. Some of the frivolous women who had made life pleasant for him were not moved in the least by the unfortunate events which were happening; but others showed themselves to be heroic and self-sacrificing, forgetting all they had done before, feeling a new soul developing within them.

The Prince suddenly found himself dragged along by the world happenings. A mysterious and irresistible force was pushing against him, causing him to lose his balance, just as he was reaching the pinnacle of his life, so pleasant, so vast, crowned with a halo of such glory. And now, once started, he was tumbling head over heels, of his own inertia, and each step he struck as he descended, gave him a harder blow, a more painful surprise. How far would this landslide take him?... What would he strike at the end of this unheard-of fall?...

His interviews with his Paris administrator seemed to him like something taking place in another world, subject to ridiculous laws. These conferences always ended with the same order on his part:

"Try and get some money. Ask for a loan.... I am Prince Lubimoff, and this cannot last. Whoever wins—it is all the same to me—order will be reëstablished, and I shall pay my creditors immediately."

But the administrator answered, with a look of dismay: "Raise money on property in Russia?..." Taking advantage of the former prestige of the Prince, he had been able to negotiate various loans; but time was passing and the enormous interest was accumulating. Lubimoff in spite of cutting down expenses and doing away with pensions, was in need of money for his current living expenses.

The fall of the Czar gave a ray of hope to this magnate who hated the Imperial government. "With the Republic the war will be over sooner and we shall come back to the proper order of things." His egoism made him conceive of a Republic as a form of government occupied chiefly with restoring the wealth of beings of fortunate birth. The meager shreds of his fortune which now and then still got as far as Paris were suddenly cut off. The fountain of wealth was dry. The crumbling of a whole world had dammed its source, and perhaps forever.

"Your Excellency must sell," the administrator was always saying. "You must do without everything that is superfluous. We must liquidate in time. Who knows how long the present state of affairs may last!"

The yacht was lying idle in Monaco harbor. Almost the entire crew, composed of Italians, Frenchmen, and Englishmen, had left it to go and serve in the navies of their respective nations. Only a few Spaniards remained on board, to keep the boat clean.

The *Gaviota II* was renamed by the English admiralty, and turned over to the Red Cross. When he signed the bill of sale, Michael Fedor felt that he was giving up his whole past. The romantic prestige of his mode of life was vanishing now for all time; the *Arabian Nights* palace was being converted into a hospital ship.... What a world!

The English millions afforded him a year of respite. The administrator paid the huge debts, and he was able to live without economizing, in Paris, a Paris nearing the end of its third year of war with inexplicable tranquillity, resuming its usual pleasures as though all danger were past. Love affairs with two distinguished women, whose husbands were called to arms—although they were not at the front—caused him to spend a few months, now at Biarritz, now on the Riviera, and now at Aix-les-Bains.

His agent disturbed these enjoyments. He was constantly repeating the same advice: "You must sell." The Prince's fortune was already like an old ship drifting aimlessly. The administrator had stopped the last leaks with the money from the most recent sale, but warned him at every moment that she was taking in water through new ones.

In the end Michael Fedor grew accustomed to misfortune, accepting it serenely.

The sale of the palace built by his mother moved him less than that of his yacht.

At the same time his desires had changed. He was beginning to tire of love adventures, which seemed to be the only object of existence. His fresh and vigorous constitution, which had amazed Castro, suddenly broke down. But this was more the result of worry than of physical wear and tear.

He felt that he was poor, and was he not accustomed to pay royally for his love affairs? Not being able to reward women with luxury, he would rather flee in order not to accept from them and be obliged to tolerate from them their caprices. He preferred to master his desires, as long as he could not satisfy them with all the grandeur of an oriental potentate. Besides he was tired of love, and all the pleasant things of life a man can find in this world!...

He thought of his friend Atilio, of the Colonel, of Villa Sirena, white and shining in the Mediterranean sunlight, among the olive trees and cypresses.

"The earth is being swept by the deluge. Perhaps the old lands will once more appear; perhaps they will remain submerged forever.... Let us take refuge in our Ark, and wait and hope."

CHAPTER IV

AFTER glancing with satisfaction at the imposing aspect of Villa Sirena, the adjoining buildings, and the surrounding groves, the Colonel said to Novoa:

"The part you see cost less than what you don't see. There is a great deal of money spent under ground here."

Turning away from the residence, Don Marcos pointed to the gardens, which lay extended before them in terraces, some on a level with the roof of the "villa," others descending like a mighty stairway almost to the water's edge.

He recalled the promontory as it was when the late Princess first thought of buying it; an ancient refuge of pirates; a tongue of rocks wild and storm-swept when the *mistral* was blowing, with deep caves gnawed by the surge, which caused the land above to crumble, and threatened to break it lengthwise into a chain of reefs and islets.

"The bulwarks we have had to build!" he continued. "You should have seen the stone we had to put in here,—enough to build a wall around the whole city!"

There were walls more than twenty yards thick, descending in a gradual slope from the gardens to the sea. In places, it was possible to see their foundations in the natural rocks which emerged from the water like greenish beads always awash in the foam; in other places the masonry went down and down until it was lost from view in the watery depths. They were like the breakwaters one sees in harbors. They covered the original hollows of the promontory, the caves, the inlets that were forming, and all the jagged spaces, which had been filled with rich soil.

These tremendous works of masonry were Toledo's pride, owing to their cost and grandeur. He called his fellow-countryman's attention to the proportions of the ramparts, worthy of a monarch of olden times.

"And they are not only strong," he continued, "but look, Professor! They are all 'artistic.'"

The blocks of stone had been cut in large hexagons which fitted together in a uniform mosaic, each piece outlined by a cement border.

At intervals there were large openings, so that the earth might rid itself of its moisture; but each one of these blind windows held some sort of wild vegetation, some hardy, aromatic plant, obstinately parasitic, spreading downward over the wall and covering it with flowers for the greater part of the year. The thick groves at the summit, and the long balustrades arched with wine-colored clematis, seemed to exude a flowery, green, inferior form of life, pouring it out seaward through the gaps in the wall.

"When you see it from a boat below you will appreciate it better. Señor Castro says it reminds him of the hanging gardens of Babylon, and of Queen Semiramis. He is the only one who would think of such comparisons. All I can say is that it meant doing all this! Imagine all the stone. A whole quarry! And I wish you could have seen the bargeloads of rich soil it took to fill the hollows, level the ground, and make a decent garden!"

He grew enthusiastic as he talked about the modern flower gardens stretching around the villa and along the iron railing bordering the Menton road; and he lavished his praise on their harmonious elegance, and the majestic regulation to which the plants were forced to conform. That was how *he* felt a garden should be, like many another thing in life: perfect order, a sense of subordination, and respect for the hierarchies, each thing in its place, with no individual rivalries to cause confusion. But he was afraid to expound his "old-fashioned" tastes, recalling the jests of the Prince and Castro. They preferred the park, which the Colonel always thought of as the "wild garden."

They had availed themselves of the extremely ancient olive trees already on the promontory as a beginning for the park. These trees could not be called old, exactly. Such an appellation would have been petty and inadequate to their age. They were simply ancient, of no visible age. They had an air of changeless eternity about them which made them seem contemporaries of the rocks and the waves themselves. They looked more like ruins than like trees, like heaps of black wood, twisted and overthrown by a storm, or piles of wood, warped and hollowed and scorched by some fire long since past. With them also the invisible part was more important than the portions exposed to the light. Their roots, as large around as tree trunks, went out of sight, wound their way through the red earth, and then appeared once more thirty or forty yards beyond. Some of the trees had died on one side, only to come to life again on the other. What had been the trunk five hundred years before, now appeared as a mutilated stump, table shaped, severed by ax or shattered by thunderbolt; and the root, showing above the soil, was flowering again in its turn, changing into a tree, to continue an apparently limitless existence, in which centuries counted as years. The hearts of other trees were gnawed away and empty; and these supported only half of their outer shell, looking like a tower with one side blown out by an explosion; but on high they displayed an almost ridiculous crown of foliage, a few handfuls of silvery leaves scattering along the sinuous black branches. Below, the gnarled roots which seemed to have preserved in their knotted windings the sap that was the first life of the earth, embraced a much larger radius on the ground than that occupied by the branches in the air. Other olive trees, that were only three or four hundred years old, stood erect with the arrogance of youth, leafy and exuberant, casting a light, trembling, almost diaphanous shadow, like that of frosted glass which swayed with the capricious will of the wind.

"His Excellency says that there are olive trees here that were seen by the Romans. Do you believe it, Professor? Can it be that any of these trees date back to the time of Jesus Christ?"

Novoa hesitated in replying. The Colonel continued his observations as they walked along between walls of well-trimmed shrubbery towards the end of the park.

"Look: there is the Greek garden."

It was an avenue of laurels and cypress trees with curving marble benches, and in the background a semi-circular colonnade.

"I would have liked to plant a great many palms: African, Japanese, and Brazilian, like those in the gardens of the Casino. But the Prince and Don Atilio detest them. They say that they are an anachronism, that they never existed in this region, and were imported by the wealthy people who have been building for the last fifty years on the Blue Coast. All those two fellows admire is the ancient Provençal or Italian garden: olive trees, laurels, and cypresses—but not the huge, funereal cypresses with bushy tops, that we use in Spain, to decorate the *calvaries* and cemeteries. Look at them: they are as light and slender as feathers. To keep the wind from blowing them over you have to plant two or three together in a clump."

They had reached the extreme limit of the park, where the leafiest olive trees were growing. They walked along open pathways through high masses of wild and fragrant vegetation, whose vigorous vitality seemed to challenge the salt breeze. The plants had stiff leaves, and gave out strong exotic perfumes. As Novoa breathed in the fragrance, it evoked visions of far-off lands; and in truth it seemed almost as though an odor of Hindoo cooking or Oriental incense were floating through that wild garden. A variety of creepers hung from tree to tree. Though it was still winter these natural garlands had already begun to bloom, owing to the warm breezes of an early Spring. They stood out with all the gay splendor of a courtly festival, against the chaste pale green of the olive trees.

"Don Atilio says that all this makes him think of a Mozart symphony."

The deep blue Mediterranean lay at their feet, its slow swells combed by a sharp reef that broke the streaming water into clouds of spray. Here the promontory divided, forming two arms of unequal length. The shortest was a prolongation of the park, carrying the magnificent vegetation which flourished on its back, into the very waters. The other descended to the sea in a chaos of rocks and loose earth, with no growth save a few twisted pines, clinging to the soil, obstinately determined to prolong their death struggle. The barren loneliness of this tongue of land drew a sad smile from the Colonel each time he gazed at the dividing wall. The rugged point was eaten away by the sea with caves that threatened to cut it in two. It had no regular place of entrance, being separated from the mainland by the gardens of Villa Sirena, and shut off by a hostile wall, which represented the inalienable rights of ownership, and was a source of constant indignation and amazement to Don Marcos.

Doubtless that was why he turned away from it, gazing out toward where Monaco lay beyond the rocky cliffs.

"It is lovely, Professor: one of the most delightful panoramas anywhere. There is good reason for people to come here from the farthest ends of the earth!"

He let his glance rest on the violet colored mountains that, at the farthest horizon, projected out upon the sea, like the limit of a world. They were the so-called Mountains of the Moors, which, with Esterel Point, form a branch of the Maritime Alps, a separate mountain chain, which juts into the Mediterranean. In the opposite direction lay a portion of the pseudo-Blue Coast, which begins at Toulon and Hyères. But this part did not interest the Colonel. What he saw, more in imagination than in reality, was a bird's-eye view of the real Blue Coast, his own Blue Coast—that of the aristocratic and wealthy people on whom he was in the habit of calling, in their elegant villas and expensive hotels.

The Maritime Alps form a giant wall, parallel to the sea. In some places they fall steeply toward the Mediterranean with the sharp slope of a bulwark, without the slightest break to mask the abrupt descent. At other points the incline is gentler, creating waves of stone, miniature mountains which stand out above the water, forming capes and placid inlets. And on these sheltered shores, from Esterel to the Italian frontier, wealthy people, sensitive to cold, arriving in pilgrimages every winter, had finally converted the sleepy provincial villages into world-famous capitals. Fishing hamlets were transformed into elegant towns; the large Paris and London hotels erected enormous annexes on the deserted bays; the most expensive shops of the Boulevards opened branches in tiny settlements where a few years before every one had gone barefoot.

In his mind Toledo went over the undulating line of celebrated places, overlooking the sea from the promontories, or nestling in the little horseshoe bays to profit more directly by the refraction of the winter sunlight from the red walls of the Alps: Cannes, which inspired in him a certain awe on account of its quiet distinction—the place where consumptives and old people of renown desire to die— Antibes, with its square harbor and its walls which, according to Castro, recalled the romantic seascapes painted by Vernet; Nice, the capital where people come together to spend their money, copying Parisian life; the deep bay of Villefranche, the harborage of battleships; Cap-Ferrat and the beautiful Point Saint-Hospice, a former den of African pirates, jutting out from it; Beaulieu, with its Tunisian palaces, the homes of American multimillionaires, who always keep open house, and who had often invited the Colonel to luncheon there; Eze, the feudal hamlet, hanging grimly to the side of the Alps, and falling in ruins around its decaying castle, while down below, the people who fled from it are forming a new town, beside the gulf which their predecessors proudly called the Sea of Eze; Cap d'Ail, which serves as a sort of portico to the adjoining Principality; the Rock of Monaco, carrying on its giant's back a walled city; opposite it the dazzling Monte Carlo; and beyond, Cap-Martin, with somber vegetation, reserved and lordly, the ultimate shelter of dethroned kings; and lastly, close to Italy, pleasant Menton, the stronghold of

Englishmen, another place for invalids of distinction, where every self-respecting consumptive feels obliged to end his days.

"Think of the money that has been spent here!" Don Marcos exclaimed.

Fifty years before, the Corniche railway in successfully finding its way through this mountain region had been considered a marvelous piece of work; but now for the convenience of winter visitors, the same work had been repeated in every direction. Smoothly curving roads, clean and firm as a drawing-room floor, extended along the seashore, ascended the Alpine heights, passing from crest to crest on lofty viaducts, or burrowing the hills in long tunnels. Where the perpendicular rock would not allow a ledge to be cut the engineer had made one with buttresses many yards high, the bases of which were lost to view in the waves.

A new dream had been added to the many which the blessed in this world's goods may realize—the owning of a house on the Riviera! Within fifty years, every architectural whim, every possible fancy of rich people bent on creating sensations, had covered this shore of the Mediterranean with villas, Greek, Arabic, Persian, Venetian, and Tuscan palaces, and dwellings of other distinct or indescribable styles. The palm tree was imported and acclimated as a native plant.

"Enormous fortunes have been invested here; three generations have been ruined, and as many more enriched. When you think what it was a century ago, and see what it is now...!"

The Colonel spoke of an Englishwoman's tomb, completely abandoned on the extreme point of Cap-Ferrat. She was a forerunner of the present winter visitors, a youthful contemporary of Byron, charmed by the beauty of the Mediterranean, and by the pathless and practically unexplored mountains. On her death, they buried her on the deserted promontory, because she was a Protestant. The fishermen and peasants of this lonely coast shunned the stranger, denying her the rights of hospitality even in their cemeteries.

"This happened less than a century ago. And such poverty as there was! The only products of the country were thick skinned oranges, lemons, and these olives. The trees are very pretty, very decorative, but they bear an exceedingly small pointed olive, all pit. Compare them with ours in Andalusia, Professor! And to-day there are millionaires, born right here on the Riviera, who have grown rich merely by selling the wretched fields of their fathers. The red land, abounding in stones, is bought by the yard, even in the most out of the way spots, like lots in large cities. When you least expect it, at a turn in the road, you come across a miserable hut with a little land around it that takes your fancy. The roof of the building sags, and the wind blows through the cracks in the wall. The owners sleep with the pig, the chickens, and the horse. This same poverty and shiftlessness you find among the peasants almost everywhere. You happen to think that you might build up a country home there without much expense. Surely the good people won't ask very much, no matter how inflated their ideas of value may be! But when you ask the price, after much talk, and many doubts, they finally say in the most casual manner: 'A hundred and fifty thousand francs, or two hundred thousand.' When you protest in amazement they reply, pointing to the mountains, the sun, and the sea: 'And the view, monsieur.'"

The red soil of the Alps amounts to little for its power of production: it is the situation that gives it its value. And the native has grown rich selling, so much per yard, the sunlight, the azure of the Mediterranean, the orange color of the mountains and the dazzling glory of the clouds at sunset, the shelter of the distant rock which, like a screen, turns aside the icy breeze of the *mistral*.

"If you only knew how inexplicably obstinate some of these people are!"

As Don Marcos spoke he turned and pointed out to Novoa the miserable strip of land that seemed fastened like a curse to the gardens of Villa Sirena. The Princess Lubimoff with all her millions, had not been able to buy the tip of that promontory. It belonged to an old married couple without any children. "That is their house," he added, pointing to a sort of yellowish cube, halfway up the mountain, beside a road that cut across the red and black slope.

The Princess, after acquiring the promontory for her medieval castle, had considered the acquisition of the small extremity a mere trifle. "Give them what they ask," she said to her business agent. And in spite of her recklessness with money, she was amazed to learn that they refused two hundred thousand francs for a few rocks undermined by the waves, and a couple of dozen dying pines.

"I was present at the interviews with the old people. The agent of the Princess offered five hundred thousand, six hundred thousand, and the couple did not seem to grasp the meaning of the figures. The Princess lost her patience, lamenting the fact that they were not in

Russia, in the good old days. She even talked of engaging an assassin in Italy—as she had read in certain novels—to get rid of the stubborn old pair. It was just like her Excellency,—but she was really very kind at heart! Finally, one day, she shouted to us: 'Offer them a million, and let us be done with it!' Imagine, Professor, more than two thousand francs a yard; you could buy land at that rate in the business district of a big city! We went up to their cottage. They didn't bat an eyelash when they heard the figure. The old woman, who was the more intelligent of the two, let Her Excellency's lawyer explain what a million meant. She looked at her husband for a long time, in spite of the fact that she was the only one of the two who was doing any thinking, and finally accepted; but on condition that the Princess should erect, on the outermost point, a chapel to the Virgin. It was a wish that her simple imagination had cherished all her life. Without the chapel, she would not accept the million. 'Don't worry, we'll build the chapel!' we said. The day set for signing the papers, we found the two old people, sitting in the lawyer's office side by side, with bowed heads. The lawyer received us, wringing his hands, and looking toward heaven with an expression of despair. They would not accept! It was no use insisting. They wanted to keep things just as they had received them from their forefathers. 'What would we do with a million?' groaned the old woman. 'We would lead a terrible life!' We tried to talk to her about the chapel, in order to persuade her; but they both fled, like people finding themselves in bad company, and afraid of being tempted."

The colonel looked once more at the dividing wall.

"Her Excellency being a born fighter, immediately had the partition raised before beginning the foundation of the castle. As you see from here, the old people can reach their property only by the beach; and on stormy days they have to enter the water up to their knees. That doesn't matter; from that time on they became more attached than ever to their land. They used to come down from the mountains every Sunday, to sit at the foot of the wall. By constantly measuring the point they succeeded in discovering an error made by the architect, who had been a trifle flustered owing to the haste enforced upon him by the Princess. He had made a mistake of eighteen inches, and half the width of the wall was on the old people's land. The peasant woman, in spite of the fact that she had a sort of superstitious fear of the majesty of the law, threatened to bring suit even though she might be forced to sell her hut and field on the mountain to fight the case. It was necessary to tear down the wall, and build it up again, half a yard farther this way. It meant some sixty thousand francs lost—nothing for the Princess—and yet I suspect at times, that the affair may have hastened her death."

Don Marcos felt that he must pause a moment out of respect for the deceased.

"The old woman has died too," he continued, "and her husband comes here only from time to time. When he finds that one of his pine trees has fallen, through the wearing away of the soil, he sits down close beside it, just as though he were watching beside a corpse. At other times he spends hours looking at the sea and the huge rocks, as though calculating how long it would take the waves to break his property to pieces. One afternoon, going on foot from La Turbie to Roquebrune, I ran across him near his hut, where he was pasturing some sheep. With his long beard he looked like a patriarch; and he is always the same, leaning on his staff, with a dirty tam-o'shanter on his head, and a rough cape about his shoulders. Besides, he always has a pipe in his mouth, though he rarely smokes. 'The million is waiting,' I said in fun, 'whenever you want to come and get it.' He didn't seem to understand me. He smiled with a look of vague recognition, but perhaps he thought I was some one else. His gaze was fixed on Monte Carlo, a bird's-eye view of which lay at our feet. He must spend hours and weeks like that. His face looks as though it were carved of wood, or molded in terra cotta; he seldom speaks, and no one can guess the substance of his reflections. But I think that every day the same identical amazement must be renewed, and that he will die without ever recovering from his surprise. He sees the expanse of waters, which is always the same, the eternal hills, that never change, the house built by his ancestors, which was old when he was born, the olive groves, the mighty rocks ... but that city has sprung up, since he was a grown man, from a plateau covered with thickets, and burrowed with caves, and it is enlarged each year with new hotels, new streets, and more domes and turrets!"

The Colonel suddenly forgot the old peasant. With his fellow-countryman, Novoa, he felt quite talkative, and he imagined that his thoughts flowed more freely and vigorously, through this contact with a man of learning. Besides, he felt a certain pride in being able to talk like an old inhabitant, of the many things of which the new-comer was ignorant.

"The fortress you see over there practically belonged to us at one time," he went on, pointing to the Castle of Monaco. "For a century and a half it had a Spanish garrison. Our great Charles V"—and the old Legitimist spoke the name with a note of deep respect—"once slept there. And there, too."

Turning, he pointed out on the mountain summit of Cap-Martin the village of Roquebrune, huddled about its ruined castle.

"The archivist of the Prince of Monaco is studying the numerous letters in his possession written by our great Emperor to the Grimaldi family. When the historians of the Principality wish to establish the indisputable independence of their tiny land, they cite as the origins of the state the treaties signed at Burgos, Tordesillas, and Madrid."

In a few words he went over the history of the little country, which came into being around a little harbor. Semitic sailors gave it the name of Melkar—the Phœnician Hercules—and the word gradually changed into the present one, Monaco. The Guelphs and Ghibellines of Genoa fought for possession of its castle, until a Grimaldi, disguised as a monk, entered the enclosure by surprise and opened the gates to his friends, making the ancient Hercules Harbor an estate of his family for all time. "This friar, sword in hand," continued Don Marcos, "is the one that figures on both sides of the coat of arms of Monaco. From that time on the history of the Grimaldis is similar to that of all the ruling houses of those days. They made war on their neighbors, and quarreled among themselves, to the extent that brother even assassinated brother. The sailors of Monaco plied the trade of corsair, and their flag was even used to give distinction to the pirates of other countries. The alliance of the Grimaldis with Spain allowed them to use the title of Prince for the first time. Charles V addressed them in his letters as 'dear Cousins,' and gave them other honorary titles. This great rock was of exceeding importance to the Spanish Monarchs who had lands in Italy and needed to keep the route safe. The Kings of France were very anxious, on their part, to do away with this obstacle and win the Grimaldis over to their side. You must realize that for a hundred and fifty years the latter kept their agreements faithfully, and that during all this time the subsidies that had been promised them from Madrid were sent only at rare intervals. Two galleys from Monaco always figured in the rolls of the

Spanish navy. Only when the decline of Austria began to cause us to lose our influence in Europe, did the Grimaldis, like people fleeing from a house that is tumbling down, abandon us. At that particular moment, Richelieu was making France a great power, and they went with him. One night amid thunder and lightning, when the garrison, composed for the most part of Italians in the service of Spain, were carelessly asleep, the French caught them unawares, disarmed them, after killing a few who tried to resist, and finally sent the remainder courteously to the Spanish Viceroy at Milan, with the notice that the alliance must be considered broken forever.

"The Grimaldis became the liege-lords of France. Later they went to Versailles, as courtiers, or served in the King's armies. During the Revolution they were persecuted, like all the other princes, and a beautiful lady of the family was guillotined. Napoleon kept them in his military following as aides-de-camp, and the long peace of the Nineteenth Century caused them to return and take up their abode once more in their tiny Principality.

"They were so poor!" Toledo went on. "They were obliged to keep up the show and pomp of a court, since in a small state where all are neighbors, the Prince has to exaggerate formality, in order to hold the people's respect. The same expenses must be defrayed as in a large nation; the maintenance of courts, administrative offices, and even a diminutive army for internal safety. And the whole Principality produced nothing but lemons and olives.... You can see for yourself how poor and how hard pressed they must have been, not knowing how to raise funds, especially since under the rule of Florestan I, the grandfather of the present Prince, there was an attempted revolution, owing to the decree of the Sovereign that the olives of the country should be pressed exclusively in the mills of his estate.

"Later under Charles III, the situation became still more difficult. The Principality was dismembered. The two cities, Menton and Roquebrune, dependencies of Monaco, full of enthusiasm for the Italian Revolution, declared their freedom, and joined the Kingdom of Savoy. Shortly after, when Napoleon III acquired the former County of Nice they fell under the control of France. And thus Monaco was isolated within French territory, with its sovereignty clearly recognized; but a sovereignty that embraced only a single city on a rocky height, a small harbor, and a little surrounding land overgrown with parasitical vegetation; about as much ground as a peaceful citizen might cover in a morning walk. How was the tiny State to be maintained?

"It was saved by gambling. Don't imagine as some people do, that the idea originated with the Ruler of Monaco. Many German Princes had had recourse to some enterprise to support their domains. It is a German invention; but gambling on the shore of the Mediterranean, under a winter sun that seldom fails, is quite a different thing from gambling in Central Europe. At first the business was unsuccessful. They established a miserable Casino in old Monaco, opposite the Palace, in what is now the barracks of the Prince's Guard. The betting was very slight. It was necessary to come by diligence, over the Alpine heights, following the old Roman route, and to descend from La Turbie by roads that were like ravines. One had to be very anxious indeed to gamble. Later the Casino was transferred to the harbor below, where the La Condamine district is to-day: another failure. The lessees of the gaming privileges went bankrupt, and were unable to fulfill their obligations to the Prince. And then the Corniche Railway was put through, placing Monaco on the road between Paris and Italy; and all the gamblers and idlers of the world came flocking here within a few years. What a transformation!"

The Colonel recalled once more the old peasant, who, pasturing his sheep on the Alpine slope, spent hours and hours with his eyes fixed on the marvelous city, stretching out below, on the very spot that, as a young man, he had seen covered with thickets.

"That was the beginning of Monte Carlo. Opposite the rock of Monaco, forming the other side of the harbor, there was an abandoned plateau, only some sixty years ago. Scattered about the gardens of the Square, among the tropical trees, there are still a few scraggly olive trees left from those times. They have been spared as relics of the days of poverty. Where we now find the Casino, the large hotels, and the most elegant tea-houses, there were caves dating back to prehistoric times, which in less remote periods served as haunts for thieves. On account of the grottoes this wild plateau was nicknamed *The Caverns*. Some of the things you have seen in the Anthropological Museum in Monaco, stone axes, human bones, etc., came from those caves. And the abandoned plateau, in some ten or twelve years, was converted into Monte Carlo, the great city of world fame, leaving on the heights opposite in obscurity and more or less in oblivion, the historic Monaco, which at present is merely one of its suburbs. Monte

Carlo has grown so that it extends from one end of the Principality to the other; the entire national territory is covered with houses, and each year it over-flows still farther beyond the boundary line. The French part is called Beausoleil. You have only to cross the Square in front of the Casino, ascend the sloping gardens, and mount a stairway to the Boulevard du Nord, to find one of the rarest sights in Europe. One sidewalk belongs to the Prince of Monaco, and the other across the street, to the French Republic. The shopkeepers pay different taxes and obey different laws, according to whether their show windows are on the left or on the right."

Toledo remained thoughtful for a moment.

"The miracles accomplished by roulette!" he continued. "The magic power of 'red and black'! They say the Casino is a marvel of poor taste, but the walls and ceilings fairly drip with gold, as in a rich church. The theater there is the first to produce many operas that become famous throughout the world. The countless hotels are like palaces. Monte Carlo bristles with domes and turrets like an oriental city. The streets with their scrupulously clean pavements, seem like drawing-rooms. There isn't a trace of dirt. And think of the gardens! The Alps, here, form a wonderful screen; we live in a sunny shelter; almost a hothouse. But at times the *mistral* blows, and it is cold. I don't know how it is possible for all those tropical plants that are so fresh and luxuriant, and all those trees that originate in a climate as hot as an oven, to live here. The poor old olives must be as amazed as I myself at finding themselves in such company. 'Trente et Quarante' must be a powerful fertilizer! I'm sure that if the gambling were to stop, all this tropical vegetation would vanish like a dream."

The silent Professor greeted these words with a smile.

"And what a transformation in the people!" the Colonel continued. "Notice the crowd some Sunday; none of them like workmen, all equally well dressed! The girls here copy what they see worn by the elegant society women; and imagine how many of the latter come here! You never see a beggar, nor a man in rags. To be born here means something: one's livelihood is assured. The Casino takes care of every one; there is always a place for every citizen in the gambling rooms, in the gardens, or in the theater; and if not, on the police force, in the administrative offices, or in the Prince's household— and the latter is paid for with the Company's money too. To achieve the dignity of being put in charge of a gaming table is the native's highest ambition. He may earn as much as a thousand francs a month, not counting the tips. That is more perhaps than you will ever earn, Professor. And he ends his days in a little villa he has built on the heights of Beausoleil, where he can look after his garden, with a view below of the Casino—the house of the Good Fairy that dispenses all blessings. They all have enough to live on as long as they know how to keep a silent tongue, and mind their own business. An old cab driver, whom I sometimes engage, was bold enough one evening to talk quite frankly with me, owing to the fact that he was slightly intoxicated. His wife has been for some twenty years now in the Ladies' Section of the Casino toilets; his daughters work as cleaners; his sons are employed in the theater. They all bring in money. Moreover, the old men retire on pay, the sick are not forgotten, and the widows and orphans of every employee that dies during service are paid pensions. 'It's a great country, sir,' the driver said to me, 'the best in the world. Every one can make a living, as long as he's wise enough to keep his mouth shut, and not make trouble.' And you can depend upon it, they are all discreet. Moreover they watch one another, and are afraid of being denounced by their best friend, if they talk about the latest scandal, or a gambler's suicide. Among strangers not one of them lets on that he knows anything."

"And supposing one of them were to talk?" asked Novoa. "Or if one of them were to make trouble?"

"They would banish him. It is a paternal despotism, and does not dare inflict harsher punishments. The police of the Prince make him go half way across the street, and put him on the French sidewalk.... Don't laugh; it is a cruel penalty. Exiles to other places finally grow accustomed to their misfortune, since they live at a great distance, and see their native land only in their mind's eye. But a man who is exiled here can almost reach out and touch his country with his hand; he has only to cross the width of the street. As the land slopes downward, he can see his house a few roofs beyond. He sees the smoke from breakfast coming out of the chimney, and yet he cannot sit down to his own table; the family is at the windows, and he has to talk to them by signs. Moreover, and worst of all, he sees that the rest who were prudent go on leading their pleasant lives in the shadow of the Casino, while he has to seek a new profession at much harder work. His torment becomes unbearable, and he finally flees to some distant city, to let a few years go by, so he may be pardoned."

Don Marcos began to praise Monte Carlo again; "People who lose their money in the Casino always retain an unpleasant memory of it; but where can one find a quieter, cleaner, or more peaceful city, with its Spring-like climate in mid-winter?

"Everybody comes here sooner or later; lots of rogues, of course; but you find famous people too, and you can enjoy society of distinction. I scarcely ever gamble, and for that reason I appreciate the beauty of the scenery. And more than that: at times I have the satisfaction one feels in getting things for nothing; and when I gaze at the lovely walks, when I attend the concerts and operas, and enjoy the sweet tranquillity of a city in which there are no poor, and no desperate revolutionists, I say to myself: 'The gamblers pay for this, and you get the benefit of it. They lose so that you may enjoy life.'"

As Novoa smiled again, the Colonel expressed his admiration still more glowingly.

"It seems impossible that roulette should have performed so many miracles! And there must be others besides those which lie before our eyes. Gambling has paid the cost of this delightful harbor of La Condamine: a harbor for yachts, with elegant docks that are really promenades. It must have had a hand also in the restoration of the castle of the Prince. It even helps to develop the spiritual life of the place, and increase the prestige of religion. Before roulette came none of the clergy were of higher rank than priests. Since the triumph of the Casino there has been a Bishop, and canons; and a beautiful Byzantine cathedral has been erected, which, according to Castro, needs only to have Time darken it a bit. The Sunday masses are one of the chief attractions of the Principality. The Nice papers print the program of the music that will be sung by the choir, alongside the program of the concert at the Casino: 'Canto piano of the most celebrated masters, the Italian Palestrina, or the Spanish Vitoria.'"

Novoa interrupted him.

"There is the Museum of Oceanography too. That alone is enough to remove any taint from the money which has come from the Casino."

He said this with the pleasing voice and the somewhat distracted expression that were natural to him; but in his words there was the mystic ardor of the firm believer.

The Colonel nodded assent. The Museum which roused the Professor's enthusiasm was the work of the Prince, and as for himself, Don Marcos felt a deep respect for "Albert," as he called the sovereign familiarly. "Albert" had been an officer in the Spanish navy. As a lieutenant commander he had sailed the coast of Cuba; in his books he had praised the old Spanish sailors, his first masters in the art of navigation. What more was needed to inspire veneration in Don Marcos?

"Whenever he attends a ceremony in his Principality he wears the uniform of a Spanish admiral. And he is a man of science: you know that better than I do."

He gave Novoa a chance to speak. Three-fourths of the earth were covered with water, and for centuries and centuries humanity took no interest in investigating the mysterious hidden life of the ocean depths. Navigators, skimming the surface, went their way, guided by routine methods or by fragmentary experience, without succeeding in embracing the fixed and regular laws of the atmospheric or ocean currents. Science, which has to its credit so many discoveries in a single century of existence, halted in dismay at the edge of the sea. The scientists in the laboratories only need material for their work, and that is easily obtained; but to study the seas, to live on them for years and years, is another matter. For that, it was necessary to have ships and men at one's disposal, to construct new and costly apparatus, to spend millions, to cruise patiently and leisurely here and there over the ocean wastes, with no fixed goal, waiting for the great blue depths casually to reveal their secrets. That meant a great outlay, with slight returns. Only a sovereign, a king, could do that; and that was what the former officer in the Spanish navy, on becoming a Prince, had done.

"Thanks to him," Novoa proceeded, "oceanography, which scarcely amounted to anything, has become to-day an important study. His yachts have been floating laboratories, cruisers of science, which have gradually made the first conquests of the deep. With his drifting buoys he has been able to demonstrate in a conclusive manner the circular drift of the Atlantic currents; with his careful soundings he has brought to light the mysteries of deep sea life at various levels of the great body of water. Scientists have been enabled to sail the sea and study, with no material restrictions, thanks to him. Through his generosity handsome books have been published, museums have been opened, and excavations have been made in the earth which throw enlightenment on the origin of man."

"And all this," the Colonel interrupted, persisting in the admiration already expressed, "with the money from the Casino! Gambling has defrayed the expenses of the cruisers of science, the coal and men for far-off expeditions, the printing of books and journals, the subsidies for young men anxious to perfect their scientific training; the Institute of Oceanography in Paris; the Museum of Oceanography in Monaco, where you are working; the Museum of Anthropology and.... And you have to figure that all this is merely a tip left by the stockholders of the gambling corporation. Just imagine what the Casino produces! And lots of people consider it terrible!"

"It doesn't make any difference where wealth comes from as long as it is put to useful purposes," said the Professor, with a note of hardness in his voice. "No one asks a government the origin of its funds, when they are used for some good purpose. Often they have been extorted with more cruelty and violence than those which come from here, where the people all flock of their own free will. It is a good thing that the money of scheming, foolish people, and of those who feel their lives are empty and don't know how to fill them, should be used for once to accomplish something great and human. Think what this Prince of a tiny State has done for science in the course of a few years. If only the great Emperors would devote the enormous forces at their command to similar enterprises! If only Kaiser Wilhelm had done the same, instead of preparing for war all his life, how humanity might have progressed!"

The Colonel, considering himself a warrior by profession, only half admitted the truth of the Professor's words. The sword, the glory won on the battle-field, were something after all, and the world would be ugly without them, it seemed to him. But he remained silent, not venturing to spoil his friend's enthusiasm.

"All the sins on the one hand are redeemed on the other." Saying this, Novoa pointed to the huge Casino, with its multi-colored domes and towers, rising from the table-land of Monte Carlo. Then tracing with his finger an imaginary arc above the harbor, he paused when it pointed to the eminence on the left, where, on the cliffs of Monaco, a large square edifice rose, the walls of which descended to the water's edge. It was the Museum of Oceanography, a fine new building in stone that, in that atmosphere so seldom streaked with rain, still retained its waxy whiteness.

Don Marcos smiled at the contrast. "Don Atilio says the same thing. Every time he gazes at the view from here, he looks at the two buildings separated by the mouth of the harbor, and occupying the two promontories. He says the one justifies the other, and adds: 'They are ...' What is it he says?—an antithesis. No; it's something else.'"

The metallic booming of a gong drifted through the trees from Villa Sirena, summoning the guests, who were scattered through the park, or had not appeared as yet from their rooms. The Colonel listened with pleasure: "Luncheon!"

He gave a last look at the two enormous buildings, one of them bristling with sharp and many colored pinnacles, the other plain and square, of uniform whiteness. Between the promontories, at the water's surface, two new breakwaters meet, closing the mouth of the harbor. At the outermost extremity of each is a beacon: one red, the other green.

The Colonel tapped his brow and looked at his compatriot with a smile. "Oh, yes, I remember. He says the Casino and the Museum are a symbol."

The little group which Castro had labelled "Enemies of Women" had now been in existence two weeks with no disharmony and no obstacles to the perfect happiness of the members. Complete freedom was theirs! Villa Sirena belonged to them all, and the real owner seemed merely like an additional guest.

Arising late in the morning, Castro saw the Prince in a corner of the garden with his shirt open at the neck and his bare arms wielding a spade. The thing that made the new life complete for him was the cultivating of a little garden, and having the gratification of eating vegetables and smelling flowers that were the product of his own toil. This man who had always been surrounded by a corps of servants to attend to all his wants, was anxious now to be self-dependent, and feel the proud satisfaction of one who relies entirely on his own hands. Vainly he invited Castro to join him in this healthy, profitable exercise, which was at the same time a return to primitive simplicity.

"Thanks; I don't care for Tolstoi. As far as the simple life goes this is all I want." And he stretched out on the moss, under a tree, while the Prince went on digging his garden. They talked for a while of their companions. Novoa was in the library, or wandering about the park. Some mornings he would take the early train for Monaco to continue his studies at the Museum. As for Spadoni, he never arose before noon, and often the Colonel would have to pound on his door so that he would not be late for lunch.

"He never gets to sleep until dawn," said Castro. "He spends the night studying his notes on the way the gambling has been going. He gets into my room sometimes when I'm asleep, to tell me one of his everlasting systems that he has just discovered; and I have to threaten him with a slipper. In his room, among the music albums, he keeps piles of green sheets that give each day's plays for a year at all the various tables in the Casino. He's crazy."

But Castro took care not to add that he often asked Spadoni to lend him his "archives" in order to verify his own calculations; and in spite of his making fun of the latter's discoveries, he used to risk a little money on them, through a gambler's superstition that attaches great value to the intuitions of the simple-minded.

After luncheon, Castro and Spadoni would both hurry off to the Casino. The Prince, when not attending a concert, remained with Novoa and the Colonel in a *loggia* on the upper story, looking out over the sea. The war had filled that part of the Mediterranean with shipping. In normal times the sea presented a deserted monotonous appearance, with nothing to arrest the eye save the wheeling of the gulls, the foamy leaps of the dolphins and the sail of an occasional fishing boat. The steamers and the large sailing vessels were scarcely ever to be seen even as tiny shadows on the horizon, following their course direct from Marseilles to Genoa, without following the extensive shore line of the Riviera gulf. But now the submarine menace had obliged the merchant ships to slip along within shelter of the coast. Convoys passed nearly every day; freighters of various nationalities, daubed like zebras to reduce their visibility, and escorted by French and Italian torpedo-boats.

These rosaries of boats so close to the coast that one could read their names and distinguish their captains standing on the bridge, caused the Prince and the Professor to talk of the horrors of war.

At times the Colonel entered the conversation, but only to lament the difficulties which such a war presented to the fulfillment of his duties as steward. Each day his task was becoming more difficult. He was no longer able to find anything worth serving at a table like that of the Prince, and even so, the prices that he paid roused his indignation when he compared them with those of peace times! And the servants! He had sent to Spain for some, now that all those from the district were in the army; but the hotel proprietors had immediately enticed them away. They all preferred to serve in cafés or in places where people are continually coming and going, tempted by the chance of getting tips and of associating with the white-aproned chamber-maids.

He had improvised dining-room service with the two Italian boys from the Brodhigera, whose families were living in Monaco. The older and livelier of the two had the name of Pistola, and treated his companion in despotic fashion, bullying him with kicks and cuffs when the Colonel's back was turned. Atilio, for the sake of the rhyme, had nicknamed Pistola's comrade, Estola, and every one in the house accepted the name, even the boy himself.

"When you think of the work it cost me to make decent respectable looking servants out of them!" groaned Toledo. "And now it seems that they are going to be called back to Italy as soldiers. More men off for the war! Even these young lads that haven't reached the age yet! What shall we do when Estola and Pistola go?"

Many evenings, at the dinner hour, the rules of the community were rudely broken. The first to desert was Spadoni. He arrived sometimes after midnight, saying that he had dined with some friends. At other times he did not return at all. After a few days had gone by he would quietly appear, with the serene ingenuousness of a stray dog, just as though he had gone out only a few hours before. No one could ever find out exactly where he had been. He himself was not sure. "I met some friends." And in the same half hour, these friends would be at one moment some Englishmen from Nice, or at another a family from Cap-Martin, as though he had been in both places at the same time.

Atilio also used to absent himself. A gambling companion had shown him, in the Casino, the little cards divided into columns, which are used to note the alternating frequency of "red" and "black." Various ladies had taken similar documents from their hand-bags, where they lay among the handkerchiefs, the powder boxes, the lip sticks, the banknotes, and the various colored chips, which are used as money in the gaming. The indications all agreed. During the morning and afternoon the "bets" were all lost, and the house was winning; but from eight o'clock in the evening on, undreamed-of fortune smiled on the players. The statistics could not be clearer; there was no possible doubt. And Castro would renounce the excellent food of Villa Sirena, satisfied with a glass of beer and a sandwich at the bar. Then at midnight he would return in a hired carriage, paying the astonished driver with prodigality. At other times he would stand in front of the gate fishing in his pockets to get together enough to pay for the cab. Fate had lied. Nor, on those occasions, would any of the prophets of the little cards have been able to lend him a cent.

Toledo muttered protests. This lack of orderly habits made him lament once more the scarcity of servants. The help always got up late on account of having to sit up and wait at night. For that reason, on the nights when all the companions of the Prince were present, the Colonel felt the satisfaction of the Governor of a fortress when he sees all the posterns locked and feels the keys in his pocket. After dinner they would listen to Spadoni. Seated at a grand piano, he would play according to his mood or according to the wishes of the Prince. Lubimoff was a melomaniac whose musical taste was cloyed, perverted, by an excessive refinement. He cared only for rare works, and obscure composers.

Castro, who was himself a pianist, at times was unable to hide his enthusiasm for the wonderful execution of the Italian virtuoso.

"And just think that after all he is an idiot!" he exclaimed, with the frankness of a man who is carried away by his feelings. "All his faculties are warped, and narrowed, concentrated on a single purpose, music, without leaving anything for anything else. However, what's the difference? He's an idiot—but a sublime idiot."

There were nights when Spadoni remained with his elbow on the keyboard and his brow resting in his right hand, as though completely absorbed in music. As a matter of fact, the visions that were then whirling in his head, beneath those long locks, were red and black squares, many cards, and thirty-six numbers in three rows beginning with a zero. The Prince, annoyed by the silence, turned to Castro.

"Tell us something about your grandfather, Don Enrique."

This grandfather had married an aunt of General Saldaña, and although Atilio had never known him personally he often talked about him, as a curious sort of person who aroused either his admiration or his bitter irony, according to the mood he happened to be in. This ancestor was a man of warlike temperament and rather perverse enthusiasms, who had succeeded in depleting the family fortune, already undermined by his predecessors. Related to a great many nobles, he usually would deny the relationship if forced to the point, as though it were something of which to be ashamed. Other members of the family might take the title of nobility if they chose. The motto which had figured for centuries on the Castro shield was an accurate summary of the man's character: "To-morrow more revolutionary than to-day." For thirty years there had not been a successful or abortive insurrection in Spain in which this somber-looking gentleman had not had a hand. He was very sensitive to insult and a great swordsman. He treated men like a despot and at the same time he was ready to die for the liberty of mankind.

"A red Don Quixote!" said Castro.

He remembered having played with the old man's sword, as a child. It was a Toledo weapon, inlaid with golden arabesques copied from the old sword of the explorer and *conquistador*, Alvaro de Castro, who had been Governor of the Indies. But toward the hilt of the blade, where his ancestors had been wont to inscribe an expression of fidelity to their God and King, Don Enrique had had engraved: "Long live the Republic!" Without this knightly sword, he refused to take part in a revolution. He had carried it from Sicily to Naples, following Garibaldi to dethrone the Bourbons. "To-morrow more revolutionary than to-day!" His companions soon appeared to him unspeakable reactionaries, and this caused him to seek new doctrines which would fully satisfy his insatiable eagerness for destruction and innovation. Finally, this descendant of Governors and Viceroys wound up in the "First International." And the most extraordinary thing of all was that in his new life he never lost the traces of his early education, his arrogance and his knightly ways, which caused him to consider the slightest difference of opinion as "an affair of honor."

Over a discussion in a committee meeting, he had fought a "comrade" laborer in Paris. No sooner had they crossed swords than the workman received a cut across the head.

"It is quite just," said the wounded man, wiping away the blood. "The Marquis, who has been able to learn the use of weapons, ought of course to beat a mere man of the people."

Don Enrique turned pale at the irony, and to restore equality, and eliminate his traditional advantages, he raised his sword and gave himself a terrible cut across the skull, while the witnesses ran forward to seize him and prevent him from doing it again.

After accompanying Garibaldi once more, in the War of 1870, fighting the Prussians at Dijon, he was drawn to Paris by the revolutionary movement of the Commune.

"I think they made him a general," Atilio said. "He must have suffered heavily in that tragic farce. It is certain that he was executed by the government troops, and no one knows where he is buried."

Atilio's admiration for his grandfather, whose life had been so romantic, was dampened by the thought of his mother. Poor, an orphan, and forgotten by her relatives, she had been obliged to marry a man old enough to be her father, and led the wandering life, outside of Spain, that is forced upon the wives of consuls. Atilio was born in Leghorn, and was given the name of his godfather, an old Italian gentleman, who was a friend of the Spanish Consul. The memory of his grandfather, saddened from time to time the life of his poor, resigned, and devout mother. In Rome, visiting Spaniards, all persons of conventional ideas who came to see the Pope, would look askance on learning of her birth: "Oh, so you are the daughter of Enrique de Castro!" And she would seem to shrink, and beg their pardon with her sad, humble eyes.

"I don't disown my grandfather," Castro added. "I would like to have known him. The only thing I blame him for is that he left us so poor; though his forefathers had already done more than he to ruin us."

On days when Atilio had lost, he was more prone to complain, recalling the immense estates of the Castros, gained in the conquests in America.

"To-day there are large cities on the fields given by the king to my forefathers. One of my remote ancestors grazed horses, and built a colonial country house on land where at the present time you will find gardens, monuments, and big hotels. There were hundreds of millions of square yards; at a franc a yard, imagine, Michael! I would be richer than you, richer than all the millionaires in the world. And I'm only a well-dressed beggar. Good God! Why didn't my ancestors keep their land, instead of devoting themselves to serving the king and the people? Why didn't they do like any peasant who keeps religiously what has been left him by his ancestors?"

Other evenings, seated in the *loggia*, the Prince listened to Novoa and gazed at the nocturnal scene of sea and sky. There was no light, save the veiled gleam from the distant drawing-room. The coast was dark. The silhouette of Monte Carlo stood out against the starry background, without a single dot of red. There were few street lights in the city, and besides, the glass of those few was painted blue. The lamps on the stairway of the Casino were shrouded like those of a hearse. The German submarine menace kept the whole Principality, as well as the French coast, in darkness. Only at the entrance to the harbor of Monaco, the two octagonal towers kept on their summit a red and a green beacon, which threw out over the water one shifting path of rubies, and another of emeralds.

In the darkness, standing and looking at the stars, Novoa talked about the poetry of space, about distances that defy human calculations. It was impossible for Spadoni to follow this talk with the same attention as the Prince and Castro. What did the so-called tri-colored star matter to him? The millions and millions of leagues that the scientist spoke of merely made him yawn; and through an association of ideas, he became absorbed in gambling, mentally, imagining that he was winning fifty times in succession, doubling each time.

He wagered a simple five franc piece—the smallest bet allowed in the Casino—and at the end of the twenty-fifth bet he stopped as though horror-struck. He had won more than a hundred and sixty-seven million francs. In only twenty-five minutes! The Casino was closing its doors, declaring the bank broken! But this was not enough to bring him out of his dream. The marvellous five franc piece remained on the green cloth beside a mountain of money which kept growing and growing. He must finish the fifty bets, always doubling. He continued for five more times and then stopped. He had already won more than five thousand million francs. They would have to hand over the entire Principality of Monaco to him, and even that would not be enough perhaps to pay the debt. The thirty-fifth time the simple "napoleon" had become a hundred seventy-one billions of francs. They wouldn't pay him; he was sure of that. It would be necessary for all the great powers of Europe to ally themselves as though for a great war, and even then perhaps, he, the pianist, Teofilo Spadoni, would not accept the credit they might offer him.

He could no longer make the calculations mentally. The twentieth time he had been obliged to have resource to the pencil which he used in the Casino to note results of the various plays, and to the cards divided in columns which were distributed by the employees. The back of the card was rather narrow for his winnings, which kept growing so tremendously that they had reached fantastic sums. He continued his triumphant playing. At the fortieth winning he stopped. Five million million francs. Decidedly neither Europe nor the entire world would be able to pay him. The nations would have to put themselves up for sale, the globe would be put on public auction, the women would all have to sell their bodies and give him the proceeds; and even so it would be necessary to ask him for several thousands of years in which to pay the debt to him, the creditor of the universe, seated on his piano stool as though on a throne.

But although he was certain that he was being deceived, since no one on earth or heaven could guarantee the bank, he went on playing. There were only ten more bets to be made. And when he had made the fiftieth he had a sudden stroke of generosity. In his mind he gave the employees of the Casino thousands, millions, and millions of millions. For himself he only kept the amount that figured at the head of his winnings, and wrote on his card:

5,000,000,000,000,000 francs.

Five thousand billions! For fifty minutes' work, that wasn't bad.

Suddenly his attention was attracted by the silence in which the Prince and Castro were listening to Novoa, and he fixed his visionary gaze on the latter, his eyes still dazzled by the golden whirl of the Vision.

The scientist too was talking about millions of millions, figures which words would not express, and was going into detail, repeating dozens of ciphers one after the other. He thought he heard the professor surmising the age which the sun would reach in time—here an interminable figure—the disappearance of the present forms of life, the recession of the heavenly body towards an exceedingly remote constellation, and its final extinction and death—here another appalling sum.

Spadoni smiled disdainfully. The sun, the constellation of Hercules, the hundred million years that it would take for the former to reach the earth, the seventeen million years that it would require to lose its incandescence, and cease furnishing warmth for life on earth, and all the other calculations of the scientist were as nothing, mere nothing! If he were to put his money on the green table fifty times more, the figures obtained by astronomy would appear paltry and ridiculous beside the winnings obtained in an hour and forty minutes. God alone could be the banker, and pay with stars as though they were money; and who knows if God himself would be able to withstand the hundredth time the five franc piece was wagered, always doubling, and if he would not have to declare his bank was broken?

Spadoni remained for some time absorbed in inner contemplation of his greatness. Coming out of his revery he became aware of Novoa's voice which still sounded a note of mystery, before that dark horizon, dotted above with the points of light from the stars, and undulating below with the phosphorescence of the waves.

The Prince urged him to talk of the sea as the regulator and origin of life. The pianist heard it said that the sea covers three-fourths of the globe, and, as it represents a large preponderance over the continents, the latter, though they consider themselves superior, are dominated by the former, just as governments are obliged to yield to universal suffrage and respect the strength of majorities. All the great atmospheric laws are established, not on the lesser surface of the land, which is rough and broken, but on the vast ocean spaces, which allow the molecules freely to obey the mechanical laws of fluids.

Spadoni touched Castro on the elbow, and tried to tell him in a low voice about the unheard-of winnings that he had just made. But Atilio, without turning around, brushed the interrupting hand aside, and went on listening.

Novoa was talking about the hot waters which condensed on the globe in the primordial atmosphere, and had been precipitated on the crust of the earth which was then in formation, dissolving and tearing down everything in their way on the new-born surface.

"With the salt that there is in the ocean," Novoa said, "one could reconstruct the entire African continent."

The pianist stirred once more in his seat. An Africa made of salt! What could you do with it?

"Castro, listen to me," he said in a low voice. "I put five francs on a certain bet, fifty times in succession, doubling each time, do you know?"

But the latter was not interested, and rejected the piece of cardboard held out to him.

Spadoni, offended, shut his eyes, deciding to isolate himself from the rest, and not listen to what did not seem to him of any importance.

If the scientist was going to talk every evening, he would dispense with the hospitality of the Prince, and go in search of other friends.

Suddenly, a word caught his ear and drew him from his shell, causing him to open his eyes. The Professor was talking about the gold that had been washed away by the boiling rains at the creation of the globe, and was still present in solution in the sea.

"There are only a few milligrams in each ton of water, but with all that there is in the ocean one could form a heap so immense, that, if it were divided equally among the thousand five hundred million inhabitants of the earth, we would each get an eighty-five thousand pound ingot, or some forty tons of gold."

The pianist craned his neck in amazement. What was the Professor saying?

"And," Novoa continued, "according to the value of gold before the war, each person's ingot would represent some hundred and twenty million francs."

The silence was broken by a whistling sound. Castro turned his head, thinking that Spadoni was snoring. Observing the pianist's staring eyes, he realized that this was a sigh, of real emotion, an exclamation of surprise.

"I'll give my share for a hundred thousand francs in bank-notes," he said in solemn tones.

And as the others laughed, he remained with his eyes fixed on Novoa. The sea! Who would have thought that the sea!... That scientist knew a great deal; and as for himself, with sudden awe and respect, he determined that hereafter he would always listen to him.

One night, Atilio and the Prince were eating alone. On leaving the Casino, the pianist had gone off to Nice with some English friends of his, who played poker in their landau. Novoa had been invited to dine with a colleague from the Museum and would not be back until midnight.

Michael was thinking of his impressions of that afternoon. He had gone to the Casino to attend a classical concert, determined to face the obsequious curiosity of the employees, and take the risk of running across former friends. From the outer stairway to the door of the theater he had been obliged to reply to the series of deep bows from the various functionaries, some with military caps and gold buttons, others in solemn frock coats, stiff and dignified like lawyers in a play. The people who were passing through the portico noticed him immediately. "Prince Lubimoff!" They all remembered his yacht, his adventures, and his parties, and repeated his name like the glorious echo of a resurrected past. He had been obliged to hurry through the groups at top speed, with a vague stare, feigning absentmindedness, so as not to see certain well-known smiles, and certain inviting faces which evoked sweet visions of by-gone days.

In the auditorium he looked for a seat where he would be entirely inconspicuous, some corner divan, close to the wall; but even there he was annoyed by the curiosity of the crowd. Around the leader of the orchestra were the most famous musicians, those who prided themselves on the title of "Soloists to His Most Serene Highness the Prince of Monaco." Some of them had sailed with Prince Michael on his yacht, as members of the orchestra. During a pause in the music, the first violin, in looking around the room to see if he could recognize any of his admirers, discovered Lubimoff, and communicated his surprise at once to the other soloists. They all smiled in his direction, and showed on their faces that they were dedicating to him alone the music which was rising from their instruments. Finally the public began to notice the gentleman who was half hidden, and who was gradually attracting the attention of the entire orchestra.

When the concert was over Lubimoff left hurriedly, afraid of being stopped by certain former women friends whom he had observed in the audience. He crossed the portico brusquely, elbowing his way through the crowd that barred the way. Here his attention was caught by a person of majestic bearing and exclusive showy appearance, with a derby of smooth gray silk, a honey colored overcoat with velvet sleeves of the same shade, and white gloves and shoes. His gray side-whiskers joined his mustache; his hair was parted away down to his neck, and over his ears strayed two locks of hair, cut short and dyed and shining with cosmetics.

"I thought it was a Russian general or some Austrian of note dressed for winter, with an elegance worthy of the Riviera, and I find it's you, my dear Colonel. I hadn't seen you outside of Villa Sirena before."

Toledo blushed, not knowing whether to feel proud or annoyed, at these words.

"Your Excellency, I always liked to dress well, and...."

"Who was the lady you were talking with?"

"It was the Infanta. She was telling me that she had lost seven thousand francs that were sent to her from Italy, and that she hasn't the money to pay her living expenses, and...."

"The tall, thin one, with the big cow-boy hat? No, not that one. I was asking you about the other."

He had only seen "the other" from behind, but she had attracted his attention for the moment because of her svelte figure and her queenly carriage.

"Your Excellency," said Don Marcos, hesitatingly, "that was the Duchess de Delille."

There was a moment's silence, and as though the Prince had caught him doing something wrong, that he must apologize for, he hastened to add:

"She is very kind to the Infanta. She gives her children clothes, and I think she even lends her dresses. The daughter of a King! The grand-daughter of San Fernando! I am an old legitimist soldier, and the least I can do is be grateful that...."

Michael cut his excuses short with a gesture. That was enough: he did not want to hear any more. And he turned to Castro. He had seen him too, near the entrance to the Casino, talking to another lady.

"And I saw you, too," said Atilio, "but you were in such a rush, going along with your head down, making your way like a mad bull. Do you want to know who the lady is? Does she interest you?"

Lubimoff shrugged his shoulders; but his indifference was feigned. As a matter of fact she had interested him, although slightly. The unknown woman was tall and blond, with an air of lithe strength, with the freedom of movement of a gymnast or an amazon.

"Well, that's the 'Generala,'" Castro continued without observing that his friend was not paying much heed. "The title of 'Generala' isn't to be taken seriously. It's a pet name. I think the Duchess invented it, for I warn you the two are very good friends. She's a 'General' in the same way that certain other people are Colonels."

Don Marcos overlooked this bit of irony. Atilio was evidently in a bad humor that evening. His nerves were on edge, and he seemed ready to snap at any one. He must have lost in the gambling.

"They call her the 'Generala' because of her somewhat masculine character, and the brusque way she has of treating people at times. An extraordinary woman! A real amazon! She shoots, does gymnastics, swims in the rivers in mid-winter, and what's more she has a voice like the sighing of the breeze, and looks as though she were going to faint at the least emotion, like a timid girl. Do you want to know who she is? Her name is Clorinda, a name of ancient poetry, or ancient comedy. I always call her Doña Clorinda; it seems as though it would be disrespectful if I didn't, in spite of the fact that she is still young. Perhaps two or three years younger than her friend Alicia. The two hate each other, and they can't live apart. One week each month they clash, call each other names, and tell the most horrible tales about each other; then they look each other up; 'How are you, my dear?' 'Are you angry with me, angel?'"

The Prince smiled at Atilio's imitation of the words and gestures of the two ladies.

"Clorinda is an American," Castro continued, "but from South America, from a little Republic where her grandfathers and great-grandfathers were Presidents, and fighters, and fathers of their country. Her title of 'Generala' has a certain basis. Over there in her native land they admire her for her beauty and for the great sensation she is supposed to have caused in Europe. At a distance, you see, everything is changed and seems much greater. Her picture is public property, and figures on every package of coffee, and every advertising prospectus in the country. She is a national beauty; and when she gets old, there will always be a spot in the world where she will be considered eternally youthful. She got married in Paris to a young Frenchman, a dreamer, rather ill with tuberculosis. That was the very reason why the 'Generala' loved him. If she had married a strong, fiery sort of man, they would have killed each other in a few days. She is a widow now. I don't think she is very rich; the war must have diminished her income, but she has enough to live comfortably. I even imagine she must suffer fewer hardships than does the Delille woman. She is an exceedingly well-balanced person."

He remained silent for a moment.

"But she has such queer ideas! She is so used to dominating! I met her in Biarritz some years ago. I have seen her here often in the gaming rooms; we have bowed to each other and had a few conversations which did not amount to much. When a woman is placing her stakes she doesn't allow compliments that might distract her attention. To-day is the first time that I have talked with her at any length. Do you know what she asked me, the very first thing? Why I wasn't in the war. It didn't make any difference when I told her that I'm neutral, and that the war doesn't interest me. 'If I were a man, I would be a soldier,' she said. And if you had only seen the look she gave when she said it!"

Lubimoff smiled a bit scornfully at the woman's words.

"In her opinion," Castro went on saying, "every man ought to work at something, produce something, be a hero. She adored her poor husband, gentle as a sick lamb, because he painted a few pale, washed-out pictures, and had been rewarded in some slight degree at various expositions. Men like you and me, in her eyes, are a variety of 'supers' hired to give life to the drawing-rooms, casinos, and bathing resorts, to keep the conversation going, and be nice to the ladies; but we don't interest her. She told me so this afternoon once again."

"Does her opinion bother you?" asked the Prince.

Atilio paused for a moment, as though to weigh his words before replying.

"Yes, it does bother me," he resolutely answered at last. "Why should I deny it? That woman interests me. When I don't see her, I forget all about her. Months and years have gone by without my giving her a thought. But as soon as I meet her she dominates me.... I want her. I know I can't come up to you in such matters, but I've had successful love affairs too. But she is so different from the others! Besides, there's the joy in conquering, the need of dominating, that you find at the bottom of all our amorous desires! Every time we talk together, and she makes quite evident, with her bird-like voice and her smile of compassion, the distance that separates us, I come away sad, or rather, discouraged, as though I had to climb a great height, of which I would never reach the top, no matter how hard I tried. To-day I ought to be happy; it has been months since I've had an afternoon like this. I've played, and look ... look! Seventeen thousand francs!"

He had taken from his inner pocket a bundle of blue bank-notes, throwing it on the table with a certain fury.

"I succeeded in winning as high as twenty-six thousand. If there is anything in the saying, 'Lucky at cards, unlucky in love,' I was as lucky as a despairing lover or a deceived husband. And yet, I'm not happy."

The Prince smiled again, as though a self-evident truth had just been completely demonstrated. Woman! That Clorinda, that devil of a "Generala," was a real "woman." With a few short minutes of conversation only, she had turned Castro topsy-turvy, and perhaps would end by breaking up the peaceful life—without exciting pleasures but without desperate sorrows as well—that the guests at Villa Sirena were leading.

"And you, Atilio," he said in a reproachful voice, "are moved by that smooth-voiced virago. You believe in love like a school-boy."

Castro replied in a cold, aggressive tone. The Prince might say whatever he liked about him; but to call her a virago!... What right had he? Nevertheless he hid the real cause of his annoyance, pretending to be hurt by the allusion to his credulity.

"I don't believe in anything; I'm more skeptical than you perhaps. I know that everything about us is false, and conventional—all a matter of lies that we accept because they are necessary to us for the moment. You love music and painting as though they were something divine and eternal. Very well; if the structure of our ears were to be modified a little, the symphonies of Beethoven would be a regular din; if the functioning of our retinas were to change, we would have to burn all the famous pictures, because they would seem like so many canvases dirtied by a child's play; if our brains were to be modified, all the poets and thinkers would become childish idiots for us. No, I don't believe in anything," he insisted angrily. "In order to live and understand one another, we have to agree upon a high and a low, a left and a right; but even that is a lie, since we live in the infinite which has no limits. Everything we consider fundamental is simply a matter of lines that have been laid down on the canvas of life to mark off our various conceptions."

The Prince shrugged his shoulders, giving him a look of surprise. Why all this, apropos of a woman?

"Everything is a lie," Castro went on; "but that is no reason why I should live like a stone or a tree. I need sweet falsehoods to sing my mind to sleep until the hour of my death. Illusions are a lie, but I want them near me; hope is another lie, but I want it to walk before me. I don't believe in love, since I don't believe in anything. Everything you say against it I have known for years; but should I give it a kick if it comes my way, and wants to go with me? Do you know any dream that fills the emptiness of our lives better—even though it lasts only a short time?"

Michael greeted his friend's enthusiasm with a sardonic gesture.

"Do you know why I look younger than I am?" Atilio continued, more and more excitedly. "Do you know I shall be young when others of my own age have become old men? I pretend to be ironical. As a matter of fact I'm a skeptic. But I have a secret, the secret of eternal youth, which I keep to myself. Let me tell you what it is. I have discovered that the greatest wisdom in life, the most important thing, is to 'while away the time'; and I fill the emptiness that every man carries inside him with an orchestra; the orchestra of my illusions. The great thing is that it play all the time, that the music rack never be empty; once one piece is played, another must take its place. At times it is a symphony of love. Mine have been beautiful but brief. For that reason I have replaced them with another which is endless—that of ambition and the desire for gain, whose orbits are infinite like those of the stars in the heavens, and like the possible combinations of cards. I gamble. In the whirl of the roulette wheel I see a castle that may be mine, a more sumptuous castle than any in existence; a finer yacht than the one you used to have; endless *fêtes*. Through a pack of cards I can contemplate things more magnificent than were dreamed of by the Persian story-tellers. Its suites are so many piles of precious gems. Most of the time I lose, and the orchestra plays an accompaniment on muted strings, with a funeral march of wondrous wild sadness and beauty; but after a few measures, the march becomes a hymn of triumph, the dawning of a new day, the resurrection of hope."

And now there was a look of pity in the eyes of the Prince. "He is mad," it seemed to say.

"This afternoon," Castro continued, "my orchestra made me acquainted with a new symphony, something I had never heard before. While I was winning money I did not think a single time about myself, nor about palaces, nor yachts, nor parties. I was thinking only of the 'Generala,' and thinking of her with real hate, wanting to get revenge. I wanted to win a hundred thousand francs—who knows, I may win it to-morrow—and spend the whole hundred thousand on a pearl necklace, on leaving the Casino, and send it to her anonymously with something like this: 'As a tribute of dislike from a worthless, miserable man.'"

A burst of laughter from the Prince woke the Colonel with a start. As a good early riser, the latter had gone to sleep in his chair. Observing that His Excellency was not paying any attention to him, he slipped out of the Hall, as though he had something of more importance to attend to than the conversation of the two friends who seemed to ignore his presence.

"But what do you find in love?" Michael asked. "For I think you know what love really is. All the illusions of adolescence, and all the idealism of poetry, are merely winding paths which lead to the same, the only goal; the physical act. And aren't you tired of that? Aren't you never daunted by the monotony of it?"

There was a certain gloomy intonation in the Prince's voice, as though he were lamenting over the ruin of all his own life. He had met hundreds of women of the sort that cause a sudden burst of mute desire as they pass. Feminine resistance was something unknown to him. More than that: women had sought him, coming half-way of their own free will, pursuing him with no regard for the conventions and modesty, obliging him, as a matter of masculine pride, to overtax his powers with a prodigality that made pleasure almost painful. And they were all alike! He understood the mirage of illusion in the things that one admires from afar, and has no hope of obtaining. It is our curiosity for what is hidden, the desire which is aroused by an obstacle, the inner fancies inspired by clothes, ornaments, everything which covers the feminine body, giving to its sameness the charm of a mystery which is ever renewed. As for him, alas, it was as though they all went nude. Nothing could stimulate his interest; it was all too familiar.

"Besides," and here his voice grew quieter, "I wouldn't confess it to any one else; but love and women make me think of the miserableness of human life, the inevitable end, death. Since I've been freed from their false seductions, I feel gayer, more sure of myself; I enjoy more frankly the passing moment. I don't want to talk to you about the shame of those bodies which we claim to be divine. Women are less wholesome than men. It was Nature's will. But that isn't what makes me flee from them."

He was silent for a moment, but then added shortly after:

"Whenever I am near a woman I can't help but see the image of death. When I caress her silky hair, I suddenly seem to feel a smooth, hard yellow skull, like those one sees protruding from the ground in abandoned cemeteries. A kiss on her mouth, or a nibble at her chin, rouses in me a vision of the bony jaw with its teeth, not so different from those of the anthropoids in the museums. Those eyes will fade; that nose with its graceful curves and rosy quivering nostrils will dissolve likewise; the only solid and permanent parts are the black sockets, and the grotesque grin of the skull, with its flattened nose. Those swelling breasts are nothing more than false padding to hide the ghastly cage of the ribs; those legs, which seem to us such wonderful columns, are stringy flesh and water that will waste away, leaving bare two long calcareous pipe-stems. We imagine we are adoring supreme beauty, and we are embracing a skeleton. The image of death fills us with horror, and every woman carries one within her, and compels us to worship it."

Now it was Castro's turn to gaze in astonishment. His eyes, fixed on the Prince, seemed to say: "He is mad."

"The trouble with you, Michael, is that you've over-enjoyed," he said after a long pause. "You make me think of the people who, when they sit down to the table, hide their lack of appetite with nausea. The most succulent meat for them suggests the horrors of the slaughter house. Bread reminds them of the hands that kneaded it, and wine calls up a picture of feet reeking with juice in the vintage-troughs. But just let their senses awaken, and their physical needs reassert themselves, and they see everything in a different light, as though the sun had just risen, and they find an indescribable charm in the very things that disgusted them. What difference is it to me if a woman has a skeleton inside? I have one too, and that doesn't prevent me from taking a great deal of joy in the pleasures of life, and considering love as the most interesting of all those pleasures."

Castro laughed with affectionate compassion as he looked at his friend.

"Let me say it again, you are satiated; you have the lack of appetite and the gloomy vision of a person suffering from a painful indigestion. You are still too young for this debility to last. You will recover. Your appetite will come back. I hope you won't find the table set exactly as in the past, that you will be swept off your feet by some obstacle, in other words, that unrequital will make you suffer; and then ... well, just wait till then!"

CHAPTER V

DON MARCOS had never seen the Prince so vexed as he was that morning, when he announced that the Duchess de Delille was waiting for him down-stairs in the hall.

"You should have told her I'd gone out; any sort of a pretext—a lunch at Nice.... There must be some understanding between you. You certainly look out for your Infanta!"

The Colonel, flushed with emotion, made an effort to reply to these accusations. If the Duchess had now suddenly presented herself, it was perhaps because he had refused to take any of her messages for the Prince.

As the latter went down to the hall, he ran straight into Alicia, who was standing close to a window, and looking at the gardens and the sea. Her back was towards him, just as he had seen her coming out of the concert. When she turned her head, Michael thought to himself that he would surely never have recognized her had he met her anywhere else. She was a beautiful woman, but scarcely like the person he had seen that last time in the "study" on the Avenue du Bois, with its weird oriental nick-nacks and unwholesome perfumes. Several years of her life had passed away since then, and yet she seemed fresher, and younger. Her eyes had lost the veiled disturbing fire, that made them look larger, and gave them a fixed, unnatural stare. The dull, sickly whiteness of her skin had taken on color from the sun and the open air. Her airy, undulating litheness had become less willowy, giving her person the calm tranquillity of bodies that are beginning to crystallize in their definitive form.

The Prince, interrupted by Alicia's smiling glance, was unable to continue his scrutiny. It seemed from her quiet easy manner as though she had been there in that very place only the day before. Moreover, Michael suddenly began to wonder how he should start the conversation. Should he talk English or French? Should he speak informally as before?... She put an end to his hesitation, speaking familiarly in Spanish, just as when they were children.

"How hard it is to get in touch with you! Practically impossible," Alicia said as she sat down, after shaking hands with him. "So I decided to pay you this visit. It isn't exactly proper for a lady to call on a person with such a terrible reputation as you have; but I'm not the first one who has come here. There have been lots of others!"

She laughed teasingly as she said this. Immediately she became serious, and said timidly:

"I came here on business—a money matter."

Not wanting to take up such a subject at once, she talked about the obstacles which had obliged her to come unannounced to Villa Sirena. The Prince could have absolute confidence in the fidelity with which his "chamberlain" carried out his orders. This Colonel was a nice fellow, but there was no approaching him, any more than a ferocious dog, when some one tries to make him disobey his master. She had vainly asked him to announce her visit; and he had even refused to accept her card for his Prince.

"I might have written you; but I was afraid you wouldn't reply, or would simply tell me to deal with your agent in Paris. It has been such a long time since we've seen each other! Our friendship has been so intermittent! So that is why I finally decided last night to come and surprise you in your den, with the hope that you wouldn't show me the door."

Michael smiled, making a gesture of indignant denial.

"I came about my debt ... the loans your mother made me some time ago. I didn't know how much they amounted to. Your agent now says they are over four hundred thousand francs. It must be so, if he maintains it. At times when I was in straits I asked for something, and the Princess, who was such a great lady, kept giving and giving, without either of us paying any attention to the amounts. Now I see how tremendously generous she must have been."

This was surprising news for Lubimoff. Then he gradually recalled that when his mother died she had left a long memorandum of all the loans she had made, and that Alicia's name figured among the debtors. But he had left the papers in the hands of his administrator, without thinking any more about the matter.

He immediately understood the reason for Alicia's visit. His agent had wanted to raise some money, and owing to the lack of funds from Russia, he was raising all he could in the West: credits ... advances made to friends or dependents, guaranty deposits, and even the loans made by the Princess, which, according to his express orders, were not to be demanded except in case of strict necessity.

The general pressure of circumstances had reached Alicia. For the last four months the Lubimoff estate had been sending her letter after letter, demanding the payment of her enormous debt. Already the agent's last note had become threatening because of her silence. It notified her that action would be brought against her in court. The estate was holding many of her letters thanking the Princess for the latter's generosity. Besides, all the money had been paid by checks cashed by the Duchess herself.

"Your administrator is certainly an insolent fellow. The other day I saw you in the Casino,—I saw you from behind as you were running away from people. You frightened me: I imagined then that you had changed, that you were very different from the man I knew, and that we would never come to an understanding. Later I thought you mustn't be quite so terrible as you seem ... and I came."

Michael, remaining silent, seemed to be saying something with his eyes, which were fixed on Alicia. Well, why had she come? What was it she wished to propose to him?

She smiled with an expression of cynical amusement.

"I came to tell you that I can't pay now—and perhaps never; to beg you to wait, I don't know how long, and to ask you to see that that disagreeable fellow who is managing your estate doesn't annoy me with his insolence."

And as the Prince made no move, she continued,

"I'm ruined."

"So am I," said Michael. "We're all ruined. The munition makers are the only people with any money now."

"Oh! You ruined!" Alicia protested. "With you it is simply a question of being hard pressed for the moment. Things in Russia will be straightened out some time or other. Besides, you are Prince Lubimoff, the famous millionaire. If I had your name, who would refuse me a loan?"

Suddenly she lost the audacious smile which she had worked up for the interview. Her eyes grew darker; the corners of her mouth drooped.

"I am really ruined. Look."

She pointed to the triangle of bare flesh visible at the throat of her low cut dress. A pearl necklace rested on her white bosom. Michael, as she insisted, finally looked at the pearls. False, scandalously false; all the luster gone, opaque and yellow as drops of wax. He knew something about pearls; he had given away so many necklaces! Then Alicia showed him her hands. Two artistically made finger rings, but without any jewels, and of slight intrinsic value, were all that adorned her fingers.

"This is a last year's dress," she added in a mournful voice, as though confessing something most shameful. "They won't trust me any more in Paris. I owe so much! Nothing but the hat is new. What woman, no matter how poor she might feel, wouldn't buy a hat! It is the most conspicuous thing about one,—something that changes all the time; and must be looked after at all costs. Luckily, on account of the war, they are not using plumes.... I'm poor, Michael, poorer than any woman you ever knew."

"And your mother?"

The Prince asked this instinctively, without thinking. A moment later he suspected that he had read, some years before, he didn't know where, perhaps while he was roving the seas, the news of the death of Doña Mercedes. He was not sure; but her daughter removed all doubt.

"Poor señora! Let's not talk about her."

But nevertheless Alicia did talk, but only to lament her mother's devout prodigality. She had given millions for the construction of an enormous hospital in Spain, on the advice of her Aragonese chaplain, the astronomer of the Champs-Élysées. Marble was used in the construction for the mere masonry; the garden fence was forged by a celebrated Parisian artist who devoted himself to molding bronze statues for drawing-rooms. But when the vicar left, tired of such generosity, the monster building remained unfinished, and the precious fence lay on the ground in pieces, like so much old iron. Later, the "Monsignor" directed the worthy lady's funds into other channels. It was necessary to spread the faith by means of the "good book," and a new publishing house arose in Paris, which was most extraordinary and unheard of. Packages of books were stored on mahogany shelves, and the leaves were folded on lacquer tables.

"The priests got everything that belonged to me," Alicia continued. "At times they egged mamma on to the most absurd outlays of money just for the sake of collecting commissions from the contractors. From numerous belfries in both hemispheres chimes rang thanks to Doña Mercedes. One entire bell foundry was kept going just on mamma's gifts. Besides, she was often carried away by a sort of loving weakness for all the saints who were not especially famous.

"In her last years she devoted herself to 'launching' saints. Every one in the calendar who was little known, or of some unusual name, aroused in her the desire to repair a great injustice. She had their lives written, churches dedicated to them; and corresponded with the high dignitaries of Rome to push many a dead man, who had waited centuries in vain for the hour when he should become a Saint."

Lubimoff finally began to laugh at the resentful tone in which Alicia spoke of her mother's mystic pleasures. Doña Mercedes was a great one! And finally she began to laugh likewise.

"In that way all our income, which was enormous, was spent. She should have left me a real fortune, unencumbered, in the bank. A lady that spent so little on herself! And nevertheless, I had to pay out huge sums for all the orders she had contracted before her death. You can be sure the Monsignor and the rest of them are much richer than I."

"How about your mines? And your lands in Mexico?"

The Duchess repeated the same gesture of despair. It was as though they did not exist! She was poor, absolutely poor.

"You say you are ruined, and you haven't suffered from the money shortage for more than the last two years, perhaps less. I haven't seen a cent of my fortune for some time before the war. Every one is talking about Russia, and Bolshevism, because it is something that concerns the Old World directly. But how about Mexico, and the situation there which goes back to the time when Europe was at peace?"

Her lands had been lost as though they were so much personal property, that could be transported and hidden. An agrarian revolution, the echoes of which had scarcely reached the Old Continent, had swallowed them up, suppressing all traces of her former property rights. The half-breeds had divided them to suit themselves, to work them, or leave them more unproductive than before. To whom could she appeal, if these lands were in provinces that were constantly changing hands, and the Mexican government had no authority over them?

The silver mines, which for three generations of Barrios had been the basis of their fortune, were in a still worse situation.

"One of the so-called 'Generals,' an Indian, has fortified himself in the territory where my mines are, and from there he defies the rulers in the Capital. They tell me that every month he takes out half a million francs in silver bars. He cuts them up in disks, puts his stamp on them and makes money thus to pay his men. You can imagine he has plenty of followers, with pure silver money, worth more than that of civilized countries! They will never be able to put him out; all he has to do to create armies for himself is to dig down into what belongs to me. This bad joke has gone on now for several years; I, who live in Europe, getting poorer and poorer every day, am paying for an endless war on the other side of the earth."

In spite of the fact that the Prince had never taken care of his own business he wanted to give her some advice. She ought to go over there and ask for assistance; she was born in the United States.

"I've already seen to that," she replied. "I have some one in New York who looks after my affairs. But would they go to war just on my account? Perhaps I shall take the trip later. Not now: I haven't the strength. There is something that is bothering me terribly just now, and it would be even worse if I were to leave France."

Her eyes began to fill with tears. Her face contracted with an expression of pain, and her hand moved toward her purse for a handkerchief. Michael recalled the young man that Castro had been noticing at Alicia's side during the last few years. Perhaps he was the cause of her emotion, and inability to make the trip.

"Love!" he thought to himself. "Love, even now when she's growing old."

He tried to change the conversation and asked about the Duke de Delille. He knew that he was at the front; and even thought he remembered a report of his being wounded in one of the early battles. Was he still alive?

In speaking of her husband, Alicia looked grave, to Michael's great surprise. Formerly she used to treat him with a certain scorn. He had accepted his wife's freedom, with all its consequences, in exchange for an enormous allowance. They lived apart, and although she found her independence very sweet, she could not help but feel a sort of feminine dislike for her accommodating husband, so little given to tragic jealousy. But at present her ideas seemed to have changed, and she spoke rapidly as though afraid of noticing Lubimoff smile as she used to smile herself, in mentioning the Duke.

"Yes; he joined the service. You know of course that he is some twenty years older than I. He was exempted from bearing arms on account of his age; but he remembered that he had been an officer in his youth, and was one of the first to go. Who would have thought it of a man who didn't seem to have any cares, and made fun of everything that didn't affect his own selfish pleasures!"

The Germans had picked him up in a dying condition during one of their victorious advances at the beginning of the war. He was covered with wounds. After two years as a prisoner they had exchanged him as useless, and he was living interned in Switzerland, with one arm gone.

"Poor man! He writes me every month. He fishes in Lake Geneva, and thinks of me more than he ever thought before. His epistles are almost love letters. What a transformation misfortune can make in a character. He says that he sees life from a different angle; and hopes that after the cataclysm, which will have made us better, we shall be able to come together again, and be happy. Oh, if only I could want to!..."

Her tone was ironical as she spoke of this illusionary happiness, but at the same time there was in it a note of respect and admiration. The Duke whom she had known as a great dowry hunter, accommodating and unscrupulous, was forgotten. At present she saw in him only the white-haired warrior, the invalid, who according to the doctors, would not live long, owing to the operations he had undergone. And she was trying to keep up the exile's hopes, replying to his long letters, with brief, affectionate notes.

"So it's on account of your husband that you don't take the trip?" Michael asked, pretending that he was inquiring in good faith.

Alicia was ruffled by such a supposition. Poor Delille! It was something else that was troubling her. Her husband wasn't the only one who had gone to war. There were others, who were younger, and had better reasons to love life, but who had suffered the same fate. How many hidden griefs there were these days!

The Duchess's eyes moistened, and her eyes and lips frankly expressed her sorrow.

"It's the little lover; there's no doubt of it," Michael said to himself. "It's the young chap Castro saw."

As though she read his thoughts and were anxious to switch them, Alicia began to talk once more about the reason for her visit, and about her situation.

The Prince nodded when she described to him her amazement at finding that wealth was not something infinite and immutable, and that it was slipping from her grasp ... slipping and slipping, without her being able to do anything to avoid the gradual ruin.

"I sold inopportunely; I took the money they cared to give me, without paying any attention to the conditions. All my jewels went; I sold some in Paris, others here in this very place. You say you are ruined. No, you don't know what it means; but I know all right! I've been shipwrecked longer than you; my boat was smaller. I don't want to bore you with an account of my poverty. I haven't a house in Paris any more. I shall never go back there again, unless my affairs are straightened out. The only house I have is a villa here, which I bought in the good old days. Don't smile; there are two mortgages on it. Almost any day they may put me out of it. It was a very pleasant sort of house before, when I had money; but now, with everything so scarce on account of the war! There's no coal, and wood is dear; it gets cold at night, and it takes a fortune to keep the old furnace going. Besides, I haven't any servants except my former lady's maid, the gardener, and his wife who does the cooking. For that reason all the rooms are closed, and Valeria and I live our lives in two rooms on the first floor. We eat there, and sleep there. Valeria is a girl from Paris, a señorita whom I am 'protecting.' Imagine how poor she must be if she trusts her future to me!"

"But you gamble," said the Prince.

Alicia seemed shocked at these words. They sounded like an accusation.

"I play, but what can you expect me to do? I have to do something to keep body and soul together, to earn my living. How else could a woman like myself do it? I know what you're going to say to me: that I've lost a great deal. True; I sold my pearl necklace here, the real one, and a great many other jewels; I have lost large amounts, more than I care to think of. But at that time I didn't know all I know to-day.... When as luck will have it, I haven't much money to play!"

Lubimoff was astonished at the way this woman spoke in all seriousness of her present adeptness.

"Besides," she added in a tone of sadness, "what would become of me if I didn't play? Surely you haven't forgotten how I was when we saw each other last. You must have noticed certain tastes of mine."

Michael recalled the invitation to smoke "the pipe," and the odor that filled the "study" in the palace on the Avenue du Bois.

"I put a stop to all that: gambling and something else made me give it up. Now I think of it with disgust. That's why I live in Monte Carlo. I have a feeling deep down in my heart that fortune will come back in search of me here, and nowhere else. Don't you play?"

Michael was annoyed at this question. Hadn't he told her that he was ruined? Was he going to follow her example, and make his situation still worse by losing the remnants of his fortune?

"Ruined!" exclaimed Alicia. "Your hard times can't last long. This Russian business will finally be settled. The great powers have too large interests at stake there, not to take a hand in straightening everything out. It's this affair of mine that won't be arranged for years. The only hope I have is to enjoy a run of luck in the Casino and win some two or three hundred thousand francs, and, with that amount, wait for things to change."

The Prince shrugged his shoulders. He knew gamblers. This woman, dominated by her wild dream, would forget the object of her visit, and go raving on about the possible whims of fortune, like Spadoni, or like Castro himself.

"And what do you want of me?"

Alicia seemed to wake up, and once more her smile became bold, and engaging, as it had been at the beginning of the interview; the smile of a petitioner who comes with the firm determination to get what he wants. She had already told him at the very beginning what her object was; that the Prince's agent shouldn't bother her any more in regard to that forgotten debt.

"I shall pay it some day, if it is possible for me.... But you had better count on my never paying it at all. Give it up as lost, and tell that horrid gentleman not to write me any more."

Michael, fascinated by the simple way in which this woman announced her extraordinary desire, imitated the tone of her voice.

"Very well; I shall tell this horrid gentleman not to bother you; to forget you."

And he laughed like a child, without paying any attention to the fact that his own interests were at stake. The only thing he thought of was the expression on the face of his solemn agent when he received such an order.

"I always thought you were kind and generous," she said. "Thanks, Michael! At times I have had a discussion with the 'General' about you, to convince her that you are a big hearted man."

"Oh, so Doña Clorinda is an enemy of mine? Why I've never seen her!"

"She's an extraordinary woman. In her eyes, every man who has a good time, and doesn't do wonderful things, is displeasing to her. Only yesterday we quarreled for good. Let's not talk about her. I have something more to ask of you."

More? The Prince looked at her in astonishment, but Alicia hastened to add that what she wanted was some advice.

War had upset their modes of life with amazing rapidity. Social values were reversed: the fortunes that seemed most solid were crumbling.

"Things will change, surely? It's impossible for this to last."

"Yes it is impossible," he said gravely.

Both of them seemed to be living in another world, surrounded by the senseless visions of a nightmare. To think that they would have to worry of money, after it had been, up to that time, a natural part of their existence, much as sunlight, air, or water is for every one! To think that they should find themselves obliged to pursue it in its flight through unknown ways! No, it wasn't logical; surely a passing whim of destiny. Their lives would again be the same as before, with the regularity of the laws of nature, which seem to swerve at times, but finally return to their orderly predestined course.

Being harder pressed, and having suffered economic hardships for a longer time, it was impossible for her to adopt the serenity with which Lubimoff accepted his momentary ruin.

"Things will change, that's certain; but in the meantime, how can I live? You have just freed me from a moral burden by forgetting about this debt. I thank you. But I must work, I want to earn some money! What is your advice?"

He was astounded. What work could Alicia do? Her question was laughable. But there she was, gravely facing him, convinced of her determination to work, and expecting illuminating counsel, as though her fate depended on him.

Fortunately Alicia herself, unable to bear the silence, began to explain her own ideas on the subject. The topsy-turvy state of things at the present time justified the wildest plans. A great lady might adopt means of support which some years previously would have caused a scandal. She knew a number of Russian ladies in Nice who used to give wonderful parties in their drawing rooms before the war, and who at present, having been reduced to poverty, were devising schemes to earn their living in their own way. One was going to open a millinery shop, and count on her former friendships to form a circle of customers. Another had changed her villa on the Promenade des Anglais into a boarding house. She would admit only people of distinction. Allied officers, from Colonels up. She intended to treat her boarders like visitors, with all the courtesy of a great lady receiving her guests; save that from now on every day in the week would be her reception day.

"What do you think of my turning my villa into a boarding house? Could you help me with a little money to renew the furniture, and buy whatever is lacking? Nothing but aristocratic guests; generals, and retired ambassadors who come here in quest of sunlight."

The Prince replied with a burst of laughter.

"Why, you're crazy. They would all make love to you. In a few weeks your establishment would be a regular inferno."

Alicia, considering his observation quite accurate, did not insist any further. The Russian lady in Nice was old and terrible looking compared with her. Besides, she thought it perfectly natural and logical that her guests should become enamored of her.

The "General" had suggested another plan to her. She might open a tea-room in Monte Carlo, a very elegant one. The attraction of seeing her at the counter would draw people. For this she would not need a financial backer.

Once more Lubimoff burst out laughing.

"The Duchess de Delille's tea-room! That would be delightful; but once people's curiosity had been satisfied the only customers you would have would be those who were interested in your charms. No; that's not business."

She gave a look of somewhat comic dismay; what was she to do? A lady who is anxious for work can find no occupation in a world controlled and monopolized by men. She had nothing to fall back on except gambling. It was an exciting pleasure which made her forget her worries, and at the same time gave her hope. Each day with gambling she opened a window to fortune, in case it should deign to remember her. Who knows but what some time it might fold its golden wings and alight on a Casino table, and allow Alicia's slender hands to caress it, like a tame eagle!

"In the first few months of the war," she continued, "I didn't feel the need of anything to distract my mind; the reality of what was happening was enough. What anguish I went through! But one gets used to everything; the deepest emotions get monotonous if they are too long drawn out. One can't live forever with one's nerves at a high tension. And this war is so long, and so tiresome! I might have had recourse to philanthropic work to take my mind off my troubles; go into a hospital, and take care of the wounded. But I've never been clever at such things, and I don't want to make a nuisance of myself and be a hindrance, out of pure vanity, like a great many other women. Besides, we are in the habit of giving orders, and always coming first, and no matter how deeply we may feel the spirit of sacrifice, we finally leave, unable to endure finding ourselves ordered about by more skillful and useful women, who have previously been our inferiors. Take Clorinda for instance; she was a nurse the first two years; she was one of the prettiest and most interesting with her white dress and her little blue cape. She is attracted by everything great; heroism, sacrifices, etc., but she finally quarreled with her superiors and gave up her fine rôle."

In gesture and facial expression Alicia seemed to be pitying her own uselessness.

"What could I do? I was reduced to worse and worse straits. In Paris my creditors were right at my heels, constantly bothering me; that's why I came to Monte Carlo, and gambled to forget, and to make a living. There is love, an old Academician, a friend of mine, said to me, with a selfish motive to be the first to make advantage of his advice. Just imagine: real passionate love, wholehearted love, as the only solution for the sorrows of life, and at such a time! Oh, if only I could! But I feel I'm old, two thousand years old. You are younger, but you can count your life in centuries too. Love, for such as you and me!"

At first Lubimoff smiled at the tone of irony and disenchantment in which she spoke. Yes, they were very old. The great remedies, useful for the majority of people, had no effect on them. They, as it were, had become insensible from satiety and weariness. Suddenly the Prince was moved by an indiscreet desire. He decided to take advantage of the opportunity to ask her a question that had often occurred to him.

"Indeed," he said with masculine frankness, as though talking with a comrade, "you still believe in love? They told me about a boy, almost a child, whom you used to take everywhere before the war. Really, we are beginning to get old," he added with a smile, "and feel we need the contact of youth. Was he your lover? Is he the reason for your worries?"

At these questions, the Duchess paled, and seemed to hesitate. Then she made an effort to speak. It was evident that she was eager to be sincere. But her pallor was followed by a wave of crimson. Twice she tried to say something, and finally, mastering her desire to talk, she forced a mischievous smile.

"Let's not talk about that. We each have a right to our secrets," she said.

And to keep the Prince from relapsing into his curiosity, she went on talking about gambling. But he was absorbed in his thoughts, and was not listening to her. He had hit the nail on the head; that young stripling was her lover, and she was suffering on his account. Perhaps he was wounded, or a prisoner. That was the great obstacle which stood in the way of her trip; which was keeping her pinned down in Europe, in the superstitious belief that we can ward off dangers better if we remain close at hand. And she seemed very much in love! Here the Prince gave vent to a series of mental exclamations.

"Forty years old, with a past that would fill a book! To feel such a powerful, such a youthful passion! Still to believe in love!"

Michael looked at her with an expression that was almost one of hatred. Her passion for the boy annoyed him, without his being able to tell just why; perhaps because of the indignation which is always aroused by people who cling to some harmful lie, accepting it as truth and consolation. Whatever the cause, her conduct annoyed him.

This sudden feeling of hostility towards Alicia finally caused him to pay attention once more to what she was saying.

"If only I had as much money as I had before, when your mother was still alive, and we used to live in Monte Carlo! But at that time I didn't know as much as I know to-day about gambling. I used to play just for excitement, just to enjoy the sensation of losing, which, as a matter of fact, didn't affect me very deeply. I used only chips for a thousand francs in betting. I thought it was beneath me so much as to touch any others; and besides, I never risked them one at a time. I always staked them in a row."

"How much have you lost?"

She shrugged her shoulders, and pursed her lips disdainfully.

"Who could possibly know? I've been coming here for twelve years or more. Even the people in the Casino wouldn't be able to calculate what I've given them. In those days, I never used to keep any track of it myself. When I needed money I telegraphed to Paris. Besides, I had your mother; and I had my own, who usually gave in to my requests, in the end. I wouldn't like to know how much I've lost: it would make me furious. It must be millions."

The smile of commiseration with which Michael listened to her, seemed to make her bolder.

"But at that time I didn't know how to play! Now I must win, and I play in a different way. What I need is capital. If I only had a working capital!"

This last expression changed his smile into frank laughter. "A working capital!" The Duchess would go on talking seriously about her "work." She lamented the slenderness of her means. Some thirty thousand francs was all the capital she had at her disposal. At times it dwindled in alarming fashion: the thirty thousand often shrunk to a single digit. Then the ciphers would reappear, and the product of her "work" expand, gradually rising above the thirty thousand; but this amount seemed to be the fatal number for Alicia, for soon after reaching it her winnings would always fall to their usual level.

"Last night I was lucky; I succeeded in winning fourteen thousand francs. But last week was bad. Sum total, I'm still at thirty thousand: impossible to get any farther. And I don't run any chances, I'm afraid, and don't take advantage of the good runs of luck I do have. I ought to go on doubling, and doubling. I'm afraid of losing it all on a single stake. If I only had a working capital! If I were to go into the Casino some afternoon with a hundred and fifty or two hundred thousand francs! That's the way to master luck. I ought to play big stakes. Imagine me, betting a hundred, and even as low as twenty franc chips, like a retired money lender! That's the reason fortune doesn't notice me, and passes by on the other side."

The Prince shook his head. He refused to help her with her follies. Wasn't it better to keep those thousands of francs, instead of losing them in no time, as would happen when she was least expecting it?

"You're not a gambler, I know," she said. "You have never felt attracted to that sort of pleasure. That's why you don't realize the mysterious power of the game, and give advice about something you don't understand. If I were to give up playing, I would feel my poverty at once; then I would be really poor. While you play, you always have money in your hands; you win, and lose, but you never lack the necessities of life. And if you lose everything you can still get what you need to start in again. I don't know how it is, but a gambler always has plenty of money. A single coin puts him on his feet again in five minutes. It's the poor man who doesn't play who goes around with empty pockets, without hope or means of improving his situation."

Michael continued his mimicry of protest. That was all an old story to him; it was the way Spadoni, and even Castro, talked, but with a certain added fanaticism, characteristic of women, who, mystics in money matters, are always inclined to believe in presentiments and mysterious influences.

"Don't count on my helping you to gamble. Besides, I'm poor. At the present moment the Colonel must have less cash in the strong box than you. I'm almost tempted to ask you to loan me your thirty thousand francs."

They both laughed at the idea of this loan. And she had come as a debtor to ask his aid!

"I don't know what I can do for you; it's impossible for me to tell just what my situation is; but I'll do what I can. Let's have hope: one must be patient. These times can't last."

"No; they can't last."

Again the thought of the ridiculousness of their being poor so unexpectedly, came over them. But was it logical to think that the world would go on in the same normal fashion after such radical divergences from the natural order?

They felt drawn together in the solidarity of misfortune; they suddenly met, like brother and sister, fallen at the foot of a mountain peak, on the heights of which they had previously avoided each other, rudely clashing in uncontrollable hostility.

At present Michael had a feeling of being attracted to her, for a reason that was absolutely novel. Since his youth he had hated the daughter of Doña Mercedes, for her pride, and for the air of overwhelming superiority which she maintained even in those moments of love when nearly every woman freely humbles herself to take shelter in a man's arms like a happy slave. She could give herself only with a manner of haughty condescension, as a haughty alms, much as a goddess might come to a poor mortal.

And now, seeing her come to him thus simply, to entreat his aid, without the rancor of humiliated pride, hiding her fear with friendly merriment, desirous of forgetting the past, he felt all his old antipathy melt away.

He had always been a protector, a lover in the oriental fashion, incapable of caring for any women except those of his harem, who owed everything to his munificence, from their slippers to the plumes in their turbans, from the jewels that adorned their breasts, to the sweetmeats they ate, the pipes they smoked, and the musical instruments which accompanied their songs. Alicia did not interest him as a woman; neither she nor any other! But he felt the sympathy of comradeship in seeing her in need of his protection; somewhat the same feeling that he had towards Castro, the Colonel, and the other occupants of Villa Sirena. He even thought to himself that misfortune was acceptable, so long as it tended to make people show their real character once more. This Alicia, so odious to him in early youth, might finally turn out to be quite a good friend, now that she found herself freed from the influence of vanity and of her bad bringing up.

"You have done enough just in receiving me here," she continued. "I know the limitation of my rights: I'm in hostile territory. This is the house of 'The Enemies of Women.'"

The Prince pretended not to hear her. Somebody had been talking; perhaps it was Castro, who could never keep anything from Doña Clorinda.

They walked through the gardens. Alicia stopped suddenly in front of a little piece of cultivated ground, where a few vegetables were beginning to spring from the soil.

"This is where you work? I know you amuse yourself working in your garden, just as other Russian princes do by making shoes."

So she knew this too? Oh, that tattle-tale rogue of a Castro!

In the Greek garden, one of the marble benches supported by four winged Victories attracted her attention, causing her to stop for a moment with a pensive expression on her face.

"Do you remember the old man on the bench near the Trojan wall?" she suddenly said.

Michael did not know how to answer her question; but after a few moments he remembered, as though her fixed stare communicated to him the vision of that night in which he had brutally left her.

"How you laughed at me! What a fool I must have seemed! Yes: I was unbearable. I was Venus; I was the center of the world; everything in existence, people and things, had been created for my special benefit. I felt it was my mission to make the world endure my whims, and that the world ought to thank me on its knees for paying any attention to it. What can you expect! It was youth, and the childish pride of our Springtime, which imagines itself eternal. And afterwards! If I were to tell you all the disillusionments, and all the sorrows that I experienced, even back in the days when I didn't have to worry about money! Winter sweeps away all our fancies of Maytime!"

"But you're not an old woman yet!" Michael exclaimed. "You still inspire romantic love in young men. You're fooling yourself or trying to make fun of me. There are still lots of men who, when they see you, would...."

"Perhaps," she replied, "but you, my dear, are not one of them. Confess it; I've never pleased you."

The Prince decided not to confess anything, and changed the conversation. These allusions to the past annoyed him. Alicia irritated him, every time she attempted to revive her charms as a siren of men.

They wandered about for more than half an hour on the various garden terraces. From time to time, in passing a clearing in the shrubbery, Michael cast a stealthy glance in the direction of the villa. No one was at the windows; but he himself felt an inner agitation at this visit. He was sure they were spying on him. Atilio, from behind the window curtains, was undoubtedly following their promenade among the trees. Perhaps Spadoni, who had spent the night at Villa Sirena, was jumping out of bed, and losing two hours of sleep, in order to contemplate this surprising spectacle. Even Novoa might have stopped reading to look in the direction of the garden.

Alicia herself noticed the fact that no one was visible, neither guest nor servants. She and the Prince seemed to be walking through an enchanted park.

As they went in the direction of the gate they met Don Marcos, who was hurriedly coming out of the gardener's lodge.

The Duchess held out her hand to Michael, who kissed it ceremoniously.

"I hope we are to see each other again in the Casino."

He shook his head. The gaming rooms bored him: he had no idea of going there.

"I would have liked to meet you there. I'm sure you would bring me luck."

For a moment she seemed undecided. She had no thought of returning to Villa Sirena, where there was no one but men: she was convinced that she was a nuisance there.

"Come and see me to-morrow. The Colonel knows where I live. Come, and we'll have a laugh at the way the Duchess de Delille is living. It's rather interesting."

She went over to the livery carriage which was waiting for her outside the gate. Before getting in she turned to urge him, in a tone of playful threat:

"If you don't come, you'll never see me again. I shall think you want to break with me, that you think I'm a bore, and don't like me. I shall expect you."

As the carriage drove off, she waved farewell.

"It was about time!" Michael exclaimed, on finding himself alone.

It had been a visit of an hour and a half. It had kept him continuously at a nervous tension, weighing his words, and avoiding too great an expression of friendliness, giving advice without any interest whatsoever, and leaving the past in silence. He preferred the confidence and lack of restraint of the conversations with his comrades.

On thinking of the latter, his feeling of annoyance returned. How Castro would smile, when he sat down at the table! He could hear his voice already saying ironically: "No women!" And the first to appear had made him as sheepishly obedient as a prior breaking the rule of the monastery to receive a Queen.

This worry caused him to speak to the Colonel, who was walking along at his side in silence, accompanying him from the gate to the house. Where was Castro?

"In the library with Lord Lewis. His Lordship arrived while Your Highness was in the garden. He has come to lunch."

He was a nice Englishman! He had taken it into his head of his own accord to choose this day, after so many futile invitations! While that

Englishman was present, Castro would talk of nothing but gaming. And Michael went in search of Lewis.

The latter was the son of the great historian, whose country had rewarded him with the title of lord. But this title was only to be inherited by the oldest son of the family, and no one but Toledo, who always exaggerated the importance of his friends, called the second son *Lord* Lewis. He had been in Monte Carlo for twenty-five years, and the old employees in the Casino, seeing his bald head sadly bowed above the gaming tables, recalled the gentleman of former times, elegant, gay, and vigorous. He had come to the Riviera, on one of his Byronic "pilgrimages," and there he had remained, not caring to see any more of the world. The passion for gambling was the one inexhaustible pleasure for this man who had tried them all, and who was bored by the majority.

The real Lord Lewis, a solemn person, who maintained the prestige of the family name, had several children, and had served his country in various high positions in the Colonies. As for the Colonel's "Lord," he was gradually losing all his former connections, and becoming a mere Monte Carlo gambler.

"Twenty-five years!" he had remarked with sadness one day to the Prince. "And I shall never be able to do anything else! It's too late now to get a fresh start. My life is ended, and they will bury me here, I'm sure; all that I inherited from my father, and all that several old aunts left me will remain here. There have been times, when I saw things as they are, and undertook to run away. But when I'm at a distance, I feel violently indignant. I remember that I've dropped more than a million here, I think that I ought not to resign myself to the loss, and in order to recover it, I come back at once to play, and lose again. I shall go on doing like that until I die. Besides, there's the castle...."

Michael was acquainted with the castle. It was on a peak of the Maritime Alps, in sight of Monte Carlo, near the village of La Turbie and the remains of the Trophy of Augustus which marks the ancient Roman road.

During his first years of life on the Riviera, the aristocratic Lewis had bought for a few thousand francs the ruins of a lordly stronghold that possessed the romantic tradition of having witnessed wars with the Counts of Provence, and scenes of family violence and murder. The son of the Historian, fonder of sport than of literature, considered it a matter of filial homage to reconstruct within sight of the Mediterranean a castle such as his father had described in telling the legends of his country. Part of his fortune had gone into this. The rest had been devoted to gambling. "With what I win," he used to say to himself, "I shall finish the castle." And since he imagined he would win fabulous sums, he started the reconstruction on a gigantic scale, directing it himself, according to the architectural fancies he had studied out from the drawings of Gustave Doré. The castle had remained half built, standing thus for many years. On the one side that was completed, the walls displayed huge gloomy-looking windows with stained glass. On the side opposite, the timber of the scaffolding was rotting; the unfinished walls stood there meeting at right angles, and the wind and rain entered the future drawing rooms, for lack of a fourth wall to shut them off. They were open to the view like a stage setting.

Whenever Lord Lewis' friends did not meet him in Monte Carlo it was because he was out of money, and was staying in his castle, sadly contemplating all that remained to be done. He lived in one of the wings that was most nearly completed, and passed the lonely hours in fighting with his peasant neighbors, the market people, and with every one in the district in fact, who considered it a duty to annoy him and exploit him in every possible way.

Whenever a remittance of a thousand or two thousand pounds sterling arrived from England, he proudly descended from his mountain to the Castle. He had a great aim in life, and he felt he must accomplish it. This time he was going to triumph! And when, after exciting fluctuations—his capital sometimes increasing, as though his hopes were about to be realized—he finally lost everything, Lewis would return to his refuge on the heights, and to his hermit's life, in hopes of new remittances, which were less frequent and more difficult to get each time.

The Prince had visited him once, in this new yet crumbling stronghold, to invite him on a long voyage on his yacht. But Lewis refused. He must continue his duel with the Casino to get back his money; he was under obligation to finish his undertaking.

The war had awakened him for a few weeks from the grip of his wild dream. His brother had died a few weeks before; but countless young nephews still remained. They had given up their comforts and pleasures in high society to offer their lives. Some of them, who were in the navy, had embarked on small vessels, torpedo-boats and submarines, seeking the greatest dangers; others entered the army as officers. A niece of his even, delicate in health, had been decorated on the firing line, for her sacrifices as a nurse.

"And I, miserable selfish man that I am," he said, in talking with the Colonel at the Casino, "go on being a mere Monte Carlo gambler. I ought to be out there, where the men are, but I can't.... I can't! My days are over; I'm a corpse that eats and sleeps just to go on gambling. Add to that the fact that some of my relatives, older than I am, are in the army!"

At the age of fifty-four, the consciousness of his moral decay, and his continual losses, had embittered his nature. Besides, the evenings that luck was against him he kept going out to the Casino bar, seeking inspiration in one whisky after another gulped down in haste. Heavy set, with square shoulders, a small head, deep blue eyes and a red mustache streaked with gray, he reminded Atilio somewhat of a wild boar, perhaps because of his aggressiveness and gruffness when he was in a bad humor. He gambled with his head sunk between his shoulders, his strong hands resting on the green baize, without looking at any one, and without allowing any one to talk to him, since it disturbed his calculations. The days when things were going wrong, and he was having arguments in regard to some doubtful play, with the employees or with those who were sitting near him at the tables, Lewis's outburst of rage broke the discreet calm of the gaming rooms. He insulted the croupiers, inviting them to step outside on the Square, while his biceps swelled like a prize fighter's. It was necessary to call one of the principal directors to pacify him with all the paternal considerations which a steady patron deserved.

This man, who in his youth had believed in neither God nor devil, lived a constant prey to superstitions which were Castro's delight. He detested strange faces, feeling certain that they exercised on him an evil influence. It was enough that he should see one across the green table, or behind his seat, to cause him to begin to growl in an undertone, until finally he would get up and go out to the bar, with the idea that a whisky taken in time would change his luck. His intimate friend, the only one who could live with him for several days in succession, was a French count, older than Lewis, and who was simply called by his title, as though he were nameless, or as though he were just naturally "The Count." The latter never gambled, but he was ever so wise, in spite of the fact that many people considered him insane! One day, thirty years ago, he had stepped out of his house in Paris, saying that he was going out to buy some tobacco, and he had not yet returned. His wife had died without seeing him, and his children, and countless grand-children, who had been born and had grown up during his absence, were anxious that he should never finish making his purchase.

While Lewis played, the Count, seated on a divan, quietly read some book, without paying any attention to the curiosity of the public, which stared at his long white hair brushed back, his enormous wild-looking mustache, his round green eyes, gleaming with phosphorescence like those of a night hawk. Castro's curiosity was aroused by the Count's books. They were always new volumes of the sort that are never seen in any book store, and are published by obscure unknown firms; conscientious treatises on the nectars and ambrosias of modern life—opium, cocaine, morphine, and ether—formulas by which one can enter into direct communication with the mysterious powers—spirits, hobgoblins, and familiar demons—old books of magic brought to light by up-to-date sorcerers.

He never deigned to give his friend advice as to gambling; his thoughts were on higher things; but Lewis felt surer whenever he raised his eyes and saw him, by chance, reading in a corner. As long as he was there, he always won, or at least he did not lose much. His presence was enough to conjure the evil power of the infinite number of enemies which the Englishman felt were surrounding the table. Besides, he was aware of the object which the Count was fondling secretly with one hand, while he went on reading.

After he had had the misfortune to lose for several days in succession, Lewis would come to him, entreatingly:

"Count, my dear Count, if you would please lend me your Satan's rosary!"

The learned personage would look up, doubtful and hesitating. But since it was his best friend who asked for it, he would hand the rosary over, which meant that one of his hands would be left without anything to do. It was a rosary like any other, with large red beads and black ones to mark off the tens. The chief thing about it was the group of objects which hung in place of the missing cross: an ivory elephant picked up by the Count in India, an authentic coin of the Emperor Constantine found in the excavations at Anatolia, and another charm which even Lewis could scarcely look upon without a sense of revulsion.

Ill luck was vanquished. At times Lewis had lost while he was secretly telling the beads of the diabolical rosary under the table; but he always lost less than when he was deprived of the marvelous talisman. He only cared to remember how one afternoon, aided by the obscene sacrilegious thing so highly prized he had succeeded in winning eighty thousand francs.

If he stopped winning it was the Count's fault. He was as fickle as a coquette. He would suddenly disappear, repeating the same unexplainable flight that had amazed his family. He never left Lewis to go and buy tobacco; but if any of the books he bought told about some narcotic used in Asia to enable one to see the future, or about a gypsy woman in Granada who could kill people by merely wishing and saying a few words, then off he would go, accepting as gospel truth the saying of some anonymous writer who had never been out of Paris. He never lacked money for these mysterious trips: doubtless his family was interested in keeping him at a distance. He might be three months or five years in reappearing. At last the rumor would reach Lewis that his friend was living in Nice or Cannes, and he would then write him frequently, inviting him to come over to Monte Carlo. He even used to go after him and the Count would allow himself to be brought back with his mysterious books and his prodigious rosary, without ever saying a word about what discoveries he had made on his trips.

On seeing Lewis, after a year's absence, the Prince was obliged to conceal his surprise. Nothing save the clear, quiet, gentle eyes, recalled the vanished freshness of the athletic and elegant gentleman. He had grown thin in an alarming manner, with the emaciation of illness. His skull seemed to have shrunk, and across his baldness strayed the few scattered ashen locks that still remained.

A remark made by the Colonel came to his mind. Toledo had made a study of the decadence of gamblers. It was when they reached the last limits of depression and despair that they began to stoop, to shrivel up, and become wrinkled. Lewis' hat was getting too big for him; each day it sat farther down on his head until it rested on his ears. His shirt collar was also getting larger, as though it were making room for his sorrowing heart to take flight.

During the lunch, Lewis, Castro and Spadoni kept up the conversation. They talked about gambling and the Casino, but no one dared ask the Englishman if he had been winning. He had a superstitious fear of this question, as if it brought misfortune. On the other hand, he talked about other people's good luck, and the great stakes that had been won in a night. He kept in his mind all that he had been told, and all that he had imagined he had seen during twenty-five years of life at Monte Carlo. An American had gone away with a million; an Englishman had won ten thousand pounds sterling with five *louis* that he had borrowed. Thus he went on talking about the wonders that had happened in the Casino. And after that could there still be people to assert that all, absolutely all, of the gamblers, lose in the end?

With eyes that glistened with astonishment and greed, the pianist listened to the tales of the "Dean of the Gamblers." Castro was more skeptical. He had heard of these extraordinary winnings, and of many others, but had never witnessed a single one of them, although he had been coming to Monte Carlo for a good many years. It was true that he had seen as much as five hundred thousand francs won in a single night. But the next day things had changed, and the winner had lost all his gains, and all the money he had brought, into the bargain, finally being obliged to ask for the customary viaticum in order to be able to return to his country.

"I think," he said, "all these stories are invented by the advertising department of the Casino. They tell me they have engaged a popular novelist, whose business it is to start a story like that every week, in order to encourage the gamblers."

The Prince smiled at this invention of his friend, but Lewis would not listen to jokes on such a serious subject, and asserted that he had witnessed everything that he related. He was lying unconsciously in making this statement. In reality he had seen the same things as Atilio: people who won to lose later on; but he felt the need of the supernatural and was inclined to believe everything in advance. He had the soul of a fanatic, who, when told of a miracle, affirms a few days later with sincerity: "I saw it with my own eyes."

Every now and then the Prince would eye Castro, expecting to surprise some ironic glance, something which would reveal his impressions in regard to the visit he had received that morning. Lewis' presence seemed to have obliterated all memory of anything unrelated to gambling.

When the luncheon was over they talked in the hall, over their coffee, about those who played for big stakes in the private rooms. The names of some of them were spoken of with respect, as though they were masters, worthy of admiration.

"So-and-so knows how to play," was the one comment.

The amusing part of it for Michael was the fact that Lewis also figured among the masters "who knew how to play," and every one of them lost, like those who were "ignorant." Their one merit rested on their ability to put off the hour of final ruin, and prolong the annihilating emotion, growing old like prisoners in the shadow of the rocky cliffs of the Principality.

The Prince looked at Castro once more, as at a clever enemy who is hiding his thoughts. He ventured to ask a question.

"And how does my relative, the Duchess de Delille, play?"

Atilio looked at him, with not so much as a mischievous twinkle in his eyes, surprised at the interest shown by the Prince. But before he could reply, Lewis broke in with an answer. The latter hated women, especially at the gaming tables. They were only a nuisance, interrupting the calculations of the men, with their nervous looks and gestures.

"She plays like an idiot," he said brutally. "She plays like any woman.... The money she's lost like a fool!"

Castro intervened as though desiring the conversation to go no further.

"How about the Count?" he asked Lewis. "Where is he? The Colonel is very much interested in him."

Don Marcos gave an exclamation of surprise and reproach. He had formed his own opinion of that person a long time ago. He was a crazy man! He would never forget the brief dialogue they had had one afternoon in the Casino, after Atilio had introduced them. On learning Toledo's nationality he had launched into a great eulogy of Spain. Oh, Spain! What an interesting language it had! And when the Colonel was about to thank him for his extreme politeness, he was dumbfounded by the following remark, that took away his breath:

"Because, as you probably know, Spanish is the preferred language of the devil, after Latin. The most powerful charms are written in Spanish. What wonderful necromancers in Toledo! What learned sorcerers in Salamanca!"

The old soldier who had fought for the Most Catholic king was always greatly disturbed when he thought of the Count and his rosary. For this reason when Lewis declared that he had no idea of the whereabouts of his friend, he solemnly replied:

"I know where he is: in a mad house."

Suddenly the roar of a train was heard passing Villa Sirena, accompanied by shouts and whistling. They were more Englishmen on their way to Italy.

This caused them to take up the subject of the war. Lewis, who had imbibed freely at the table, was overcome at once with an intense sadness, the talk of gambling having reminded him of the worthlessness of his life. His intoxication was of the solemn, melancholy kind.

"Two of my nephews died in the Jutland naval battle. Six of my brother's sons were killed in France, in a single afternoon: they belonged to the same battalion. They were all young, spirited, and anxious to do something. I'm the only man left in the family; I'm the worthless one, the old man, good for nothing. It's terrible!"

No one said anything, realizing the shame and despair of this man, who seemed to be weeping over the ruins of his aimless existence. Novoa nodded slightly, as though approving of his words.

"My family is extinct. And there were so many young men in it! Life is strange. Time goes by without anything extraordinary happening, and then all of a sudden the hours are like months, the days like years, and in a few minutes things take place that usually require centuries. All dead! None left but my niece Mary, the nurse. She is here; her superiors ordered her away almost by force, to take a rest and recuperate. But, anxious to resume her service, she got away to Menton and Nice, where there are wounded men. If at least she would only marry! But it can't be: she will die like the rest. And I shall remain alone, and be a lord, the third Lord Lewis; Lord Lewis the Historian, Lord Lewis the Colonel Governor, and Lord Lewis the Wastrel...."

At this point they all stopped him in affectionate protest. The misfortune of his family had been extraordinary, but he ought not to torture himself like that.

"If you don't mind, Prince," said the Englishman, changing the conversation, "some day I shall bring my niece to let her see your gardens. She is so fond of such things! She is the only one of the family to inherit my father's spirit."

After saying that, Lewis showed signs of desiring to go. It was necessary for him to forget, and he knew where oblivion was waiting for him. For a gambler like him, it was no more possible to sit still than it would be for a drunkard who is thinking of a bar with its rows of glasses. Castro and Spadoni exchanged several glances with him.

"What do you say to dropping in at the Casino?" one of them proposed.

And all three disappeared.

The Colonel also left, and the Prince spent the remainder of the afternoon talking with Novoa, walking about the gardens, and looking at the sunset. Finally, he sat down in the hall under a tall rose-shaded floor lamp, to read.

Castro returned alone, long before the dinner hour. He was sad; he whistled occasionally. His smile was a savage grin. It had been a bad afternoon. He had lost everything! The next day he would have to ask his relative for a fresh loan in order to return to his "work."

Once more Michael felt compelled to talk to him about the call he had received that morning. It was better to have a frank explanation and avoid ironical allusions.

"Yes, I saw her," Castro said. "I watched you from a window while you were walking through the gardens."

The Prince looked at him, astonished at his brevity. Was that all he had to say? At present he felt he would have preferred his joking.

"What of it if she did come?" at last he said brusquely. "That's natural; poor woman! I warn you that you've begun the conquest of an enemy."

He had met "the General" in the Casino. She and Alicia had just had another reconciliation, and to seal their renewed friendship with a fresh burst of confidence, the Duchess Delille had related her interview with the Prince.

"Doña Clorinda used to be unable to stand you. She considered you a frivolous fellow, a worthless loafer. But now she praises you to the skies, because of your cancelling that enormous debt, and proposing to help the Duchess. She says you are like a knight of old times, and that you are big hearted."

Michael shrugged his shoulders. A lot he cared what Doña Clorinda thought! This exasperated Castro.

"Why shouldn't your relatives come here?" he said sharply. "You're getting bored living just among men all the time. You don't believe it, but it's true. It's the same with all of us. One has to talk with a woman from time to time, even if it's only out of friendship. What you claimed when you came from Paris is impossible."

"Perhaps you think I'm going to fall in love with Alicia?"

And the Prince laughed for a long time, as though never tiring of seeing the funny side of such an absurd supposition.

"You'll find that out later on," Castro replied. "All I have to say is that we can't live much longer as enemies of women. Look at the Colonel: he's your 'Chamberlain,' your Aide, the man who obeys you blindly. Well, even he is deserting you. Just notice: whenever he can, he spends his time in the Porter's lodge. He has to talk to the gardener's daughter, a little brat he used to see crawling around on all fours, but who is sixteen now, and not bad looking. She worked in a millinery shop in Monte Carlo, but follows the styles like a young society girl. The Colonel keeps her provided with high-heeled shoes, short skirts, tams, and smart hats, and buys her imitation amber beads. That's how he spends all the money you allow him to take for his services. Sometimes he follows her at a distance in the street, admiring her seductive outline and her ankles, much in evidence, and always in silk-stockings. He patiently cultivates his garden; and smiles like a fool when he thinks of his future harvest."

CHAPTER VI

ONE Sunday, as he got out of bed, the Prince felt like singing. Perhaps he was unconsciously following the example of some birds, which, deceived by the Spring-like warmth of a midwinter's day, had been warbling in the eaves of Villa Sirena since sunrise.

He looked out of his bedroom window. The Mediterranean, without a single sail, stretched away in far-off undulations, to where it met the sky. The gulls were wheeling in circles, continually drooping into the water, folding their wings, and letting themselves be carried along by the waves. The sandy depths, stirred by the swells, gave the blue sea a lighter shade, which attained, along the shore, an opalescent hue, like that of absinthe. Around the promontory, white luminous foam was constantly being churned among the projecting rocks of the reefs.

The Prince heard voices above him. Castro and Spadoni were talking from window to window. The mysterious call of the early morning beauty had caused them to jump out of bed. They were admiring the sky, which did not have a trace of mist to dim the brightness of its farthest reaches. The mountains stood out in extraordinary relief: they seemed larger and nearer. Above Cap-Martin, the Italian Alps descended to the sea, their outlying buttress, at the water's edge, white with the frontier towns: Vintimiglia and Bordighera.

Through some freak of the atmosphere, a dense, elongated cloud, like a snow-covered island, was floating directly overhead in the clear sky. Its whiteness seemed to radiate an inner light.

"I recognize it," Atilio said with a tone of conviction to the musician, who did not seem to tire of looking at it. "I have seen it often. When the day turns out too bright, the Directors of the Casino are afraid that the patrons may be bored by so much sunlight, and the vast expanse of azure: blue sea and blue sky. 'Have the big cloud brought out,' they order over the telephone. You must have noticed that that cloud always appears from behind the mountains. That's where the Casino has its storehouses. They don't neglect details here when it comes to entertaining their patrons."

Michael heard two exclamations: one of surprise and the other of indignation. Next he heard the sound of a window suddenly closed. The pianist, not in a mood for joking at so early an hour, was going back to bed, to sleep until lunch time.

The Prince hurried through his toilet. He felt the need of getting out and going somewhere, as though his gardens seemed too small for him. In the distance the bells of Monte Carlo were ringing, and still farther off those of Monaco were replying; and the merry pealing of the chimes caused the clear brittle air to vibrate like a crystal glass.

He went down stairs slowly, trying not to make any noise, and when he reached the gate he breathed freely. He had not met any of his companions, not even the Colonel. As though attracted by the Sunday morning atmosphere of gaiety which, as the afternoon wears on, changes to tiresome ennui, he decided to walk to the city alone.

Outside the gate, a girl was waiting for the street car. She was very young; but her feet slanted at a sharp angle on her high-heeled shoes. Her skirt, falling scarcely below her knees, showed her well-rounded calves. The finely woven stockings revealed the whiteness of her flesh. Prominent against the salmon colored silk sweater, was a necklace of large imitation amber beads. Her hair, cut short just below the ears, fell smoothly from underneath a jaunty velvet tam o'shanter of graceful line. The air of profound respect with which she spoke to him made him recognize her. It was the gardener's daughter. But at the same time she looked at him in a sly way with ill-concealed curiosity, as though her eyes made a distinction between the master and the man whom women adored and of whom she had heard so many things.

The Prince went on, after speaking to her as he would have to a young lady of his own social rank. He was gay that morning, and he laughed inwardly as he thought how later on that little bundle of mischief and ambition would keep men busy. Then he thought of Don Marcos, and what Atilio had told him. Poor Colonel! Imagine a person, at his age, trying to tame a young wildcat!

He walked lightly, with a springy step, in the direction of Monte Carlo. He passed the villas and the gardens as though contact with the ground had given his step fresh vigor, and as though the Spring-like air had abrogated to some extent the laws of gravity.

When he reached the city he stopped in front of the steps of San Carlos Church. Through the door he could see the twinkling tapers, smell the odor of flowers, and hear the droning of the organ, and the voices of young girls singing. He felt like a boy once more, buoyant and fresh as the morning, and had an impulse to follow the various families, in their Sunday best, who were ascending the steps. He was a Catholic through his father, a member of the Greek church through his mother, and nothing by his own inclination. Suddenly he felt a certain repugnance for the cave-like darkness, laden with perfumes, and dotted with lights. So he went on, breathing the open air with delight.

"Oh, your Ladyship! Good morning!"

A long, thin female hand shook his with masculine vigor. The brass buttons of her khaki colored uniform, like that of an English soldier, were gleaming in the sun. The uniform, instead of being completed by breeches, ended in a short skirt and tan leather leggings.

It was Lewis's niece. She had spent two afternoons at Villa Sirena rambling about the gardens. Once more Michael observed her unhealthy emaciation, which was beginning to take on the miserable appearance of consumption. Her Sam Brown belt buried itself in her blouse, as though failing to meet the resistance of a body underneath the cloth. The face under the visor of the military cap was as sharp as a knife. Her skin, drawn and lined in spite of her youth, showed all the bones and hollows. It was impossible to judge her age: she might have been twenty-five, or she might have been sixty. Only the eyes had retained their freshness; eyes that still kept the guilelessness of adolescence, and looked one squarely in the face with the serene confidence of a virgin sure of her strength.

She had gone through the horrors of war, as through a flame that dries up and parches everything it touches, and in the end converts it to dust. She was like a mummy, burned by the fire of the blazing towns that she had seen, and shaken by the tears and moans of thousands of human beings. "Think what those ears have heard!" Michael said to himself. And he understood the sad expression of the pale mouth which hung wearily between two drooping furrows. "And think what those eyes have seen!" he continued mentally. But the eyes did not care to remember and smiled at him, happy in the present moment.

She had just come out of a large hotel converted into a hospital, and was waiting for the street car to go to Menton. More wounded soldiers had arrived there, and owing to the scarcity of nurses the doctors had been obliged to accept her services. For the present they would not bother her any more with solicitude about her health! As she thought of the hard work that lay before her, of the long night watches, and the fight with death to save so many lives, she was filled with joy. She was anxious, as though she were going to a celebration to take the short trip as soon as possible, and seeing the car coming, she shook hands with the Prince again, with a firm grip.

"I shall go on abusing your permission. Next time I shall pillage your gardens even worse. Flowers ... lots of flowers! If you would only see the joy they give the poor fellows when you put them beside the beds! Some of the doctors are vexed; they think it is silly. But all I say is: as long as we have to die, why not die with a little poetry, with something around us to remind us of the beauty we are losing. It doesn't hurt any one."

Lubimoff went on his way, but his heart was less light. This woman, fighting death so generously and so manfully, seemed to have torn away the rosy veil that had made his eyes rejoice.

Everything was the same, but of a darker hue, as though he were looking at the landscape through smoked glasses. He noticed things which he had not observed until then. The large hotels had been converted into hospitals. Their porches and large balconies were filled with men basking in the sun; men whose heads were white balls, bound with bandages that left only the eyes and mouth visible; half finished men, as it were, lacking a leg or an arm, like a sculptor's rough models. Others were lying motionless, with both legs amputated, like corpses in a dissecting room, but still breathing.

On the sidewalks he met soldiers of various nations: French, English, Serbian, officers, and a few Russians, who reminded him of the former importance his country had had in the war. Every variety of uniform worn by the various armies of the French Republic passed before his eyes: the horizon blue of the home troops, the mustard color of the soldiers from Morocco, the yellow fatigue caps of the Foreign Legion, and the red fez of the Algerians and the negro Sharpshooters.

Each one was maimed. This sunny land, with its lovely views of sea and sky, seemed peopled with a race that had survived a cataclysm. Elegantly dressed officers, with handsome figures, limped along, cautiously dragging one leg, or else stepping gingerly on a foot so swathed in bandages that it was several times its natural size. Some of them were leaning on canes, bent over like old men. Men of athletic proportions trembled as they walked, as though their skeletons were rattling about in the hollow wrapper of their bodies wasted by consumption. Fingers were missing on hands; arms had been cut off until the shapeless stumps looked like fins. Under their pads of cotton, cheeks retained the gashes made by hand grenades, scars like those left by cancer; the horrible cavity of the nose, which had been torn away in some of the men, was hidden by a black tampon attached to the ears. The faces of others were covered by masks of bandages, leaving nothing visible save the eyes—sad eyes that seemed to look with fear to the day when they would have to grow accustomed to the horror of a face that a few months before had been youthful and now was like a vision in a nightmare. The bodies of some were intact, retaining their former strength and agility in all their limbs. Seen from behind they had kept all the vigor and suppleness of youth. But they walked abreast, holding tightly to one another's arms, their eyes lost in darkness, tapping the pavement with a stick which had taken the place of the vanished sword, and which would accompany them until the hour of their death.

And this procession of sadness and resignation, this grievous masquerade comforted by the joyousness of the morning, and feeling love of life once more renewed, was coming from the gardens. Others were going in the direction of the Casino and its terraces, passing among the Brazilian palm trees, with smooth, hollow trunks covered with elephant hide; among the cacti, held up by iron supports like a tangle of green reptiles bristling with thorns; among the prickly pears as high as trees; among the Himalayan fig trees, with towering trunks and wide spreading domes of branches which seemed to have been made to shelter the motionless meditation of the fakirs; among all the trees that come from tropical and temperate America, from China, Australia, Abyssinia, and South Africa. A tiny rivulet descended the slope in zig-zags through the openings in the green lawn, forming back waters among the bamboos and Japanese palms, until it flowed into a miniature lake, bordered with foliage, as tranquil, pleasing, and dainty as one of those centerpieces in which the water is represented by a mirror.

Michael stopped in the upper gardens to look at the Casino from a distance. He had never realized before the fussiness and bad taste of the architecture of this building, which was the heart of Monaco. If the "gingerbread monument"—as Castro called it—closed its doors, all Monte Carlo would be wrapped in a deathly stillness like the loneliness of those cities which in former centuries were ports, and now are sleepy and deserted, far from the sea, which has withdrawn. It was the work of the architect of the Paris Opera House, an ornate, gaudy, childish structure, of the color of soft butter, with multi-colored roofs, balconied turrets, niches with nameless statues, many tile friezes and gilded mosaics. At the corners there were green porcelain escutcheons, imitating roughly cut emeralds. The outstanding decorative motif of this building, famous throughout the world, was the imitation of gold and precious stones.

Owing to the prosperity of the establishment, they had added to the main body flanked with four towers, an extensive wing in which the best gaming rooms were located. Various green and yellow cupolas of different sizes revealed the existence of the latter, rising above the upper balustrade. On this balustrade a number of bronze angels or genii, entirely nude and with golden wings, had been set up. With black extended arms they were offering golden tributes, the significance of which no one had been able to guess. Other white or metal statues of half nude women were sheltered in the niches in the walls, and the names and significance of these were likewise a mystery.

Although the edifice was erected with the pretense of dazzling and charming with its gold and soft colors, those who went there paid scarcely any attention to its splendors.

"The ones who are arriving," Castro would say, "go in on the run; they want to get placed at the gaming tables as soon as possible. The ones who are coming out take a gloomy view of everything; and even though the Casino were as beautiful as the Parthenon, they would take it for a robber's cave."

The Prince looked to the right of the building, where a strip of blue sea was visible, with the hairy trunks and rounded tops of a few Japanese palms standing out against the blue. There at the entrance to the terraces along the Mediterranean rose the only two monuments of the city, dedicated to the fame of two musicians from the simple fact that some of their works had been played for the first time in the theater of the Casino. Carved in marble, Berlioz and Massenet greeted with a vague stare in their sightless eyes the cosmopolitan crowd that came to the gambling house. "They are honorary *croupiers*," Castro used to say.

"Massenet—that isn't so bad," thought Michael. "He was fortunate, he had money, and his gifts were recognized during his lifetime. But imagine Berlioz, who spent his years struggling against poverty and public indifference, standing guard after death over the Casino's millions!"

Next, he looked at the foreground, observing the open Square in front of the edifice. There was a round garden in the center. People called it the "cheese" and some even particularized and called it the "Camembert."

Around the garden rail and on the benches backing up to it, one could observe the living soul of Monte Carlo. Here people gathered, to exchange jokes and gossip, ask news from those who were coming out of the Casino, and comment on the good or bad fortune of the most celebrated gamblers.

In the immediate neighborhood, there were no business houses except jewelry stores, branches of the government pawn shop, and millinery shops. Women who played small stakes felt like satisfying their longing for an expensive hat on coming out of the Casino. Those who needed fresh capital to carry out their systems had only to take a few steps to pawn their valuables. In the show windows of the jewelry shops, pearl necklaces worth a million francs and emeralds worth three hundred thousand, were exhibited during the winter, waiting for a buyer; and in summer they were sent to the fashionable bathing resorts to continue being a mute and dazzling temptation. The jewelers, with Semitic profiles, were waiting behind their counters, more for sellers than buyers, and calmly offered a fourth of the price for a gem bought in that very shop the year before.

From a distance it was easy for the Prince to guess the character of the many people who at that early hour were sitting on the benches opposite the stairs leading up to the edifice. Here those condemned to misery by gambling, and accursed by fate, remained all day, suffering the most atrocious torment of living close to the door of the sanctuary without being able to enter. They had lost their last cent, and the directors of the establishment, who generously send ruined gamblers back to their respective countries, had handed over the *viaticum* to them for their return. But they had staked the money given to aid them and had lost; and since they were debtors to the Casino they could not reënter it until they had fulfilled their obligations. So there they remained, stranded in the Square for all time, with the false hope of getting some money. None of them had any idea of how or from what source. They mingled together there in the companionship of misery, watching for fellow-countrymen who were better off, to besiege them with requests for a loan; or else they spent their time discussing numbers and colors. Perhaps they would succeed in getting together a few francs after turning all their pockets inside out, and they might choose, as the emissary of their illusions, a comrade who was as poor as they, but who had not "*taken the viaticum*" and was free to enter.

Michael saw a crowd of people extending as far as the Japanese palm trees, near the Massenet monument. They had just arrived by various street cars from Nice. They were all hurrying, anxious to enter the motley edifice as soon as possible, as though fortune were expecting them in the gaming rooms and might leave at any moment, tired of waiting.

He looked at the clock above the façade. It was ten o'clock. The daily occupations were being resumed and the devotees who lived in Monte Carlo were likewise flocking there, and mingling with the people who had come from other places. They all mounted the marble steps, following the three stair-carpets held in place by brass rods that glistened in the sun.

"And to think that we're at war!" Michael thought. "And many of those who have gotten up early to make the trip, and those who live here, too, have sons or brothers or husbands, who at the present moment are fighting, and dying perhaps!"

Love of life, love of pleasure, and the vain hope of winning, worked like an anæsthetic, causing them all to rise above their worries and forget, so that they were able to live entirely in the present moment.

This general rush for the opening of the gaming hall disgusted the Prince and caused him to halt in his descent of the gentle slope of the gardens. It was repugnant to him to mix with the crowd that was loitering in the neighborhood of the Casino.

His desire to retrace his steps gave him an idea. "Supposing you go and surprise Alicia at her home? She would be so pleased!"

She had been at Villa Sirena twice since her first visit. A chance meeting in the street with the Prince, when she was walking along with her friend Clorinda, had served as a pretext for another visit to the refuge in their beautiful gardens of "the enemies of women." He found the "General" less hostile and dominating than he had imagined; but he could not understand Castro's passion for her. In spite of her beauty it seemed to him that he was talking to a man. They had been accompanied by Valeria, a young French girl, who had been a protégée of Alicia's, a traveling companion in the days of dazzling wealth, and who now accompanied her in poverty, out of gratitude and fidelity. Later the Duchess de Delille had returned alone a second time to consult him about various projects for her future, all of them lacking in common sense; and she had finally accepted a loan of a thousand francs. Luck was against her in gambling: she needed new "tools to work with." The capital that had irritated her so by never varying, never going much above thirty thousand, had finally heard her complaints, and dwindled with lightning rapidity, leaving merely a few remnants of its former self.

In spite of the Prince's loan the Duchess had complained.

"I'm always the one who is looking you up: you never deign to visit my house. How poor I really am!"

Remembering her humble protest, the Prince no longer hesitated. Turning his back on the Casino, he began to ascend the sloping streets in the direction of the frontier line separating Monte Carlo from Beausoleil; streets that displayed names recalling Spring: the Street of the Roses, of the Carnations, of the Violets, of the Orchids.

He entered a short avenue formed by a double row of garden fences. He caught a glimpse of the houses between the columns of palm trees, and the firm leaves of the large magnolias. As he went along he read the names of the small estates carved on little plaques of red marble, placed at the entrance to the grounds. "Villa Rosa", here it was. He pushed open the iron gate, which was ajar, without hearing the sound of a voice or the barking of a dog to greet his presence. He saw a small garden half deserted, overgrown with weeds at the foot of the untrimmed trees, and covering the space that had formerly been occupied by flower beds. The rest was more carefully tended, but it was a vegetable garden with rectangles of kitchen stuffs intensively cultivated.

Lubimoff approached without meeting anyone. It occurred to him that the gardener must have been the man with the dog, whom he had met as he turned into the street.

Then he mounted the four steps at the entrance. Here too the door was half ajar, and upon pushing it all the way open, he found himself in a hallway with stairs leading to the upper story.

There was no one in sight. He tried the doors of the adjoining rooms and found them locked. There was not a sound. It was as though the house were deserted. But the silence was suddenly broken by a voice floating down the stairway. It was a faint voice, singing a slow, sad English air. The song was accompanied by a sound of dull blows, as though hands were beating and shaping up some large unresisting object.

Michael thought he recognized Alicia's voice. He coughed several times without result; he was not heard. He was about to call to let her know that he was there, but refrained, through a sudden impulse to play a little joke on her. Why shouldn't he surprise her by going up-stairs the one part of the house where she was now living, he thought? His hesitation vanished. Up-stairs he would go!

From the first landing he saw several doors, but only one was open; and it was from that one that the sounds of the song and the thumping were coming. A woman bending over a bed, was holding out her arms and vigorously shaking up a pillow. Instinctively she felt that some one was standing behind her, and turning around she gave an exclamation of surprise on seeing Michael in the doorway. The latter was no less surprised to recognize the woman as Alicia; an Alicia dressed in an elegant but old négligée, with crumpled gloves on her hands, and a veil wrapped around her hair.

"You! It's you!" she exclaimed. "How you frightened me!"

Immediately she recovered her composure, and smiled at the Prince, as the latter tried to excuse himself. He had not met any one; the gate and the door had been open. She, in turn, now excused herself. It was Sunday; Valeria, her companion, had gone to Nice to take lunch with a family she knew; her maid and the gardener's wife were at mass; the old man had gone out a moment before to see some friends.

After these mutual explanations they both remained silent, looking at each other hesitatingly, not knowing what to say, but still smiling.

"You making your bed!" he remarked, just to say something.

"So you see. This is rather different from my bedroom in Paris. It is hardly the 'study' that I took you to either. Times have changed!"

Michael gravely nodded assent. Yes, times had changed.

"At any rate," she continued, "you must confess that there is a certain novelty in seeing the Duchess de Delille, madcap Alicia, making her bed."

The Prince nodded again. Indeed it was a novelty: something one could not see every day.

Alicia persisted in her explanations. It had not been at all hard for her to do housework. She cleaned her room herself, in order to save her elderly maid the extra bother. She did not want Valeria to help her.

They were each keeping their own rooms in order, now that help was scarce. Besides, she herself sometimes went into the kitchen, and she would have liked to help the gardener cultivate the little garden, just for her own pleasure.

"We are living in war times; things are getting dearer every day, and as for me, I'm poor. We ought to return to the simple primitive life. But I don't dare work in the garden, on account of the neighbors. They watch you all the time from their windows. There is a Brazilian gentleman, even, who seems to have fallen in love with me."

She herself was proud of her industriousness. Who would ever have guessed such qualities some years before in the mistress of the luxurious residence on the Avenue du Bois, who was in the habit of getting up at three o'clock in the afternoon?

"I owe it all to mamma. She had me educated in a girls' school in England, when it was the fashion to substitute domestic work for the physical exercise of sports. I think it's called 'Corinthianism.' And I feel better than ever. In the old days I had to get up several mornings a week with Valeria and Clorinda and go to a tennis club and play until I was exhausted. Now, after taking care of my room and helping with the others I don't need any exercise. I'm doing poor man's gymnastics."

There was a long silence. Michael looked at the room; a woman's bedroom, still in disarray, with clothes lying on the arm chairs, giving out the perfume of a fastidious femininity. Through a narrow door he saw a corner of the adjoining bath room, where a wet spot had been left on the mosaic floor, from the morning bath. An odor of eau de cologne and tooth paste hung in the air. From several toilet jars, in disorder, vague scents of more precious essences were escaping. Mingling with the toilet articles and objects of intimate apparel, he could distinguish cards such as are given out to the patrons of the Casino, to mark their plays; some with red or blue marks in the columns, others pricked with a hat pin, for lack of a pencil. He observed larger cards, with a roulette wheel indicating the numbers and colors; and also many books of the sort sold by the stationers and at newspaper stands; illuminating treatises on "How to win without fail in all kinds of play." On the mantelpiece, half hidden by various fashion magazines, was a small roulette wheel, a real one, used undoubtedly in studying out and trying various theories. On the lamp stand beside the bed the latest copy of the Monte Carlo Review was lying open, with statistics of all the winning numbers during the past week at the various tables; interesting reading, with mysterious annotations which had kept Alicia up perhaps till dawn.

In the meantime she was dexterously causing to disappear everything which she considered prejudicial to her appearance since the surprise. When Michael looked at her again the old gloves had vanished from her hands and the veil was hidden somewhere. Her hair, now left free, was black and lustrous, a trifle coarse, perhaps, but it rose luxuriantly in large ringlets in disarray.

They prolonged the silence with an embarrassed smile, as though neither of them could find a way of relieving the situation.

"Go on with your work," Michael said, somewhat timidly. "Now I'm here, I don't want to be in the way."

As though seeing a challenge to her embarrassment in these words, and anxious at the same time to show her skillfulness, she bent over the bed to continue her work. Michael regained his high spirits at this display of confidence. It wasn't chivalrous to allow her to work alone: he must help her.

"You! You!" exclaimed Alicia, laughing, as though such a proposition seemed to her unthinkable.

The Prince pretended to feel hurt. Yes: he! Wasn't he a sailor, and hadn't his adventurous life compelled him to know how to do a little of everything? More than once in his explorations in the wilds, he had had to make a bed as best he could, wrapped in blankets beside the embers of a fire.

He had gone over to the other side of the bed, and was imitating all the movements of the Duchess with comic exaggeration. He petted the pillows after her, with such violence as to make the bed resound. While she lifted it slightly toward her to shake it better, he lifted it completely with his strong hands.

"You don't know how! You don't know how!" Alicia exclaimed with childish glee.

Then, seeing his fingers seize the linen with a powerful grip, she added:

"Good heavens, let go of that: You'll tear the pillow, and just now, in these hard times!"

They both laughed, finding this work very amusing.

"Take hold!" she said in authoritative tones, and flung in his face a sheet that she was holding at the opposite side.

Michael found himself wrapped in a cloud of filmy linen fragrant with feminine perfumes. It was for an instant only, but to him it seemed like something extraordinary, of limitless duration, extending beyond the bounds of time and space. He had a presentiment that this insignificant event was going to be a turning point in his life. He felt his former self suddenly awaken with fresh vigor. Perhaps it was the stimulation due to continence. He thought of Castro's ironic smile, and of himself, living like a hermit there in Villa Sirena, and preaching hostility to women! There was a buzzing in his ears; his eyes, momentarily blinded, seemed to be gazing on a vast expanse of rosy sky, the pale, luscious rose color of a woman's flesh. There was something intoxicating in the sudden breath that caused his brain to reel, communicating the sensation to his whole organism, as violently as though struck with a lash. When the sheet had fallen back on the bed, Michael was deathly pale, with a look of intenseness gleaming in his eyes. She thought he was angry at the jest, and she laughed mischievously, leaning on the pillow with her hands. As she shook with laughter, the lace of her low-necked négligée trembled seductively on her breast and shoulders.

Suddenly the Prince found himself on the other side of the bed close to Alicia. Finally they both sat down on the edge of the bed, turning their backs on the forgotten sheet. He took one of her hands without realizing what he was doing. Then he bent so close to her face that one of her Medusa-like tresses brushed against his temple. He felt no desire to talk, but seeing her eyes, so close to his, he broke the pleasant silence.

"You have been weeping!"

The woman protested with a strained smile and grew pale as she stammered her excuses. No; perhaps it was the dust shaken up by the cleaning, or the effort of working. But he went on studying her eyes which were indeed slightly reddened.

"You were crying when I came in," he continued, with insistent and troubled curiosity.

Now Alicia's protest took the form of a harsh, shrill laugh, that was decidedly forced and unnatural. And by one of those modulations of which only great actors know the secret, the burst of her laughter died gradually into a sigh, then a groan, until, letting go the Prince's hand, she covered her eyes, and hung her head, while a fit of sobbing shook her whole body.

She was crying. It was enough that Michael should have discovered her recent weeping to cause the tears to rise in her eyes again, renewing her former anguish. She gave in to her grief with a sort of cruel delight, finding it preferable to the torture of feigning, which his unexpected visit had imposed.

The Prince remained silent for a few moments.

"Is it for that young fellow of yours?" he plucked up courage to ask, with a shaking voice as though he too were undergoing an unexplainable emotion.

She replied with a slight movement of her head, without taking her hands from her eyes. It was unnecessary for Michael to see them. He had guessed the truth on discovering the traces of tears. It could be only for him that she was weeping: the lack of news; the worry of thinking that he was a prisoner, far off, suffering all sorts of privations; and that perhaps she would never see him again.

"How you love him!"

The Prince was surprised himself at the tone of voice in which he said these words. There was a note of despair, envy, and sadness at the thought of the passing years, bequeathing to the coming generation the haughty privileges of youth.

The guests at Villa Sirena would also have been astonished to hear him talk in this fashion. Alicia's surprise caused her to forget all precaution as a pretty woman, and lift her head, as she took away her hands. Her face was red, her eyes tremulous and overflowing. A tear hung from a lock of hair. She realized that she must be looking terrible, but what did she care?

"Yes, I love him; I love him more than anything in the world. It is on his account that I go on living. If it weren't for him I would kill myself. But he isn't what you think. No, he isn't."

With her face so reddened with weeping, it was impossible to detect a blush; but her gestures, the expression of her face and the tone of her voice, rebelled with shame and indignation against the suspicion of the Prince.

She went on talking in a low voice, without daring to look at him, hurrying her words like a penitent anxious to get through with a difficult confession as soon as possible. On various occasions in talking with the Prince, the truth had come to her lips, and at the last moment the reticence of a woman still desirous of pleasing through her beauty had caused her to conceal the facts. But to whom could she reveal her secret better than to Michael? She considered him one of the family: he had received her in friendly fashion in her hour of need, when so many men had turned their backs on her. Besides, between a man and a woman, love is not the only feeling that can exist, as she had thought in the days of her mad youth. There were other less violent things, more placid and lasting: friendship, comradeship, and brotherly affection.

She paused for a moment, as though to gather strength.

"He is my son."

Michael, who was expecting some extraordinary, some monstrous revelation, worthy of her mad past, was unable to restrain an exclamation of astonishment:

"Your son!"

She nodded: "Yes, my son." With lowered eyes, she went on talking in the same nervous tone, as though she were making a confession. She went back over her past. How surprised she had been, how angry, at the cruel trick love had played in cutting off the best years of her life! Her indignation was like that of the citizens of Ancient Greece who began a riot when they learned of the pregnancy of a courtezan who was considered a national glory, a beauty whom the multitude came from afar to see, when she showed herself nude in the religious festivals. They were bent on killing her unborn child, as though it had been guilty of a sacrilege. Alicia, too, used to consider herself a living work of art, and wanted to punish the sacrilege of her child with death. What criminal attempts she had made to rid herself of the shame that was throbbing in her vitals! Besides, what tortures she had undergone in her efforts to hide it, to go on leading her life of pleasure as before, and suffer anything rather than permit her secret to escape! Returning from parties where she had seen herself admired as formerly yet always with the dread that her secret had been discovered, she would fall into fits of homicidal rage and rebelliously curse the being that persisted in living within her; and in paroxysms of wild hysteria she would devise ways and means of encompassing its destruction.

There were tears in her voice as she recalled these scenes.

"But how about your husband?" Michael asked.

"We separated at that time. He could tolerate my love affairs in silence: he could pretend not to know about them ... but a child that wasn't his own...!"

She recalled the attitude of the Duke de Delille. He had shown a dignity worthy of him. There had been many deceived husbands in his family: it had almost become a tradition of nobility, an historic distinction. He did not feel dishonored by selling his name in getting married in order to increase the pleasures and comforts of his life. His name that belonged to him was a tool to work with. But it was impossible for him to let that name get out of his family, to give it to an intruder to continue the line. His forefathers had had many illegitimate children; but it had never occurred to any of his gay women ancestors to introduce into the family descendants in whose creation their husbands could assume no responsibility whatever.

The Duke had separated from her, granting all her demands save that one. It was an adulterous son and it must disappear. And no one, except they two and the maid—who was still with her—were to know of the birth.

"There were times when I was quite happy," Alicia continued. "I learned to know new unsuspected joys. I would suddenly leave Paris: lots of people thought I was traveling with some new lover. No; I was going to see my little boy, my George; first in London, later in New York, but always in a large city. I could live with him, and play at being a mother, with a living doll that kept getting bigger and bigger ... bigger! Do you remember the night I invited you to dinner? I had just come back from one of those trips, and in spite of that, just think of the foolish things I said. I imagined myself Venus, or Helen, passing before the old men on the wall. And in order to give myself up completely to a paroxysm of maternal pride I was thinking of my heroines, who were also my rivals. Helen had had children, and men went on killing one another for her. Venus had not escaped maternity, and gods and mortals continued to adore her in spite of the fact that she had a son fluttering about the world. Maternity meant neither abdication of rights nor loss of prestige; she could go on being beautiful and being desired, like other women, after an incident that had seemed to her irremediable. So I went on living my life. Oh, when I think of how I sometimes shortened the time that I had intended to stay with him, in order to follow some man that scarcely interested me! Now that I haven't him, I think of the hours that I might have lived by his side, and that were given up to the first male that aroused my curiosity! It's my most terrible remorse; it gnaws at my conscience all night long, and drives me to gambling as the only remedy. I am certainly to be pitied, Michael."

But a fixed idea seemed to dominate Michael as he listened to her.

"And the father? Who is the father?"

The tone of his voice was practically the same as before: a tone of hostile curiosity, of aggressive spite.

Another wave of astonishment swept over him when he saw that she was shrugging her shoulders.

"I don't know; it doesn't make any difference to me. Other women, in like circumstances, fasten the paternity on the man they are most interested in. As though you could tell! I haven't picked out any one in particular from among my memories. They are all the same. I have forgotten them all. My son is mine, mine only."

She had the majestic indifference of the serene and fertile forest that opens its blossoms to the pollen scattered through the air like a golden rain of love. The new plant springs up. It belongs to the forest, and the forest keeps it, without showing any interest in learning the name and origin of the wandering source of life borne hither willy-nilly on the wind.

There was a long silence.

"One day, on arriving in New York," she continued, "I made a terrible discovery. I found my George almost as tall as I was, and strong looking, with the serious air of a grown man, though he wasn't quite eleven. I'm ashamed to think it; but I mustn't lie: I hated him. Venus might have a son, as long as the son remained eternally a little child through all the centuries, like one of those amusing babies that are dressed in a whimsical fashion, and are the mother's pride and amusement. But my own son, with his powerful body, his strong hands, and solemn face! It meant that I should grow old before my time; I should have to renounce my youth if I kept him by my side! I could never resign myself to declaring that I was his mother. And I fled from him, letting a number of years go by, without paying attention to anything in regard to him, excepting to send the means for his complete education. Oh, when I think how fate has punished me for my selfishness!"

She remained silent for a few moments to dry the fresh tears that were reddening her eyes and giving her voice a husky resonance.

"He came to Paris when I was least expecting him. The venerable friend who was looking after his education there in America, had died. I found a man, a grown man, in spite of the fact that he wasn't over sixteen. My first feeling was one of annoyance, almost anger. I should have to say farewell to youth, and change my mode of life on account of this intruder. But there was something in me that kept me from doing anything so heartless as to send him back to a foreign country, or off to a boarding school in Paris. I grew accustomed to him at once. I had to have him in my house. It seemed as though, when I was near him, I felt a certain serenity, a deep quiet joy that I never thought myself capable of feeling. You don't know what it means, Michael. You could never understand, no matter how much I tried to explain it to you. I swear it was the happiest time in my life. There is no love like that. Besides, we were such good comrades! I suddenly felt as though I were a girl of his age again; no, younger than he. George used to give me advice. He was so wise for a boy of his age; and I used to do what he said like a younger sister. He let his mother drag him along and introduce him to a world of pleasure and luxury that dazzled him, after his sober, athletic life with a stern educator. And I leaned proudly on his arm, and laughed at the false ideas people had of our actual relation. How we used to dance, the year before the war, without any one suspecting the true nature of the affection that bound me to my partner!"

Alicia paused to linger on these delightful memories. She smiled with a far-away look in her eyes, as she thought of the malicious error people had made.

"Every tango-tea in the Champs-Élysées found the Duchess de Delille dancing with her latest crush! And, Michael, as for me, I was proud that they should be making such a mistake. I went on being the beautiful Alicia, restored to youth by the fidelity of an adolescent who accompanied her everywhere, with all the enthusiasm of a first love. This seemed to me a much better rôle than that of the passively resigned mother. Besides, what fun we used to have laughing and talking it over afterwards when we were by ourselves! Many of my former lovers felt their old passion revive again out of a sort of unconscious envy—the instinctive rivalry that the man of ripe years feels toward youth—and they began besieging me with their gallantries again. George used to threaten me in fun: 'Mamma, I'm jealous!' He didn't want any other man to be showing attentions to his mother, so that she might belong to him completely. On other occasions I myself had better reasons to protest. I surprised a greedy look in the eyes of many women of my own class when they gazed at him—some with a boldly inviting look, since, being younger, they felt they had a right to take him away from me. And he was so good! He used to joke with me about these passions that he inspired; and tell me about others that I had not been able to guess! You don't know what young people are like nowadays, in the generation that has followed us. They seem to be made of different flesh and blood. Our generation was the last to take love seriously; to give tremendous importance to it, and make it the chief occupation of our lives. Now they don't understand people like you and me: we seem monstrous to them. My son is only interested in one woman: his mother; and in addition to her, automobiles, aeroplanes, and sports. All these strong, innocent boys seemed to have guessed what was awaiting them...."

As she spoke, the momentary serenity with which she had related this happy period in her life gradually vanished. She went on talking in a subdued voice, choked from time to time by sobs.

Suddenly war had come. Who could have imagined it a month before? And her son was ashamed not to be one of the men who were hurrying to the railroad stations to join a regiment. One morning he had overwhelmed her with the announcement of his enlistment as a volunteer. What could she do? Legally she was not his mother. George bore the name of a pair of old married servants who had been willing to play that game of deception by posing as his parents. Besides, he was born in France, and it was not extraordinary that he, like so many other youths, should have wanted to defend his country before he was called to arms by law.

The Duchess lived for a few months in a tiny village in the south of France, near the Aviation Camp where her son was in training. She wanted to be with him just as long as she possibly could. If only he had become a soldier at the time when she was living separated from him, and was concealing her actual relation to him! But she was going to lose him at the sweetest moment of her life, when she was beginning to think she might be at George's side forever.

"It did not take him long to become a pilot. How I hated the ease with which he learned to manage his machine! His progress filled me with pride and anger. Those young fellows are regular fanatics so far as aviation is concerned. It is something that has come into existence in their time, and they have seen it grow before their school-boy eyes. He went away, and since then I have been more dead than alive.

Three years, Michael, three years of torture! I've paid dearly for all my past life! Though the mistakes that I made were great, I've made up for them, and more too. You may well have compassion on me. You can have no idea what I'm suffering."

The first year that Alicia had spent alone, she had lived in constant expectation of his letters, which arrived irregularly from the front. Her joys were few and far between. George had come to Paris only once on leave, and had spent half a week with her. At long intervals she also received visits from the aviator's comrades, greeting the news they brought with tears and smiles. Her son had received the War Cross after an air battle. His mother had cut out the short newspaper paragraph referring to this event, sticking it with two pins on the silk with which her bedroom was hung. She would spend hours staring as though hypnotized at these brief lines: *"Bachellery, Georges, aviator, gave chase to two enemy planes beyond our lines and ..."*

This "Bachellery, Georges" was her son! It made no difference to her that other people were not aware of the fact. Her pride seemed to grow because of the mystery surrounding it. The handsome strapping fellow, strong, and innocent as the heroes of ancient legend, had been formed in her body. All the men whom she had known in her past life seemed more and more petty and ugly; they were inferior beings, sprung from another race of humanity, the existence of which should be forgotten.

Suddenly a stupid, unforeseen accident plunged her into the darkness of despair. One beautiful morning with the joyous confidence of a young knight setting forth in quest of adventure, the aviator started out in his pursuit machine, rising through the silvery clouds in search of the enemy. Suddenly, he noticed some slight motor trouble—due to the negligence of the mechanics in getting it ready, a matter of slight importance under ordinary circumstances ... and he was forced to descend, absolutely unable to continue his flight, and the wind and bad luck caused him to land within the German lines.

"A hundred yards this side, and he would have landed among his own men.... What can you expect? I was too happy. I had still to learn what misery really means! I confess that at the very first I was almost glad, with the selfish gladness of a mother. A prisoner! It meant that his life would be safe; he wouldn't be killed in an air battle; he was no longer in danger of being crushed to pieces or burned to death under his broken machine. But later on!..."

Later this security, that placed her son outside the limit of actual war, became a source of torture. She envied herself the times when he used to go out each day and face death, but still remained free. The newspapers talked about the suffering of the prisoners, their being herded together in vast unsanitary sheds, and the hunger from which they were suffering. The life of ease and comfort which the mother was leading was a constant source of remorse. When she sat down at table, or looked at her soft bed, or noticed the warm caress of a fire, and saw that the window panes were covered with the traceries of frost, she felt she was usurping in a shameless manner something that belonged to another person. Her boy, her poor boy, was living like a stray dog, lying on the straw, with hunger gnawing at his stomach! She had produced a human being—she, a miserable woman, who for so many years had believed herself the center of the universe, was enjoying all kinds of luxuries—and this flesh of her flesh was agonizing under the tortures of want such as are felt only by the most poverty stricken.... She never could have dreamed that such an irony of fate would be reserved for her.

During the first few months she scurried wildly about, with the fierce irrational love of the female animal that sees her young in danger. She went from one government bureau to the other, taking advantage of all her social connections! But there were so many mothers! They were not going to open diplomatic negotiations for a woman in her position.... Every day she sent large packages of food to the offices that had charge of prisoners' relief. They finally refused to accept them. The entire service could not take up all its time doing nothing but send aid to a mere protégé of the Duchess de Delille. There were thousands and thousands of men in the same situation as he. And she could not cry out: "He is my son!" A scandalous revelation like that would not help matters. She kept on sending the packages regularly even if they did not go to her George. They would be used to satisfy some one's hunger. She felt the magnanimity roused by great sorrow; she made her offerings like a mother who, in praying for her child when all hope has been given up, prays for other sick children also, feeling that through her generosity her prayers may be heeded.

Besides, the suspense was cruel. When the clerks took her packages, they smiled sadly. She was practically certain that her shipments of food were being appropriated by the guards. All the expensive eatables intended for her son were doubtless used by the old German reservists in charge of guarding the prisoners, to have a joyous feast, with the greedy merriment of fierce mastiffs, toasting to the glory of the Kaiser and the triumph of their race over the entire world! Good God! What could she do?

At long intervals, after tremendous delays, she would finally get a postcard passed by the German censor. There would be four lines, nothing more, written as children write at school, under the eye of the teacher standing at their backs. But the writing was George's. "In good health. We're not badly treated. Send me eatables." She would spend long hours gazing at these timid, deceiving lines. For her they acquired a new meaning. They told something else: the truth, namely. She recalled the stories of dying captives who had come from those torture camps, and the lines seemed to stammer with groans of a sick child: "Mamma ... hungry. I'm hungry!"

There were times when she thought she would go mad. Everything about her brought to memory the image of her George, well groomed, and cared for by her with such fond and exaggerated attention. She had looked after his clothes, taking an interest in the respective merits of his tailors. She had had to endure his masculine protests when she had tried to provide him with underwear of fine silk like her own. In the morning she used to go and surprise him, as he lay in bed, like a little child, and kiss her own flesh and blood, metamorphosed into an athlete. Everything seemed to her too mean and poor for that strong fellow, handsome as a god of old. She looked after his bed, his dresser, and his person with all the passionate fondness of a sweetheart. She inspected his pockets in order continually to renew her gifts of money. Her Mexican mines were his, and so were the frontier lands, and everything she possessed. And later on—she hated to think when—she would see him married to some one after her own heart. Then his obscure birth was to be glorified by the splendor of enormous wealth. But suddenly the world, losing its balance, had been plunged into a furious madness, and this Prince of Fate, whose mother, in conference with the chef, had invented gastronomic surprises for him alone, was crying from some far off snow-swept plain in the icy north:

"Mother ... hungry. I'm hungry!"

"I went to Switzerland three times, Michael. I even proposed that in Paris they should provide me with means of getting into Germany, offering to go as a spy. But they laughed at me; and they were right! What was I going to spy out? My son, of course ... what I wanted to do in Germany was to see my son. In Switzerland I met two crippled soldiers who had just been exchanged, and came from the camp where George was. They knew the aviator Bachellery. He had tried to escape five times. He enjoyed a certain fame among his companions in misery for the haughtiness with which he faced the cruelest guards. The latest news was uncertain. They had not seen him lately. They thought that he was then in another prison camp, a punishment camp, farther inland, near the Polish frontier, where the refractory and dangerous prisoners were forced to undergo a cruel disciplinary régime, and suffer terrible punishments."

Her voice trembled with anger as she said this. She could see her son dragging a chain, and being whipped like a slave. Oh, if she were only a man, and could be left alone for a moment with that tragicomedian with the upturned mustache who had made many millions of women groan with sorrow!

"And to think that there have been fanatics who have killed good or insignificant kings! And not one of them has lifted a hand to do away with the Kaiser! Don't talk to me about anarchists. They are idiots! I don't believe in them."

This outburst of wrath vanished immediately. Once more grief and despair tore a sob from her. She remembered a photograph she had seen in one of the newspapers: the torture called "the post," applied by the Germans in their punishment camps; a Frenchman in a tattered uniform, fastened to a wooden stake, as though it were a cross, on an open snow-covered plain, suffering for hours and hours from the deadly cold. It was the death penalty, hypocritically applied, with savage refinements of torture. It was impossible to distinguish the features of the poor fellow suffering like Christ, with his head falling on his breast. Even if it wasn't George, surely he had also suffered the same torture.

"How can I live in such endless anguish! They wouldn't let me go back to Switzerland. They held up my passports. I don't know what's happened to him. There are times when it seems as though my head would burst. That's why I avoid living alone. That's why I gamble, and have to see people, and talk, and get away from my thoughts. Since then I've only received one postcard from my son, without any date, and without any indication as to where he is. It says about the same as the other one. The writing is his, and nevertheless it seems to be in another hand. Oh, what that writing says! I see him like the other man, like the poor fellow fastened to the post covered with rags, as thin as a skeleton.... My son!"

Michael was obliged to take both her hands in a strong grip, and draw them towards him, holding her up, to keep her from falling on the bed in hysterical convulsions. He was sorry that he had come, and, by his curiosity, invited a confession that aroused the woman's grief.

As for her, she looked at him with wide-open staring eyes, without seeing him. Finally, concentrating with an effort, she noticed Michael's emotion. This calmed her somewhat.

"You can be glad you don't know what such torture is like. There's no end to it: there's no help for it. When I think of him, I feel as though I were going to die. Not to know about him! Not to be able to do anything! I ought really to find some diversion and learn to think of something else. One must live: one can't be always weeping. But whenever I succeed in getting interested in anything, I immediately feel remorse. I call myself names: 'You're a bad mother, to forget your sorrows.' A day seldom passes that I eat without crying. I'm tormented by the thought that he would be happy with what is left from my table, with what the servants eat, or perhaps with what they give to the dog! And when Valeria and Clorinda see my tears, they can't explain such constant grief. They don't know my secret. They think like every one else, that it's simply a question of a mere protégé or a young lover. They can't understand such despair over a mere man. That's why I gamble so much. It's the only thing that really keeps my mind occupied, and makes me forget for a time; it's my anæsthetic. Before, I used to play just for the excitement, for the pleasure of struggling with fate; and because I was flattered by the amazement of the curiosity seekers who watched me stake enormous sums with indifference. Now it's on his account—and for no other reason."

Alicia's mind reverted to her financial difficulties. As a matter of fact, her fortune had been seriously impaired some years earlier, but she had always had hopes of some sudden recuperation. Besides, the period before the war had been the happiest time of her life. She had her son and she lived her life, without any thought of business matters. Later her financial ruin had come along with the loss of George.

"If only I had the wealth I used to have! I know the power of money. I could have moved men and even governments. I would have written to the Kaiser, or to Hindenburg, sending them a million, two million, or any amount they asked. 'Now that you are reëstablishing slavery and pillaging towns, here is money for you. Give me back my son.' And now I would have him back at my side. But I'm poor! If you knew how I love money now, just for his sake! I dream of winning big stakes, five hundred thousand francs or maybe a million, in two or three days. How happy I am when I come back from the Casino with a few thousand francs to the good! 'It's to send my poor boy a box with something good to eat,' I say to myself. Then I write to the stores, or go there myself, keeping in mind the things he liked best. You are rich and don't understand how hard it is to get along now, how scarce things are getting, and how much they cost! I didn't have any idea of such things before, either. And I send him boxes of the nicest things; and I feel proud that in my mind I can say to him: 'It's with the money mamma won for you ... it's with my work!' Don't smile, Michael. That's what it is—work! Besides, what else could I work at? The one thing that worries me is how to address these shipments. 'For the Aviator Bachellery, prisoner in Germany.' That's all I know, and there are so many prisoners! Almost all my shipments must be lost; but some at least will reach him. Don't you think he'll get some of them?"

The Prince greeted this anxious question with a vague gesture of agreement. "Yes;—perhaps, almost certainly!"

Immediately Alicia showed a certain reassurance. Eight months had gone by without her hearing anything about him; but other mothers were in the same situation. There was no use despairing. Men who had been given up for dead in the early battles of the war were returning home after a long period of captivity. Besides, did it seem reasonable to believe that a son of hers was going to die of hunger and want, like a beggar?

Lubimoff again nodded assent. "Really, it didn't seem reasonable!"

"There are moments," she said, "when I feel an unexplainable joy, a mysterious intuition, that I'm going to receive good news,—the feeling I have on the days when I go to the Casino sure of winning,—and do win. I wrote to the King of Spain, who is interested in ascertaining the fate of prisoners, and who often succeeds in getting them sent back to their homes. I have had a great number of friends write to him. If he could only give me back my George! At least I expect to learn good news; to find out where he is, and convince myself that he is alive. I would be satisfied if they interned him in Switzerland, the way they do with the seriously wounded, and I would go and live with him. How happy I would be if he were in Lausanne or Vevey, beside the lake, like my husband!"

There was a sad, kindly smile on her face as she thought of the Duke.

"Oh, I haven't forgotten him, I assure you. Everything that's left over from George's boxes, I send to him by way of Geneva. 'For Lieutenant-Colonel de Delille.' Oh, it reaches *him*, without any difficulty! Poor fellow! His answers are almost love letters. I send him sausages and canned things, in memory of the twenty louis bouquets he used to send me when he was courting me. What are we coming to, Michael! Who could ever have imagined that everything and everybody would be so topsy-turvy!"

Already she was talking more calmly, as though the memory of her son was no longer in the foreground of her thoughts.

"Everything seems to tell me I'm going to get good news. Misfortune can't last so very much longer. Doesn't it seem that way to you? It's like bad luck in play: it finally goes away. The main thing is to save your strength in order to resist it. I ought to feel satisfied. I was so excited I could hardly sleep last night. I went above the thirty; you know: the thirty thousand francs that used to be the limit of my luck. Last night I won eighty thousand. Your friend Lewis was furious. He says it takes a woman to do a thing like that: to win, playing haphazard, defying all the rules."

From the look on the Prince's face she guessed his surprise at her merriment following so closely on her recent tears.

"I can't stay by myself. I have such memories! Perhaps you heard me singing, as you came up-stairs. It's an English song my son used to sing. In the morning I used to go and listen at his door like a sweetheart who, while waiting for him to appear, is glad to hear the voice of the man she loves. Whenever I'm alone I sing it over mechanically; I try to imagine it is George singing, and my eyes fill with tears, but with tears of tenderness that are very sweet. While I was making the bed it seemed as though I heard him, going back and forth in his bedroom, with me waiting and listening in the hall. My voice was his voice. That was why I fairly trembled when you came in. For a moment I supposed you were he. How wonderful it will be when I see him!... I'm sure I shall see him. Misfortune can't last forever. Don't you think I'll see him?"

Her closed eyes seemed to smile on a far-off vision of hope. And Michael, who had remained silent for a long time, spoke to give her encouragement. Poor woman! Yes; she would see her son. At his age a man can stand any hardship. He would return; they would both be happy once more, talking over their present troubles, as though it had all been a bad dream.

"Besides, I will help you. We must get busy and take steps to have your son returned to you. I shall write to the King of Spain. I knew him. He had lunch on my yacht once when I was in San Sebastian. I have friends in Paris, men in politics, and diplomats; I shall write to all of them. And if worse comes to worst, and there's no other way out of it, I shall try through the medium of some neutral government to get a letter through to Wilhelm II. Perhaps he may pay some attention to me. He must remember me, and his visit to my boat."

Now it was her turn to look at him fixedly through a mist of tears, smiling, at the same time, to express her gratitude.

"How kind you are!" she exclaimed after a long silence. "The day when I was in Villa Sirena for the first time I was convinced that I had made a great mistake. How little we knew each other! We needed adversity to see each other as we really are. First you offered to relieve my poverty, and now you are going to try to get me back my son!"

She let herself be carried away by an impulse of affection. Michael saw her bend her head, and suddenly felt the contact of her lips on his hand. He heard two loud kisses and a voice whispering: "Thanks ... thanks." The Prince rose to his feet. He could not tolerate such expression of humility. But at the same time she too stood up; their eyes were on a level. As though desiring to complete the recent caress, she took his head impulsively in her hands, and kissed him on the brow.

A sudden wave of human fragrance, like that which had enveloped him when the sheet had been thrown on his face, once more stirred the depths of his being. He realized that the caress meant nothing:

that it was merely a kiss of gratitude, a sudden outburst of feeling on the part of a mother expressing her emotion with unusual impetuousness. In spite of this, he felt himself dominated by passion, cruel and at the same time voluptuous, causing him to reach out his arms to master and embrace what he held within reach.... But his hands touched empty space.

Repenting her act, she had stepped back, retreating a few steps. She was standing in the doorway, ready to continue her flight, mechanically straightening her hair, and drying her tears, as a deep blush spread over her features.

"I didn't know what I was doing!" she murmured. "Forgive me. I was so grateful to learn that you wanted to help me!"

At the same time she pointed to the balcony. Below, in the garden, the voice of the gardener could be heard telling his dog to stop that barking all the time at the foot of the stairs, as though a thief were inside the villa.

"Let us go," she commanded gravely. "The servants will soon be coming back from mass. I shouldn't like to have them find us here in my bedroom. They might think...."

Calming down, Lubimoff noted the unconscious modesty, and the evident uneasiness with which she said this. He suddenly recalled the woman of the "study" on the Avenue du Bois, and her daring theories. Was it really the same person?

As they went downstairs she turned her head to talk to him, as though she had read his thoughts.

"You must be amused at me. What a change from the Alicia of former times! I'm not so bad as I seem, that much is certain, isn't it? Tell me you don't think I'm so bad; tell me you think I'm only mad; mad, and always unlucky."

She opened the rooms downstairs to show how orderly they looked, but the chill of the deserted drawing room, the covers on the furniture, and the musty odor, like that of a damp cellar, prompted them to go out into the garden and, like two people prolonging their farewell, continue their conversation at the foot of the stairway.

The elderly maid of the Duchess, and the gardener's wife who looked after the cooking, passed them repeatedly on various pretexts. They bowed to the gentleman, with a look of adoration and a pleasant smile. They seemed to be saying to themselves: "That nice fellow is Prince Lubimoff, the one that's so much talked about." They had often heard his name in Villa Rosa, and they both venerated him as a providential being who could restore the vanished days of abundance with a mere wave of the hand.

Michael thought it best not to prolong his visit.

"Come and see me," she said in a low voice, as she accompanied him out to the gate. "Now you know everything. You're the only one who does. It will seem very sweet to me to talk with you, and have you console and help me."

The Prince spent the next few hours, pensive and silent. So many new things had come up all at once! First there had been the revelation of a son, whose existence he never could have imagined; next, the untamable creature of love changed into a mother; her tears, her silent suffering, which she was bearing, like a convict's chain, in expiation of her mad past. And the crowning surprise of all had been what he had felt within himself, the resurrection of his former being, his new surrender to the domination of the flesh, and the double lashing his nervous system had received in breathing the perfume of the soft linen and feeling the imprint of her lips on his brow.

This latter he wished to forget, and to succeed in doing so he concentrated all his attention on the revelations she had made, and on her maternal sorrows. Poor Alicia! Finding her impoverished and tearful, with no other help than that which he might give, he began to feel a lasting affection for her. It was the affection of the strong for the weak; a paternal love which did not take into account the similarity in their ages, nor the difference of sex; a tenderness made up for the most part of a certain sweet pity. He was moved by the memory of the humble kiss with which she had caressed his hands. It was the kiss, almost of a beggar. Unhappy woman! This was enough to make him feel obliged never to abandon her.

Alicia's pride, her desire to dominate, had formerly irritated him. Accustomed to protecting women generously without ever submitting to their will, considering them in the light of something agreeable and inferior, he could not compromise with her haughty character. They were both people too strong and domineering to be able to tolerate each other. But now everything was changed.

He remembered her as he had seen her in the bedroom, sorrowful, weeping, with pearls hanging from the corners of her eyes, which were tragically beautiful, as in the images of the Virgin, where

Mary is holding the body of the crucified Christ on her knees. *Mater Dolorosa!*

But there seemed to be another person within the Prince protesting with cold, clear-sightedness against this image. No, she was not the Mother of Sorrows. A mother never abandons her son. She renounces all of the vanities of this world for him. She gives up her present and her future, as though she had no other life than that of her son, part of her own flesh. At all hours she gives him the milk of her breast. Moment by moment she follows his development, fighting with illness, laughing at danger. To love him she does not have to wait for him to grow to the full splendor of adolescence. Whereas she...!

She was the *Venus Dolorosa.* Even in the moments of deepest despair she maintained her beauty, and her grief seemed a new means of seduction. She was a mother; but she continued to be a woman, that terrible, destructive woman whom the Prince had always hated. Look out, Michael!

But with a smile of superiority he replied inwardly to this reflection.

"Perhaps I am going to fall in love with her," he said to himself. "I am fond of her as I never thought I could be, but only as a friend, a companion worthy of pity, one whom I ought to protect."

At lunch time Spadoni did not turn up at Villa Sirena. Atilio had seen him at the Casino with some English friends from Nice. They were probably lunching together at the Hôtel de Paris to work out some new system or other. The last thing they had tried was for the four of them to play at different tables, but with the same system of combinations, a device that the pianist boasted would prove infallible.

After they had had their coffee, all the guests of the luxurious villa seemed possessed by the same restlessness, which would not let them sit still.

Castro was the first one to leave, announcing that he was going to the Casino. He had a feeling that it was going to be a "great evening." He had had his eyes on a *croupier* who started work at half-past three. He knew this man's style of starting the ball. Every *croupier* has his own mannerisms. Some do it with a long sweep, and others with a short jerky motion of the arm. This particular one made it fall most frequently in seventeen, and that was Castro's number.

Novoa was the next to go, but he was less frank about it. He stammered blushingly as he said good-by to the Prince. Perhaps he would spend the afternoon with some friends from Monaco. Perhaps he would take a short trip on the Nice road as far as Cap d'Ail or Beaulieu. His was the embarrassment of a man who does not know how to lie.

The Prince was left alone. He looked at the sea for a while. Then he changed windows, and gazed at the gardens. He pressed a button to call Don Marcos. He did not know what he was going to say to him but he felt he must see him in order not to remain alone. One of the old women servants appeared, and announced that the Colonel had gone to Monte Carlo.

"He, too," the Prince said to himself.

In order to escape the tediousness of spending a Sunday afternoon alone, he took his hat and overcoat. Some power beyond his comprehension was impelling him toward the neighboring city. Turning away from the villa, he walked through the gardens.

The edifice, thus deserted, appeared larger, and its frowning and angry silence seemed to be asking him why anybody had ever been such a fool as to waste so much money and material on a box like that.

Along the nearby road, street cars and carriages were gliding, filled with city people who were coming out for a glimpse of the smiling sea, or of a group of pines, or to find a height that might afford a panoramic view.

And he, the owner of the famous gardens of Villa Sirena, was deserting all this beauty to go to a city from which others were trying to escape.

Lubimoff recalled the splendid scheme of life he had worked out a few months before: a community of lay brethren shut off from the world in a spot like paradise: music, astronomy, pleasant conversations, wholesome work. And now the monks were running away on all sorts of pretexts, and he, who was their prior, also was feeling an unexplainable impulse to follow their example. Even Toledo, the faithful admirer of that estate which he had considered the best work of his life, seemed to be suffering from the same feverish desire to get away.

Near the gate he turned to contemplate his beautiful domain as if to beg its pardon. There was a silence like that surrounding an enchanted palace. The gardens seemed asleep like dream woods.

He thought he saw at the end of a long avenue a flutter of two large birds. It was Estola and Pistola, in afternoon coats too long for them, running toward the end of the promontory. It was as though Villa Sirena had been constructed for them. They could play with the active joy of youth in these gardens, to the envy of those who lingered at the gate out of curiosity. As they ran along they were free to trample on rare plants brought from the other side of the globe; free to jump from rock to rock in search of the little fishes left by the waves in miniature lakes in the hollows of the rock, until their coat tails were wet and their shoes full of holes—to the despair of the Colonel, who made the servants pass in review before him every day.

Michael preferred not to ask himself where he was going. He surely had some end in view when he started his walk, but he felt it a nuisance to think about it. Suddenly he saw two currents of people coming from opposite directions, meeting and mingling, as they both mounted a short winding stairway which was divided by two hand-rails, and was covered by three red carpets.

He was in front of the Casino. On one side, were arriving the people who had just come by train, on the other, those who had been gathered in by all the street cars from the towns on the Riviera between Nice and Monte Carlo.

That evening a celebrated Italian tenor was singing, and many of the people, forgetting their game for the moment, were gathering in the theater.

Lubimoff found himself immediately attended by two solemn gentlemen in frock coats with black ties and their heads bare. They were two inspectors from the Casino.

"We are very sorry, Prince, but everything is full. There are people even in the aisles."

But since it was he, one of the two men accompanied him as far as the box belonging to the Prime Minister of Monaco. The man who governed for the Sovereign Prince recognized him and was anxious to give him the best seat, but Michael, disliking public curiosity, preferred to remain in the second row.

It was a theater without any balconies. The auditorium was wider than it was deep. The rows of comfortable seats were all alike and all sold at the same price. The stage was used for concerts and, on rare occasions, for plays and operas.

The architect who had built the Paris Opera House had repeated the same dazzling display in this hall. There were gold ornaments on every side, elaborate moldings, caryatids and immense mirrors. There was not a hand's breadth of the wall without its gilded stucco, raised in bold relief.

In the hall at the rear above the seats that rose at a decided angle, were five boxes, the only ones there were.

They were reserved for the Sovereign Prince and his high officials.

While listening to the singing, Michael examined the crowded mass of people, as well as he could, from his seat. He recognized many as he gazed over their heads.

Toward the front he distinguished a man with gray hair that was parted from the forehead to the nape of the neck, and brushed forward mingling with his side whiskers, in an Austrian fashion. It was the Colonel, who was listening with a certain air of authority, swaying his head to show his approbation of the celebrated tenor. But he was not alone. The Prince saw him bend toward a girl with curly hair and a string of large amber beads. Oh, the traitor!

There was no doubt about it. It must have been the gardener's daughter. That was why he had fled in such a hurry. The milliner's apprentice had insisted. She was anxious to hear the singer she had heard the ladies talk so much about.

When the huge nightingale had retired to the wings, the Colonel offered his protégée a cornucopia full of caramels. Caramels in wartime! An extravagance, indeed, that only a lover could allow himself.

In the intermission, the Prince slipped away, for fear that he might meet Don Marcos and spoil his aide's pleasant afternoon by his presence. Besides, he was not interested in the opera or in the highly praised artist.

He crossed the large ante-room with its columns of jasper supporting a gallery with balusters surmounted by bronze candelabras. At one end of the room the latest news was posted on panels. The Prince read it without any curiosity.

Nothing new. The same as ever. The monotonous trench warfare was continuing. Ground gained and lost by the yard. There would be no end to it.

He slipped out between the groups of people during the intermission, taking care that the Colonel should not see him.

Poor Don Marcos! He was walking along gravely and proudly by the side of his protégée, who might have been his granddaughter. He glanced with hostility at all the young men, while behind his back, she made eyes at every passing uniform.

The Prince was obliged to force his way through a motionless compact group made up of wounded officers. French, Canadians, Australians, and Englishmen. Mingled with them were nurses of various types—some with nunlike veils and with a delicate appearance; others with a masculine look, having neckties and uniforms with gold buttons, without any feminine apparel except their skirts. Some who were older and had short hair, red faces, and large shell spectacles had to be examined closely before one could be convinced, from their hybrid appearance, that they were women. They crowded together in front of the three double curtains leading to the gambling rooms. Those who belonged in any way to the army or navy of any nation whatsoever were not allowed to pass this limit. Soldiers could enter only the theater and the ante-room of the Casino. And those people who in their far-off countries had often heard of Monte Carlo, finding themselves there by chance of war, were crowding at the curtains with childish curiosity, admiring, for an instant, as the draperies rapidly opened and closed, the vision of gilded rooms, all in a row and filled with people. Afterwards they would withdraw, giving up their places to other comrades. At last they had seen it! Now they could say they knew all about Monte Carlo!

The employees in their black frock coats opened one of the curtains, greeting the Prince as though he were an old acquaintance. It was the first time Michael had entered the gaming rooms since his return. It seemed to him as though he had awakened miraculously into the world of things before the war. Everything that was afflicting humanity remained on the other side of the door, as the action of a drama, unreal but exciting, remains on the stage of a theater which we leave behind us. He found even a certain attractiveness in the architecture of these drawing rooms, because of their vague familiarity, recalling the pleasant days of his life. He was in the Renaissance hall, but his whole attention was taken by the adjoining parlor, the central rotunda of the Casino, called the "Schmidt Drawing Room," the one on which all the other rooms converge and which seems to be prolonged under the dividing archways to the farthest ends of the building.

A pulsing silence arose from the mass of human beings around the green tables. Every one was talking in a low voice as though in church. From time to time this murmur was broken by a long swishing sound, a noise like that of pebbles on the shore swept by a wave. It was caused by the rakes of the employees sweeping the green cloth and carrying with them the clashing coins and ivory ships—all the spoils of the losings. The voices of the *croupiers*, like those of officers giving commands, arose above the feverish silence which reminded one of a humming hive.

"Faites vos jeux. Vos jeux sont faits?... Rien ne va plus."

The hall gradually lost the suppressed noises which served to accentuate its silence. People breathed more naturally, as they craned their necks to see better over the shoulders of those in front of them. Some of the women were standing on one foot only, with the other raised behind them like dancers bending over to touch the ground with their hands. They all crowded together, paying no attention to the sex of the persons against whom they were pushing. During this pause, marked by long faces, frowning eyebrows, drawn mouths, and converging glances, there resounded with its noise increased by a diabolical echo, the rattling of the tiny ivory ball as it whirled in the grooves along the wooden rim, while the colored rows of the roulette wheel kept spinning in the opposite direction, like a kaleidoscope. Suddenly there was a sharp click. The ball had ended its circular flight, falling into a number. The silence was prolonged. The spectators' necks were craned even more. There was a nervous clenching of fists. Again there was the sound of pebbles washed by the sea. The rakes were sweeping the green table. It was a bad number for the players. Whenever a stifled uproar occurred, caused by a hundred bosoms suddenly breathing freely, it took the *croupiers* several minutes to resume play. They had to pay the winners and settle disputes between those who claimed the same bet. At the end of each play various groups at a table would disengage themselves to go over to another; but the ring of people always remained compact through the arrival of new spectators.

From the central skylight a dim splendor descended. Outside the sun was shining on the azure sea. This light was like that of a wine cellar, a light, according to Castro, like that of a Hall of Congress.

It was a yellowish light gold which seemed to increase the magnificence of the drawing rooms. The architecture was of the rich and majestic sort that attracts the crowd and the newly rich. The columns and pillars of onyx and bronze held up a magnificent ceiling, broken by the circular stained glass of the skylight. In the four triangles of the vault were statues representing *Air*, *Earth*, *Fire*, and *Water*, as though these four elements had some relation to the business which gave the vast edifice its reason for existence.

Four metal spiders, huge and glistening, completed the heavy sumptuousness of the decoration. Where there were no gilded ornaments or mirrors, the walls were covered with showy pictures. These paintings and all of the rest that adorned the Casino were the object of Michael's jests. Some of them were fairly acceptable. The majority appeared very ancient in spite of the fact that they were not over forty years old. But there was nothing noble about their antique appearance. It seemed rather as though they had lain for centuries in scorn and oblivion. Atilio accounted for the appearance of these canvases in a way of his own. According to him they were the work of various patrons ruined by gambling, whom the Casino felt obliged to advertise.

The Prince began to notice well-known faces in this crowd which was being constantly renewed, and was changing each moment. The whole world, sooner or later passed that way. That floor with its various inlaid woods was one of the most frequented spots of Europe. It was something like the ancient Roman forum, a point on which all roads of the entire world converged. Idlers from the entire globe were attracted to this room. They all dreamed of being able to go sometime and risk a coin in the great Mediterranean gambling house. Men from other continents disembarking in the old world wrote Monte Carlo on the itinerary of their travels. But this human river which constantly glided along, receiving new waves of arrivals, kept leaving in the crannies of its shores, pools of stagnant waters, clogged by uprooted plants and the naked trunks of trees.

Lubimoff nodded to certain persons, who looked at him with a sort of cordial surprise, as though they were looking at a dead man brought to life. An old man, with a short bristling beard on a face pale as a corpse, bowed deeply as he passed, without seeming in his humility to be offended at not receiving an acknowledgment. He was the man most sought after and coaxed by the women who frequented the Casino. He wore a sort of black cap like that of a priest, and carried a hat in one hand. On his coat lapel was a medal of enamel work with the Sacred Heart of Jesus. Atilio and Lewis had also sought him frequently. Michael was sure that this man was a friend of the Duchess de Delille and that on more than one occasion he had seen her tears. He loaned money at 5 per cent (for every 24 hours), and spent the time, he was not busy, watching new arrivals from a distance to see if they might turn out to be new clients.

The Prince received smiles, also from certain respectable looking women who were by no means ugly, though they were stout in some parts of their body and slender in others, like persons who have taken a course to reduce flesh without obtaining a uniform result. They were seated on the divans in the corners, talking among themselves, and watching the groups of gamblers, with the air of employees resting after having done their duty. They had come to Monte Carlo many years ago with jewels, with thousands of francs, and men who endured all the unevenness of their tempers and in addition gave them money. And everything had vanished on the Casino tables. But they went on clinging to the reef on which they had been wrecked— perhaps beyond salvation, living on the jettison of many another who had followed the same route, only to be dashed on the same rocks and perish. They offered their services to strangers as persons acquainted with the mysteries of the house, advising honey-moon couples what number they should play, as though they knew the secret. Besides they came to the Casino at the opening hour to get the best places at the tables and later give up their chairs to wealthy players, steady clients, who rewarded them generously if luck favored them.

He met still others also. A number of women passed close to him. They were old, but of an age incapable yet of frankly facing the free air and the open sunlight. Their appearance of antiquity was accentuated by their strange apparel, which recalled no particular style— dresses of bright colors that had faded, and which seemed to have been cut from old curtains, and smelled like a musty old house;— and monumental hats or spherical turbans made of mosquito netting. Some were thin as skeletons; others were mountains of living fat; but all of them were painted scandalously with vermilion and had blue rings around their lightless eyes.

"A *louis*, Prince," murmured the most daring. "I am sure that you will bring me luck." As she spoke, her false teeth, too large for her gums, rattled; a stench of the grave accompanied the smile on the painted lips.

Michael knew who they were, from Toledo's tales. The Colonel, as an admirer of fallen royalty, accepted their conversation with melancholy deference. One of them had been a sweetheart of Victor Emanuel; another, who was older, recalled, with sighs, the days of Napoleon III, and of Morny.

They had come to die in Monte Carlo, the last spot on earth able to remind them of the splendors of sixty years before; some of them, in memory of their vanished jewels, calmly displayed brass ornaments and beads of glass. According to a paradox of Castro's, they had died many years before, spending the night in the Monaco Cemetery dressing themselves with the spoils from other corpses and coming to the Casino from force of habit to contemplate once more the scenes of their remote youth. The Prince gave them a few bank notes and went out, while they ran to gamble this money, after having thanked him for the gift, with a death-head grin that was the last remnant of their former professional charm.

Suddenly Michael stopped, observing the various parasites who lived by clinging to the gearing of the terrible machine and feeding on the crumbs it pulverized. He became interested in the crowd which was always apparently the same, though always with distinct individuals. There were some who walked along leaning on canes, invalids' canes tipped with rubber—the only kind allowed in the gaming room for fear of quarrels. He noticed flaccid old women slowly hobbling along, paralytic gentlemen leaning on the arm of tall, robust fellows in braided uniforms who led them in a fatherly fashion toward the roulette wheels and eased them into their chairs. A few paralytics arrived at the foot of the stairway in little carriages like children's carts, and thence were carried on hand chairs through the rooms to their favorite spot. At certain moments it seemed as though the gambling hall were a famous health resort, or a place of miracles, like Lourdes. They came just as incurable invalids come to other places, impelled by a last hope; but in this case the hope was not for health. That was the least of their cares. What galvanized them here was the hope of fortune, and dreams of wealth, as if riches would be of any service to these poor bodies lacking all the appetites which make life pleasant.

Mentally the Prince summed up all human passions in two pleasures which are the springs of all action—love and gambling. There were people who experienced equally the attraction of them both— Castro, for example. He himself had been interested only in love and could not understand the pleasures of gambling. Whenever he had gotten up from the gaming tables, each time with winnings, he had never felt any temptation to return. But looking at these ailing people, some of them very aged, at those incurables, all of them dragging themselves toward the roulette wheel as though toward a miraculous bath, he condoned them pityingly. What other pleasure was there left for them on earth? How could they fill the emptiness of their lives prolonged so tenaciously?

What he could not understand was the intense attitude, the hard faces, of the other gamblers who were healthy and strong. Young men moved among the women around the tables with hostile brusqueness, quarrelling with them harshly and treating them like enemies. Women suddenly lost their grace and freshness, becoming masculine all at once as they looked at the rows of cards of *trente et quarante* or at the mad whirl of the colored wheel. Their gestures were those of prize fighters. Their mouths were drawn. There was a look of fierceness in their eyes. As though warned instinctively of this transformation, no sooner did they tear themselves away from the tables than they took out their vanity case—the little mirror, the powder, and the rouge—to correct or efface the passing ravages of the play. Those of more dignified and normal appearance showed themselves at times to be the most reckless. In a place where all the women were doing the same as they, gambling had something official about it, something worthy of respect; it was possible for them to indulge in a vice without fear of gossip, without the risk of being criticized.

The Prince smiled as he remembered a story Toledo had told him a few days before: the despair of a woman of about forty who came from Nice with her two daughters every afternoon, and had finally lost fifty thousand francs.

"Oh! If I had only taken a lover," the mother had groaned with tears in her eyes. "It would have been better if I had chosen love."

Michael entered the other rooms that had no skylight. The clusters of electric bulbs lighting them with senseless splendor made him think of the burning sun and the azure sea just beyond those walls of gold and jasper.

Above the tables were oil lamps with two enormous shades each one sheltering four fixtures which hung by bronze chains several yards long, attached to the ceiling. Thus if the electric current was cut off, there was no danger of the patrons feeling tempted to appropriate the money on the tables.

Occasionally a little bell would sound, rung by one of the employees in black frock coat who directed the playing. A chip, a coin, or a bank note had fallen under the table. Suddenly with the promptness of a scene shifter waiting behind the stage, a lackey dressed in a blue and gold uniform appeared, carrying a dark lantern and a hook to rummage about among the players' feet until he found the lost object.

The discipline observable in these vast rooms was like that on a warship, where everything is in its place and every man at his post. In order to make sure that everything was going properly, various respectable gentlemen with decorations on their coat lapels, walked back and forth among the tables, with the air of officers on duty. Whenever voices were raised, these men appeared with rapid strides, to cut short the arguments in some tactful manner. When two gamblers claimed the same bet, they immediately settled the dispute by paying both. The money would finally come back to the house any way!

According to Atilio, the Casino was honeycombed in all directions with secret galleries, hidden openings and even trap doors, like the stage for a comedy of magic—all these for the sake of immediate service, and to avoid any annoyance to the patrons.

Sometimes the invalid fainted at the table or fell dead through too violent emotion. Immediately the wall would open and eject two attendants with a stretcher who would cause the troublesome body to disappear as though by enchantment. Those at the adjoining table would scarcely have a chance to be aware of it.

At other times it would be a suicide. Lubimoff knew a table called the Suicide Table, because an Englishman had killed himself there in melodramatic fashion, shooting himself with a pistol when he had lost his last penny. His brains had been scattered in shreds on the green baize and on the faces of his neighbors, and even on the frock coats of the *croupiers*. There are always people who have no tact, and who do not know how to behave in good society! But the attendants emerged from the wall, carried away the corpse, and cleaned the blood from the carpet and table.

Shortly afterwards, from the oval of people crowding against the green table, the consecrated words arose: *"Faites vos jeux.... Vos jeux sont faits?... Rien ne va plus."*

The Prince recalled the famous suicide bench in the gardens of the Casino. It was all a magazine yarn. No such bench had ever existed. When several persons killed themselves on the same bench, the administration had its position changed immediately! Besides, the number of suicides was much exaggerated. There were two or three each year, no more. According to Castro, it was no longer the fad to kill one's self at Monte Carlo. It showed an unpardonable lack of taste. The proper thing to do was to go a long way off and disappear without making any commotion.

Besides the house police were quick to detect those who were in despair. Such people received a railway ticket at once and they were advised to kill themselves, like good fellows, in Marseilles, or if not so far away, at least in Nice or Menton.

Michael was near the "Suicide Table" close to the entrance to the private rooms, when he noticed a certain commotion in the crowd. Groups were seeking one another to exchange news. The old patrons were moved by professional feeling. Something important was going on. The Prince knew the meaning of these sudden bursts of curiosity: a player was winning or losing in remarkable fashion.

He heard indistinctly a name that brought him to attention.

"The Duchess de Delille—two hundred thousand francs!"

All those who had permission to play in the private rooms hurried toward the large glass door which gave access to them. Michael followed this living current.

He found himself in an enormous hall with a lofty ceiling. On one side four large balconies opened out on the terraces, and the Mediterranean. Because of the war they were covered with dark curtains to hide the light from within. The wall opposite was adorned with various gigantic mirrors. On the ceiling seventeen white, full-breasted caryatids, bending under the weight of the roof, supported the wide bands of rock crystal, with electrical bulbs, which shed a sort of moonlight.

Those whom curiosity had attracted, passed the first gaming tables with an air of indifference. Everybody was crowding around the last, the *"trente et quarante,"* at the foot of a large picture, in which three buxom lasses in the nude against a background of dark trees like those in the Boboli Gardens, represented the *Florentine Graces.*

The great phenomenon was taking place there. Craning his neck above the shoulders of two sightseers, Michael caught a glimpse of Alicia seated at the table with an anxious expression on her face. All eyes were upon her. In front of her, were heaps of bank notes and many columns of chips. There were the five hundred franc ovals, and the one thousand franc squares, "little cakes of soap" as they call the latter, in the language of the Casino.

Suddenly she raised her head as though realizing instinctively the presence of some one interesting to her. And her eyes fell straight on Michael. She greeted him with a happy smile. There was the suggestion of a kiss in her glance. And all the people there, with the submission of a mob when dominated by enthusiasm or amazement, followed her eyes to see who the man was whom the heroine was greeting in this manner. The vanity of the Prince was flattered, as it used to be when some celebrated actress greeted him from the stage and went on singing with her eyes fastened upon him to dedicate to him her trills. Once, when he was a boy, a bull-fighter had bowed to him in a friendly way before giving the final death thrust in the arena. Alicia seemed to be choosing him as her god of luck.

But immediately she fell back into the deep absorption of the play. She was not alone. An invisible and powerful person was standing behind her chair, bending over her to whisper in her ear some word of unfailing counsel, to suggest some unlooked for resolution, some original and daring idea. Her eyes, lighted by a mysterious fire, were gazing on something that no one else could see. Her mute lips trembled with nervous contractions, as though she were talking with some one who did not need sound to be able to hear. Michael felt there was a demon-like power beside her, the inspiration of the unforgettable hours which reveal to artists a masterful harmony, an illuminating word, or a supreme stroke of the brush; the inspiration which prompts the final slaughter in battle or the decisive move in some business venture, that means either millions or suicide.

She had begun to plunge. Her hand carelessly pushed forward a column of twelve rectangular chips, with an extra oval one: twelve thousand five hundred francs, the maximum amount that could be risked in "*trente et quarante.*" The crowd, with the idolatry which victors inspire, was hoping for the Duchess, as though each one expected to share in her winning. They all knew she was going to win. And when as a matter of fact she did win, there was a murmur of satisfaction, a sigh of relief from that oval of sightseers pressing against the backs of the chairs occupied by the players. From time to time she lost, and profound silence expressed their sympathy. Sometimes after advancing a column of chips, she closed her eyes as though listening to some one who remained invisible, and moving her head in sign of assent, withdrew the stakes. Once more there arose a murmur of satisfaction, when the public saw that she had withdrawn her money just in time, and had scored, as it were, a negative triumph.

Many of them computed with greedy eyes the sums amassed in front of her.

"She's in the three hundred thousands already—perhaps she has more—Oh! if she would only succeed in making it millions! What fun it would be to see her break the bank!"

To these comments spoken in low tones were added the laudatory exclamations of a few elderly women who looked at the conqueror with adoring eyes. "How nice she is!—a great lady and so beautiful!—Good luck to her!"

A dark shoulder over which the Prince was looking moved and the Prince saw Spadoni's face close to his. The pianist did not show the slightest surprise; as though they had separated only a few minutes before. He did not even greet Michael. The astonishment which caused the pupils of his eyes to dilate, the indignation and envy that this insolent fortune inspired, made it necessary for the pianist to express his feelings in a protest.

"Have you noticed, Highness—she doesn't know how to play—she goes against all rules, all logic. She doesn't know the first thing about it, not the first thing!"

Immediately his eyes returned to the table, forgetting the Prince on hearing once more a stifled outburst from the crowd. A little more and some of the people would be applauding the repeated triumphs of the Duchess. Those who had lost during the previous days, were rejoicing with the joy of vengeance. "What an evening! You don't see this every day." They smiled and nudged each other as they noticed the coming and going of the inspectors, the presence of high officials who strove to hide their concern, the long faces of attendants as they returned from the head cashier with new packages of one thousand franc chips to pay this lady who had swept the table bare of money three times. The news of her extraordinary run of luck circulated throughout the entire edifice. At that moment the gentlemen of the management must have been discussing in their offices on the top floor the bad trick that chance had dared to play them. A mood of anticipation and excitement, akin to the whispering of a revolution, spread through every nook and cranny. Those who had no tickets for the private rooms asked for news from those who were coming out, repeating what they had heard with exaggeration born of enthusiasm. In the wardrobe, in the lavatories, in the inner corridors, in all the subterranean and winding passageways where the servants, maids and firemen lived under an eternal electric light, this news shook the sleepy calm of the humbler employees. The atmosphere of excitement was similar to that which circulates through the half deserted corridors of the Chamber of Deputies while in the semi-circle teeming with emotion, a Prime Minister is fighting to survive a crisis. The news gathered momentum as it passed from group to group with that satisfaction mingled with uneasiness which is inspired in employees by the reverses of their employers.

"It seems that upstairs a Duchess is winning a million—no: now they say it is two millions."

And by the time the news had circulated throughout the entire building, the two millions had married and given birth to another. Half an hour later they were four millions, according to the lesser servants, who had grown old living off gambling without ever seeing it at first hand.

Michael suddenly felt a great wave of anger against the fortunate woman. Since her smile of greeting she had not looked at him again. Several times her eyes had glanced mechanically in his direction, without taking any notice of him. He was merely one of the many curious spectators witnessing her triumph. At that moment there were only two things in the world, the pack of cards and herself.

Her indifference caused him to feel the indignation of the moralist. It did not make any difference to him that Alicia was forgetting him. He repeated this to himself several times: no, he did not care about that. They were not lovers, nor was there any deep affection between them. But how about her son! He remembered that morning a scene with her tears and despair. And the mother was there abandoning herself completely to the pleasures of chance and with no feeling for anything except her perverted passion.

If some one had spoken to her about the aviator who was a prisoner, she would have had to make an effort to recall his existence. And a few hours before she had wept sincerely on thinking of his imprisonment!

This was too much for the Prince. His sense of dignity could not accept this thoughtlessness! He elbowed his way through a crowd of onlookers, after freeing himself from Spadoni's shoulder, while the latter as though hypnotized, remained with his eyes fixed on the ever-increasing treasure of the Duchess.

Lubimoff began to pace the drawing room. He scorned Alicia's self-absorption, but lacked the strength to go away. It was necessary for him to be near her, perhaps in order to see just how far her slight of him would go.

He came across a gentleman who was walking about among the tables, beating his hands behind his back and muttering unintelligible words. It was his friend Lewis.

"Have you seen how she plays," he said in a tone of anger, as he recognized the Prince; "like a fool, like a regular fool! They ought not to allow women in here."

All afternoon he had been losing according to rule and experience. He did not have enough money left even for his whiskies and had had to charge them at the bar. But suddenly he remembered that the Duchess was a relative of Lubimoff.

"I am sorry if I offended you, but she plays like an idiot."

And he turned his back to continue his furious monologue.

Don Marcos passing in a hurry without seeing the Prince opened a path in the crowd of onlookers with all the authority of a dressy personage. He had just left the gardener's daughter in haste. The news had crept through the theater causing many of the spectators to give up seeing the close of the opera in order to be present at this unheard of run of luck, which was for them a spectacle of the greatest interest.

At one of the roulette tables he saw Clorinda who was playing cautiously, with Castro standing behind her chair.

"The General" had witnessed the first part of her friend's triumph. "She's going to lose: this cannot last," she thought each time. Then she had moved away from the table, explaining her attitude to Castro and other friends. It was impossible for her to watch Alicia tranquilly as she risked such heavy stakes. It was more excitement than she could endure.

"I hope she wins a great deal, a great deal, indeed," she added with the generosity of a friend. "Poor Alicia, she needs it so much! Her affairs are going so badly!"

She had just seated herself at another table with the faint hope that luck would remember her, too; but the murmurings which reached her from the trente et quarante table, announcing the news of fresh victories, made her nervous and she attributed the loss of several twenty franc pieces to this cause. When she found she had lost two hundred, she felt that she must take her spite out on some one. Atilio, who followed her everywhere, was standing there, greeting her expressions of bad humor with an adoring smile.

"Castro, go away; don't stand there behind me. You must know you bring me bad luck. Go somewhere else."

The Prince observed how his friend, with a look of annoyance, left the widow and walked toward the door.

He thought he would follow him. By talking with Atilio, he might forget the irritation which the other woman had caused him; but as he went toward the end of the room he had a new surprise.

In one of the dimly lighted corners he saw Novoa, who was going to spend the afternoon in Monaco or take a walk on the Nice Road. Perhaps the latter was true. He might have been waiting for Valeria who was coming back from her luncheon party. They must have both been there for a long time, in the dark corner, unaware of what was going on about them and deaf to people's comments.

The scientist, with his back turned, was unable to see the Prince. As for the lady, her eyes were fixed on Novoa with the affectionate seriousness of a girl who has taken advanced studies, has the bachelor's degree, and is able to understand a man of science. Michael heard a snatch of the young professor's conversation.

"And when the glacial currents from the pole reach that spot they take the place of the warm waters that rise to the surface...."

He was explaining the formation of the Gulf Stream.

No one could have guessed it from observing the caressing and timidly amorous glances behind his glasses.

She was listening with admiring fervor, but Michael, who knew women, imagined he guessed her real thoughts. She was weighing, with the cunning of a poor girl alone in the world, the possibilities of this man as a husband. He was ignorant of everything not to be learned in books, and she was calculating the modifications necessary to improve the person of this careless male who always wore a necktie badly tied, and never pulled up his trousers before sitting down, to keep them from bagging in a grotesque manner.

Lubimoff spent more than an hour deeply sunk in an armchair in the bar, listening to Castro. The branches of the large trees on the terrace wove soft shadows like spider webs on the window panes in the twilight dusk.

Atilio was giving vent to his melancholy by lamenting the meagerness of the afternoon tea. On account of the war, burnt almonds and potato chips were the only gastronomic delicacies to be offered, in this place frequented by the wealthy.

The crowd roused in him the same sad reflections. There were people there, but very few compared with the numbers that flocked to Monte Carlo some years before. Then they came in limited trains direct from Vienna, Berlin, and the farthest parts of Europe. The square in front of the Casino was a second *Babel*. Around the "Cheese," people of all races walked up and down, speaking every known language. At present the absence of the Russians, who were spirited gamblers, was to be lamented, and likewise the absence of the Austrians and the Turks. The last persons to be attracted by Monte Carlo were the Germans, but Castro had seen them come in great numbers during the past few years, applying to gambling the same quiet minutely scientific thoroughness of method they used in military discipline, the organization of industries, and laboratory work.

He was always able to recognize them as soon as they entered the rooms. When they sat down at the table they surrounded themselves with books and papers: statistics of the most favored numbers of past years, manuals on how to gamble, their own calculations and logarithms that only they themselves could understand.

"They held on to their money more tenaciously than the rest," Atilio continued. "They were as patient and tireless as stubborn oxen; but they lost in the end like every one else. Who doesn't lose here— even the Casino, that always wins, is losing now. Before the war it brought in an income of forty million francs a year. At the present time it clears not more than three or four millions and since enormous expenses have to be covered, it has had to ask for loans to go on living, the same as a State."

Michael observed those who were passing through the bar. There was only one man for every ten women.

"That's the war, too," said Castro. "You can see women, women everywhere! Before the war, if you recall, even in peace times, the proportion of women was always larger. There are fewer men but they play higher stakes. They risk their money with more daring; three-fourths of the crowd around the tables were composed of women. When women are afraid of love, or disillusioned by it, they give themselves up to gambling with passionate intensity. It is the only means they can find to express their imagination. Besides, when one takes into account their love of luxury, which is never proportionate to their means, and considers the needs of present day women which were unknown to their grandmothers.... Look—look over there." He pointed discreetly to a lady advanced in years, modestly dressed and with a face that was daubed with rouge, who was being approached with supplicating looks and gestures by two other young and elegantly dressed ladies. It was easy to guess that they had come in there purely for the sake of discussing some business affair, away from the prying eyes in the gambling rooms.

"They are asking for a loan and she is refusing," Castro continued. "Perhaps it is the second or third time in the afternoon. This lady is a rival of the old man who wears the Sacred Heart on his lapel. He is quite a character, that old usurer! He began as a waiter in a café and must have some two millions now after thirty years of honorable toil. Everything he owns is to be given to the village of La Turbie, which has named him its benefactor. He pays for images of Saints and has rebuilt the church—. Notice: the lady is softening. They are going to get the loan."

The three women had disappeared through the mahogany door leading to the women's lavatories. As the loan agent kept her funds in her petticoats, it was necessary for her to pull up her skirts to carry on her negotiations. Shortly after she came out and walked rapidly in the direction of the gambling room. She had to go on watching several women to whom she had loaned money, to see if they were winning. The two young women followed her with their purses still open, hurriedly counting the bank notes they had just received.

Castro, who had suffered the humiliation of similar operations more than once, began bitterly to attack the vice which maintained this enormous edifice and the whole Principality.

He played to win, played because he was poor; but so many rich people came there and risked the foundations of their well being!

"Gambling is a functioning of the imagination. That is why you must have noticed that men with real imagination, writers, and true artists, seldom gamble. Many of them have caused great scandals by their extraordinary vices, reaching the point of monstrosity. But none of them have ever distinguished themselves as gamblers. They have other more exciting subjects to which they may apply their imaginative powers. On the other hand the great mass of human beings feel the charm of gambling and the more commonplace the individual, the more strongly is he attracted by the fascination of chance. Our acts are guided by the desire of obtaining the maximum of pleasure with a minimum of pain and effort; and you cannot obtain this better than by gambling. We all obey our hopes that do what seems most advantageous. We like to exaggerate the probability that what we most earnestly want to happen will occur, and we end by taking our desires for reality. Every day those who come in here have a feeling of certainty that they will come away taking a thousand, twenty thousand, or a hundred thousand francs with them, and, as a matter of cold fact, they come away with empty pockets. It doesn't make any difference, they will come back the next day, guided by the same illusions."

He stopped talking as though depressed by the thought that he was painting his own picture. Then he added:

"What is the difference? Without these illusions, which gently stimulate the imagination, life would overwhelm us. It is perhaps fortunate for us that our hopes are not mathematically exact, that our destiny is largely shaped by luck. Besides, life is short. The future is uncertain; if fortune is to be ours, should we not prepare the way so that it may come swiftly? And what better way than that of gambling? When we put our hope in some far-off future time, it is not worth much. If we are to win, let it be soon and once for all. Our life is nothing more than a game of chance. We are gamblers all, even those of us who have never touched a card. Professions, business, and love itself are pure gambles, pure luck, a matter of chance. Cleverness and intelligence may cause our life games to turn out favorably, but chance still retains its hold on us, and the luck of an individual is what is most important. To become rich, even in the most stable business enterprises, one must be favored by a combination of extraordinary circumstances, a continual run of luck. A man never has become rich or celebrated merely on his own merits."

Lubimoff, one of the world's great millionaires a few years before, nodded his head at this statement.

"Even Governments keep up the habit of hope in the public by recourse to chance," continued Castro. "There are very few that do not authorize a lottery. A person who takes a ticket, buys a little hope and the possibility, if he has any imagination, of building for a few days every kind of wonderful dream, and feeling deeply stirred at the time of the drawing. The betterment of our material well-being by means of our own efforts is a laborious and difficult task; but there is a way to give the humble a certain relative happiness: by giving them hopes of becoming rich, of freeing themselves from every kind of servitude, and of realizing the ideal of freedom to which they aspire. As a matter of principle the State shows itself an enemy of games of chance; and considers them immoral because they are based on what is uncertain; but all classes of commercial, financial, and industrial operations represent chance and oftentimes the ruin of one or two parties. They are all games quite similar to the gambling that goes on here." Atilio smiled ironically before continuing.

"Let the moralists talk against gambling until they are weary. This much is certain. The sums that are played on horse races and in the Casino increase each year with rapid progression, more rapidly in fact than public wealth. The general improvement in ways of living which is developing, exerts no influence toward decreasing gambling. On the other hand, the complexity of modern life, with the increase of our needs and wants, favors this passion, and even aggravates it."

The Prince interrupted him. He was quite right, perhaps, in what he was saying, but what a degrading vice gambling was! The more reasonable people allow themselves to be mastered by it and even lose their ordinary intelligence.

"That's certain," confessed Atilio. "In gambling our human weaknesses and the tendency which we all have towards superstitions are shown most clearly. What madness.... Just as though the past could influence the present! How many useless efforts to conquer luck! More wealth and imagination has been wasted in the invention of new systems in gambling than in the attempt to find perpetual motion—and just as uselessly. All these wonderful systems lead the gambler infallibly toward ruin with more or less rapidity, but always with certainty. And how strong our faith is! I feel that it is greater than that of religious martyrs. When we think we have a combination which is sure to win, there is no use trying to persuade us to the contrary. Nothing can convince us. It is curious that the failure of his system and the consequent losses never discourage a good gambler. He immediately seizes upon some new combination, a true one this time—which will enable him to make a fortune—one hope followed by another, and thus he goes on living until death overtakes him."

The melancholy of these last few words was brief. Castro seemed suddenly to recall something which made him smile.

"How many inconsistencies in the lives of gamblers! They are not afraid to risk their money and there is no class of people that is more stingy. Notice the women who play most passionately. They are all badly dressed; some of them are often careless about their persons. They must have money to gamble, and postpone buying necessities until the next day. There are men who carry their hats in their arms all afternoon in order to save the ten cents which it costs to leave them in the vestibule of the Casino. To-day when I came in I saw an elderly gentleman who waits for a friend every day standing by the cloak room window. They leave their hats and coats together and that way each one has to pay only five cents. Later on, at the roulette table, I saw them handling rolls of thousand-franc bills."

From the tables people called to the players who were entering the bar:

"Is she still winning?"

They referred to the Delille woman. The various reports did not agree. Some of the people seemed indignant: "Yes, she went on winning with luck that would make you tired." The enthusiasm of the first moment had vanished. There was a note of envy concealed in words and glances. Others moved by some selfish sentiment were pleased to point to a decline in her marvelous luck. She was losing and winning. Her runs of luck were not so frequent as in the beginning, but at all events if she were to stop at once, she might well take away three hundred thousand francs.

Atilio and the Prince noticed Lewis standing at the bar, drinking the whisky which always restored his peace of mind, and permitted him to resume the complicated systems that were to give him back his paternal inheritance and restore his castle.

They called to him to inquire about the luck of the Duchess. Lewis shrugged his shoulders with an expression of indignation and protest. It was absurd to win like that, playing so badly.

"She must have the Count's rosary hidden in her skirts," said Atilio, gravely.

Lewis was puzzled for the moment as though he took the words seriously. Later he blushed like a proper Briton, as he remembered the strange ornaments on his friend's rosary. Suddenly he burst into a violent fit of laughter. "Oh, Mr. Castro!——-" Mr. Castro's supposition seemed to him so witty that he laughed till he nearly choked himself coughing, and then he decided to get another whisky to regain his serenity.

The two friends returned to the drawing room of the *Florentine Graces*.

The Prince saw Novoa and Valeria on the same divan continuing their conversation, but constantly becoming dreamier as they gazed into each other's eyes, as though in some deserted spot.

He came near them without their seeing him, and was able to hear some of what Alicia's companion was saying.

"I don't know Spain, but I am so interested in it. I adore all of the romantic countries where love is everything, and men are disinterested, where dowries don't exist, and a woman may marry even if she is poor."

The Prince, in passing, gave the scientist a casual glance of pity.

CHAPTER VII

A new personage entered the lives of the dwellers in Villa Sirena. The Colonel announced with enthusiasm this friend whom Doña Clorinda had introduced.

"He is a Spanish Lieutenant in the Foreign Legion. He lives in the hotel which the Prince of Monaco gave up for convalescent officers. His name is Antonio Martinez, a very common name which reveals nothing of his character; but he is a great soldier, a hero, and I don't know how he manages to survive his wounds."

The "General" who kept track of all the soldiers of a certain reputation, as soon as they arrived in Monte Carlo, had been anxious to meet this Lieutenant, and had taken him under her protection. The Duchess de Delille was also interested in him, and the two women, proud of being his *marraines*, showed him off in the anteroom of the Casino, rented carriages to promenade him around to the most beautiful spots on the Riviera, and treated him to the finest war-time foods and pastry that they could find. With his lungs injured by German poison gases, he had also received a hand grenade wound on his head, and suffered from time to time from nervous trouble, which caused him to fall to the ground unconscious. The doctors talked despairingly of his condition. Perhaps he would live for years, perhaps he would die in one of these crises; the important thing was that he should live a quiet life, without any deep emotion. And the two ladies, who knew the real state of his health, lamented it when he was not present. He was so young, so affectionate, and so timid? On the breast of his mustard-colored uniform, attached by red ribbons, as a symbol of bravery given to the foreign battalions, were the War Cross and the Legion of Honor.

Clorinda, who considered that she had greater rights over him because of having "discovered" him, thought for awhile of taking him to live with her in order to be able to take better care of him. But as she was at the Hôtel de Paris, she did not, like Alicia, have an entire villa at her disposal. And the latter, although tempted by her friend's suggestions, did not dare to take the convalescent into her home. People liked to talk, and she, without saying why, was afraid of their gossip.

In the meantime, they both took the Lieutenant everywhere, protesting that, because of his uniform, he was not allowed to enter the rooms of the Casino. One afternoon, Doña Clorinda, with all the natural boldness of her character, took him to Villa Sirena. It was a shame that the handsome building and its vast gardens should be given over to five men who did nothing for humanity at all. Often in her imagination, she had converted it into a Sanitarium filled with invalid soldiers, with herself at the head of it as director and patroness. But her suggestions had no effect whatever on the Prince. "A selfish fellow," she said to herself, returning to her former opinion.

As long as it was impossible to occupy the Villa with a band of convalescents, she took the Spanish officer to show him the gardens, without first asking Lubimoff's permission.

The latter was able to see at first hand the hero of whom Don Marcos, during the last few days, had talked so much. He saw nothing in him to indicate extraordinary deeds. Martinez was a youth, ready to blush when forced to tell what he had done in the war. Without his uniform and his insignia of honor, he would have seemed like a poor office clerk, modest and resigned and incapable of being anything else. His appearance contrasted with the deeds which, after much pleading, he would finally be persuaded to confess. He was twenty-six years old, and seemed much younger, but it was a sickly sort of youthfulness, undermined by wounds and hardships.

Lubimoff, who hated the swagger of boastful heroes, felt at first disconcerted, and then attracted by the simplicity of this officer. If he had not known from Don Marcos the authenticity of his prowess, he would have taken no stock in it.

Somewhat intimidated in the presence of the famous owner of Villa Sirena, Martinez confessed his humble birth with neither pride nor timidity. He was poor, the son of poor people. He had tried to study for a career, but the necessity of earning his living had caused him to abandon books, trying the most diverse occupations, one after the other. It was so difficult to earn one's bread in Spain! After fighting in the Spanish campaign in Morocco, he had wandered through various South American Republics, struggling all the while against poverty and ill luck.

"There where so many common rough people get rich," he said, "all I found was poverty, like that in my own country. When this war broke out, like many other people, I was indignant at the conduct of the Germans, and their atrocities in the invaded countries. At the time I was in Madrid. One night some of my café acquaintances agreed to go and fight for France. The person who backed down was to pay ten dollars. They all repented their decision, except myself. Don't imagine that it was to avoid paying the wager. I have my own ideas, and have read more or less. I believe in republics—and France is the country of the Great Revolution. I entered a battalion of the Foreign Legion, which, composed for the most part of Spaniards, was being organized in Bayonne. There are a very few left by this time; most of them are dead; the rest are living scattered throughout the various hospitals, or else are crippled for life. I knew what war was like from mountain warfare against the Moors in the Riff country, and without seeking the honor I had gotten as far as being a Lieutenant of Reserves in my own country. Perhaps that is why they made me a Sergeant in the Legion after a few weeks. But it certainly was hard! I had never imagined they would receive us with a brass band! France has too many other things to think of; but it was sad to see how badly our enthusiasm was interpreted. Men called to arms by the laws of their country, and who were obliged to fight, looked at us with jealousy and suspicion. The other regiments considered us adventurers; or even escaped convicts. 'How hungry you must have been at home,' they said to me at the front, 'to have come here to be able to get something to eat!' And among us there were students, newspaper men, young men from wealthy families, fellows who had enlisted with enthusiasm—but let's not talk about that. In every country there are vulgar minded people incapable of understanding anything beyond their selfish, material wants."

His military experience was confined to trench warfare, endless and monotonous, and to short distance attacks. He had arrived late at the Battle of the Marne; and he, who imagined that he would take part in gigantic combat, involving millions of men and the firing of immense cannon, merely witnessed a series of struggles between small forces hidden in the earth, and hand-to-hand encounters to win a few yards of ground. Life at the Dardanelles was the worst of his memories. He hated to think of that horrible campaign. The struggles in France seemed rather placid compared to that fighting on a few miles of coast, with the sea at their backs and unconquerable lines ahead of them.

After saying this he fell silent, and the Colonel had to insist, with a certain paternal pride, that Martinez go on talking.

"Wounds, many wounds," he added simply. "I have lost count of the hospitals that I have known in three years, and of the trips I have made through France in Red Cross ambulances. When we are not killed outright, we are like the horses in bull fights. They patch up our skins outside the ring, strengthen us a bit and back we go into the arena, until we get the final goring."

Toledo, becoming impatient at the young man's modesty, told the story of his wounds. He received some in every period of the fighting. Some belonged to modern warfare, produced by fragments of high explosive shells, others came from machine guns, and even that cough which interrupted his speech from time to time was caused by asphyxiating gases. Others were made by knives, by clubbings from gun stocks, by flying stones, and even by the teeth of the Germans in night encounters and surprise attacks, in which men fought as they did in the infancy of human life on this planet.

Prince Lubimoff could not help admiring this slight, dark young man, who looked so insignificant. It seemed impossible that a human organism could resist so many blows, and that his weak body could sustain so many shocks without succumbing.

But Martinez, with the solidarity of all those who face danger, refused all personal glory. He talked about the Legion as a soldier talks about his regiment, as a sailor talks about his ship, considering it the finest of all. He saw the entire war in terms of the Legion. The French were all brave. Besides, no one could guess where the enemy would attack, and wherever the latter assumed the offensive, they found troops that withstood them and kept them from passing. But the Foreign Legion!

"The soldiers who fight at the front are men," he said, "men torn from their families through the needs of the country. But we are fighters. That is why in the difficult operations, when flesh and blood have to be sacrificed, they send us forward. I am always, of course, only one of many. But the Legion!... Every six months a new Colonel: He is killed and another takes his place, he, too, is destined to die. And how the enemy hates us! There is one thing we are proud of. Among the prisoners that there are in Germany, there is not a single one from the Foreign Legion. Any one of us who ever falls into the hands of the *Boches* knows that he is a dead man: we are outlawed.

And for our part, well, we do our best too!... Even when they insult us from trench to trench, we are proud of belonging to the Legion. One night, the enemy opposite, hearing us speak Spanish, began to shout in our language. They must have been Germans from South America. 'Hey, *Macabros*! Wait till we get hold of you, and then!...' They threatened us with the most terrible tortures. And they always nicknamed us 'Macabros!' I don't know why."

The Duchess de Delille admired the hero, feeling at the same time a certain sense of uneasiness at the horrors which she guessed from his words. "The war! When would the war be over?"

The Lieutenant shrugged his shoulders, smiling. People who live far from the front were more impatient for peace than those who risked their lives in the front lines. They had become accustomed to contact with death. The war would last as long as was necessary: five years, ten years; the main thing was to win the victory.

But Toledo, fearing that the conversation would get away from his hero, insisted once more on his great deeds.

"I'm only one of many," said Martinez. "But as far as brave men are concerned, I can recommend the Legion. That is where you'll find them. And all have died!... At first we had men from every country. But the Americans left as soon as their Republic intervened in the war; and it was the same with the Italians and Poles. On the other hand, many Russians, when their regiments were disbanded, joined the Legion. There is nothing extraordinary to tell about myself. And they have rewarded me so highly for the little I have done! Being a foreigner I have two ribbons. Besides, I shall never forget the moment when the Colonel, a week before they killed him, called me, and said, 'Martinez, the General has given me four Crosses of the Legion of Honor for our Legion. One of them is yours.' And he put it on my breast in front of a whole battalion of brave men presenting arms. It was unforgettable: it was worth a life time."

It was the truth. Colonel Toledo affirmed it, nodding his head, his eyes wet with tears. Later, with selfish jealousy, Don Marcos tore him away from the ladies, who were busy for the moment, talking with the Prince and his friend.

Walking through the gardens, the Colonel gazed at his hero with a look of tender protection, such as an artist who has exhausted his talents gazes at the increasing triumph of a younger, fresher, and more successful colleague.

"Youth, youth!" he said. "You, Martinez, belong to the Spain of the future; I belong to the Spain of past days, the Spain that will never return again. I am convinced that the world is progressing in new directions."

The Colonel kept up a frequent correspondence with many Spanish volunteers in the Legion. He looked after them with all the affection of a *marraine*, sending them chocolate, select edibles, everything that he could spare from the Villa Sirena pantry, without impairing the service. Some of the letters which came from the front made him weep and laugh. One volunteer asked him to send a good Spanish knife, having broken his own in a night attack. Another dreamt of a Browning revolver. Who would give him a Browning? He had only an ordnance revolver, an undependable weapon that had failed him twice in an attack on a trench and had prevented him from killing the German who finally wounded him.

With Lieutenant Martinez, the Colonel could let go all his enthusiasm and give free rein to prophesies in favor of the Allies.

In the presence of Atilio and Novoa he was less talkative as he feared their ridicule.

In order to tease him and make him mad they recalled the enthusiasm of the Carlist party in Spain for Germany. Castro even pretended that he was surprised that the Colonel was not a pro-German, the same as his political friends.

"I am where I belong," said Don Marcos with dignity. "I am a gentleman, and belong with decent people."

This was his supreme argument. Humanity was divided, according to him, into two classes—the decent and the indecent. It was the same with nations, and Germany was not to be counted among the decent.

As a patriot he suffered at seeing Spain outside the struggle, making an effort to remain unaware of what was going on in the rest of the world, putting its head under its wing, like certain long-legged birds that imagine they can avoid danger by not seeing it. Happily, his country did not figure among the indecent nations, nor was it any too decent either. It was allowing a chance for glory to escape, and this stirred the Colonel's wrath deeply.

For the last three months a fixed idea has been disturbing his happiest moments. The Allies had entered Jerusalem. What a great joy for an old Catholic soldier! But his joy afterwards made him smile bitterly. A Protestant nation freeing the sepulcher of Christ for the third time!...

"Imagine, Martinez, if only Spain had been with the decent nations! We have missed the chance of obtaining this glory, we who belong to the nation that has showed the greatest faith. Even I, in spite of my years, would have gone on the crusade. The Spanish entering Jerusalem victorious! What do you think of that?"

But the officer replied, with a vague smile, "Yes, perhaps." It was evident that the entry into Jerusalem and the empty tomb of Christ made very little difference to him. Don Marcos was somewhat disappointed with his hero, but he consoled himself with the thought that after all his own ideas belonged to the Middle Ages. Decidedly, he and Martinez were men of two different periods. "Youth, youth! You belong to the Spain of the future; I to the Spain" ... and so on.

Yes; the world was progressing in new directions. He, himself, a few days later, worried by the gloomy aspect of the war on the Western Front, had forgotten all about Jerusalem. The Germans, freed from the peril presented by Russia at their backs, after making peace with the Bolsheviki, were concentrating all their troops in France, in order to make a drive on Paris. The Allies, facing this overwhelming offensive, could count only on their regular forces and those which the recent intervention of the United States might bring.

In regard to aid from this latter source Don Marcos held a fixed and decided opinion. In the first place he had felt towards the United States a certain antipathy which dated back to the Cuban war. They might possess a large fleet, because anybody can buy ships if he has money enough, and the Americans were immensely rich: but how about an army? Toledo believed only in armies belonging to monarchies, with the exception of that of France, since in the latter country the glory of military tradition was attached to the history of the first Republic.

At the beginning of the war, he had even been irritated by the importance which every one had given President Wilson. Both sides had turned to him, appealing to his judgment, and protesting against the barbarities of the respective adversary. Even Wilhelm II cabled him frequently to make a show of sincerity for his frauds, as though he considered it important to gain Wilson's good opinion.

"Just as though this man were the center of the Universe! The President of a Republic that had only a few thousand soldiers, a professor, a dreamer!..."

He understood only heads of States in uniform, their breasts covered with decorations, with both hands on the hilt of a sword, and with an immense army before them, ready to fight in obedience to orders. And this gentleman in a cut-away coat and stiff hat, with eyeglasses and a smile like that of a learned clergyman, was now the man on whom the eyes of half the world were focused with looks of hope, and he was the deciding power that some were anxious to win over and others were afraid of arguing with!

Atilio Castro laughed at Don Marcos. He was always out of sympathy with the Colonel's opinions, and seemed impressed by this new marvel in history.

"Times have changed since your day, Don Marcos. We are going to see something new. America, which a century ago was merely a European colony, will perhaps protect and save Europe now. In the meantime, we are witnessing the curious spectacle of a former University professor being the arbiter of the world. What would Napoleon say if he were to see this ninety-four years after his death?"

Toledo gloomily assented. Yes; his days had passed. Democracy, Republicanism, all these things that had made him smile, as though they were something transitory, ineffectual and out of date, were very powerful in the present world, and perhaps would finally take charge of directing its affairs. Even he felt their irresistible influence. When he saw how the President of the great American Republic protested against the torpedoing of defenseless ships, the crimes of the submarines, and finally declared war on the German Empire, Don Marcos affirmed, stammering out a confession:

"This man Wilson ... this Wilson is a decent sort of a fellow."

For him it was impossible to say more.

He approved of the man through instinctive worship of personal power, but refused to believe in the military strength of the United States. It was a land of liberty, according to him, where all considered themselves equals and this made it impossible to create a real army.

The Prince and Castro occasionally talked in his presence of the war of secession, the first war in which millions of men had taken part, applying, moreover, innumerable inventions, in which all the progress in modern armament found its source. Toledo listened, with a doubt inspired by distant events. This struggle had been among themselves: militia warfare; but to raise an army of millions of men in a country that did not have compulsory military service; to transport this army across the ocean with all the immense quantity of supplies and munitions, and to get them there, besides, in time to save Europe from the great danger.... Mere dreams! "What they call over there 'bluff'!"

Don Marcos clung to this word in order to maintain his incredulity. This race is accustomed to accomplishing tremendous things; Americans conceive of everything on a large scale: cities, buildings, industries, wealth; but afterwards they exaggerate considerably when they come to advertising and describing what they do. Everybody knew that, and the American military forces which were to crush German militarism and re-establish peace on earth, although well-intentioned, were nothing but one bluff more.

Castro approved of the Colonel's words for the first time, without any intention of making fun of him. The President had declared war, but the country did not seem disposed to follow him.

"They will probably send money, munitions, supplies, all the immense power of their wealth and production. But a big army? Where can they get one? How is an immense people accustomed to the volunteer system, and living amid the greatest prosperity, going to take up arms? What would they gain by doing so?"

But the Prince, who had often been over there, replied with an ambiguous gesture:

"Perhaps! But if they really want to enter the war, who knows! Anything might happen in that country, no matter how impossible it seems!"

The Colonel was gradually won over by the irrational enthusiasm of the general public. Since the beginning of the war, the masses, who believe in mysterious predictions and supernatural interventions, had always had some favorite people, some nation that it had been the fashion to regard as invincible and in which all hopes could be concentrated.

At the beginning it had been Russia, with its millions and millions of men, the Russian "steam roller" that had only to advance in order to crush Germany. Poor steam roller! When it had fallen to pieces, the fickle enthusiasm of the public had turned toward England. Now it was America, all the more miraculous and omnipotent because little known.

In all conversations one heard the name of an American, both at elegant teas and in humble cafés; the one American well known in Europe: Edison, the inventor. He would settle everything. Up to the present time he had remained out of sight and silent, but now that his country had entered the war they would see something miraculous. In a few hours, invisible and implacable powers would crush to bits the invading armies; the submarines would burst like shells under a sort of frozen light which would pursue them in the ocean depths; the aeroplanes that bombarded defenseless cities would be forced to descend, drawn by electric magnetism, as a bird is drawn toward the mouth of a boa constrictor. Edison, the wonder-worker, meant more to the popular imagination of Europe than all the soldiers and all the ships of his country.

And Toledo, who decorated his bedroom with pictures of Joffre and Foch, but believed at the same time that St. Genevieve, the patron saint of Paris, had intervened in the victory of the Marne, felt attracted by all the miracles of the American wizard, announced by every one as something sure. Science, being somewhat apart from religion, inspired in him a feeling of respect and fear. For this reason he believed blindly in its wonders, much as a zealot believes in the immense powers of the devil.

At other times his incredulity was renewed. The war could only be determined by troops. Up to that time the forces of both sides had been equal; but now Germany was bringing new divisions—those from the Eastern Front,—and was preparing the decisive blow. On the side of the Allies an equivalent or greater number of soldiers was lacking; they needed the last few drops which would fill the glass, cause it to overflow and tip the scales. America might do this. But their forces were arriving so slowly! The obstacles were so great! A few battalions of the regular American army had already marched through Paris. After that months went by without the constant tiny stream of reënforcements becoming a torrent.

Everywhere on the Riviera, Toledo observed wounded soldiers from various countries. Only from time to time was he able to distinguish a few American uniforms, worn by men of the Medical Corps, who did not seem to have much to do. The newspapers talked about forces from the United States that occupied a sector on the front, but they were so few!

"All that talk about a million or two million men before the end of the year is mere bluff," said the Colonel. "I know something about such things, and it is easier to build a skyscraper with a hundred stories than to transport a million soldiers from one hemisphere to the other. And how about the great drive that is beginning! And France is worn out, after four years of heroism that has drained her blood!"

Every day he walked up and down in the ante-room of the Casino, waiting impatiently for the big bulletins which were written out by hand in large letters and posted on the panels by the employees. In scanning the latest telegraphic dispatches he was looking only for the beginning of the offensive announced by the enemy. This menace had shaken his faith in the victory, and kept him in a state of constant worry. Oh! If only the Americans would come in time, and in enormous numbers.

He felt it his duty to lie unblushingly to the friends who surrounded him in the ante-room, asking his opinion as a soldier.

"We will triumph; and William will have to shoot himself."

The question of his shooting himself was the one thing that will be his end, in case of a defeat.

"I know the Kaiser very well," he continued. "He is only a Lieutenant, a Lieutenant that has grown old, keeping the cracked brain swagger of youth. But he has the sense of honor of an officer who, finding himself defeated, raises his revolver to his head. You will see that that will be his end, in case of a defeat."

"He writes verse, music, and paints pictures, giving his opinion on every matter, and making people accept it, like one of those young officers who on entering a drawing room of civilians monopolize attention with their insolence and conceit, emboldened by the silence of the guests, who are afraid of provoking a duel. He is the eternal twenty-two-year-old Lieutenant whose hair has grown gray under the imperial crown, whose head has been turned a bit by the constant triumphs of his personal vanity. But once Fate turns her back on him, he will act in the same decisive manner as an officer who has gambled away the funds entrusted to his care, or committed other crimes against his honor.

"Never fear; the Lieutenant will know how to act when the hour of adversity arises. He is a mad man, a vain comedian, but he has the sense of shame of a warrior. Let me repeat: He will shoot himself."

And in his imagination he could hear the Imperial revolver-shot.

What disgusted Don Marcos was not to be able to talk about this, nor about the danger of the offensive, when he was in Villa Sirena. The friends of the Prince lived like guests at a hotel. They never were all together except during the early morning hours. They rarely sat down together at table. Some power from the outside seemed to attract them away from the Villa, driving them toward Monte Carlo. Even the Prince often lunched or dined at the Hôtel de Paris, sending word at the last minute by telephone.

This domestic disorder was accepted by Toledo as providential.

The service had suffered an unavoidable decline through the departure of Estola and Pistola. One morning they appeared, stammering and filled with emotion, minus the dress suits which were too large for them. They were going away. They were to cross the frontier that very afternoon to appear at the Barracks. They had received orders from their Consul.

They did not seem filled with enthusiasm for their new profession; but Don Marcos, through a sense of professional duty, tried to buck them up with a bit of a speech. He, too, at their age, had gone off to war of his own accord. "Respect for your officers ... love them as you would your father ... for honor ... for the flag."

The appearance of the Prince cut short his harangue. The two boys kissed their master's hand as though they were taking leave of him for eternity, and in their confusion they did not know where to put the bank notes which were given them. Imagine Estola and Pistola converted into soldiers! Even these two boys were being driven along the road of death! And the whole thing seemed so extraordinary to Michael, so absurd, that while he felt sorry for them, he also felt like laughing.

Half an hour later he had forgotten all about them. The Colonel would manage to organize new service with women, now that owing to the war it was impossible to get other servants. Besides, he was bored at Villa Sirena, and living at Monte Carlo would be something of a novelty for him.

The idlers who promenaded around the "Camembert" frequently saw him enter the Casino with an absent-minded air, like a gambler who has just thought of a new combination. The crowd in the gambling room had also seen him approach the tables as though interested in the fluctuation of chance, but they waited in vain to see him place a bet, imagining that he would play nothing save enormous sums.

His eyes seemed to see in all directions, and no sooner did the Duchess de Delille leave her seat to go over to another table, than the Prince came forward to meet her, extended his hand and smiled youthfully.

They remained motionless in the spot where they greeted each other, gazing into each other's eyes, until, warned instinctively of prying glances behind their backs, they went and sat down on a divan in a corner, and continued their conversation there. Suddenly, a murmur from the crowd around a table would cause her out of professional curiosity to leave Lubimoff and to hasten thither.

Alicia would smile the proud bitter smile of a dethroned queen. During the preceding day people had talked of nothing save her. Her name had traveled as far as Nice and Menton. In the evenings, at the dinner hour, families who dwelt permanently in Monaco and who are forbidden to enter the Casino, asked for news of her luck. In the cafés and restaurants, her name resounded, mingled with those of the Generals who were directing the war. In front of the bulletins giving the latest news, people interrupted their comments on the coming offensive, asking one another, "How did the Duchess de Delille come out yesterday?" Afternoons, when she arrived at the Casino, sight-seers crowded about her to get a better view, and her friends greeted her, proudly kissing her hand. It was a silent ovation, consisting of glances and smiles, like that which greets the entry of a famous soprano on the stage which has witnessed her triumphs.

Her battle with the Casino lasted about two weeks; she won, lost, and won again. She began her "work" at three o'clock in the afternoon, and remained at it until midnight. The tea hour passed, then the dinner hour, without her being aware of it. When the gambling was closed she came away, leaning on Valeria's arm, greeting every one amiably, exhausted and victorious. Sometimes, like an invalid fed against her will, she accepted the sandwiches and a cup of tea which her companions brought her at the gambling table.

One night—a memorable one—she had won continuously up to the closing hour of the Casino. She counted the bank notes that the head employees had given her with a hard, enigmatic smile. There were four hundred of them, each of a thousand francs. They protruded from her hand bag and from Valeria's. Even her friend, "the General," was obliged to help her, by taking care of several packages of them.

"If they hadn't closed I would have broken the bank," she said with the vanity of a conqueror.

Clorinda accompanied her in the carriage as far as her house, repeating prudent advice: "Don't go on; keep the money. It is impossible to go any higher." Valeria, during the course of the evening, kept repeating the same words: "It is tempting God to keep on."

But Alicia refused to listen to her. Her inspiration was not exhausted. There still remained great things for her to do; and when the time came for her to stop, she would be aware of it sooner than the rest.

Michael had been present at this struggle, which had been annoying to him. Every afternoon, when he entered the Casino, he called himself names, as though he were doing something cowardly. Why did he come to witness the acts of that mad woman? She did not seem to be aware of his presence! At first a look, a smile, and during the remaining hours she had eyes for nothing save the gambling and the *croupiers*. In spite of this, the Prince kept coming regularly.

To excuse himself, he recalled certain words which the Duchess had said. The day following her first famous winning, she had arisen on seeing him enter the room, taken both his hands in hers to speak to him privately.

"You bring me good luck," she murmured in his ear. "I am sure that this is so. I have been winning since we became friends. Come, come all the time! Let me see you every time I raise my eyes."

She raised them, however, very, very seldom. She had other more urgent things to think of. But Michael, to quiet his angry conscience, told himself that he was there to keep his word. Besides, who knew but what she was telling the truth! The tendency to superstition, common to all gamblers, the Casino's surroundings and even Alicia's luck itself, had finally influenced the credulity of the Prince.

He tried to avenge himself for these long waits and her indifference by looking at her with scornful eyes.

"How ugly she looks!"

Yes, she was ugly, like all the women who gamble and seem to suffer at an ever increasing rate, the weight of years crushing out their youth under the stress of emotion. Every loss meant another year, every winning meant a look of tenseness which spoiled the regularity of their features. Michael took a certain joy in noting the wrinkles which fixed attention formed about her eyes. Her nose seemed to grow sharp, and two deep furrows drew down the corners of her mouth, giving her an expression of premature old age. All the little feminine attentions disappeared as the hours went by. Her hat tilted to one side; locks of hair made an effort to escape, as though disarranged by currents of human electricity darting among their roots. She seemed ten years older.

But a second voice within gave forth a different opinion. "Yes, she was very ugly, but so interesting!" Surely when she arose from the table she would be once more the same Alicia as ever.

One afternoon, on entering the Casino, he had a sense of something extraordinary happening. People were talking together, asking news, all of them hurrying toward the same table.

His friend Lewis passed him without stopping.

"It was bound to happen. She doesn't know how to play. I expected it."

A little farther on Spadoni came forward to greet him.

"She would never listen to me. She acts on her whims. She doesn't follow any system. She is done for."

All the gamblers were talking as though they were lamenting somebody's death; but it was a question of hypocritical compunction, inwardly they felt a sense of envious triumph on seeing at an end that absurd run of luck, which had embittered their evenings.

Lubimoff, thrusting his head between the shoulders of two onlookers, saw Alicia at the same time that she raised her eyes. Their glances met. She looked at him with dismay, as though lamenting, making him responsible for her misfortune. "Why did you abandon me?"

The Prince fled: it hurt him to see her with that humble look of rage, like that of a cornered sheep, bleating in pain and defending itself.

At nightfall he returned to the Casino. A few people were still talking about the Duchess, but in low tones, with sad gestures, as though referring to a dying person. The crowd had thinned about the table. He saw Alicia in the same place. Valeria stood behind her chair, with a sad face, while Doña Clorinda bent over her friend, talking in her ear. He guessed her words. She was pleading with her to come away: next day she would have better luck. But she did not seem to hear, and remained with her eyes fixed on the few five hundred and a thousand franc chips, which were all that remained. Suddenly she lost her patience, and turning her head she said one word, nothing more, something very strong, but nothing without precedent in that intimate friendship which was broken off at least once every week. Doña Clorinda immediately retorted, looking daggers, and went away, haughtily and disdainfully, while Valeria looked at the ceiling in despair.

Michael fled once more. He was frightened by the expression on Alicia's face and the nervous hostility in her voice, which he had not been able to hear, but which was easily guessed from the trembling of her lips. He wandered about the rooms for half an hour, listening at a distance to the words of those who were still talking about the Duchess. One afternoon had been sufficient to sweep away all that she had won in many successful days. Her misfortune was as extraordinary as her good luck had been. She had not won a single bet.

Suddenly he felt the contact of a nervous hand on his shoulder. He turned his eyes. It was Alicia, but with an eager gesture, and with an expression which was both bold and imploring.

"Have you any money?"

Her voice and the expression on her face were not unknown to Michael. Before the war, the Casino had been the scene of his most unexpected and dazzling conquests. Women who were very cold and treated him with visible antipathy, and women of well-known virtue whose very looks repelled all audacity, had approached him with an air of sudden decision, requesting a loan, and immediately asking point blank at what hour the Prince might offer them a cup of tea at Villa Sirena. He thought of the Colonel, who considered gambling the worst of women's enemies. It caused them to lose all sense of shame. In a few hours the standards built up during an entire lifetime were suddenly demolished. In order to go on gambling, they offered of their own free will what they had never thought of granting.

The Prince replied, with surprise, at this sudden request. He carried very little money on his person: he was not a gambler. How much did she want?

"Twenty thousand francs."

She mentioned the figure in the same manner as she might have said a hundred thousand or five thousand. It was the same to her at that moment. Besides, during the last few days she had lost all sense of values.

Michael replied with a laugh. Did she imagine, by any chance, that he came to the Casino with twenty thousand francs in his pocketbook, as though he were a money lender or a pawn broker?

"Ask for a loan," said the Duchess. "They will give you anything you ask for."

He went on laughing at this absurd proposition, but was won over immediately by the simplicity with which Alicia formulated her request.

"How about you? Why don't you ask for one?"

Oh, as for her!... In the midst of her proud triumph, she had forgotten to pay various debts contracted before her sudden burst of luck. At present it was useless to ask. It was a difficult moment for her; every one considered her ruined, and incapable of recouping.

"And they are mistaken, Michael; I feel the inspiration of luck. You shall see how I get on my feet again after a few days. It is my secret. If I tell it to you, fortune will abandon me. Do me this favor! Ask for the twenty thousand from that little old man over there who is looking at us. He can't refuse you; you are Prince Lubimoff. If you like we will form a partnership: I shall share half my winnings with you."

Michael kept on smiling, while inwardly he was scandalized by this proposition. Imagine the things in which this woman was trying to involve him! He, asking for money from a money lender in the Casino!

But, like certain invalids who do things most contrary to their will, no sooner did he leave Alicia with gestures of protest, than his legs mechanically took him in the direction of the divan where the old man with the short beard, and the badge of the Sacred Heart on his lapel, was squatting, with his hat in one hand and a silk cap on his bald head.

"I need twenty thousand francs."

The Prince seemed to be in doubt as he faced this little man, who had arisen, surprised and suspicious on seeing that he was talking with so lofty a personage. Was it really his own voice that he heard? Yes, it was his voice, but he felt a sensation of immense surprise, as though it were some one else who was talking. He felt a desire to withdraw without waiting for the gnome's reply; but the latter had already responded, stammering:

"Prince ... such an amount! I am a poor man. From time to time I do favors to distinguished people, two or three thousand francs ... but twenty thousand! Twenty thousand!"

He muttered this sum with a groan of torture, but meanwhile his shrewd eyes were penetrating Lubimoff like a probe. This look irritated Michael, causing him to take an interest in the operation as though his honor were at stake. Doubtless, the usurer was thinking about Russia, and the disaster of the revolution and of the impossibility of being paid this loan even though the great man were to offer all his fortune.

"You must know me," he said in an irritated tone. "I am Prince Lubimoff; I am the owner of Villa Sirena. I need twenty thousand francs; not a franc less. If you are unable...."

He was about to turn his back on him, but the dwarf humbly restrained him, considering useless on this occasion all the excuses and delays which he usually made his clients endure, like a slow torture. He slipped out between the groups of people, begging "His Highness" to wait an instant. Perhaps he did not have the entire sum with him, and was obliged to ask for aid from the Cashier of the Casino; perhaps he was going to secrete himself for a moment in the lavatories, to take bank notes from various hiding places in his clothes, even from his shoes.

Michael felt a discreet hand touch his own, thrusting between his fingers a roll of paper. The old man had returned without his seeing him come; bobbing up between two groups, small and sprightly, like an imp from a trap door on the stage.

"You know the Colonel? To-morrow he will interview you about the payment and the interest."

And the Prince turned his back without more words, leaving the usurer satisfied with his discourteous brevity. A great gentleman could not talk in any other way. He liked to have dealings with men of that sort.

Alicia, who had followed the scene from a distance, came forward to meet him, holding out her hands inconspicuously.

"Take it!" Michael's right hand thrust the bank notes forward so rudely that the offer was almost a blow.

His shame for what he had just done expressed itself in a confusion of protests.

"Women! Of all the fool things I have ever done!"

But Alicia, with the bank notes in her hand, was already thinking of nothing but the tables.

"You will see great things. You know we have formed a partnership: you get half."

Mastered once more by the invisible demon that was singing numbers and colors in her ear, she went away without thanking him.

He also left. He was afraid of meeting the money lender again, and having him bow familiarly; he imagined the entire crowd in the rooms had followed attentively his interview with the old man and had smiled when he received the money.

He left the Casino. He would never come back again: he swore it!

Castro, whom he had seen from a distance gambling at one of the tables, returned to Villa Sirena at the dinner hour. He was in a bad humor; but he forgot his own misfortune long enough to console himself by relating Alicia's mishaps:

"After losing everything in *trente et quarante*, she appeared at a last minute with more money: a roll of thousand franc notes. And she, who never felt any special inclination for roulette, began to play the wheel. And how she played! At first she won a few long shots, two or three; but after that nothing: she kept losing and losing! She left everything on the table. I did not see her go out, but they told me she looked like a corpse, leaning on Valeria's arm. They say she suffers from heart trouble. All I say is: it isn't every one who pretends to be a gambler that is one; you need a strong constitution. The 'General' doesn't play so much, but she is cooler and doesn't lose her head."

Michael slept badly. He was angry with Alicia. Instead of lamenting her misfortune he considered it logical. Imagine a woman trying to make money! Women can only get it from men's hands, and it is useless for them to try and get it for themselves, even by appealing to gambling. Gambling also is an enterprise for men.

In the mental twilight when one is half asleep and half awake, the Prince, lying on his bed, remembered a scene from his happier days, when his yacht was anchored in the harbor of Monaco. It was one night when he was coming from a banquet in the Hôtel de Paris. He was slightly intoxicated and was leaning in a sort of a mental haze on the arms of two pretty women, who, smiling and unsuccessful, were competing to see which one would get him. Behind him, like a retinue, came his friends, his brilliant parasites, and various women guests, his entire court. They had entered the Casino. He was not a gambler; it bored him to sit motionless at a table; he considered it childish to get interested in the whirling of a little ball of bone, or the combinations of little colored cards. There were so many more interesting pleasures in life! But that night, proud of his power, he felt a desire to fight a battle with fortune. Fortune is a woman, and he was determined to conquer it by the power of wealth, as he had conquered many another woman. The rich finally defeat even destiny with all its mysteries. He placed in front of him an enormous quantity of money to begin the struggle, and fortune refused it; or rather, began to give him money of her own, with scornful prodigality. The multi-millionaire wanted to lose and he could not. He varied his game capriciously, committed voluntary errors, and success always came forward to meet him. Finally he grew tired. It was before the war, and instead of with bone chips representing a hundred francs, they played with handsome gold coins of the same value. In front of him he had numerous and dazzling columns of this metal; and packages of bank notes.

"Who wants money?"

He began to fling it about in an enchanting rain. All except the most aristocratic women came running, tense and pale, swarming around the table, struggling for a single *louis*. They shoved one another, rolled on the carpet, bruising each other with hands and feet, to gain a single drop of this golden manna. Some of them struck and scratched each other, while their right hands clutched the same thousand franc note, tearing it. Hats rolled about on the ground; the hair of some of the women fell down their back, or was scattered in a cloud of false curls.

"Me, Prince! Me!"

And with clutching fingers they danced about him, in a body, as though possessed.

"Who wants money?"

The head employees intervened, angry but smiling, seeing who was the cause of the disturbance. "Your Highness, please! You are interrupting the play! Such a thing has never happened here before." But he continued flinging his money, until he had exhausted his winnings—more than sixty thousand francs—and the games went on again, with more players than before. Every one who had gathered something from the floor or caught it in the air, ran to risk it on a card or a number.

Michael dwelt on this memory which was like a triumph. He could repeat it any time he pleased; he was sure of it. He recognized that in the end every gambler finally loses, and he did not consider himself an exception to this rule. But his will dominated fortune at first, and—by withdrawing in time before the latter had a chance to recoup with the perverse cunning of an untamable female!...

The Prince finally went to sleep thinking of Alicia.

"Poor woman! She doesn't know how to play; Lewis is right: She doesn't know how.... How should a beautiful woman know, who has never thought about anything save her own person! I must help her. I am a man. Perhaps to-morrow ... to-morrow!" ...

The following day, at the breakfast hour, Don Marcos had a great surprise which worried him considerably. The Prince, who never bothered about money, allowing his "Chamberlain" to make negotiations directly with his Paris manager for the house expenses, asked him what amount he had at his disposal.

The Colonel made a mental calculation. He did not think he kept just then any more than fifteen thousand francs. He was expecting a check from the agent.

"Give it to me," Lubimoff commanded.

And immediately, as though suddenly recalling something, he calmly mentioned the debt he had contracted the afternoon before. Toledo was thoughtful for a moment on learning that he was to come to an understanding with the old money lender to return the twenty thousand francs and the payment of extraordinary interest, which might double in a few days. He recalled the luncheon during which the Prince had proposed their present solitary life. Where were the ferocious "enemies of women" now? For the Colonel suspected that behind these squanderings of the Prince and this sudden passion for gambling, lay the influence of some woman. And he who never dared stake more than a few odd coins from time to time, thinking of the enormous sums entrusted to his loyalty, was deeply worried.

While Don Marcos was on his way to the bank where the house money was deposited, the Prince walked about in the neighborhood of the Casino, waiting impatiently for the rooms to open. In the morning the crowd was very slight and very few tables were operating. Only the most desperate gamblers, after spending a sleepless night, anxious to try their new combinations as soon as possible, and sickly people who hoped to find a good seat vacant, came at that early hour.

Impatiently Lubimoff entered the anteroom, after secretly thrusting into a pocket a roll of bills which Toledo handed to him. The employees of the first shift were arriving slowly, like clerks entering an office. The cleaning women and porters in shirt sleeves had just swept up the sawdust scattered on the floor. They all looked at him from the corner of their eyes, pointing him out to one another by discreet nudges. Imagine the Prince there at that hour, when people of his station in life were still in bed! Instinctively they looked all about expecting to see some coyly dressed lady waiting to meet him unobserved at that early hour. His well-known reputation did not permit them to imagine anything save a rendezvous.

It was ten o'clock. The curtains were opened, and Michael entered brushing against the first gamblers to arrive, modest timid folk. He felt the same nervousness, impatience, and dull anger that he felt on the mornings when he had fought duels. He walked with a heavy step; his hands kept contracting as though ready to strangle the empty air. At the same time he felt the same proud confidence of a marksman, sure of hitting the bull's-eye. He defied Lady Fortune before facing her, the wench whom he had once conquered. "By God! She would see she was dealing with a man this time!"

He jerked a chair away from a hand already stretched out to take it, and sat down at a roulette table, between two dirty, badly dressed old women, who looked like witches. The employees exchanged looks of amazement, eyeing one another discreetly. The Prince betting, and at such an hour!...

"Faites vos jeux!"

The game began. Michael had no particular combination and had not thought of any. His eyes wandered over the thirty-six numbers, but only for an instant.

"That's the one," he thought. And he placed all that he could, nine *louis*, the maximum, on thirteen.

The ball spun about the mahogany border, and when it finally came to rest was greeted with a murmur of amazement. "Number thirteen."

A few thousand franc notes thrust in his direction by the rake of the *croupier* remained in front of the Prince, who sat there impassively, retaining a hard willful look. He knew it; he was sure he was making no mistake. Thirteen once more.

People looked in amazement. What folly to bet twice on the same number! But when thirteen won a second time and the Prince was paid the maximum again, a murmur from the crowd applauded the victor. Onlookers came hurrying, leaving the other tables devoid of spectators. This was going to be as famous a morning in the Casino, in spite of the smallness of the crowd, as the most celebrated afternoon and evening, when wealthy players fought with luck.

Lubimoff changed his number. It was absurd to go on with thirteen. And he placed nine *louis* on seventeen. The ball spun around. It was thirteen once more. He lost.

His look became harder and more aggressive. Dame Fortune was beginning to laugh at him for his lack of will power. A conqueror should feel no vacillation; it was his fault, for having given up his number. Men like him should go ahead, and impose their will, or perish without abandoning their first attitude. Thirteen as before!... And it was seventeen that won.

For a moment he thought the ground was falling away beneath his feet; he seemed to be floating in air, surrounded by mysterious forces that were weakening and finally breaking his will. He passed his hand over his forehead, as though trying to brush away, far away, his momentary weakness.

"The she-devil," he exclaimed, mentally, insulting Fortune, sure once more that he was going to enslave her.

And he went on playing.

At three o'clock in the afternoon he came out of the Hôtel de Paris. He had lunched alone, without paying any attention to the glances he had received from other tables, avoiding friendly greetings that might have started a conversation.

In his mouth was a fat cigar, and his legs, although perfectly steady, inwardly felt a certain voluptuous sensation. The food had been bad; he had scarcely touched the dishes; on the other hand he had drunk a bottle of famous Burgundy, and several glasses of cordials immediately after finishing two cups of coffee.

From the hotel steps he gave a glance of destructive hate at the square, the Casino and the Gardens. He thought with satisfaction of the possibility of a cruiser belonging to one of the nations which were carrying on war on the seas of Europe anchoring in front of that gingerbread house, and firing a few shells at it. What a wonderful sight! Then, in his imagination, he had a landing party with their machine guns disembark, to take prisoner all the people who were filling the square, men, women and even children. The world would lose nothing by it. What a city of corruption! Why the devil had his mother taken it into her head to buy the promontory of Villa Sirena, obliging him to live near this den of thieves? He even upbraided the dead Princess, with the stern uncompromising morality of every gambler who has just found himself tricked.

As he glanced over the gay, well-dressed crowd that he was condemning to slavery, he saw Alicia, alone and on foot, on the edge of the sidewalk around the "Camembert," looking at the Casino.

"Are you going in?" he said, approaching her.

The Duchess became indignant, as though he was proposing something humiliating, something that she had never done before. She enter the Casino?

"It's a rotten den, and the employees are rotters, and those who gamble—rotters too."

It was all rotten! After saying this they took each other's hands as though they had just suddenly recognized each other.

When Michael, still harping on his kind wishes, told her about the bombardment and landing party with machine guns that he had been enjoying in his imagination, the Duchess almost applauded. As far as she was concerned, she would be very glad if they destroyed everything, if they even took the sovereign Prince himself prisoner, and if, into the bargain, the invaders returned the money she had lost, she could want nothing better.

Suddenly, as if these charitable fantasies of Lubimoff told her of something, her eyes scrutinized him closely, much like those of a suspicious invalid who is able to recognize his own symptoms in those of a neighbor.

"You have been gambling."

Michael nodded sadly.

"And you have lost," she continued; "that goes without saying: I don't need to ask you. You, gambling!"

But her surprise was short.

"You have been gambling for my sake: I have guessed it. You said to yourself: 'I'm going to win what that crazy woman loses; men know more than women.' Oh, my poor boy, my poor boy, how grateful I am for your friendly intention!... How much was it?"

On hearing the sum she gave him a look of compassion, but smiled immediately, as though the comradeship of misfortune made her own losses easier to bear.

They remained silent for a moment. Then she explained her presence on the square. The night before she had sworn she would never again come near the Casino, but habit...!

"I'm alone. Valeria went away immediately after lunch. She goes around like a crazy woman on account of that scientist you have at your house. They must have made an engagement somewhere. All she talks about is Spain, because the women there marry without dowries. As for 'the General,' don't talk to me about her: I don't want to hear her name; she is dead—dead forever, as far as I am concerned! And I'm so bored all by myself; I think of things that make me weep; I go out, and my feet take me here without my realizing it."

Then she added with a graceful entreaty:

"Take me somewhere, wherever you feel like. Let's go a long ways from here. Where can we go?"

The Prince showed the same hesitation. They continually moved in the same circle, from their houses to the center of Monte Carlo, the Casino, and seemed lost if they tried to go any farther. The war had done away with private automobiles; to go on an excursion it was necessary to get a permit in advance. One could find nothing save carriages drawn by feeble horses, rejected by the Army.

"Suppose we go to Monaco?" Alicia proposed.

Monaco was in sight, on the other side of the harbor; a street car ran from there to Monte Carlo every twenty minutes, and nevertheless she made this proposal as though speaking of some remote country.

They had both spent some twenty years there, continually seeing the rock which bore on its crest the old city of the Princes; but, as though those places were painted on a back drop in the theater, it had never entered their heads to go that far. Alicia vaguely recalled a visit to the Palace of the Sovereign and another to the Museum of Oceanography, without being able to formulate her impressions.

Lubimoff also from his automobile had seen the garden, the old houses, and a large square, the one day that he had visited the Prince of Monaco in his old castle.

They decided on the trip with the glee of school children, and when the Duchess went to call a cab, Michael showed a certain hesitation as he searched through various pockets.

He had no money. He had dropped it all in the roulette, absolutely all. At the hotel he had asked them to charge his lunch, handing over his last few francs to the waiter as a tip.

Alicia greeted his worried look with bursts of laughter. Lubimoff unable to pay a cabman! Monte Carlo was the only place where you could see things like that.

"Poor boy, I'll pay. You can deduct it from the twenty thousand I owe you. No; not that, no; it will be a gift. You have given women so much money, let me be the first to pay a bill for you. What a luxury! I 'keeping' Prince Lubimoff."

They had gotten into the carriage, which was beginning to descend the slope toward La Condamine harbor.

"How people stare at us!" said Alicia. "They will think I am carrying you off by force. The Duchess de Delille, ruined, seduces a multi-millionaire Prince to make him her lover and get money out of him ... and they don't know that I am the one that is paying! Come laugh a little. Are you annoyed that I should pay? Don't you think it is amusing?"

She talked of her lack of foresight and her folly with a certain pride, as though it were something which placed her above people of regular habits. The evening before she had been afraid of not having enough money left to buy food for the next day. But Valeria had spent the morning making valuable discoveries in the closets! Bank notes lost among the clothes, Casino chips forgotten among the books, and even a thousand franc bill used to wrap up an old cake of soap.

She suddenly stopped enumerating these finds.

"Look! Look!"

They were beside the harbor. She pointed out a lady who was walking along the shore, among the tall rose-bay bushes trimmed in the shape of trees. It was Clorinda. A gentleman who seemed to be waiting for her rose from the bench, and came forward to meet her. They both recognized Atilio Castro, and observed how he and "the General" greeted each other, and how they continued their promenade together, so absorbed in mutual contemplation, that they did not notice the carriage.

Michael smiled slightly. Himself there, beside Alicia, who was causing him to commit every sort of folly; and the other man waiting there for Doña Clorinda's arrival with all the emotion of a youth! Poor enemies of women!

"Don't talk to me about her!" Alicia exclaimed in a rage, in spite of the fact that her companion had said nothing. "I hate her.... Think of poor Martinez forgotten. She quarrels with me to get him, takes him away from me, and then comes in search of Castro, while the other unhappy fellow is wandering about Monte Carlo. What a woman! She has done me so much harm! She is to blame for everything."

And as the Prince looked at her with a questioning air she explained her complaints with a tone of conviction. Her losses which had been so rapid and so complete, could not be explained logically. She had won for two weeks, and in a few hours had lost everything. How could that be? The evening before, as she was leaving the Casino, a respectable friend, an Italian Marchioness, a former dancer, who was very wise in matters of luck, and who had been gambling for the last thirty years in Monte Carlo, had revealed to her the cruel truth: "Duchess, there is some one who hates you; an envious friend who comes to your house and has cast an evil spell over you. That is the only way to explain what has happened. You must drive out the evil luck, turning it back on the person who gave it to you.

"So you see it couldn't be clearer: an envious friend who comes to my house—Clorinda; it can't be any one else. And no later than to-morrow I am going to drive away my bad luck, in the way the Marchioness recommended. Other gamblers follow her advice and are very successful."

It was the Three Wise Kings who possessed the power of undoing evil spells. It was necessary to cleanse away the rooms which "the General" had entered by burning in a small pan gold, incense and myrrh, the three presents of the monarchs who had come from afar. She had no gold; it was inaccessible on account of the war; but, according to the Witch-Marchioness, it would be the same if she burned wheat.

"And at the same time recite a prayer in Italian, a very pretty entreaty to the Three Kings, that sounds like a song, that says—that says—"

Unable to remember it, she opened her hand bag. She kept the prayer in her coin purse, written in lead pencil on one of the cards furnished by the Casino to keep track of bets. Michael looked at the contents of the purse with the curiosity always inspired by every object belonging to a woman who interests a man. Beside the mussed handkerchief he saw a little leather case, and hanging from it a gambler's fetish, a hand with the index and little finger extended like horns, to ward off bad luck. But beside the hand there hung another golden fetish, of such an unexpected, unheard of form, that Michael refused to believe what had passed before his eyes like a rapid vision.

Alicia drew back, pushing aside his inquisitive hand: "No, no!" And she closed the purse so rapidly that the silver rings almost caught his fingers. Blushing and smiling, she held him off, giving him a sly look, and at the same time shrinking like a naughty child.

"It is a gift from the Marchioness. The best she knows, to bring luck. Mine has gone. That is all you need to know. How curious you are!"

And while she pretended to be somewhat angry in order to avoid new explanations, Michael recalled the Rosary of Satan belonging to his friend Lewis and its strange ornaments.

The carriage began to ascend the slope towards Monaco. The ships and the harbor seemed to sink with each turn of the wheel. Verdant shades cooled the road, within sight of the luminous sea and of the yellowish mountains, that were taking on a rosy color under the afternoon sun.

Michael explained to his companion the strange features of the promontory that serves as a base for old Monaco. On the Southern part, among the rocks covered with century plants and prickly pear, the vegetation of the warm countries becomes acclimated with a facility that if one takes the latitude into account is truly extraordinary. On his visit to the palace of the Prince he had found in the warmer moats of the fortress, which are like natural hothouses, the same damp sticky heat that one finds in the forests of Equador, with their Brazilian palm trees that rise many yards in quest of light. On the other hand, without leaving the rock, one finds on the northern side, where there is little sunlight, ferns from the cold countries, vegetation from the Vosges Mountains, which got here no one knows how, and took root beside the Mediterranean.

Alicia, not wishing to seem less informed, talked about the San Martino Gardens. She had not seen them, but she imagined that they were between the Museum of Oceanography and the Cathedral. Valeria had not been able to talk about anything else during the last few weeks, and described them as though they were the most interesting gardens in the world. She had seen them in good company, and this had exerted a strong influence on her powers of vision. It was doubtless Novoa who had revealed to her this Paradise.

"Supposing we were to meet them!" said Alicia, laughingly.

The carriage passed between two little towers, capped with tiles, that marked the entrance to the walled enclosure of Monaco. The harbor lay far below, with its boats that seemed so tiny. On the other side of the sheet of water shone the cupolas of the Casino and the many Monte Carlo hotels, with their multi-colored façades, the windows of their balconies and belvideres. It was impossible to make out the people. Automobiles were gliding along like tiny insects on the slope that descended to La Condamine.

They followed the asphalt avenue, between two narrow dense gardens, leading to the Museum of Oceanography.

"Look at them!" said Alicia with an expression of triumph, as she nudged the Prince at the same time.

When the latter turned his head all he could see were two indistinct forms hiding in a side path.

"It is they, you may be sure," continued the Duchess, laughing. "They were walking in the middle of the avenue. Valeria is very quick; she turned when she heard the sound of a carriage, and recognized me immediately. She hurried the scientist away as though she were dragging him along."

She stopped laughing, and her features took on a look of sad solemnity.

"Happy pair! What dreams! We have all gone through the same thing. The worst of it is that we want to keep on going in quest of something further, when we ought to remain satisfied with what we have."

The Prince nodded, repeating briefly:

"Happy pair!"

His voice sounded like a *requiem*. These successive meetings had made him think of the end of the community of which he was the ridiculous head. First of all, Castro; then, Novoa. Even the Colonel at that very moment was walking up and down in front of a millinery shop waiting for the gardener's little girl. Spadoni was the only one left, but his loyalty counted for little. As far as the latter was concerned, nothing feminine existed except the roulette wheel.

The carriage stopped beyond the Museum of Oceanography, where the San Martino Garden began. Alicia paid the driver.

"We must economize," she said gravely. "We shall return on foot."

They followed a network of winding paths, ascending and descending the gulleys of the slope. The tiny plateaus had been converted into stone lookouts, from which the view embraced an immense expanse of sea. Occasionally at dawn one could distinguish the distant profile of the Mountain of Corsica. Since the gardens were far above the Mediterranean, the horizon line was so high that one seemed to be looking upwards when viewing it. The pine trees rose in slender black colonnades and between the thin trunks one could see the dark Mediterranean suspended like a curtain. Only the murmuring tops of the sharp trees emerged in the diaphanous azure of the skies. Below the vegetation was composed of wild hardy plants breathing out strong odors, plants that were unaffected by the salty exhalations of the sea; prickly pear, lobes of which were surmounted by red fruit; small century plants whose twisted blades intertwined like tentacles of green pulp.

Alicia admired this garden. According to her it was a maritime garden, in harmony with the nearby Museum and the landscape. The trunks of the trees seemed like the masts of ships; the plants amassed at their feet had the radiating enveloping form of the monsters of the ocean depths. Other vegetation of a foreign origin recalled images of warm countries, and of distant parts, filled with odors and swarming with crowds of yellow and copper-colored men. Through the straight trunks of the trees, one could see five schooners, motionless on the horizon with their sails hanging.

A train of smoke followed the evolutions of a slim torpedo boat steaming around the white, timid flock, like a watch dog.

Looking over the stone balconies one could peer into the ocean to enormous depths. The bold red cliff buried itself vertically in the waters darkened by shadows, or took shelter behind landslides of rocks continually surrounded by foam. On one side Cap-Martin advanced, repelling the onrush of the waves, circles of white caps that constantly succeeded one another, rising from the azure meadows;

still farther on lay the Italian coast, showing rose-colored through the melancholy afternoon mist, and on the opposite side lay Cap-d'Ail and Cap-Ferrat, above whose backs embossed with the green of the seas, and dotted with the white of the villas—the golden winding sheet, which was to enshroud the dying sun, began to rise.

"Beautiful! very beautiful!"

Alicia displayed a girlish delight. They sat down in view of the sea, slowly drinking in the vibrant calm, in which mingled the trembling of the pines, the deep churning of the invisible foam, the breath of the azure plain, and the rustling of the earth, grazed by rosaries of ants, by chains of caterpillars, and by the busy work of the black beetle, and at the same time deeply stirred by the awakening of the roots.

From time to time human footsteps sounded on the sand of the winding path. They came from invalids or convalescents who were passing through the gardens on coming out of the Museum; people from Monaco returning to their homes after having taken the sun on a bench; fat housewives who kept their knitting in a bag; old men leaning on canes, who perhaps had never gone to sea, but who looked like old Genoese sailors. Also a few pairs of lovers passed slowly. They would appear at a turning of the path with their arms around each other's waists, silent, looking at each other, and observing that there was another couple on the bench, they unclasped, and suddenly pretended to be carrying on a conversation. As soon as possible they gained the nearest turning to resume their tender entwining, not without having first greeted the Prince and the Duchess with a smile, as though they saw in them another pair of lovers.

"And just to think that we have never come here before!" said Alicia. "You, at least, own magnificent gardens; but I, living in a villa which is simply a house with a few trees around it and has no other views than the opposite building, have been so stupid to have spent the afternoon in the Casino, dark and shut in like a wine cellar. How awful!"

She shuddered on thinking of the Casino. It seemed impossible to her now that during the very hours when this garden lay stretched out beside the sea, with its luminous sylvan splendor she should have been able to live in that half light of artificial illumination or in that nasty, unwholesome atmosphere.

"There are many beautiful things in the world," she continued, "for which money is not necessary. Just to think that if we had not lost we would not be here! It is almost better to be poor."

Michael laughed at her earnestness. No; it was not pleasant to be poor; but she was right in saying that to enjoy many beautiful things it was not necessary to have money.

"We, ourselves," she added, after a long pause, "have known each other only since we lost our wealth. Who knows but what if we had been born poor we would have understood each other better when we were young! I have often thought so."

Of course! And since Michael had been there on the bench, beside her, he had been thinking the same thing. Alicia's joy at the splendor of the afternoon, her enthusiasm on seeing this rustic garden overlooking the sea, far from certain people, without whom she formerly would have thought life intolerable, far from gambling, which was the only remedy to fill the emptiness of her life—all this flattered and delighted the Prince, like a discovery in harmony with his desires. At present he saw her in a very different light from that in which he had imagined her in former years. And he, too, surely seemed like a very different person in her eyes than he had in the past. Before, they had been separated by an enormous wall, wealth, that gave rise to pride and eagerness for domineering.

He felt the need of going on talking. Something was surging within him, causing words to rise to his lips in an irresistible tide.

A voice within seemed to warn him. "You are going to commit some monstrous folly. Look out!—You are on the road to mixing up your life again—" It was the old Lubimoff in him that was talking; the Lubimoff who had recently arrived from Paris to take refuge in his Ark, far from the vain longings that make up the happiness of the majority of men; it was the stern chief of the "enemies of women."

But the harsh, mournful inner voice awoke no echoing response. The Prince despised this phantom that still remained within him, lamenting over the ruins it found there.

Up to that moment he had been inhaling with delight the perfume of that woman. It seemed to mingle with the perfumes of the afternoon, communicating its essence to all Nature. He saw the sky, the sea, the trees, and everything in fact in terms of her, as though she filled all space.

He, too, had made a discovery that afternoon. He thought with horror of the loneliness of Villa Sirena, just as she had been thinking of the Casino. These gardens which every one might enjoy, seemed to him more beautiful than those he owned, and which every one envied him. How had he ever been able to walk around his villa, through its magnificent and lonely avenues, when there existed in the world the marvelous pleasures of sitting on a public bench beside a woman, or walking close to her, with an arm around her waist, like those poor soldiers and sailors?

Once more he heard the voice: "Fine, Prince! In love like a school-boy when you're over forty. Go on with your foolishness, if it amuses you!... What would the other 'enemies of women' say?"

But he refused to listen to this last protest from the other hostile and forgotten half of his personality.

"Our life has been a mistake," he said aloud, with a certain vehemence, in order not to show his emotion. "You, too, must realize that I think the same—that I acknowledge my error—because I—because I, for some time—have been in love with you!... Well, I have said it! Now laugh if you like."

She did not feel like laughing. She gave a slight exclamation, looked at him for a moment, and turned away as though avoiding the questioning glance in his eyes. She had had a presentiment that this was coming, sooner or later, but her breath was taken away on actually hearing it!

There was a long silence.

"What is your answer?" the famous Prince Lubimoff, adored by so many women, finally asked with timidity.

Alicia looked at him again.

"Aren't you joking? Isn't it a mere whim inspired by the beauty of this afternoon—so poetic?"

Michael protested with a gesture. How could she take as a caprice the grave decision that he had finally reached after so long and difficult a debate within, the way one evolves a truly great decision!

"If I were like most women, I would reply: 'How many women have you said the same thing to?' But such a question is stupid. One may have said: 'I love you,' to a woman, in all sincerity and some time later repeat the same words to another, with still more sincerity. I'm not going to ask you to how many you have said what you have just said to me. Perhaps you never said it to any one before. To fulfill your desires it wasn't necessary to exert yourself, playing a comedy of deep affection: they sought you passionately; like a Sultan, you needed only to throw your handkerchief as a signal.... But when it comes to me! Remember, Michael: as children we hated each other; later on, when I was willing, you were not. And now we are beginning to grow old! Now that I possess only the remains of what I once was and haven't the same freedom any longer, since I have—you know what...! It is absurd, and that is why I laugh. No: never!"

It was the Prince's turn to speak. They had hated each other, that was true, and now he considered that hate as fortunate. What a misfortune for both of them if marriage had united their two enormous fortunes and their two prides, more enormous still.

"We would have separated a week later; perhaps the same day," Michael continued. "I even suspect that I would have beaten you."

"And I you," said the Duchess. "No place would have been large enough to hold us both. It would have been necessary for one of us to give in to the other. And neither one of us would have thought of making such a sacrifice."

"I might say the same," he continued, "about the night when we dined together. I am glad of my absurd and ridiculous conduct on that occasion. Had I given in, there would be an invincible barrier between us now; we would never have met again, and we would not be here saying to each other what we are saying now."

She assented.

"We would not be here, that is certain. You would have kept a frightful memory of me; I know very well what I was like then. Neither would I have sought you out, even though my life depended on it. Thanks to your flight that evening we can still be friends, eternal friends, brothers if you like; but why do you talk to me about love? It doesn't belong to our age. The time has passed. What do you see in me now that you did not when I was young?"

"I see your misfortune."

The voice of the Prince sounded grave and deeply sincere as he said this.

He had reflected for a long time, before answering, when he had asked himself the same question as Alicia's. He was sure that he had begun to love her the day when she had come to Villa Sirena to confess her ruin and to ask him to forget her debt to him. Poor Duchess de Delille, accustomed to spending millions each year, the proprietress of precious mines, and having to live by gambling like an adventuress!... Afterwards, beside her bed, seeing her tears, and listening to the great secret of her life, the hidden motherhood that had made her weep, he had become definitely conscious of this love. During the last few days, seeing her victorious in the Casino, his love had been clouded; he cared less for her. Later, finding her ruined and sick with sadness, his affection was renewed; and to help her, he had even become a gambler, he, who was incapable of doing this even for his own salvation!

"You can't understand me; you are a woman. Often in my life, other women have said to me, after some unexplainable act of theirs: 'It is useless to try: men can never succeed in understanding us.' I say the same: A woman cannot understand a man either. I love you now because you inspire pity in me, and pity leads to tenderness and tenderness is true love, love such as I have never felt before. Each one loves in his own way. The majority of women need to feel proud when they love; the person they love must arouse the envy of others through being brave, handsome, wealthy or talented. Man almost always loves through pity, through tender compassion inspired by woman. He never feels more in love than when a woman's head reclines against his breast with the abandon of weakness; and when his hand is buried in her hair, it finds a tiny delicate head—smaller than he had ever imagined—a head that is filled with divine words, irresistible charms, and noble impulses, but which rarely has that force of thought which makes man superior to her. Her adorable arms are not strong enough to protect her. And man, seeing her so lovely and so weak, feels his passion increase with pity and the desire to protect her."

"No," she said. "Woman, too, knows the meaning of compassionate love. A man for whom she feels indifference suddenly interests her, when she sees that he is unhappy; and a woman, who hates her lover one day, returns to him the next, when she feels that he is in danger. She never speaks more tenderly than when she says, 'My poor little boy!'"

The Prince assented with a gesture. That was all very well. But immediately he returned to the subject which interested him.

"To-day we both know misfortune; I, as well as you, since I have lost what distinguished me from other men, and which I shall never perhaps recover. But your situation is still worse; you are a woman, you are poorer, and I feel attracted to you and tell you what I never would have told you if, shut up within our own pride, we had both kept our former places in the world."

He went on talking in a soothing tone almost in her ear, coming closer to her, and breathing the perfume of the fur boa around her neck, which seemed to have concentrated in itself the perfume of her whole body.

He repeated what he had thought in the nights when he had struggled with his former dread; thoughts that he had vigorously resumed shortly before, as he was sitting silently by her side in the carriage. He talked of the future. They might still be happy; the love he offered her was of the quiet, lasting kind; an autumnal love, a love that would be for all time, with no dramatic complications, peaceful, tranquil, sweetly uneventful, like the long winter evenings beside a fire.

She laughed with a pained expression.

"You forget who I am; you talk as though the past did not exist, as though you were not yourself and as though all the stories that weigh against my name did not exist. If some one else were to make me this proposal, who knows!... I am weary and the thought of a quiet future attracts me. But you!... With you it would be impossible: It would end disastrously. I prefer that we be friends, without any thought of love. It is safer and more lasting."

On seeing his look of dismay, Alicia went on talking. She was not afraid of living with him because of what people might say. It is true that she had a husband, who now in the throes of a senile passion would refuse to grant her a divorce. But what did she care for an obstacle like that, or for what people would say about it!... She had done more daring things in her life!

"It is simply that I do not want to. Don't ask me why: I could not explain it to you; or I should say, you would not understand me. I repeat what other women have said to you: 'You are a man, and cannot understand women.' No, I don't want to. I shall speak more plainly: Another man might succeed in interesting me—I don't know. We are so weak! Our wills play us such strange tricks! But with you, no.... We know each other too well: It is impossible."

Michael spoke in a tone of sadness and chagrin.

"I don't interest you: that is easy to see."

Alicia once more laughed heartily and with one of her hands she tapped those of the Prince which were clasped together.

"Silly! Do you really think I don't care for you at all. If I felt indifferent toward you would I have sought you formerly, and would I be here with you now?"

He was disconcerted. "Well, then?" And he made an effort to discover what obstacle stood in the way of his desire. If it was on account of what had happened in her past life, he had forgotten it. He, Prince Lubimoff, had had many affairs that it was better not to recall.

"Let's not talk about the past at all. You are a different woman. I know what your life has been during the last few years; besides, the other morning you told me what you have been since your son began to live by your side. I take you from the time you recognized the seriousness of life, on seeing beside you a man formed from your own flesh and blood. I have forgotten the Venus of former years, the Helen of the 'old man on the wall.' I desire you, seeing you as you are to-day, the Venus Sorrowful, weeping, suffering and in need of consolation and care that will sustain and sweeten life."

She stopped smiling. Her lips trembled with a pitiful expression of gratitude; her eyes were moist with tears.

"No," she said in a humble voice. "It is impossible for that very reason. My son! How my son has changed me! I know what all this love means. We are not two children to be deceived by dreams of purity and talk about the soul and heaven, while our bodies are drawn together by a natural impulse. If I accept your love, I know what that means at once, perhaps before the dawning of a new day. Can you imagine such a thing? My son,—I don't know where he is, perhaps he is dead. At least he is suffering at the present moment hardships which a beggar woman would not allow a son of hers to suffer, and I, in the meantime, abandoning myself to a great love, to a passion such that it would absorb all my time and thoughts, as though I were still in my early youth.... Oh, no! How shameful! I know what love between us fatally demands, and it frightens me. I feel powerless in the face of things which formerly seemed to me as nothing. You have spoken the truth: I am a different woman."

The Prince regained hope on learning the nature of the obstacle. Her son was still alive: he was sure of it, He had written to the King of Spain and to influential friends of his in Paris; he had even sent letters to Germany through diplomatic channels. They might find him any moment; he would succeed in returning him to his mother's side. Why should the poor boy stand in the way of both their futures? Her son knew life; the years that he had spent with his mother had familiarized him with the irregularities which are so common in the world of the fortunate. He would not consider it unusual for her, submitting to a marriage that was not a lie, to rebuild her life discreetly with a man whom she had known since her youth. Besides, he would love him like a younger brother. He could count on influential friends capable of helping the boy if he wanted to work. When he died what was left of his fortune would go to him.

Alicia clasped one of his hands with the tenderness of gratitude. "How good you are!" But suddenly she dried her tears, and her eyes shone with a glow of energy that seemed to reflect her struggle with herself, and she continued, in a firm tone:

"No, no. I don't want to. I am looking to the immediate future: to what would happen to us if I gave in to your glowing words; I can see my son—or I should say, I cannot see him, I don't know what has become of him, I don't know whether or not he is alive. I tell you no. It is useless for you to insist."

There was a long silence. A soldier passed with his head bandaged beneath his *kepis* and a flower behind his ear. He was smiling at a red-faced girl, who was leaning on his arm. They were both humming a tune. The Prince and the Duchess separated slightly on the bench, and remained in silence, he, looking on the ground, absorbed and frowning, she, with her eyes on the horizon line, following the slow progress of the schooners, the sails of which were filling with the breeze that announced the coming twilight.

The obstinacy with which Michael kept his eyes riveted on the ground caused Alicia to make a mistake. Her ankles showed somewhat owing to her posture and her short skirt; trim ankles with the whiteness of her skin visible through the meshes of snuff-colored silk.

"You are looking at my stockings?" she asked, her mood suddenly changing from sadness to gaiety. "Look. What you see on the side there is not embroidery, it is darning. My maid mends them nicely. What can you expect? We are poor."

And doubtless, for the sake of amusing her frowning companion, she went on to enumerate in gay tones the various difficulties arising from her poverty. Oh, the war, with the terrible cost of living! Silk stockings were so bad! One got holes in them after putting them on once, and they came only at fabulous prices. She preferred to prolong the existence of those that she had kept since the days of her wealth, because they were stronger. She might say the same of her dresses. It had been two years since her wardrobe had received any replenishing, so frequent before.

"We are poor," she repeated, with mock solemnity. "Besides, we are fond of gambling, and, like all gamblers, we lose thousands of francs and economize on the little things that make life pleasant."

She had been waiting for an enormous stroke of luck after which she would stop playing and begin to think again of the wardrobe.

But the Prince, by his gestures and the expression on his face gave her to understand how little he was interested in these confidences. It was useless for her to try and change the conversation. Michael, offended by Alicia's negative reply, was still absorbed in his question. Perhaps with another man she would have shown herself more clement.

She realized that she must return to the subject which interested her companion, and said with masculine frankness:

"I know what is the matter with you. I am going to forget we belong to different sexes and talk to you like a comrade, just as I talked to you that night in my study. I know the life you are leading; I know also all about the 'enemies of women': a silly idea. What you need, after several months of living alone like a maniac, is a woman. Choose from those about you; you can find them whenever you like, younger and more beautiful than I, who am beginning to see myself as I am. Why do you choose me? Why do you disturb my tranquillity, now that I have forgotten all about such things?"

The Prince smiled bitterly at the suggested remedy. He had often thought of it. The censor that he kept within had repeated the same advice: "Find a female, and it will all pass away immediately; a woman who inspires only a momentary interest; no women and no love complications. Do what you recommended to Castro." He had frequented the Casino with the resolute air of a slaughter-house man about to choose his prey from the flock. He would glance over the troop of girls in the gambling rooms, who kept one eye on the green baize, while with the other they watched the men who were walking about behind them.

He felt physically attracted by certain women; by one, because of her features, by another, because of her figure or stature, and by some, because of their strange ugliness or stimulating irregularity of form and feature, which affected his nerves much as sharp or biting food affects the palate. He had had only to make a sign or say a brief word to many who, seeing themselves noticed by that famous person, smiled ready to follow him. But suddenly he felt the dislike which is inspired by things repeated to the point of satiety, and by the emptiness of what is familiar to the point of weariness. He could not expect anything new; he was horrified at the thought of the vain prattle of an unknown woman desirous of appearing interesting; of the lies inspired by a sudden and false sentimentality; and by the gross animalism of the pairing which would end the tiresome preliminaries. No; he couldn't. Only once, with a desperate energy of a patient gulping down a disgusting medicine, he had followed one of these beautiful animals, and shortly afterwards he felt disgusted with his baseness and ashamed of his backsliding.

"It is you; you and no one else," he said gloomily. "You, or no one."

Alicia replied in the same grave tone. She knew by experience what this meant "We desire with greater eagerness what is impossible for us to obtain; we single out as unique whatever is beyond our grasp."

But these reasonings exasperated Lubimoff to the extent of making him unjust.

"I know you," he said, drawing nearer on the bench, as he gazed at her more closely, with angry, passionate eyes. "I know what you women are like; you're all vain and revengeful. You can't forget the evening you wanted me and I was not willing, and now you are taking delight in my torment; you enjoy making me suffer."

"Oh, Michael!" she interrupted, in a tone of protest.

The Prince continued to express his rancour, and his indignation stirred Alicia more than the humble question of a few moments before. It was the desperate pleading of a patient who is past recovery and desires to return to normal life.

"I love you.... I need you. I'll get you!"

Above the promontory of Cap-d'Ail the orange-colored globe of the sun was descending. Its lower edge was already touching the undulating line of garden and buildings. For a moment its rays were concentrated in a sheaf seen through the colonnade of a pergola, as though showing itself through an arch of triumph before dying. A dark azure light seemed to emerge from the sea driving the fading gold of the afternoon from the gardens.

"No!... No, I won't!"

Alicia's voice suddenly broke the vibrant silence with the tremulousness of surprise, and immediately changed to a long gasp, as though something were weighing on her lips. Michael had thrown both his arms around her shoulders, mastering her, drawing her breast forward, pressing it against his own. His lips sought hers, but she made an effort to resist, by turning away with a violent straining of her neck. Finally the moan of protest ceased. Both heads remained motionless.

"Michael ... Michael!" she sighed, freeing herself for a moment from the caress. But a moment later she submitted again to those lips which pursued hers so eagerly.

She spoke in a tone of surrender. She was suddenly back in her past life, trembling at the contact of all those foreign things which seemed absolutely new through long continence. His ardent lips had overpowered her, awakened her from a dream that had lasted for years, in a sleep longer and deeper than Michael's.

She forgot everything around her. Her eyes were still open but the vision of the sea, the golden sunset in the sky, and even the pine boughs forming a canopy above their heads, had disappeared from her gaze.

Suddenly she saw them all once more, and at the same time she drew back her shoulders repelling him.

"No, I won't.... Stop! They might see us. How crazy of us!"

The Prince was an athlete, but his emotion weakened him. Besides, his energy was scattered in the double effort of trying to master the woman and at the same time of enjoying her caress in the overwhelming fury of passion. She bent and straightened several times, with all the suppleness of a reptile, finally succeeding in escaping from the chain of his arms, as she gave a sigh of weariness and relief.

Lubimoff, coming to himself again, saw Alicia standing in front of him, smoothing her disordered clothing, and raising her hands to her hair, to her tilted hat and her boa, which was slipping from her shoulders.

"Let us go," she said, with angry brevity.

And the Prince followed her, crestfallen, repenting his violence. After walking a few steps, she seemed moved by his silence, which showed his repentance, and smiled again:

"It is quite evident that from now on I must not see you alone. I forgot that you were a sailor, accustomed to making port in a hurry without caring to lose any time." They walked along slowly, in a tranquillity like that of the serene twilight.

On leaving the gardens, they found themselves cut off by the Museum. Must they return by the way they had come? Michael discovered on one side of the building a rustic stairway cut at intervals in the rock, the hollows of which were filled with brick steps. It descended to the edge of the sea in various flights of stairs, and at the farther end, a walk following the edge of the coast led to the harbor.

She hesitated for a moment at the archway of the entrance.

"I warn you," she said, shaking her finger at Michael, "that if you return to your old tricks, I shall call for help. Do you promise me you'll be good? Word of honor?... All right; go on ahead: I don't trust you."

He went ahead down the stairway to explore. The walls of the Museum seemed to expand as they continued to descend. Besides the building with its roof at their feet, there was a second building below, rising with its stone walls pierced by large windows, from the rocky slopes. At a turn of the path, the Prince faltered to wait for his companion. She was slowly descending, maintaining a distance of several steps between them. Her feet were higher than Lubimoff's head, and it was only necessary for the latter to raise his eyes slightly to see the stockings the darning in which Alicia had explained.

With the lightness of a spring released, he slipped up the various steps that separated them.

"Michael! I'll shout!" she exclaimed on seeing him coming, and she held out her hands to repel him, trying at the same time to flee.

With his arms he had embraced the lower part of that adorable body. He could not climb any further; Alicia's hands repulsed his head with a nervous violence. And he in passionate madness pressed his lips to her feet and her ankles, kissing her skirts wherever he could reach them.

She was angry at feeling that she could not stir and would be unable to escape.

"Let me go! It's ridiculous! Stop!"

The Prince's hat rolled down the steps, knocked off by a blow from her slender hands, as, blindly, she defended herself.

This incident brought him to his senses. Yes; as a matter of fact, it was ridiculous. And as he saw that Alicia intended to retrace her steps, returning to the garden, Michael to inspire her confidence ran down the stairway without turning his head, to see whether she was following him.

They met at the edge of the sea, on the wide path that wound among the loose rocks bordered with foam, and the nearly vertical walls of the cliff. The flat places and hollows in the stone had been made use of, on this promontory, that had so few soft surfaces, to construct the few houses that sheltered the families of the employees in Monaco. Along the upper edge of the cliff appeared the green line bordering the lofty gardens and cut at intervals by the old works of fortification.

They were the sloping bastions, with sentry posts, like those one sees in old engravings or in stage settings. Huge stone facings with Latin letters sang the praises of the various sovereign Princes, who had built these costly works of defense, now antiquated and worthless. Lubimoff expected to see appear from these sentry posts a grenadier in a white uniform with scarlet facings, wearing, above his black mustache and powdered wig, a golden miter.

They walked slowly along in the twilight. Above them shone the orange light of the setting sun, casting a mild red glow on the jutting rocks, the trees, and the white and yellow façades of the buildings. At the edge of the sea, the shadow was a deep blue shade, like moonlight shadow. The sky, blood-red in the West, was invisible for them behind the rocky cliffs of Monaco. They could see it only in the direction of Italy, and there it was growing darker and denser every minute, preparing for the first luminous piercing of the stars.

They met various fishermen who were returning home loaded down with baskets and nets.

Alicia felt worried in certain bends of the path so completely deserted. Later, on seeing a house or a passerby approaching, she resumed the conversation. What she was afraid of was stopping along the way, and sitting down with the Prince on the little parapet bordering the seashore. In the meantime they continued walking!

Without protesting, she allowed Lubimoff to put his arm in hers, leaning upon it. He expressed such deep humility! He seemed repentant for the liberties he had taken; and asked her forgiveness with a pale smile. Besides, he talked to her about her son with soothing optimism. All her fears were unfounded; her son would return: he was sure of it. She would receive good news almost any moment, perhaps that very night.

Her George was a man, and no matter how much he might love his mother, some day he would fall in love with another woman whom he would care for more deeply, and would build up a separate existence, like all the rest.

"And you, who may still consider yourself young, you, who have the right to long years of happiness, do you want to give up everything like an old woman? Why? Why be in a hurry about that?"

She bowed her head without knowing what to reply, and her emotion was such, that she made not the slightest movement when his arm freed itself from hers and encircled her waist. Thus they walked along, closely linked, forming a single body, taking step after step mechanically, without watching where they were going. With his eyes fixed on hers, he closely watched her face, hoping for a glance, or a monosyllable that would mean acceptance. Alicia was afraid of meeting those imploring eyes, and turned her own away.

"Tell me yes," Michael murmured, "tell me that you will. It isn't for nothing that we have met; it is not for nothing that you sought me out. We shall rebuild our lives that have been so nearly wrecked by our vanity and pride. Let us be, although it is rather late, what we ought to be to one another."

"No," sighed Alicia. "I can't.... My son!..."

And immediately afterwards she hastened to murmur, as though repenting:

"Yes; perhaps ... later ... but not now. How shameful! When my mind is at ease, when I don't feel this worry that is killing me. I love you; is that enough? I love you."

These two words sufficed the Prince. He, who had gone to the farthest extreme of domination with so many women without ever feeling satisfied, contented himself with these brief words, which sounded in his ears like happy music.

Instinctively, his arm dropped below her waist, while his other arm drew her head to one of his shoulders.

There was a kiss, a long kiss, without either of them pausing in their walk. Alicia offered no resistance, and shortly afterwards, her lips, animated by a feverish awakening, responded to his kiss, making it more passionate, more vibrant and endless. She no longer felt any fear; they were walking along, and it was impossible for her lover to repeat the liberties he had dared to take in the garden. Moreover, she inwardly confessed, with a certain shame, the delight aroused in her by that violence.

"I love you!" she sighed, without knowing what she was saying. "I love you; but not that, no! Let us love each other like children. It is ridiculous at our age—but so sweet."

At that moment Lubimoff's spirit was like her own. This simple kiss seemed to him the greatest pleasure he had ever known. Life opened up enchantments of which he had never dreamed. It seemed to him that he was gazing on the most beautiful landscape in the world. How interesting were the old fortifications! What a great man Albert of Monaco was to build that lonely asphalt path, so that he might walk along it with his lips pressing the lips of a woman.

They walked along as though they were intoxicated, in a continual zigzag between the parapet and the wall of the cliff, their lips pressing, their eyes almost touching, as though nothing existed beyond them, and they actually imagined that they were walking in a straight line. From a distance one would have thought they were two adversaries struggling, staggering, as they jostled each other in the fight.

Suddenly mastered by desire, he stopped and refused to go on.

"No, no!"

Her will still shaken by her recent emotion, Alicia protested at this danger, but she forced herself to reiterate her refusal.

His lips had separated from hers. There was an aggressive gleam in his half-shut eyes. His hands fell upon her hips, and clinched like claws.

"I won't: I told you I won't! Come!"

She struggled in his arms with the agility of a gymnast, and in breaking free from his grasp there was a sound of tearing clothes.

"Look, you villain! Look what you've done!"

She was standing motionless, a few steps away, with her fur boa falling from one of her shoulders, while at the other she was looking for the tear that her dress had just suffered.

Michael, behind her, saw that one sleeve was almost torn away, giving a glimpse of her white flesh, and the seductive hollow under her arm.

He repented his violence, and the clumsiness of his hands, which like those of a drunken sailor broke what he caressed.

Once more Alicia took pity on his childish embarrassment.

"No, don't worry about that. It is a dress I have had for two years: it is so old, that it tears just by looking at it. That is one of the inconveniences of walking with a beggar."

But she finally became worried by this tear which was so visible. She was going to enter Monte Carlo on foot or by street car. What would people say, seeing her in such a state!

"A pin: have you got a pin?"

This request increased the remorse of the Prince. Where could a man find a pin? While Alicia was feeling for one without avail, he thought of returning to the Museum or scaling the rocks to one of those houses where the employees of the Prince live. He would have given a hundred francs for a pin—but he remembered that his pockets were empty.

He began to search his clothes while she searched hers, although he was certain that it would be useless.

Suddenly he smiled triumphantly.

"Here is your pin."

It was from his necktie! A famous pearl, admired by the women, and which he had never been willing to give away, because it was a gift of the Princess Lubimoff.

He was obliged to mend the tear at the shoulder himself, sighing with vexation.

"You don't know how," said Alicia laughing. "Look out that you don't prick me. How clumsy!"

But he finally felt glad of his clumsiness. He had to touch her naked arm with his fingers; and he quivered as he touched the soft skin, which preserved in its velvety shadows a certain mystery of passion.

"Look out!" she called. "Don't go back to your old tricks: I shall get angry. It is all right as it is. Come on!"

She threw her scarf over the clumsy repair, and the pearl, which stood out against it, with odd magnificence. They were walking along once more, without any new attempted audacities on Michael's part. The last incident had made him circumspect. Inwardly he called himself names, considering himself a savage, incapable of living among real ladies.

As they reached the last bend they left the azure shade of the cliff. Above their heads extended the last angle of the bulwarks, and a stone sentry post; across the harbor, with its mouth flanked by two illuminated towers, and on the opposite bank rose the heights of Monte Carlo, with its huge buildings, and its glistening cupolas, which were reflecting the last rosy fire of the twilight.

They both halted instinctively. In the middle of the harbor, the yacht, the white yacht of the Prince of Monaco, lay motionless, tugging at her buoy. Beside the nearby dock a few latine rigged boats were pitching, moving their single mast, and a Spanish steamer, displaying its neutral flag, was unloading sacks of rice, and barrels of wine. The presence of various groups of men gathered in front of the boat made them prudent. They were no longer alone. Once more they had entered the life of the City.

"How short the road was!" exclaimed the Prince.

She thought the same. "Yes; how short!"

They could no longer walk together. It was necessary to say good-by there, far from the crowd.

Alicia held out both hands.

"Nothing more?" sighed Michael.

The Duchess hesitated a moment. Then, with the agility of a young girl, as though she were still the wild Amazon of the Bois de Boulogne, she sprang for his open arms.

"There, there, and there!"

There were three rapid fiery kisses, that only lasted for a second; three kisses that made Lubimoff think he had never felt one in all his life, since he had never experienced the quivering that swept his body from head to feet.

"More! Give me more!"

She laughed at his imploring look.

"Enough folly. Another time, who knows!—For the present I am worried again. I am afraid to enter my house: I feel terror and hope. Oh, the news that I may receive at any moment! Tell me; do you really think that nothing has happened to him? Do you think he may come back?"

CHAPTER VIII

SPADONI entered Novoa's room with the intention of getting him to talk. At present he was an ardent believer in the professor's knowledge, and seeing him well disposed toward gambling and inclined to meditate on its mysteries, he hoped with simple faith that the scientist would discover something miraculous, some brilliant idea that would make them both wealthy. On that account the pianist arose earlier than he was wont, to surprise the professor during his toilet, considering this the proper time for matters of confidence.

"The word 'chance,'" said Novoa, "is a term devoid of meaning; or, I should say rather, chance does not exist. It is an invention of our human weakness, our ignorance. We say that a phenomenon takes place by chance when the causes either are unknown to us or seem impossible to analyze. We are ignorant of the causes of the majority of things that occur and we get out of the difficulty by attributing them to chance."

The musician opened his eyes wide, and his olive features contracted with a look of respectful attention. He did not understand the scientist's words very clearly, but he admired them in advance, as a prelude to revelations which would be more practical, and of immediate application.

"Every phenomenon," continued Novoa, "no matter how slight it seems, has a cause, and the man with an infinitely powerful brain, infinitely well informed of the laws of Nature, would be capable of foreseeing everything that might happen within a few minutes or within a few centuries. With a man like this it would be impossible to play any gambling game. Chance would not exist for him. Having the secret of the small causes that at present escape our intelligence, and a knowledge of the laws that control their combinations, he would know absolutely everything that might arise from the mystery of a pack of cards or from the numbers of a roulette wheel. No one could hope to win from him."

"Oh, Professor!" sighed the pianist, in admiration.

Inwardly he prayed that his illustrious friend would go on studying. Who knows but what a professor might become that all-powerful person, and, taking pity on a poor pianist, allow him to follow in his trail of glory!

Novoa smiled at Spadoni's simplicity and went on talking.

"The number of facts which we attribute to chance (and chance is nothing but a fictitious cause created by our ignorance) varies, in the same ratio as our ignorance varies, according to the times and according to the individual. Many things which are chance for an uneducated person, are not chance for a man of learning. What is chance to-day will not be perhaps within a few years. Scientific discoveries finally diminish considerably the domain of chance, just as our ignorance decreases."

The pianist's face beamed with a rapt expression.

"You are a great scholar, Professor, a great scholar!... Don't shake your head; I know what I'm saying. I have a feeling of certainty that, if you go on studying these important matters, you will find a system which...."

The Spaniard interrupted him, pointing to a pack of cards on a nearby table. It was easy to guess that he had been studying during the night, before going to bed. These cards were for Spadoni evidence of scientific studiousness, worthier of respect than all the books from the library of the Prince, which lay forgotten in the corners. At present the Professor was interested in the mysteries of chance, and Spadoni was certain that he would discover something better than anything which had been invented thus far by ordinary gamblers.

But his hope vanished at Novoa's gesture of dismay.

"Look at that pack of cards: A few pieces of cardboard and, nevertheless, they contain the immensity of the universe! They cause in one the feeling of dizziness inspired by the Infinite, just as when you look upward with a telescope or downward with a microscope. Do you know how many combinations can be made with a pack of fifty-two cards? I don't know how to express it: nor will you find the figure in a dictionary or an arithmetic, as it is useless, since it lies beyond human calculations. Let us coin the word: eighty unidecillions, or the figure eight followed by sixty-six ciphers. Two men who began to play with a pack of fifty-two cards and played a hand every minute, each hand being different, would not be able to exhaust all the possible combinations in five million centuries."

There was a long silence, as though the walls of the room had shrunk under the weight of these inconceivable numbers. Spadoni bowed his head.

"Now, tell me," continued the Professor, "what can a poor human being, with all his calculations of probabilities, do against this infinity!"

And seizing a handful of cards, he let them fall again like a whispering rain of colors on the table.

"Everything depends on chance," he added, "or I should say, on error. We lose through error and win through it likewise. Our error is the result of an infinity of infinitesimal errors due to another infinity of small causes, the analysis of which we cannot even attempt. These tiny causes are all independent of one another, and since they are directed by chance, they operate in one way as readily as in another. When the infinitesimal is positive, it causes us to win, when it is negative, we lose."

Spadoni nodded his head, although he scarcely understood. The one thing clear to him were the infinitesimal errors which cause us to lose. He was acquainted with them; they were like microbes, malevolent germs, which always clung to him. He wished that his learned friend might discover an antiseptic that would put an end to them.

"Besides," said Novoa, "if there are probabilities of winning, these probabilities are in proportion to the wealth of the gamblers. A poor gambler has less chance of winning than one who has capital at his disposal."

"Then, how about us?" the musician asked in a melancholy voice.

"We are the under dogs and were born to be victims. Gambling is an image of life: the strong triumph over the weak."

Spadoni remained thoughtful.

"I have seen wealthy gamblers," he said, "who were finally ruined like the rest."

"Because they don't stop in time, at the point where the resisting power of their capital brings the hour of winning. In life, as well, the great devourers, soldiers, multi-millionaires, and rulers, are in turn devoured in the final leveling: death. But before that time, they triumph through a powerful means that fate has placed in their hands. We who are poor, never triumph continuously for a whole day. Trying to win a great fortune with small capital is equivalent to wanting to lose that small capital."

They both fell silent, discouraged; but Novoa seemed to have suffered the contagion of his companion's dreams, and felt the necessity of bolstering him up again with some fantastic meditation fit for a gambler.

"You know, Spadoni, how much one can win with a thousand francs? Last night I undertook to make the calculation."

He pointed to a piece of paper covered with figures which was protruding from among the cards. So Novoa was up to the same tricks as the pianist!

"With a thousand francs, doubling each time in forty-three games (some four hours), one could win a block of gold a hundred thousand million times as large as the sun."

"Oh, Professor!"

They both looked at each other with mystic ardor, as though they were actually contemplating this immeasurable block. Beside such a vision what did the winnings of a few paltry millions mean?

Toledo was beginning to realize, little by little, the gradual transformation of his friend, the scientist.

Novoa was greatly interested in his personal appearance; he had asked the Colonel to recommend him to his tailor in Nice; and the Professor made frequent trips to the latter city, merely to make purchases.

Besides, he was gambling. Don Marcos frequently surprised him beside a table in the Casino, standing and meditating before risking one of the few chips which he held tightly in his hand. He seemed dazzled by the ease with which he won. The amounts were small, but so large in comparison with those which he had received for his previous work as a Professor! In half an hour he could win a month's salary. In an afternoon he had succeeded in amassing three thousand francs; half a year's work at teaching and in the laboratory.

Monte Carlo seemed to him an interesting place and life there a quiet relaxation, which stood out above the grave, laborious monotony of his previous existence. The Museum of Oceanography could wait; it would not move away during his absence from the point on the rock of Monaco. The science of maritime zoology was not going to be revolutionized in a few months. And when the director saw him with a gay excited look enter, from time to time, the quiet silent atmosphere of the Museum, and when he observed his gay clothes, and the closeness with which he followed men's style, he sadly shook his head. Novoa was not the first. Oh, Monte Carlo! The old professors looked with the stern face of prophets at the city opposite. Young men who arrived from various places in the world to study the mysteries of the ocean, ended by making mathematical calculations on the probabilities of roulette.

"Besides, he is in love," said Castro, communicating to Toledo his impressions in regard to Novoa. "When he isn't gambling he is with that Valeria woman."

They were engaged. The professor, with an air of mystery, had told this to all his friends, asking each one to keep the secret. After idle gallantries as a student, this was the first, the great love of his life. He was worried somewhat by the humbleness of his position. When they were married what would Valeria say on learning how little he earned as a scientist? But immediately he placed his hope on gambling, the undreamt of fortune which at present offered itself each day.

"If this goes on a few months," he told the Colonel, "I will have gotten together a tidy little sum before I have completed my studies. Every day I lay something aside, and nevertheless I am spending more than ever. I must dress smartly like my fiancée."

And Don Marcos replied with an ambiguous smile.

Novoa's happiness was accompanied by a certain pride. He considered his future life companion a great lady, of higher intellectual capacity and capable of more serious pursuits than the majority of women of her class. She was poor, and for that reason accepted a position bordering on that of a servant. But seeing her on familiar terms with the Duchess, he considered her of as high rank as the latter, and finally blended the affairs of both women in a common interest. And since Doña Clorinda was at present an implacable enemy of Alicia's, and since Atilio blindly espoused the whims and ideas of "the General," a hidden animosity began to spring up between the two men, who up to that time had treated each other with amiable indifference.

"Women!" murmured Toledo on observing the progress of this dislike. "The Prince was right...."

But other more important preoccupations tormented the Colonel. The greatly feared offensive had begun. The telegrams from the front were brief and bad. The Allies were retreating before the German advance. Their lines were not broken, but were wavering, and curving backwards under the overwhelming blows of the enemy. Every day dozens of villages and great stretches of territory were lost.

Don Marcos, with the bursts of anger of a Polytechnic freshman, protested against the lack of foresight of the Generals, mingling his complaints with those of the crowd.

"I knew it would come," he said, with a self-sufficient air to the groups of idlers in the ante-room of the Casino, where he was listened to because of his military title. "The Kaiser has massed in France all the troops that he had in Russia. Who wouldn't have expected it? And our forces are doubtless inferior in numbers."

The bombardment of Paris finally routed all his ideas of strategy. "Lies!" he roared, standing in front of the telegraphic despatches on the bulletin board, and reading of the first shells that had fallen in Paris. It was impossible: he was ready to stake his word, and was well informed as to the range of modern artillery. And on learning the existence of cannon that fired more than a hundred kilometers, he was disconcerted. "What times we're living in! What a war this is!"

When the ladies consulted him in the Casino or in the Hôtel de Paris, he displayed unshakable optimism in the face of the bad news.

"This is nothing: The reaction is going to set in. Our men are withdrawing in order to be better able to take the offensive."

But when he was alone his sense of security collapsed, and he could not hide from himself that his faith was shaken like that of the rest.

"They will reach Paris, if God does not take a hand," he said to himself. "A miracle is necessary, another miracle like that of the Marne."

For the good Colonel still firmly believed that the first battle of the Marne had been a miracle wrought by Saint Genevieve, by Joan of Arc, or some other beatific person able to intervene in human combats, much as the false gods sung by Homer had intervened. Did not St. James fight in the battles of Spain, whenever the Christians attacked the Moors?

"And the miracle has been rendered worthless," he said bitterly. "It will have to be repeated, they will have to begin again, after four years of war."

With the bombardment of Paris the population of the Riviera had increased considerably in a few weeks. The trains were arriving packed with fugitives. The streets of Nice were filled with strangers just as in peace times, when the Carnival was celebrated. Monte

Carlo found its crowds largely increased and new gambling rooms were opened in the Casino.

Toledo spent the afternoon and the early evening hours in the ante-room, always expecting good news, and accepting the bad with an easy optimism which found excuse and justification for everything.

The circle of his friends was gradually increasing. Every day he came across well known faces that he had not seen for a long time. He shook hands, and returned greetings. "You here!" The cannon firing on Paris from an extraordinary distance filled the gambling rooms with a well-dressed crowd, almost as numerous as that of peace times.

Don Marcos continued to announce the reaction, the counter-offensive for the following day, as though he were in touch in some mysterious way with the General Staff. And the anger aroused by the daily failure of his predictions was taken out on the gamblers. "What a life, what an indecent life! Appetites that know no morals! The selfishness of brutes!"

The people around the Colonel seemed to be sorry for a moment as they read the bad news. Then, the majority entered the Casino. Perhaps it was a lack of thoughtfulness on their part, or perhaps it showed a desire to forget, to seek in gambling the illusions of alcohol. But the tiny ivory ball whirled tirelessly in the many roulette wheels. The cards did not cease to fall in double row on the *trente et quarante* tables, and the crowds around the green boards kept on increasing.

The people were nervous, argumentative, and irritable, and lost their manners over a mere gambling incident. The activity on the far-off battle line spread like a fierce wind, around the tables; there was an aggressive look in the eyes of the women. Every cannon shot fired on far-away Paris reverberated like an echo in the rain of money falling in Monte Carlo.

When Toledo, the strategist, attempted to put forth his opinions and plans in Villa Sirena, he found a less attentive audience than in the ante-room of the Casino. The Prince had much more interesting things to think of. Novoa displayed a certain selfish joy, as though considering this period the best in his life, and the world's misfortunes merely something which gave a keener zest to his secret happiness. Spadoni listened to war talk as though people were talking of some ancient fiction.

As for him, reality was what he wanted, and he interrupted the Colonel to tell him about more interesting matters. At present he scorned the Casino, and was frequenting the *Sporting-Club*, where there gathered the boldest gamblers who preferred to use chips of five thousand francs. A Greek, who had been a common sailor in his youth, reigned there like a hero of epic legends, admired by the ladies in ball-room dresses and the solemn gentlemen in evening clothes who gathered together in that aristocratic club. He had learned to read and write after he had grown up, but he possessed an immense fortune. The night before, after dealing for three hours, he had won a million two hundred thousand francs. Spadoni had seen it with his own eyes, and imitated the hero's gestures as he rose from the table, with a little wicker basket held in both hands, a miserable little basket containing, as so much sweepings, heaps of blue bills, and piles of five thousand franc chips. Why should they talk to him about Generals and battles? There was a man for you!

Castro had been listening to the Colonel in a silence that augured ill, and with a coolly aggressive look. Suddenly, he interrupted the plans of strategy of Don Marcos.

"And when are they going to promote you?"

Many of the Generals who at present were celebrated, had been mere Colonels at the beginning of the war. It was about time that Toledo was shoved up a notch on the Army Register.

And poor Don Marcos, wounded by this cruel jest, replied in a dignified manner:

"I am satisfied with what I am, señor de Castro."

He knew perfectly well what he was: a Colonel, and he did not care to be anything more. And several times he repeated to himself that he did not want to be anything more.

In spite of the fact that at Villa Sirena each one was preoccupied with his own affairs, appearing absent-minded when the other guests were talking, Atilio's bad humor was making their life in common rather unpleasant.

Toledo had a feeling that he knew the reason for this conduct. Doña Clorinda was doubtless treating him badly, and he, in turn, was getting revenge for these humiliations and vexations by showing himself harsh and ironical with his friends. The Colonel had been obliged to calm Clorinda when he met her (discussing the news of the war) in the Casino. She felt a strong antipathy to every man who was not in uniform, a little more and she would have insulted them.

"Slackers! Cowards! If I were a man!"

Although she was not, she felt the need of doing something, and was consumed with impatience at not being able to use her energies among the whistling bullets at the front. Finally, she found a means of being useful.

She decided to leave for Paris. When every one who was able to run away from there was hastening to do so, she determined she would go and take up her residence in her former house, defying with her presence the cannon and aeroplanes of the enemy.

Castro took the liberty timidly to suggest that this sacrifice would have no effect. The Colonel added, with his professional judgment, that it seemed to him foolish, but she was in no way disposed to modify her determination.

The outcome of the war concerned her passionately, and she entered into the spirit of it with a nervous vehemence like that which disturbed her friendly relationships.

"If the Allies shouldn't win, life for me would be impossible. How those miserable wretches would laugh! I would rather die."

The miserable wretches were the friends she had formerly had before the war, people of various nationalities who, through pose or through personal interest, sympathized with the Germans. The "General" with a feeling of pride that inspired fear, really and sincerely wanted to die, rather than see triumphant those whom she had chosen as enemies.

"If I were a man!" And Atilio, who sought every occasion to be near her in the Casino, or exaggerated the beauty of certain spots, in order to induce her to take walks with him there alone, hastened to flee at these words, in which he detected an insult.

Later, on finding himself at Villa Sirena, his submission as a lover changed to hostility for the rest.

He had discovered that he hated Novoa, or, rather, that logically he ought to hate him. Doña Clorinda was quarreling with Alicia, and the blue-stocking for whom the Professor felt such enthusiasm was the companion and protégée of the Duchess. For that reason he ought to be an enemy of Novoa. They were like two men who have never done each other any particular harm, but belong to two nations which are at war.

Besides—and he would not have been willing to confess it—the air of satisfaction and triumph of the scholar caused him a certain envy. Novoa was never squelched nor treated with indifference, it was the woman who sought him, making an effort to flatter his tastes, pretending scientific interest in things which made no difference to her whatsoever: merely for the sake of keeping him under her sway. Happy man! And how disagreeable! As always happens when one is beginning to be disliked, Atilio discovered, almost daily, various sources of annoyance of which he told Toledo.

His friend, the Professor, was trying to make fun of him, and he was not disposed to tolerate it. One day Atilio had to wait half an hour at the barber's. The Professor was in his chair and using *his* manicure. Such nerve! He was doubtless trying to outshine him, and for that reason he even got his clothes from the same tailor in Nice. Another piece of insolence! Besides, he didn't know how to wear clothes. And he even suspected that, to please his fiancée and the latter's mistress, that book-worm was probably taking the liberty of saying mean things about a certain lady, and if he ever found it out!...

But the Colonel paid no attention to such threats. The sad news from the war made the matters of daily life seem unimportant.

The Germans were continuing to advance on Paris. Under the repeated blows of the enemy the retreat of the Allies seemed endless, and Toledo's hopes diminished from moment to moment. By this time, he was prepared for anything! The invaders had an over-whelming numerical superiority!

He had only one hope left. If the aid promised by the United States were actually to materialize! Supposing it did not turn out to be a bluff, as many people thought! Now in his imagination, all he could see was America, its harbors filled with armed multitudes, and the blue surface of the ocean plowed by thousands of boats, bringing endless armies to land on European shores. And as weeks went by without his dreams being realized, he began to give advice to Wilson from the Groves of Villa Sirena, or from among the jasper columns of the ante-room of the Casino.

"What is the man thinking of? Why don't they come? If they don't hurry, it will all be over before they arrive."

War and discord made their appearance nearer at hand, within his own domains, causing him for a few hours to consider the general conflagration as a matter of secondary interest.

He never knew for sure who started the row, but one night during dinner, he noticed that Castro and Novoa, with studied coolness, were exchanging words like sword thrusts. The Prince could not suspect any hostility between his two friends, since never in his presence did they depart from the usual forms of courtesy. Besides, occupied with his own thoughts, he did not realize that the Professor, stirred up, doubtless, by Atilio's animosity, had become somewhat quarrelsome. Novoa made a slight allusion to the war-like "General," who was talking about going to Paris, as though her presence there could have any effect on the war. Castro saw in this remark a reflection of the enmity of the Duchess. Doubtless, Valeria and Novoa had laughed together over Doña Clorinda's enthusiasm. And he turned against Alicia's protégée, calling her a penniless blue-stocking, who was always rubbing elbows with great ladies though she was only a servant herself! He could not understand sentimental love affairs with women of that class. He felt a temptation to attack the Duchess de Delille also, but, remembering that she was a relative of the Prince, he refrained.

The two men sat there pale and silent, looking daggers at each other.

The next day, Atilio, before leaving for the Casino, called Don Marcos aside. Perhaps he would soon have an affair of honor on his hands; and could he count on the Colonel as second?

The Colonel drew up to his full height, with a grave frown. Several years had passed since he had performed that solemn function, for which he seemed to have been born. His last duel dated some eight years back: a meeting on the Italian frontier between two gentlemen who had exchanged blows over cheating at cards.

His face became even more gloomy as he bowed in sign of consent, raising his hand to his breast. Since with Don Marcos every action carried with it proper details in dress, he felt that it was impossible to perform a certain act without the corresponding costume, and he suddenly remembered a certain frock coat, which had long been forgotten in his wardrobe, and which he called his "duelling uniform," a black garment, of Napoleonic cut, with long tails, which he brought to light whenever he was a second and, owing to his military name, was called upon to direct a combat.

"I accept. One gentleman cannot refuse another gentleman such a favor."

And he accepted with true thankfulness, thinking how proper it would be to take this suit, as solemn as death, from its prison among the moth-balls, and give it an airing.

But that same afternoon Novoa came to look him up. The Professor spoke timidly, without the elegant indifference of Castro, and with a certain sense that he might be acting foolishly. Perhaps he would soon have an affair of honor on his hands.

"Since I don't understand such matters, Colonel, you will be my second. I have studied along other lines; but when a lady is insulted and when I see a young defenseless girl trampled upon, I consider myself as much a man as the bravest."

Don Marcos started. No, indeed! His eyes were open to the truth. He forgot about airing his frock coat; it might remain in its odorous tomb. And since the Professor was less to be feared than the other man, he let loose all his wrath on Novoa. Imagine fighting over mere nonsense, when millions of men were giving their blood for great ideals! and he, who had referred so frequently to his many experiences as a second as heroic actions, made a gesture of disgust, as though something offensive to his honor were being proposed to him.

A few days later, Novoa spoke to the Prince, with the brevity that ill concealed his emotions. He was very thankful to the owner of Villa Sirena; he would never forget his pleasant life in that retreat, but it was necessary for him to return to his former lodgings. He had important work on hand which would not allow him to live far from Monaco; the director of the Museum was complaining of his absences.

And he went away, to live in a poor house in the old city, renouncing all the comforts and luxury of the mansion in charge of the Colonel.

In spite of such excuses, the Prince expressed his doubts to Toledo. He did not clearly understand this flight. Perhaps there were some other reasons which he could not guess.

"Yes; perhaps there are," replied Don Marcos, with a knowing smile. "It must be a question of women."

Michael nodded. Doubtless, it is on account of Valeria. Living in Monaco he felt himself freer to meet the girl.

"Women!" the Prince exclaimed. "What a power they have over us!"

"And what a mess they make of friendships among men!"

Toledo's voice as he said this was as sad as the Prince's had been on enumerating to his friends the advantages of living away from women. On the other hand, Michael was now himself submitting to a woman's domination, and almost envied the scientist returning to his former modest life in order to meet the woman he loved more frequently.

As for himself, Michael was less happy. Days went by without his being able to repeat his promenade with Alicia in the gardens of Monaco.

"I love you!" she said. "You may believe that I haven't forgotten that afternoon. Later on we will take the same trip, but not now, I know how it would end. It is impossible for me.... I am thinking of my son."

Michael had no doubt that this was true, but something more than worry over the absent one was at the time in her thoughts. She had abandoned herself once more to gambling with the money she had found in her house. The Prince even suspected that she had sold or pawned the pin with which he had repaired the tear in her dress. After giving her the Princess Lubimoff's pearl, he had not seen it again. Alicia seemed unmoved at the first splendor of Spring.

"Some day we shall go there," she said, when he recalled to her the gardens of San Martino, "I promise you. But I must be free from worry, I must lose everything or win everything. I must make the most of my time. As you see, luck seems to be remembering me again."

She was winning little, but she was winning, and this caused her to hope that that sudden burst of good luck which had stirred the Casino, would be repeated.

In the evening she withdrew contented. She had three or four thousand francs more, but what did that amount to? She lamented the smallness of her capital. She wanted to play the "grand jeu" and win back all that she had lost. Winning thus little by little, she would never get anywhere. If she could only get together again the thirty thousand francs, which rose and fell, but always remained faithful!

Michael remained in the Casino for hours at a time near her table, watching for a propitious occasion, without being able to obtain more than brief conversation when she was resting from the play, or taking tea in the bar of the private rooms.

One morning he went to surprise her in her villa. It was ten o'clock. He met Valeria who had just put on her hat, and seemed annoyed at this visit. Perhaps she was going to Monaco, perhaps her man of Science was waiting for her in one of the side streets of Monte Carlo.

"The Duchess has gone," she said, smiling, "she must be in the midst of her work."

Among the gamblers the Casino was known as the "factory," and they really meant it, when they referred to their worry and scheming around the tables as their "work."

Doubtless she had spent a large part of the night figuring, in order to be on hand at the Casino, at the opening hour, her eyes still heavy with sleep, and without paying any attention to her personal adornment, as though there were all too little time for carrying out some wonderful combination she had just discovered.

Whenever he met her, the Prince, with a childish rather ill-concealed motive, alluded to her son's fate. It was only thus that he could rouse her from her preoccupations with gambling, which kept her constantly distracted, talking and smiling automatically, like a person walking in her sleep.

One day, Lubimoff showed her various telegrams and letters from Madrid, Paris, and Berne. Kings and Ministers had taken up the task of finding out the fate of the aviator who had disappeared. A promise came over from Berlin, through the medium of a neutral nation, to look for the young man in every prison cantonment. They suspected that he might be confined in Poland, in a punishment camp.

Alicia began at once ardently to measure time, as though the longed-for notice might arrive at any moment.

"In Heaven's name, please, Michael! Write, telegraph this very day. Tell the gentlemen who have been so kind to send their answer directly to me. The telegram or letter might come to your Villa while you are away, and I would be hours and hours without knowing anything about it! No, have them write to me. Every day, when I go out, I tell my gardener that if there is a telegram he should bring it to me at the Casino. Imagine my impatience! Tell me you'll do this. Promise me you won't forget!"

The one thing that the Prince was at all able to forget, while he was by Alicia's side, was his own personal business. His mind was entirely taken up with discovering the forgotten captive, on whom his happiness depended.

"The day I learn for certain that he is alive!... you will see then how different I am. I shan't bore you with my troubles: you will find a different woman."

And as a matter of fact, her smile and her glances, full of promises, caused him to see in her once more the Alicia who had walked beside him on the path along the seashore, with her lips pressed closely to his in an endless kiss.

When he found himself alone, he was assailed by his own troubles and worries. He had received news from Russia through various fugitives who had just been freed from the persecution of the Revolution. The men who formerly administered his estate there had been murdered. The Lubimoff palace was being used as the headquarters of a Bolshevist Committee. His mines were national property, although no one was working them; his land had been divided; various persons of obscure origin, former old clothes dealers and liquor merchants, had become the owners of his houses, no one knew how. And at the same time that he received this news, which made his future so uncertain, he learned other details which embittered his pleasantest memories. A great lady of the Court, with whom he had had a love affair, the memory of which he cherished, was now selling newspapers on the sidewalks; another very elegant lady, who had set all the fashions in Saint Petersburg, was sweeping snow on the streets of Petrograd, and had lost several fingers by freezing. He could count by the dozen friends of his who had been killed; some of them shot with revolvers like rats, in the depths of some dungeon, others executed by firing squads. Several had perished of hunger, just as years before those of the lower classes, who now were taking revenge, had died.

All these horrors aroused his selfish instincts, causing him to take fresh delight in his own situation. The world had been plunged into a bloody madness. East and west men were rushing about like wild beasts, while he remained quietly beside the most smiling of seas, with love and desire filling his life, which had been so empty before, and awakening anew the ardor and enthusiasm of youth. At the very hour when thousands of human beings were dying in crowds, and the whole villages were being swept from the surface of the earth, he was living under the sway of a woman, and finding his servitude very sweet.

One afternoon, in the bar of the private room, Alicia spoke to him with an air of resolution. She must play big stakes. She was tired of "working" on small capital, and gaining small returns. Besides, she scorned the Casino with its limited bets, its roulette and *trente et quarante*, almost mechanical games in which you cannot see the banker sitting opposite, but instead mere employees.

"All that gives you the impression of struggling with a formidable machine, that functions monotonously, with no imagination, no soul. I must play *baccarat*."

She had gotten her thirty thousand francs together once more: either enormous winnings or nothing! She preferred to lose everything and end it once for all at a single stroke.

"To-night in the Sporting Club. Don't say no: I need you. I have a feeling that this is going to be the decisive night for me—and perhaps for you. Sit opposite me so that I can see you. Remember that on the lucky afternoons you were near me. You will bring me luck. Don't shake your head; you will bring me luck, I tell you."

And she said it with such conviction, that Michael could no longer withhold his consent.

"Come, you will gain by it: I promise you. You will gain by it, no matter what the result. If they clean me out, to-morrow we will go for a walk in the Monaco Gardens, as we did before. And if I win—if I win,—all you want!..."

She did not need to say any more. The look in her eye and her smile filled Michael with enthusiasm. He would see her at the Club.

That night, Castro and Toledo were surprised at seeing the Prince sit down at the table dressed, like themselves, in a Tuxedo.

"The Boss isn't staying home," said Atilio to the Colonel. "He too is going to the opera."

He went to the Casino theater, to while away the time until midnight. He would not have been able to tell for a certainty with whom he talked during the intermission, nor with whom he shook hands. He was obliged to make an effort several times to recall the name and composer of the opera. The music made no difference to him. It was a lulling sound which rocked his thoughts to sleep, calming his emotion—an emotion made up of hope and of fear.

During the first act, he wanted Alicia to lose everything, absolutely everything, thus she would be his more completely, depending absolutely on him, in sweet bondage. Later, during the following act he thought of Alicia's despair after such a loss. She was full of temperament, and she felt the pride of an artist in her play. Perhaps more than the lost money, she would lament her personal defeat. No, it was better that she should win. But how long the music was lasting!

How slowly his watch seemed to go! After eleven, when the lobby was lighted and the crowd was leaving the opera, Michael got into an elevator, which took him down into the bowels of the earth, and then he followed a subterranean passageway, the multi-colored stucco walls of which brilliantly reflected the electric lights. He was walking along under the square front of the Casino, where at that moment many carriages were passing back and forth. Another elevator took him up to a large room filled with columns. It was the great hall of the Hôtel de Paris. He saw women in evening gowns and gentlemen dressed in Tuxedos, the usual crowd of fashionable hotel people who put on uniforms for dinner, and then sit around in deep armchairs, to digest what they have eaten, looking at one another without talking, or else conversing in low tones, as though they were in church, until they are overcome by sleep.

He bowed distantly to various friends who arose, on seeing him, to begin a conversation. He pretended not to see certain ladies who smiled at him, motioning with their heads to call him. He entered another elevator, and descended once more underground. He found himself in a curving passageway, the walls of which were decorated with Pompeian paintings. It extended under two hotels and their gardens. Once more he entered an elevator, which brought him above the surface of the ground. He opened a glass door. An old lackey, in a blue livery, with knee breeches and white stockings, bowed, somewhat surprised at recognizing, after a moment's hesitation, Prince Lubimoff. He was in the Sporting Club.

He had not entered it for years, since before the war. He was not a gambler, and it was only because he had been interested in certain women that he had spent his nights amid elegant society in that place which, like many others of the same class, was merely a gambling den.

The drawing rooms were too small, after midnight; one walked along stepping on the trains of women's gowns. One had to be very dextrous to slip through between the various groups. Every one was smoking, the women more than the men, and the atmosphere grew thicker and thicker with tobacco smoke and the perfumes of the boudoir. The wealthy people scorned the crowds at the Casino, considering it a sign of distinction to be packed in together in this club. They gambled with their own set, considering themselves safe from bad neighbors at the tables, and from contact with suspicious characters who were so frequent in the public rooms. To get in here, it was necessary to give guarantees; some one must vouch for the honor of a person before he could be presented.

The Prince was well acquainted with this brilliant gathering. Here one might meet people of royal blood, heirs to thrones, who were passing through the Riviera, famous bankers, millionaires from all parts of the world, women celebrated for their nobility, their beauty, or their jewels, and many famous and aged *cocottes* and a few, young and fresh looking, who were anxious to grow old as soon as possible, as though that were a means of attaining celebrity. They had all appeared on the stage, at one time or another, in a trained-rabbit act, perhaps, or in some wretched dance, or with a song which they sang in spite of the fact that they had no voices. They were admitted to the Club under the rather vague classification of "artists."

Michael came forward through the atmosphere warm from the crowds and heavy with fading perfumes. He still had to watch where he stepped this time as he had done on his visit here before. Now, to be sure, women's skirts were very short, and their legs were shown uncovered, with a placid lack of shame. The war was shortening their skirts, as though the women, obliged to run in the open field, had taken as a model the ancient Vivandière. But almost all of them, in order not to break completely with a majestic tradition, had added to their stylish overskirts, a sharp and narrow tail, tongue-shaped, which dragged far behind as they walked.

A lady came forward to meet Lubimoff, and it was a moment before he recognized her. It had been so many years since he had seen Alicia in evening dress! Her gown dated back to pre-war times, but was of rich material and the Duchess wore it with the same smartness as in the days of her wealth. The long pearl necklace gained an air of genuineness on her person, as did her other ornaments. It was evident that she had made extraordinary efforts to present a proper appearance on her visit to the Club.

She came here seldom, the crowd composed of former friends talked too much, disturbing her in her gambling calculations. She preferred the Casino, with its large rooms and its motley crowd, talking in various languages. She was a proletarian in the matter of gambling: she had a superstition that fortune prefers to come where its devotees gather in large bands. Her intuition that she would be lucky at *baccarat*, a game to be found only here, had persuaded her to abandon her usual custom for this one night.

The Prince complimented her on her lovely appearance, her dress, her pearls....

"False, scandalously false, my dear," she said, laughing and looking about her. "But you know very well that the majority of those worn by the other women are no better. Ah, pearls! If all that shine in the world were brought together, the sea would not be large enough to have produced a tenth part."

She led the Prince toward the bar. She had a favor to ask of him. At midnight the game of *baccarat* commenced: she had asked for "the bank," but the rules of the Club prevented her from getting it. Alas for women! Even in gambling they were condemned to a position of degrading inferiority. Lost in the common crowd of "ponteurs" they might lose a fortune, but they were forbidden ever to hold the bank. The directors of this Club and other similar ones doubtless feared that women were more given to cheating than men. She, the Duchess de Delille, could not be the equal of a Greek sailor, who dealt every evening with unheard-of luck, causing the crowd to feel suspicious and think evil thoughts.

"They insist that I get a man to deal for me. He must appear as my banker, although every one knows that the capital is mine. I thought that you might do me this favor. I like to think of our going together into this business which means life or death to me! Besides, I am sure of success if you deal. And what an event! How they would bet! Prince Lubimoff playing the banker!"

But she did not continue. Michael interrupted her with a decisive gesture of refusal. It made no difference what she said. He was indignant at the very idea that people should see him seated at the green table, playing with money that did not belong to him, and having Alicia at his back. Besides, he was sure of losing.

The Duchess hastily left him. Time was flying, and any minute they might give out the bank. She believed once more in her good star as she saw a young man timidly slipping through the crowd.

"Spadoni! Spadoni!"

The pianist grew pale on hearing her. "Oh, Duchess!" He trembled and stammered with emotion. *He* dealing in the *Sporting-Club* before an elegant opera night crowd, handling thousands of francs, with all eyes fixed on him! It was the crowning moment of his career; after that he could die happy.

Two players had asked for the bank, the famous Greek and a manufacturer from Paris, who had gotten fabulously rich making munitions. Spadoni also presented himself, carrying in a purse the fifteen thousand francs which were necessary in order to take charge of the bank. Lots were to be drawn among the three petitioners. An employee of the Club took a wicker basket that held ten numbered balls and after shaking it, threw out three on the table: one for each. Alicia mingling with them with masculine familiarity, almost clapped her hands with joy. Luck had favored Spadoni, the bank was his. But the pianist, respectful of the privileges due to genius, showed his sense of profound humility in smiles and expressions of face and eyes that seemed to beg pardon of the Greek, his rival.

The Greek was a stout man with a figure that almost formed a square, with a dark shiny complexion, black mustache and eyes that were somewhat slanting, and had a fixed aggressive look, suggesting those of a wild boar. His ancestors had been pirates in the Archipelago, and he, finding this heroic career cut off, had become a smuggler in his youth. Spadoni, somewhat intimidated by the majesty of the great man, stammered excuses with his eyes fixed on the Greek's shining shirt-bosom, adorned with pearls, and his gray silk vest that covered a heavy paunch. But the Greek replied, with an ill-humored grunt, walking away after favoring the Duchess with a bow like one of those he had seen on the stage. Although he scarcely knew how to read, the Greek was posted on the proper way of treating a lady who declares war.

It was twelve o'clock. The gambling stopped at the roulette wheels and the *trente et quarante* tables. The crowd was gathering in the baccarat room. The news had gone around: The pianist Spadoni, considered by every one as a pleasing parasite, was going to occupy the place that had been held on former evenings by the Greek, but in reality the bank belonged to the Duchess de Delille.

A triple row of people formed around the table, jamming together to get a better view over adjoining shoulders.

Spadoni smiled, but finally the ironic curiosity fixed on his person began to make him nervous. Many of those who were gazing on him were important personages and had always inspired him with deep respect. Fortunately, he felt the Duchess at his back, seated there with an air of ownership, and watching him with a look of authority. If he made any mistake, the great lady was capable of striking him.... Courage and forward march! The *croupier*, sitting opposite to collect and pay the bets, was shuffling the cards, before putting them in a small double box, from which the banker was to draw them. Poor banker! The crowd, considering his elevation something quite extraordinary, was ready to laugh no matter what happened. As he sat down in the presidential chair, the onlookers considered the pianist's embarrassment very amusing, and an unrestrained laughter greeted his appearance in the seat of authority. He asked the *croupier* a question in a low voice, and the same explosion of merriment was repeated. The women were the most demonstrative as they thought their ridicule might pass over Spadoni's head, and reach the woman who had placed him there. The musician's look of surprise at this unexplainable hilarity only served to prolong it to the point of a general uproar. They all laughed contagiously on seeing his comical inability to understand the situation. But a rough voice put an end to the merriment.

"Bank!"

It was the Greek. He had seated himself on Spadoni's right, with the angry look of a person who is conscious of an enormous injustice and feels it is necessary to remedy it. He could not tolerate the fact that this grotesque person should occupy the same place in which he had been admired every evening. Neither did he consider it admissible that a woman should mix in affairs that belong entirely to men. He had the same scandalized and astonished feeling of a person witnessing some disarrangement in the rhythmic order of Nature. The world was upside down: apprentices were trying to be masters; class distinctions were not being respected, such nonsense must be stopped once for all. "Cards!"

The Prince trembled. Alicia's fifteen thousand francs were in danger. That man was going to prevent the bank from continuing. If the Greek were to win, the entire capital bet by Alicia would vanish; if he lost, her money would be doubled. But he was sure to win. When a man as lucky as he dared do that!...

Spadoni was overwhelmed on hearing the great man's voice. Instinctively he turned his eyes in the direction of the Duchess, but withdrew them at once, still more overwhelmed by her motionless features and the hard look that seemed to strike his shoulder, as though he were to blame.

The double box, quite ready, was awaiting his reach. He dealt cards to the right and left, and then drew his own.

The Greek showed his cards, throwing them down on the board. "Eight." A murmur of approval arose around the table. The admirers of his good luck rejoiced as though it were a triumph of their own. From the opposite side he took cards which the *croupier* offered him, and showed them after a previous rapid examination of them. The murmur was now one of amazement. Eight again! He was going to win. It was almost impossible for the banker to make a higher point than that.

Spadoni, pale, his brow glazed with sweat, turned his cards over. The public greeted them with a suppressed exclamation: "Nine!"

The very ones who had laughed at him, considered this result quite natural. "Luck always protects the simple-minded."

And as the Greek handed over the fifteen thousand francs to the *croupier*, who acted as a depository for the bank, the pianist bowed modestly. A few superstitious gamblers considered that the Duchess had showed excellent judgment in confiding her fate to this simple fellow.

Alicia's eyes sought Michael in the triple oval of heads. She smiled at him slightly. Her features had lost the hard, fixed look with which she had faced the exciting moment. She felt entirely sure of her triumph. And anxious to amaze the onlookers by her imperturbable calm, she took a golden cigarette case and an ivory mouthpiece from her purse and began to smoke.

The pianist, after this first moment of success, played with a certain assurance. The Duchess, sitting motionless at his back, seemed to communicate her confidence to him. He dealt several times successfully, and as the money in the bank was considerably increased, the cupidity of the gamblers was aroused. Those who laughed at Spadoni's clumsiness, now frowned with aggressive interest, taking part in the playing. Thus as the capital increased, the stakes grew higher. Every one felt there was going to be a great and exciting game. The banker had forgotten the Duchess and his own humbleness. He imagined that what he was winning was his own; he believed he had discovered the secret mentioned by Novoa, which was going to win those fabulous sums, on which his imagination had played so often as he wrote dozens and dozens of zeros on a piece of paper. What a night! And to think that his friend, the scientist, was not there to witness his triumph!

Lubimoff withdrew from the table. It hurt him to see Alicia's forced serenity, and her manner of smoking while she watched the progress of the gambling with feline eyes. Luck was going to change any moment. This mad continual winning could not go on. The Greek was making an effort to hide his anger, playing and losing like an ordinary bettor. He could not call "bank" until a second deal began after all the cards in the double box were exhausted. But he stuck to his original bet with the tenacity of a bull dog, convinced that sooner or later he would succeed in getting the better of this mockery of chance. He had more money than Alicia and her representative, he would be able to hold out against fate, and in the end could beat them.

The Prince went to the bar, passing the time by sipping two American mixed drinks, which were sweet and bitter at the same time, and heavy with alcohol. He wanted to become slightly intoxicated, in order to feel himself on the same level with the woman who was appealing so desperately to luck.

He found himself alone. The entire Club was huddled together in the *baccarat* room. Michael lamented the fact that Castro was not at the Sporting-Club. They would have been able to chat together as they had the afternoon that Alicia succeeded for the first time in clutching the golden wings of the Chimera. Perhaps his absence was due to an order from the "General". He himself had come there dragged by a woman!

A dull murmur came from the gambling room. Shortly afterwards he saw a few of the onlookers entering the café, and standing at the bar to drink. They were talking in tones of wonder and amazement. Hearing the name of the Greek repeated several times, Michael listened. The former had shouted "bank" at the beginning of a new hand, when the bank contained a hundred and forty thousand francs. No one but that lucky fellow was capable of such daring. He drew eight, but the pianist immediately showed his cards. Nine once more. And the *croupier* had swept the Greek's one hundred and forty thousand into the bank. What a night! And to think that that fool of a Spadoni was the man who was doing such wonders!

A few women passed the door of the bar with an ill-humored air, gesticulating among themselves. They appeared scandalized and annoyed by the Duchess de Delille's good fortune, in spite of the fact that none of them had lost a cent in the play. Such luck was unnatural; there must have been some cheating. They could not say in what the cheating consisted, but it existed undoubtedly.

Later they saw the Greek, followed by two admirers. His face was sweating, his shirt-bosom wrinkled, and his vest had worked up, showing his shirt between the gray silk points and his belt. He was shrugging his shoulders scornfully. The world was upside down: there was no such thing as logic any more. That was why the war was going so badly!

And the Greek walked away in the direction of the subterranean passage, to return to the Hôtel de Paris. He did not care to see any more of it: it was a night for lunatics!

Neither did the Prince care to be a witness, and he remained in his armchair, asking for another cocktail. In front of the door he could see passing those whom another's good luck had embittered, and were fleeing, and those who were arriving, attracted by the news of the event.

He remained alone, like a spectator who stays in the lobby of a theater and listens to the far-off pulsing thrills of the audience. Long intervals of silence passed. Later, there was a murmur, a sigh from the crowd, a buzz of exclamations circulating in low tones. Was Alicia still winning? Or was he going to see her appear like the Greek, shrugging her shoulders at the absurdity of fate?

He asked for still another glass; and gazing at the spirals of smoke from his cigar, he was falling asleep. Suddenly he sat up, imagining he had received a sharp blow on his shoulders. It was a mere illusion! He was alone. Gazing about him, he noticed the clock. It was two. He stood up and slowly walked toward the *baccarat* room.

The crowd had thinned out, but all those who had remained were taking a hand in the play. The enormous sum amassed by the Bank was a temptation. No need to fear that the winners would not be paid! Even the mere spectators who spend the night on their feet, sharing other people's emotion, were risking their money *louis* by *louis*, hoping that this burst of luck which wholly favored the bank, would change in favor of the crowd.

The first thing that Michael saw was an enormous heap of thousand franc notes, five thousand franc chips, and chips and bills of various amounts. It was a fortune. Then he noticed Alicia, sitting motionless in her seat, just as he had left her, with the expressionless face of a caryatid. Her eyes merely looked mechanically back and forth from that heap of wealth to the hands of the banker. She was smoking, smoking. On a tray which a lackey had placed reverently beside the victorious woman there was a pile of gold-tipped cigarette butts.

She seemed stupefied by her success, by the monotony of her constant luck.

The pianist was beginning to display a certain somnolence in his looks and in his voice. Mere winning seemed something insipid to him, after the flight of that admirable Greek. Similarly other famous gamblers had disappeared, as though not caring to authenticate by their presence such an absurd run of luck. The only real competitors were some English people from Beaulieu, whose automobiles were waiting below. This extraordinary game interested them, as though it were some unusual sport; they were anxious to fight against the Bank's good luck, with British tenacity, merely for the pleasure of overcoming it. The women, bony and distinguished looking, with very low necks and long trails to their gowns, ejaculated "oh!" in amazement, each time the *croupier* with his rake carried off their heavy bets, while the men drew from inner pockets of their Tuxedos, new handfuls of bills, greeting their defeat with metallic laughter.

In one blow Spadoni lost twenty thousand francs. Lubimoff had the fatal presentiment of a sailor who feels beneath his feet the shudder of the ship about to be torn open, of the soldier who feels instinctively the beginning of his rout.

Another blow; and the bank lost again.

Michael cautiously drew near the chair occupied by Alicia.

"It is two o'clock. It is time to go home," he murmured, whispering his words into her hair as he bent over her. "You are going to have a run of bad luck: I can feel it coming. Tell Spadoni to get up."

She raised her eyes and looked at him in surprise. She seemed intoxicated, unable to make out what he was saying, and showed her refusal by a slight shake of her head. She had faith in her own luck.

Fortune saw to it that her confidence was justified. The banker was winning again, carrying off all the sums placed on both sides of the table. But this did not convince the Prince. He continued to feel afraid, and his worry made him brutal.

He went over and stood at Spadoni's back, in order to drop a word to him discreetly, while looking in another direction. "You ought to stop at once. Call the game off. It's long after closing time anyhow."

The banker turned his face and looked up at him in order to see what sage was dropping these words of wisdom from on high. "Oh, your Highness!" This discovery was accompanied by a proud smile, evincing satisfaction that Prince Lubimoff should have witnessed the greatest deed of his life.

And he went on dealing.

Michael grew angry. This idiot, overwhelmed by his triumph, did not understand him, and if he did understand him, he was refusing to obey. The voice of the Prince, falling with a slow tremor, reached the ears of the man below. "Spadoni, you incredible fool of a pianist"— here two or three oaths in various languages.—If Spadoni did not obey him at once he would jerk him out of the chair with a thud, and give him a kick that would send him flying through the windows!

"The last deal!" said the banker.

And when he stopped dealing, many of the spectators breathed freely, satisfied and relieved by the end of a game that seemed to have been under an evil spell. Others gazed with astonishment and envy at the enormous heap of money in the bank, as the *croupier* put it in order, forming bundles of bills, and straightening the various colored chips in columns.

The sum ran from mouth to mouth: four hundred and ninety-four thousand francs! A little more and it would have been half a million. Rarely had such a rapid winning been seen.

Spadoni, as though he were the master of these riches, was putting them into a little wicker basket. He was trembling with emotion. He was going to walk through the crowd of onlookers carrying this treasure, just as on former nights he had seen his hero pass, with the air of a conqueror. In comparison with this what did he care for the applause he had received as a pianist!

But eager hands snatched the basket from him.

"No! let me! let me!" It was the Duchess; it was no longer necessary any more for her to claim indifference. That money was hers. She had become transfigured by coming out of her eager trance-like silence. Her eyes were shining with a triumphant gleam, her brow was pearled with sweat, her cheeks, which were intensely pale, quivered. Carrying the basket, with her arms held out before her, she slowly passed among the groups, with priestly majesty, walking in the direction of the cashier's cage.

Spadoni remained beside the Prince. He, too, was perspiring, and his features were pale with emotion.

"What a night, Your Highness! What a night!"

He looked proudly at every one, but smiled humbly at the owner of Villa Sirena. He must make the Prince forget his refusal of moments before, and the terrible threats which had been visited upon it.

A moment later Alicia returned to them, carrying a paper in her hand-bag.

The pianist's enthusiasm overflowed.

"Oh, Duchess! Divine Duchess!"

He kissed one of her bare arms, then a shoulder. Alicia smiled at this public homage. The poor pianist, no matter what he might do, could not compromise her.

"Thanks, Spadoni, you may count on my gratitude. Go ahead and decide what you want, a house, a yacht, or perhaps a piano with golden keys."

Michael listened in amazement. She was speaking in all sincerity: as though her fortune had turned her mind.

But the pianist left them. He felt he must be alone. By the Duchess' side he was obliged to share his glory, contenting himself with but a fragment of it. And he went off to join the English people from Beaulieu, who, proclaiming him the most interesting phenomenon they had met in all their travels, were anxious to meet and share a bottle of champagne with him.

Alicia and the Prince walked toward the cloak room.

"I have deposited my winnings with the cashier of the Club," she said, showing him the receipt. "I am not going to carry so much money home at night. To-morrow I shall come to take it to the bank. I need some one to accompany me. Send me the Colonel: he is a fighter and must have a revolver."

Then, remembering something important, her features took on a grave look.

"I need not say that to-morrow we will straighten our account. Don't think I have forgotten what I owe you: the twenty thousand francs from the other day, and your mother's three hundred thousand. It will all be paid."

Michael showed the astonishment which this promise caused him by a prolonged laugh. Really, her winning had affected her brain. A piano with golden keys for the other man, and now hundreds of thousands of francs for him. The fortune recently acquired in two hours seemed to her as extraordinary and limitless as her good luck itself had been.

"What I want," he added, in a low tone, ceasing to laugh, "what I want from you, you know very well."

She stopped him with a caressing look and a discreet whisper which was equivalent to a promise.

They descended the large stairway in the Club, and were standing in the vestibule, she wrapped in a silk cape embroidered with gold and adorned with rich furs, which recalled her evenings after the opera in Paris; he, with his overcoat open and a soft silk-lined hat on his head.

The employees in the vestibule, informed of what had happened in the gambling rooms, hurried to the glass door in a hope of a handsome tip. "A carriage for the Duchess!"

But she wanted to walk in the silence of the night. She was numbed from remaining motionless so long, and felt the need, like every one who feels happy, of prolonging the joy of her triumph by a long walk.

She descended the outer stairway leaning on Michael's arm. They passed between the drivers and the few chauffeurs who were standing about in groups, waiting for the owners of their machines, or for possible patrons.

They went down into the cool night air, with their eyes still tired, from the splendor of the illumination, their skins hot from the heavy atmosphere of the gaming rooms. They both noticed that it was a moonlight night, with a sad, waning moon that was beginning to drop behind the dark barrier of the Alps. The submarine menace kept the city in darkness. At long intervals, pale lamps, the glass of which was painted blue, cast above themselves a narrow circle of funereal light.

After a few steps, they grew accustomed to the darkness. In the street the ground was divided into two bands, one a pale, dim white reflected from the dying moon, the other dark, with the heavy black shade of ebony. Instinctively, they walked along the dark sidewalk, as though afraid of being seen. They wound along through a curving, sloping street, the same that made its way underground by the Pompeian corridor and which the Prince had taken a few hours before.

At their backs they could still hear the conversations of the drivers hidden by a turn in the street, the voices of the Club servants calling by the owners' names for the carriages; the stamping of the horses, shaking off sleep as they waited, and the first humming of the motors that began once more to function. Michael, who was walking along in silence, with a desire to get away from there as soon as possible and seek absolute solitude, on seeing her pause, was obliged to stop. She had anticipated his thoughts: she did not care to go any farther.

"I must reward you!" she murmured. "I told you that at any event you would gain by coming, even though I should lose. There ... there."

Her bare arms, freeing themselves from the silken cape, closed about his shoulders, forming a tight ring; submissively her mouth sought his, humbly abandoning itself, with a desire of giving happiness.

At the end of the street a sudden illumination flared up, making the scene stand out against the shadows, like a flash of lightning. It was the searchlight of an automobile. She did not move, she was not afraid of being surprised: people were mere phantoms, without any reality whatsoever. Nothing existed in the world at that moment save themselves and the heap of paper bills, and pieces of ivory guarded in the steel vault.

All his life Michael remembered that night. The clocks were doubtless mad, turning like his head, which seemed in a whirl, following the rhythm of sweet music. He had a feeling that they passed the same place several times, going back and forth as they walked, without knowing what they were doing. What difference did it make? The important thing was that they were together. There was a moment in which they both seemed to awaken, finding themselves seated on a bench, in the Casino Square. The Prince was sure of it. He had looked at the clock on the façade. It was three o'clock! It seemed impossible, he firmly believed that only a few minutes had passed since they left the Club. And they were obliged to walk away, annoyed by the curiosity of a civilian who was doing police duty in war time, a member of the Prince's militia in citizen's clothes, with a colored band on his arm and a revolver at his belt.

Once more they walked through the deserted streets or along the public gardens, closed at that hour. Her body was thrown back, with her cape open, she was hanging limp upon his arm which was thrown about her waist, and she offered a tensely drawn throat and an upturned face to a rain of kisses. She looked up at her companion, with eyes dreamy with love. Her caresses rose slowly and voluptuously in a crescendo, as sea flowers and stars arise from the blue depths in search of light.

Replying to the mute appeal of the eyes that were imploring from above, she murmured several times, in a faraway voice, as though talking in a dream:

"Yes, all you wish ... all you wish!"

More aggressive in his passion, he buried his free arm in the warm circle of her cape, drawing her closer to him.

They walked along in a wavering course, imagining they were going in a straight line; in certain spots they both stopped at the same time, without knowing why. Their loitering caused a commotion in the villas. The gardeners' dogs howled furiously at these intruders, thrusting their noses against the iron gates. This howling sounded to the lovers like barbaric but agreeable music, feeling benevolently toward everything that surrounded them, they imagined themselves the lords of creation, just as at that moment they were masters of the night. Nothing save themselves existed in the world.

Michael, obeying an obscure impulse he did not understand, spoke to her of her son. She would recover him at any moment now, and her happiness would be complete.... Immediately he repented having awakened this memory, which might break the enchantment in which they were living. But she showed no emotion.

"Yes, I will recover him," she murmured. "I am sure of it. My good luck will not forsake me. It was time, after suffering so long."

And once more she abandoned herself to the present moment. They were both surprised to find themselves in the street where Villa Rosa was located. After wandering about at random, instinctively they had finally come there.

The Prince, emboldened by the long walk filled with kisses and abandonment, became urgent.

"Let me come in," he murmured. "No one will see me.... I will go away before the break of dawn."

Alicia stopped short as though suddenly awakening. It was her first gesture of refusal during the entire night. The gardener was surely waiting, perhaps Valeria had not yet gone to sleep. "Oh, no!"

Lubimoff, in desperation, spoke of their walking together to Villa Sirena.

"So far!" continued Alicia, growing calmer at every moment, as though she were entirely awakened. "Besides, that place is a barracks; a house full of men. And that Castro who tells everything to the 'General'! No, no, I shall never go there. What madness!"

Michael's look of sadness, his gesture of dismay, touched her. She passed her hand over his features with a motherly caress.

"My poor boy: Don't look like that, be patient awhile. To-morrow; I promise you that it will be to-morrow."

She, who in former times had dared the most atrocious scandal with tranquil lack of shame, hesitated and stammered as she spoke of the next day. She seemed like a young girl struggling between love and a fear of compromising her future in society.

To-morrow! To-morrow he might come at three in the afternoon.... No, not at three; four o'clock was better. Valeria surely would have gone out by that time. She would send her maid to Nice to do some shopping; the gardener and his wife would be busy outside the house.

"But in Heaven's name, be careful! If you can manage so that the neighbors don't see you, it will be much better."

And the famous Prince Lubimoff visibly moved, like a boy planning his initiation into love, and prematurely stirred by its mysteries, assented to this counsel.

He insisted, in spite of her protests, on going with her to the gate of the Villa.

"If you were any one else, all right! It is quite natural that a friend should accompany me at such an hour; but you!... I am afraid that every one will guess our secret."

It was not until the gate was closed and Alicia's adorable figure was lost in the darkness, that the Prince could decide to go away.

He was obliged to walk the long distance to Villa Sirena, and nevertheless the road seemed short to him. Memories and promises accompanied him. His step had never been lighter, he seemed to be advancing through air in which the laws of gravitation had been lessened, on a planet wrapped in a perpetual night of springtime, in which the air, the dim trees and the objects lost in the darkness about him, vibrated with a poetic rhythm.

His sleep was restless, but he arose serene and in high spirits. He remembered the errand Alicia had asked him to do. She needed a warrior, with a revolver if possible, to escort her in transferring her fortune from the Club vaults to the bank. The Colonel, deeply impressed at her stroke of luck, went out to perform this task. "Poor Duchess! In the end God always protects the good."

Michael spent the entire morning attending to his personal adornment. His attempts at leading a simple, country life in retirement at Villa Sirena had not made him forget the hygienic care to which he was accustomed since his childhood. But now it was a question of something more; he wanted to make himself look well, and heighten with exquisite and intimate attentions the individuality of his physique, which he suddenly felt had been rather roughly treated by time.

He had his old valet go over the wardrobe he had acquired in former days. He remembered certain under-garments that had merited women's praise. He was as desirous for novelty and seductiveness as a woman dressing for a long-awaited rendezvous. Besides, he chose a suit that he had never worn before in Monte Carlo, a new hat, and a modest tie. He recalled her apprehension, and her request that he should enter unseen.

As he was doing all this, a sinking feeling, of lack of confidence in himself, began to assail him. It was the feeling of uneasiness like that of a student before examination, like that of a dramatist watching from the wings for the fate of his play, like that of a man about to fight a duel. He had spent so many weeks desiring without avail! He had renounced love so long ago! And the thought of Alicia aroused in him both eagerness and terror.

The Colonel returned about noon. He had performed his duties. He told the news with modest brevity, as though he had just accomplished something very important. Michael almost envied him, because he had seen Alicia. "How is she?"

"Beautiful, as beautiful as ever. Somewhat pale, as was natural after such an excitement as that of last night! But gay, very happy, talking constantly about the Marquis. It is easy to guess that she feels a strong affection for him."

They had lunch alone. Spadoni was going out in society, after his triumph. Perhaps he was in Beaulieu with his new friends, the Englishmen. Toledo had met Castro going into the Hôtel de Paris, where Doña Clorinda lived. Doubtless they were having lunch together to talk over the winnings of the Duchess. Atilio had even pretended he did not understand when the Colonel talked to him about the event. Envy, of course! The Prince shrugged his shoulders. People were mere phantoms as far as he was concerned, and evil passions were illusions. There were only two realities: he and what was awaiting him.

After lunch he dressed with such attention to the minutest details that the absurdity of it made him smile. He even changed his tie, after he was dressed, looking for another of a quieter color. "Half-past two." He looked at himself from head to foot in the mirror: a dark gray suit, tan shoes, and a light felt hat with broad brim turned down to protect his eyes from the sun. No one had ever seen Prince Lubimoff dressed in such a manner. From a distance one might have taken him for one of the travelers who visit the Riviera in passing, and come to make the acquaintance of roulette at Monte Carlo in an afternoon, and go away again immediately.

Three o'clock! He left Villa Sirena. It was a long way and he wanted to walk it. The exercise would fortify his will and dispel the doubt which was assailing him anew. He thought of how he had performed the same supreme intimate act so many times in former years, as something ordinary and almost mechanical. His suspicious isolation during the last few months seemed to have numbed him. He felt the lack of confidence of an athlete who has left off exercising and doubts whether he can summon all his former strength again. Fear at the mere idea of a failure restored his confidence. Such a thing was impossible! Forward march!

On reaching Monte Carlo, he climbed the long stone steps as far as the streets of Beausoleil. He considered it advisable to go out of his way thus to carry out in the fullest detail the counsels of prudence that Alicia had given him.

He planned to enter her street from above, where there were no houses. In this way he would avoid any of her neighbors who at that hour might be going down town.

Above the building plots where houses were going up and the stairways which were winding down the slope, he could overlook a large expanse of sea, and on the shore the groves of the gardens, with a bird's-eye view of the huge mass of the Casino, with its green tiles and the yellow cupolas of its halls, the wide square, the little circular garden of the "Camembert," and around it numerous people the size of ants.

The Prince had a feeling of pity for those pigmies. Unhappy men! They were going to gamble, to shut themselves up between four walls, under artificial light, with no other dreams than those of money. For him something better was awaiting; for a few hours he was going to experience the one interesting intoxication of life. Then he laughed with pity at a certain lunatic, his double, who had tried to found a club group of "women's enemies." Imagine hating love, and trying to live without women; poor Prince Lubimoff!

It was now four o'clock. Passing among tiny gardens which seemed miles away from a crowded city, he entered Alicia's street. The red roof of Villa Rosa was peeping out from among the trees, almost at his feet. He kept on descending. His legs trembled slightly, and he stopped for a moment to regain his poise, raising his hand to his breast. Rounding a bend, all of the street that was built up appeared, straight and gently sloping down to where it joined one of the avenues of Monte Carlo.

No one was in sight, and he hastened to slip into Villa Rosa before any neighbors appeared. He passed the gardens rapidly, with the air of a man afraid of being late at a game of cards. He found the gate half open. It was a good sign: Alicia had thought of facilitating his entry.

He crossed the little garden, and thought he saw the frightened face of the gardener, peeping over some shrubbery for a moment, then hiding again precipitously. There was something strange about that man's curiosity and his look of fear. But he was hurrying away, and the Prince was pleased at his discretion.

With a flutter of emotion, he climbed the four steps of the door. With each one there awoke in his imagination a fresh dream picture, softly rose-colored like women's flesh, a sweet unconfessable vision which suddenly brought back his past. More with his memory than with his sense of smell, he perceived in the atmosphere a well-known perfume, her perfume. Everything seemed to be whirling about him with hazy contours. There was a buzzing in his ears; desire electrified him drawing his muscles taut, just as in his happiest days. And with the bearing of a conqueror, he pushed open the door, which was unlocked.

A woman came forward to meet him in the vestibule, a woman whose presence caused him to draw back.

Valeria! What was she doing there? What sort of a farce was this?

The young woman tried to speak, and he, too, wished to speak at the same time. But neither was able.

Another woman appeared, opening the door abruptly. It was Alicia, with her clothes in disorder and her hair wildly streaming. On seeing the Prince, she raised her arms and came forward, impetuous and silent, as though to embrace him. At last!... What did he care if Valeria were present: he did not see her. On the other hand, Alicia seemed different to him; taller than ever, and paler, with eyes that suddenly inspired fear.

Her arms fell about him, and immediately her whole body seemed to totter, bereft of strength. He felt a panting breast against his own; her arms were as cold as those of a corpse; a rain of hot tears began to bathe his neck.

"Michael! Michael!" Alicia groaned.

It was all she could say. She was choking, the sobs catching in her throat as though a strangling lump were fixed within it.

The Prince was obliged to summon all his strength to sustain the inert body. A voice sounded in his ear, with the same low monotonous tone that is heard in a chamber of death.

It was that of Valeria, who was also weeping, feeling afresh the contagion of tears.

"He is dead! He died a month ago!"

And she showed him a little yellow paper that had arrived half an hour before: a telegram from Madrid.

CHAPTER IX

SPADONI, after greeting Novoa in the Casino square, told him about the dreams which were troubling his sleep, and about his disillusionment on awakening.

"It is your fault, professor. When we were living together at Villa Sirena, I used to listen to the interesting things you knew and talked about and then I would go peacefully to sleep. Now I am practically alone. The Prince and Castro are unbearably ill-humored; they talk scarcely at all and pay no attention whatever to me. As you yourself would say, I lead an 'inner life,' always alone with my thoughts; and when I spend the night there, I sleep badly, and suffer from dreams, which are very wonderful in the beginning, but turn out very sad in the end. Oh, what wonderful evenings we used to spend, talking about scientific things!"

Novoa smiled. In the eyes of the musician, gambling and its mysteries were scientific matters. All the paradoxes that he had taken delight in uttering had been stored up in the mind of the pianist as irrefutable truths. Novoa tried to head him off by asking for news of the Prince. But Spadoni, absorbed in his mania, continued:

"Last night's dream was terrible, and nevertheless it could not have begun better. I had the secret of your infinitesimal errors; I had mastered the hidden laws of chance and was King of the world. I had a special train, composed of a sleeping car, a drawing-room car, a dining car, a swimming-pool car, and goodness knows how many special kinds of cars! It was a regular palace on wheels that was always awaiting me at the railway station, with the engine constantly keeping up steam, ready to start at any moment. I got out of the train in all the cities famous for gambling, just as a person gets out of an automobile. And seeing me coming, the owners of the Casinos, the employees, and even the green tables fairly trembled. 'Hurrah for the Avenger!' all those who had lost their money shouted in the anteroom. But I passed on, serene as a god, without paying any attention to these ovations from the common herd. Imagine what it would cost the possessor of the secret of the infinitesimal errors to win! My twelve secretaries placed on the various tables a million or two, following my instructions. 'Ready, play!' I walked about like Napoleon, giving orders to my marshals. In half an hour, they declared the bank was broken and the Casino bankrupt. 'The house is closing its doors!' shouted the employees, just as in a church when the services are over. And on coming out, the same starving wretches who had greeted me with acclamations rushed on the guards escorting me, with sudden hate, trying to kill me. The place where their fortunes were buried was closed to them forever. Now they could not return the next day and lose more money with the vague hope of squaring accounts. I had taken away all their hopes."

"Exactly," said Novoa.

"Also I had a yacht, which was larger than Prince Lubimoff's; something in the nature of a first-class cruiser. And I needed one that size, for a band of followers as large as mine. I had with me hordes of secretaries, a crowd of strong-arm men whose duty it was to defend me and my treasure, and a great number of blasé people, who considered me a very interesting person, and followed me all over the globe, like that misanthropic fellow who followed a lion tamer from city to city, hoping that the wild beasts might some day devour him. There was no longer a single Casino functioning in Europe: the one at San Sebastian had been turned into a convent; the one at Ostend was being used as a laboratory for experiments on oyster culture. In all the bathing resorts and all medicinal springs, people became interested exclusively in taking care of their health; and when they wanted distraction, they went to the promenades and played marbles and other children's games. In the meantime I went traveling through the Americas and the South Seas, breaking one bank after another, in all the big gambling houses. I was followed by journalists who made up another army larger than my own. The newspapers and the cable and telegraph agencies announced my arrival in advance, making a great stir. 'The invincible Spadoni is coming!' And the gaming establishments, feeling their end was near, tried to exploit their death agony by selling seats at fabulous prices to every one who wanted to witness my triumph. In the United States a steel king, or a king of something or other, gave a hundred thousand dollars for a seat, in order to follow my irresistible playing close at hand. Never before had such a sum been paid to see the long hair of a concert singer or the diamonds of a soprano."

"And how about Monte Carlo?" asked Novoa, interested by the gambler's wild dreams.

"We are coming to that. I kept Monte Carlo to the end of my trip, thinking of the money that I had lost here. The fatter I let the victim grow, the greater would be my vengeance. And such business as Monte Carlo was doing! Since there was no gambling left anywhere else in the world, all the gamblers gathered here from every part of the globe. The city had grown, until it reached the summits of the Alps; the forty millions that the Casino used to win in favorable years, had now become four thousand million. The stockholders were marrying persons of royal blood: two Balkan kings were declaring war, quarreling over the hand of the daughter of a fourth Vice-President of the company that was managing the Casino. The equilibrium of Europe was imperiled: the great powers were dreaming of annexing Monaco in the name of ancient historical and ethnological rights, since they had all had and still had many people of their race living on that tiny piece of land. But suddenly the Invincible appeared."

Spadoni, as though still dreaming, looked at the Casino, the Square, the entrance to the terrace, and the curving slope of the avenue which descended to the harbor. He could see it all, perhaps no differently than he had seen it in his imagination.

"What a crowd there was! For six months previously the whole world had talked of nothing else. 'Are you going to see the fun?' 'Aren't you going?' Cook's Agency had announced in every country of the globe an inexpensive trip 'personally conducted' to witness this world event. The Paris-Lyon-Mediterranean was giving round trip tickets at reduced prices, and all Paris was on hand. The owners of hotels and restaurants, out of gratitude, were placing my portrait in the most conspicuous part of the dining rooms, which were always filled. The newspapers published my biography, and in mentioning my wealth were obliged to break their columns, placing a line of zeros clear across the page, and even then there was not sufficient space. I forgot to tell you that I found myself obliged to establish a bank, just to take care of my treasures. And whenever the Bank of London or the Bank of France were pressed for money, they sent me a polite note, asking me to get them out of their difficulty."

Novoa laughed at the naïve way in which the pianist related his greatness. He still seemed obsessed by his dream.

"My yacht was obliged to anchor outside the harbor among other ships. There were many trans-Atlantic liners there: four from the United States, one from Japan, another from South America, and a few from Australia and New Zealand, all filled with travelers who had come from the other hemisphere to see Spadoni. After greeting Monaco with a twenty-one-gun salute, I sprang ashore amid the hurrahs of the foreign sailors. You easily understand that a man like myself could not arrive at the Casino seated in a mere automobile. Who hasn't an automobile now-a-days! On the dock there was waiting for me a single seated carriage which I was to drive myself, but a carriage with gilded wheels, drawn by six women, six beautiful women, all of them celebrated, whose pictures figured not only in the principal illustrated papers, but also on perfumery bottles and cigar boxes."

The Professor was extremely amused. He noticed the satisfaction with which the pianist dwelt on this detail of his triumphal entry. The degradation of these six elegant and famous women seemed to flatter his woman-hating propensities. He spoke with a coolly revengeful look, as though witnessing the abject humiliation of his greatest and deadliest enemy.

"It was merely a matter of paying the price: and I was not going to bargain over a million more or less. The one thing that annoyed me was having to choose among several thousand beauties who were clamoring to be selected. I was obliged to risk offending many big theater managers, business men, and statesmen, by rejecting the many ladies whom they recommended to me. A monarch even withdrew the title of Duke which he had just given me, because I had refused his favorite 'friend.' All six wore the latest frocks designed in the *Rue de la Paix*. The reporters, cameras in hand, were taking snap shots of the gowns which were to set the latest style. Besides, their harness was covered with pearls, diamonds, and every sort of precious stone, and they were careful not to injure them, knowing that at the end of their trot they would be able to keep the gems as souvenirs. I had a large whip to use on occasion: a whip of flowers, to be sure. One must always be chivalrous with ladies."

He smiled ironically. Once more Novoa noted his look of rancorous misogyny.

"But inside, the whip was made of sharp steel; and lashing my six handsome steeds, we started out. What a long time it took to climb the slope making our way through the crowd! The foreigners greeted me with acclamations. The sounds of the clicking cameras blended into an endless buzzing. Every one wanted to carry away the image of the king of the world. I could pick out the natives of the city by their sad faces. The men were imploring me with their glances, like miserable captives; the women held up their children; the old men fell on their knees. I was the conqueror who, in ruining the Casino, was utterly destroying their home land, condemning them to poverty and hardship. The square was black with people. On getting out of my vehicle, I saw that the steps of the Casino were filled with a great delegation. First of all, was Monsieur Blanc; next, his general staff of advisors, the principal stockholders, the inspectors, and the entire body of *croupiers*, all dressed in black, with long alpaca coats of a funereal cut. In the background were well known people, whose presence there might move me. In order to recall to my mind the fact that I had been a mere pianist, they had waiting for me there, baton in hand, directors of concerts and operas, orchestra soloists with their instruments; singers—the men with swords at their belts, the women with long trains, and all of them painted and bewigged; girls from the ballet, with pale pink legs and masses of tulle standing out horizontally from their waists. Instructed in advance, they were all ready to groan.

"'One word with you, Signor Spadoni.'

"It was Monsieur Blanc who took me aside, and handed me a small paper.

"'Take this and don't go in.'

"I looked at the paper: a check for a million. Humph! What can a man do with a million? And on noticing that I was crumpling it, and throwing it on the ground, the master of the Casino gave me another paper.

"'Make it five then, and go away.'

"Since this did not move me either, he kept on taking checks from all his pockets: ten million, fifteen, forty....

"My twelve counselors came forward with huge purses filled with bank notes; my escort cleared the way among the imploring crowd on the stairway; my horses were getting impatient, because certain connoisseurs had availed themselves of the crowding to take liberties with them.

"'One more word, Signor Spadoni: the last. We will cause a revolution, we will dethrone Albert, and give the crown of Monaco to you. If you like, you might marry the daughter of an Emperor: with money you can do anything. We have it and so have you....'

"'I have told you no! What I want is to get into that Casino, bust the whole business, and take away the keys.'

"This threat tore from him the supreme concession.

"'You shall be my partner; I will give you fifty per cent of the winnings. Don't you want to? Well then, seventy-five.'

"On seeing that I continued to advance up the stairway without listening to him, he raised a whistle to his lips. On his face was a look of a Samson, clutching the columns of the Temple. He would rather die than see his house bankrupt! A terrible explosion resounded, as though the world were being rent apart. They had mined with all the high-power explosives of the war, the Casino, the square, and the whole city. I was blown off my feet and driven, dazed, up into the clouds, but I was still able to see how Monte Carlo was disappearing, and even the dock of Monaco, as the sea in one enormous wave, was sweeping over the site of the vanished land. And when I came down to earth again...."

"You woke up," said Novoa.

"Yes, I woke up, and on the floor beside my bed; and I could hear Castro's voice in the corridor calling me names for having spoiled his sleep by my cries. Don't laugh, Professor. It is very sad to dream of such grandeur, as though you had had it in hand, and then to find yourself as poor as yesterday, as poor as ever, and besides with bad luck still clinging to you."

This mention of poverty and bad luck by Spadoni caused Novoa to protest. People still recalled his amazing fortune as the banker in the Sporting Club. That had been an epoch-making night. Besides, he knew through Valeria that the Duchess had made him a handsome present.

"Wonderful Duchess!" the pianist said enthusiastically, "Always a great lady. Poor woman, in the midst of her despair she remembered me. 'Take this, Spadoni, and I hope you have lots of luck.' She gave me twenty thousand francs. If I were to ask her for a hundred thousand she would give them to me just the same. And to think she is so unfortunate!"

As the Professor still looked at him questioningly, he continued:

"Well, then; of the twenty thousand francs I haven't even a hundred left."

The same evening he had hurried to the Sporting Club to repeat his great deeds. He had never happened to have so much capital before, not even when he returned from his concert tour in South America. The terrible Greek was there, and in spite of the admiration Spadoni paid His Eminence, the Helene treated the musician with implacable hostility. "Bank!" said the Greek on seeing the pianist in the banker's chair, with fifteen thousand! With what remained the musician had struggled along for a few days as a mere bettor, and now the Duchess' generous gift was merely a memory.

"If she would only return to work! I am sure that I would be once more the man I was that night, with her behind me. But who would dare talk to her about gambling."

They both lamented Alicia's misfortune. Since the day the telegram arrived telling of the death of her protégé, she had been a different woman. Spadoni attributed her overwhelming grief over a young soldier who did not belong to her family to her excessively kind heart. The Professor assented, with an enigmatic air. In her sudden burst of grief, Alicia had doubtless let a portion of her secret escape in the presence of Valeria, and the latter probably had told Novoa about it.

Then they talked about the isolation in which the Duchess was living.

"It has been a month since any one has seen her," said Spadoni. "People are beginning to forget about her; a good many people think she has gone away. That's the way Monte Carlo is: quite tiny for those who go to the Casino, and rub elbows all day long; enormous, like a great metropolis, for those who do not come near the gambling rooms. The Prince frequently asks me about her with a great deal of interest. It seems he has not been able to see her since the afternoon of the telegram."

Novoa repeated his enigmatic look on hearing Lubimoff's name. He knew through Valeria that Michael had gone repeatedly to Villa Rosa, without being admitted. And more than that; the Duchess had shuddered in terror at the thought of his visit. "I don't want to see him, Valeria; tell him I am not in." Colonel Toledo had suffered the same fate; obliged to hand his card, sometimes to the Duchess' friend and at other times to the gardener. Several letters from the Prince had remained unanswered. Alicia showed a firm determination not to see her relative, as though his presence might quicken the grief that was keeping her away from society.

Spadoni, unaware of all this, continued to praise the Duchess.

"A noble heart! She always has to have some unfortunate person around to look after. Since the death of her aviator, she seems to be feeling a deep affection for that Lieutenant of the Foreign Legion, the Spaniard who is so ill, and who may die almost any moment, like the other man. He spends whole days at Villa Rosa; he lunches and dines there; and if the Duchess takes a walk in the mountains, it is always with him. He does everything but sleep at the Villa! When he doesn't show up for some time, she immediately sends a messenger to the Officers' Hotel."

The Professor remained silent, but knew that Spadoni was telling the truth. It agreed with what Valeria had been telling. Martinez was constantly at Villa Rosa, often against his will. The Duchess needed his presence, but nevertheless on seeing him, she would burst into sobs and tears. But the poor boy, with a submission born of awe, accompanied her in her voluntary seclusion, deeply thankful that such a great lady should take an interest in him.

"Doña Clorinda must be furious," continued the pianist, with malignant joy such as rivalry among women always aroused in him. "She no longer has any influence over Martinez, in spite of the fact that she was the one who discovered him. The other woman has cut her out. Weeks go by and the 'General' doesn't get a chance to see her Lieutenant; I believe she has given him up, as a matter of fact. She criticizes her former friend for this monopolizing, which she considers 'dangerous.' They even tell me that she accuses the Duchess of flirting with the poor boy, of arousing false hopes in him, and of still worse things. Quite absurd! Women are terrible when they hate. Imagine! A poor officer—practically a dead man...."

Novoa said nothing, so that the pianist would stop talking. He was afraid Spadoni might say some awful thing, repeating Doña Clorinda's gossip, with the rancorous joy of a woman-hater. Novoa, through his relations with Valeria, considered himself a partisan of the Duchess, and could not tolerate anything being said against her.

They separated after a few minutes more of inconsequential talk.

That evening Spadoni spoke to the Prince about his conversation with the Professor, and it gave him a pretext for repeating what Doña Clorinda thought of her former friend. But immediately the pianist repented of having done this, seeing the look of wrath which Lubimoff gave him.

"What a cad," thought Michael, "peddling around a lot of female gossip, just because he has a grouch against women in general."

He understood how Alicia might feel interested in the soldier. His youth and his uniform reminded her of her son. Besides, Martinez was alone in the world, a foreigner, a piece of wreckage from the war, a man whom every one considered irrevocably condemned to death.

Yet Michael could not avoid an immediate feeling of jealousy toward the poor young fellow who was friendless and ill. Martinez was living constantly by Alicia's side, while he himself was unable to gain admittance to the Villa, even as a mere visitor. Why?

He had spent several weeks making conjectures, and watching for a chance to meet Alicia. Since the afternoon when he had held her in his arms, drying her tears and restraining her from hurting herself, as she writhed in grief, and kissing her on the brow, with brotherly compassion, the gate of Villa Rosa had closed behind him forever. "Come to-morrow," groaned Alicia on saying good-by to him. And the following day Valeria had halted him with the embarrassed look of a person telling a lie. "The Duchess cannot receive you. The Duchess wants to be alone." And this inexplicable refusal had been repeated each successive day, with increasing sharpness. At present the gardener, who was the only one who came to answer the bell, talked with him through the gate.

This rejection caused him to commit a great number of childish and humiliating actions. He circled about the neighborhood of the Villa like a jealous husband, facing the curiosity of the passersby, and taking advantage of the most absurd pretexts to disguise the real object of his vigil, hurriedly concealing himself whenever the gate opened, and any one left the house. This vigilance had only served to arouse his anger. Twice Michael had been obliged to hide himself while Lieutenant Martinez, erect in the old uniform which the Prince had given him and which was rather a bad fit, steadied his weak sick body in a desire to appear proud and healthy, and entered Villa Rosa through the wide-open gate, as though he were the owner.

One afternoon he had seen them from a distance, the Lieutenant and Alicia, in a hired carriage, which was going in the other direction, on the opposite side of the street, toward the Heights of La Turbie. She was looking after the wounded man, taking him, in maternal solicitude, to a spot where he could breathe the upland air. And the Prince might just as well have not existed!

In vain he wrote her letters, and his torment was even greater owing to the fact that he could not talk openly with his friends. The Colonel, obedient to his veiled suggestions, had unavailingly paid several calls on the Duchess.

"What unexplainable grief!" said Don Marcos. "It is impossible to understand such despair over a young aviator who was merely a protégé of hers. Unless, perhaps, he were her...." But his sense of delicacy would not allow him to insist on such an ignoble suspicion.

Nor could the Prince talk with Atilio. In the latter's eyes, the prisoner who had died in Germany was the same young man he had known in Paris before the war: the Duchess' lover, who followed her everywhere and danced with her at the Tango teas. Besides, Michael felt afraid of what Castro might add, reflecting the "General's" way of thinking.

The latter, at first, on learning of Alicia's despair, had felt like forgetting the quarrels of the past, and had gone of her own accord to Villa Rosa to console the Duchess. Since the "General" was very patriotic, the boy who had died in Germany seemed to her a hero. But the sudden monopolizing of the Spanish Lieutenant, and the passionate sympathy which obliged Martinez to spend all day with the Duchess, renewed Doña Clorinda's cool hostility.

The Prince guessed what she and her friend were thinking, and what Castro might tell if he dared talk to him about Alicia. "She has just lost a lover, and while she is weeping with theatrical vehemence, she is getting ready for another, as young as the first. A crime indeed, since poor Martinez is condemned to death, and only prolongs his days, thanks to absolute quiet. The slightest emotion means death to him."

Lubimoff could not tell the truth. His secret was Alicia's. Only they two knew the true identity of the prisoner who had died in Germany, and as long as she kept silent, he must do the same.

One night, the Colonel gave him some interesting news. At nightfall, when he was returning from the Casino, he had seen the Duchess de Delille from the street car. Dressed in mourning she was getting out of a hired carriage, in the Boulevard des Moulins, opposite the church of St. Charles. Later she had ascended the steps leading to the place of worship: she was doubtless going to pray for her protégé. And Don Marcos said this with a certain emotion, as though the visit to the church cancelled all the gossip he had been hearing in the previous few days.

Michael had a presentiment that this would be the means of rescuing him from his incertitude. He would meet Alicia at the church. And the following day, toward evening, he began to walk up and down the Boulevard des Moulins, without losing sight of the one church in Monte Carlo, the place of worship of gamblers and wealthy people, which seemed to maintain a certain rivalry with the Cathedral of silent, ancient Monaco.

This continual going and coming finally caught the attention of the shopkeepers on the street and of their clerks, girls with hair dressed high on their heads in a complicated fashion, who seemed to be dreaming behind the counters, waiting for some millionaire to lift them from their position of unjust obscurity. "Prince Lubimoff!" They all knew him, and his fame was such that immediately a hundred eyes curiously sought the object of his promenading. Doubtless it was a woman. On the deserted balconies women's heads began to appear, following his maneuvers more or less overtly. Window shades went up, revealing behind the panes questioning eyes and smiling lips. "Might it be for me?" This unexpressed question seemed to spread from one window to the next.

Annoyed by such curiosity, he ascended the double row of steps from the tiny deserted square in front of the church, using the same strategy there as when he had lurked in the neighborhood of Villa Rosa. He peeped into the interior of the sanctuary, dotted with red by a number of lighted tapers. There were only two women, within, both of them dressed in mourning and kneeling. They were women of lowly fortune, wives or mothers of men killed in the war. On returning to the little square, he passed the time reading and re-reading the headlines of all the papers displayed on the newsstand. Then he started off down a street, turned into another, walked across the square with an air of unconcern, and hid behind a corner, taking care not to lose sight of the entrance to the church. It was not bad waiting there: there were no passersby. The traffic on the nearby boulevard was invisible, as though going on in the depths of a ditch. Through the low branches of some trees, he could just see the roofs of carriages and street cars.

Night fell and she did not come.

The following day Michael returned, but discreetly, so as not to arouse the curiosity of the shopkeepers. He remained for long hours in the little square in that old part of the city, with none to watch him save a melancholy old woman who sold newspapers at a stand that had no customers. Nor did Alicia come this time.

The third day, when he was beginning to doubt whether there was any use of waiting, Alicia's head and shoulders suddenly appeared above the line of the top step. Then her whole body emerged, by waves, so to speak, as her feet advanced from step to step. Night was falling. On the façades of the buildings on the boulevard, above the green mass of the trees, the fugitive sun drew a golden brush stroke along the rows of roofs.

It was his heart that recognized her even before his eyes, just as on the day when he had seen her at a distance in the carriage accompanied by the officer. He had a feeling of shock at her black bonnet, with a long mourning veil falling on her shoulders. The emotion he felt on seeing her and the spying habit he had recently acquired, caused him to draw back, and she entered the church without seeing him. Ah, now he had her! This time she could not escape, he would have a great many things to tell her, very, very many! But at the same time he became rancorously conscious of the just indictment against her which he had prepared in advance; and, in spite of himself, he felt afraid, desperately afraid of the possibility that she might meet him with a curt reply, or perhaps not speak to him at all.

He allowed a long time to elapse. Then he was torn by the desire of seeing her again, even from a distance, and he entered the church, but cautiously, trying to avoid a premature encounter.

He advanced between a double row of deserted benches. There in the background were the same women who had been there the other day, still kneeling, as though their grief were unconscious of the lapse of time. In the darkness the pale gold of the altar pieces became gradually distinguishable, and two masses of color, two clusters of flags—those of the Allied countries, which adorned the high altar. On seeing the two praying figures alone in the church, and in motionless silence, he thought that Alicia must have fled through an exit of which he was unaware. But she appeared from a door on the side, followed by an acolyte who was carrying two tapers. Alicia seemed to be watching how the tapers were lighted and placed in their sockets in front of the Virgin. Then she knelt, remaining in a rigid posture on her knees.

Some time went by. And Michael watched her, as she became, like the two poor women, a mere shape in black, motionless in prayer and supplication. The only distinguishing features of her person that he could make out, were the soles of her elegant shoes, two tiny light-colored tongues, which stood out against the black silk of her skirt. He could also see her white neck writhing from time to time, as though trying to throw off the twining veil of sorrow.

He felt that the rancor which had caused him to desire this meeting was vanishing. Poor woman! He knew, and no one else knew, the identity of the young man whose death she had come to mourn in this temple. A picture of the Princess Lubimoff suddenly arose in his memory, vague and covered with the dust of oblivion. The Princess had been insane; but she was his mother, and he had loved her so dearly!

Immediately afterward his egotism revolted against this feeling. It was natural for Alicia to weep for her son, but it was not natural that she should have broken with him without any explanation what-soever.

Mechanically he advanced toward the high altar, desiring to see her closer at hand. A slight movement as she prayed caused him to retrace his steps. It was better that she should not recognize him. He considered it preferable to wait for her outside the church, with the advantage of taking her by surprise, without allowing her time to invent excuses to justify her conduct.

It was beginning to grow late, when Alicia came out, running straight into Michael Fedor who was blocking her path.

Not the slightest quiver revealed any feeling of surprise.

"You!" she said simply.

She was very pale, and her eyes were red and moist, as though she had just been weeping.

Perhaps she had seen him within the church, and was expecting this meeting on coming out. The natural manner in which she greeted his presence was for him a just disappointment.

He felt he must speak at once, relieving himself of the burden of complaint and accusation, which had been gathering within him during the preceding days. There were so many, that they clouded his thoughts. But Alicia, as though afraid of what he was going to say, came forward and began to talk in sad, monotonous tones.

She had been coming to this church several afternoons as she suddenly felt the need of leaving Villa Rosa with its terrible memories. Oh, the arrival of that telegram!

"Now I am a believer," she announced simply.

Immediately afterward she corrected the statement, rather through humility than pride. She wanted to be a believer, but in reality she was not. She remembered the mother, poor, simple-minded Doña Mercedes! What would she not give to have the confidence in the Great Beyond which that good lady had had! That faith, which in former days had provoked her laughter, seemed to her now like something superior. What a pity she could not feel the resignation of humble souls! The irreligiousness of her happy days still remained with her. Those who enjoy the pleasant things of life do not remember death, nor do they think of what may be beyond. No one feels religious sentiments in his soul at a dance, at a banquet, or at a rendezvous with a lover! She had to believe, because she was unhappy! She clung to religion as an invalid condemned to death by the doctors in whom he believes, implores in despair the services of a quack, in whom he has no faith.

"Grief makes mystics of us," she continued. "What I regret is not being able to be one in the way that others are. I pray, but resignation does not come to my aid."

She revolted against the thought of annihilation at death. That flesh of her flesh was rotting in an unknown cemetery in Germany! And was that the end? Could it be there was nothing more? Would she die in turn and never meet again in a superior existence the son in whom she had concentrated all her love of life? Would they both be blotted out of reality, like two infinitesimal points, like two atoms, whose life means nothing?

"I must believe," she said with all the energy of her maternal egotism. "My one consolation lies in the hope that we shall meet again in a better world: a world that knows no wars, nor death. But suddenly my confidence fails, and all I see is annihilation—annihilation! I am greatly to be pitied, Michael."

These words did not move the Prince, in spite of the despair which Alicia put into them. His amorous yearning let him think only of the present.

"And I," he said in a reproachful tone. "You deserted me in the greatest moment of our lives! You are unhappy; all the more reason that you should not drive me from you. I can put cheer into your life. I can guess what you are thinking. No, no, I do not insist on talking to you of love. Perhaps later on, but now!... Now, I want to be your comrade, your brother, whatever you want me to be, but at your side. Why do you avoid me? Why do you shut your door to me as you would to a stranger?"

And incoherently he continued his laments, his protests, his rancor, at her unexplainable estrangement.

"Am I to blame for your misfortune?" he finally asked. "Am I a different man to-day than I was the last time we saw each other?"

She shook her head sadly. She could not convince Michael no matter how much she might talk; it was beyond her strength to explain her new feelings. She seemed dismayed at the obstacle which had arisen between them.

"Leave me, forget me; it is the best that you can do. No; you haven't changed, my poor boy. What harm could you have done me, you who are so kind, so generous? You have helped me to learn the horrible truth; it was through you that I discovered it; and although it is killing me, I feel that it is preferable to uncertainty. You are not to blame, you have done all that I asked you to do. But listen to me, I beg of you: do not seek me, avoid meeting me, leave me! It is the last favor I ask of you. It is only away from you that I can find a certain peace of mind."

Michael's voice lost its tones of supplication and began to quiver with a vibration of anger. How could he be an obstacle to her tranquillity? Hadn't he just said that he wanted to be a comrade in her misfortune, without desires, oblivious of love, with a sweet dispassionate affection, like that of friendship? Now that she was unhappy he felt more vehemently a desire to be by her side. What absurd caprice made her avoid him?

Alicia looked at him with tearful eyes, which reflected the hesitations of her thoughts. Finally she seemed to have made up her mind.

"You haven't changed," she said, in a subdued voice, "but I am different. Misfortune has made another woman of me. I do not recognize myself. I am dominated by a fixed idea. An absurd one it may well be; if I tell it to you, I know that you will protest with holy indignation. No; you are not to blame; but it is better for me not to see you. Your presence increases my remorse. Seeing you, I feel extraordinary shame, a desire to die, to kill myself. I have a feeling of suspicion that it was I who killed my son. I remember all that took place between us; and I recognize God's punishment."

Lubimoff's anger vanished at these inexplicable words. Automatically he took her hands with caressing gentleness, as though they were those of a poor sick patient at the height of delirious ravings. She should be calm! What was she saying? What remorse was she talking about? Her gloved hands, in passive resignation offered no resistance to his touch; but suddenly they woke to life, violently freeing themselves from those of Michael, as though they had just received a hard shock. "No! No!" And the Prince had a sort of feeling that there was a current of repulsion between them, something that he had never experienced until then: the fear of his person.

He remained so disconcerted and humiliated by this movement of withdrawal, that he did not know what to say. She took advantage of his silence to go on talking, but as though she did not see the man who was standing before her eyes.

"When I remember all that ... what a shame! My son, my poor boy, living like a slave, suffering from hunger, being whipped, he, who was so noble and so handsome ... and his mother here acting like a young girl, going into ecstasies over ideal love, taking poetic promenades through the gardens, exchanging kisses. An old woman's romantic fancies. The gambling follies might even be pardoned. I thought of him as I played; the money was for him; but love!... it seems impossible that I could have done all that while my son was a prisoner and I was getting no news from him. What diabolical spell was upon me? And God has punished me; and if not God, whoever or whatever it may be; fate, a mysterious power which makes us expiate our shortcomings, call it anything you like."

Michael attempted to protest, but she went on talking:

"I know what you are going to tell me; but it won't do any good. All that you might say I have said to myself again and again, to convince myself that my belief is absurd. And what would that prove? All that we are not acquainted with is absurd, and we know so little! No; my remorse can never be overcome. No matter what you may say will not keep me from spending my sleepless nights puzzling things out, and thinking of certain dates in my recent life. When I began to be interested in you, my son was still alive, and I forgot him. When we were walking through the gardens of San Martino, he was perhaps suffering the agonies of hunger, and martyrdom, and I like the heroine in a novel, like a crazy schoolgirl, was kissing you, and making you promises! Besides, the arrival of the telegram the same afternoon that you were going to come, seemed like something definitive in my life! Don't you see the intervention of a superior power, the punishment for my badness?"

The Prince tried to speak again, but in vain.

"That is why I am avoiding you; that is why I have not replied to your letters. You are not to blame; but you mean remorse to me, and your presence recalls my crime. Besides, I know myself; I am only a poor, weak woman, the very personification of thoughtlessness, and neglect. If I were to accept you as a comrade in grief, since I am not indifferent to you, perhaps I might give in to what you want. And that would be horrible, still more horrible even than what has gone before; one of those offenses which people maddened by passion commit against natural laws. Don't try to see me; I don't want to see you. If I had been a true mother, thinking only of him ... who knows!... Perhaps he would still be alive. But some one was bent on punishing me for my unnatural conduct, and that some one killed him, so that I might awaken, at the very moment when in my shameful love, I felt myself happiest."

Michael no longer cared to say anything. He looked at this woman with pity and dismay in his eyes. He recalled the Princess Lubimoff with her extravagant beliefs in the mysterious; and of Alicia's own mother, with her religious manias. Whatever he might try to say would be useless. That absurd and sorrowing conviction of hers had opened a gap between them like a gulf that could be bridged over only by time.

The silence of the Prince caused her to lose the nervous exaltation that had made her express herself with such fervor.

"Leave me now," she murmured gently. "What could I do for you? I am only a woman now; I am an old woman, centuries old, as old as sorrow itself. You need a sweetheart, and I am simply a bad mother, a mother tormented with remorse."

Her renunciation of the past, and the feeling that she was only a despairing mother caused her voice to break with a groan, and at the same time her eyes filled with tears. With a timid hand Michael drew away the handkerchief that she had raised to her face to hide her weeping. He murmured incoherent phrases, with the intention of consoling her; but immediately he was mastered once more by anger.

"If you really were alone," he said in bitter tones, "I could wait, and perhaps time would silence the after scruples that torment you. But your loneliness is a lie. A man enters your house at all hours as though it were his own, while I must go away, so that, as you say, you may recover your tranquillity."

With a feminine instinct, Alicia had hastened to raise the handkerchief to her face again, on feeling herself free from Michael's hand. She felt she must be ugly with her watery eyes, her pale lips, and her nose red with weeping. But the words of the Prince gave her such a shock of surprise, such a desire to refute the offensive supposition, that she took the wrinkled batiste from her face.

"You are referring to Martinez? Poor boy!"

He was giving up the gay society of his comrades, their promenades in company, and even the parties to which the convalescent officers were invited, to come and be bored at Villa Rosa beside a woman who could do nothing but weep. When she wanted to come to church she had to oblige him to go for an hour or two to join his comrades-in-arms in the ante-room at the Casino. The visits of the invalided soldier meant so much to her. They were pure charity on his part.

"I dream that he is my son. His age and his uniform aid in this illusion. You have never had any children; it is impossible for you to know the necessity we feel, when we have lost them, to transfer our bereaved affection to other beings, imagining that they look like those who are gone. I need to go on being a mother, nor can I be anything else; and this unhappy boy never knew his own mother. He has no one in the world, and is as much alone as I am. Please, let me enjoy a little illusion wherever I can find it. The poor fellow is so grateful for my affection! He feels so happy beside me! Remember: he is condemned to death, and only maternal care, and pleasant quiet surroundings, can possibly prolong his days."

She wanted to accomplish this task, perhaps for a selfish reason, to obliterate from her memory, with a great generous deed, all the evil she had done before. She wanted him to be her son, a son born of her grief, to whom she might devote everything that it was now impossible for her to do for her real son.

Now, Michael, too, was silent, realizing the uselessness of insisting any further. He knew Alicia's character. Behind her plaintive voice, he guessed the resolute will to keep by her side that young man who refreshed her maternal feelings and was at the same time a means of consolation for the remorse which she had taken upon herself.

The consideration of his powerlessness finally irritated him, made him feel a cruel desire to hurt that woman.

"You are doing wrong, Alicia. Society is unaware of your secret. You know what people said before about you and your son. You laughed, yourself, finding such a mistake amusing. Now the equivocation continues with more reason. Many people imagine you have substituted another young man for the young man that died."

Alicia lost her sad serenity.

"How disgusting!" she said. "How can they think that. Poor Martinez! He is so good! So respectful!"

Then she continued arrogantly:

"Let them say what they like! I want to forget society; let society forget me. I am dead as far as people are concerned."

But Michael in his spite still dwelt on the subject.

"The other man was your son, and I knew he was. This man is not, and I know the power of seduction that you exercise, even against your will. Remember 'the old men on the wall.'"

Wherever she went, men's glances would cling to her rhythmic body; and that young man, that queer fellow, would finally....

He was unable to continue.

"You, too!" she exclaimed. "Good-by, don't come after me. I shall always think of you; but it is better for us not to see each other. Don't bear me a grudge. Perhaps some day!..." And she resolutely turned her back on him, and descended the steps toward the boulevard.

The Prince remained motionless for a few minutes. Then he advanced toward the top step, but all he could see was a carriage with the hood raised, and two horses starting to trot away.

And the meeting with Alicia he had so ardently desired had come to this! The feeling of spite caused him to judge himself harshly; he hadn't known how to talk. Later he recalled all his reasoning and his accusations, and felt amazed at the slight effect they had had on her. Yes, indeed, she was a different woman. Some one had changed her; some one was to blame for this absurd situation.

He spent a great part of that night reflecting. It did not occur to him to blame Alicia. He even repented of his angry words. Unhappy woman! Her extreme over-sensitiveness was causing her to find reason for shame and remorse in all that she had ever done.

"Besides, women," he continued to himself, "at the least nervous shock lose their logical faculty first of all."

He felt a need of concentrating all his anger on some one besides her; and Michael, never imagining that he himself had lost his logical faculty, put the responsibility for everything on Martinez. The latter was the one person to blame. If he had not come between them, Alicia, on finding herself alone in misfortune, would have sought once more the support of the Prince. What a gift the "General" had made them, presenting this adventurer!

His reason vainly argued that it was not the officer who was seeking Alicia, but the latter who was keeping him in her home, cutting him off from his old friendships. Lubimoff was not willing to give up his spite. It was Martinez and no one else who had come between them.

Up to that time he had not paid much attention to the boy whom Toledo called the "hero." There were so many heroes at that moment! In his hatred he began to strip him of the prestige given him by his deeds and his misfortune, Michael saw him without his uniform, without his war crosses and his wounds, such as he must have been before the war; a poor employee, a business clerk, whose dreams of love had never gone beyond a milliner or a stenographer. And this was the interesting personage who had the temerity to face him! Prince Michael Fedor Lubimoff. What intolerable times!

The following day he walked about his garden all morning, resolved never to return to Monte Carlo. He was filled with scorn at the thought of the tenderness with which Alicia had spoken of her protégé. It was better that he should not encounter him. But in the afternoon the loneliness of his beautiful Villa weighed on him. It seemed deserted. Atilio, the pianist, and even the Colonel were all at the Casino. He, too, decided to go, to mingle with the crowd which was dividing its attention between the hazards of war and the hazards of chance.

In the anteroom he walked toward the groups who were gathered around the bulletin board reading the latest telegrams. The crowd considered the news good, since it was not extremely bad as on the preceding days. The Allies had stopped the enemy's advance, holding them at a standstill on the ground they had just conquered. The bombardment of Paris with long range guns was still continuing. And that was all.

There was a man making comments in a loud voice. It was Toledo, who, as was his custom every afternoon, was giving a lecture on strategy to a semi-circle of admirers. With his back to the Prince, he was spouting a stream of clear optimism, with a simple faith that misfortune and reverses could not move.

"Now they have nailed them in their tracks: they won't advance any farther. In a short time will be the counter-attack. I am sure of it; it is clear as daylight to me."

Don Marcos rubbed his hands, and slyly winked one eye.

"And the Americans are coming and coming. There are days when as many as ten thousand of them are landed here. A wonderful people! I have always said so! That fellow Wilson is a great man. I know him well."

They all listened with delight to this voice of hope that refreshed their hearts before they gave themselves up to the strain and stress of roulette and *trente et quarante*. He talked with the authority of a man who has influential connections, and is informed of everything. "He knew Wilson," he had just said so himself. Besides, he was a Colonel—although none of them knew in what army—an expert, capable of expressing an unfounded opinion. And many of them lost no time in hastening to the gambling rooms to repeat his views, as though they had just received some inside information.

The Prince withdrew, afraid that his presence might put an end to that professional triumph of Toledo, which was repeated every day.

As he walked about the anteroom before entering the gaming halls, he saw beside a column, a group of French officers, all of whom were convalescents. Denied the permission to go any further, because of their uniform, they were standing there, looking with a certain envy on the civilians. A few of them were standing erect, without any visible infirmity, with the sharp features of an eagle, aquiline nose, bold eyes, and wild mustache. Others, with youthful faces, were bent over like ailing men, leaning on canes, and wearing wrinkled uniforms much too large for their sunken chests. Each time they decided to move their legs they made a long pause as though to muster every bit of their will power available. Some of them had come to Monaco as incurables, after a long captivity in Germany. The rest came from hospitals on the firing line. On the faces of all of them was an expression of joyous bewilderment at finding themselves in this corner of the earth, that was like a Paradise, where people seemed to have forgotten the rest of the world, and women's eyes followed them with enigmatic glances, half amorous and half maternal!

One of the soldiers raised his hand to his cap to salute the Prince. The latter looked at the yellowish color of his *kepis*, then at his uniform which was of the same color, and at the multi-colored line of decorations. It was Martinez, the lieutenant in the Foreign Legion, who was saluting him with a certain timidity, but pleased at the same time that his comrades were seeing him on friendly terms with the famous personage, who was so much talked about on the Riviera.

Michael returned his greeting mechanically and went on. That moment remained fixed in his memory all his life. Age and the discretion that accompanies it seemed to fall from him like dry bark from a tree in springtime. He felt as though he were back in his youth. For a few moments he was the same Captain Lubimoff of the imperial Guards, who had trampled on obstacles and braved scandal when any one opposed his will.

He turned to look at the group of officers from a distance. That little insignificant Lieutenant, who looked like a bookkeeper, promoted by mobilization, was his enemy! It seemed as though he were seeing him for the first time. Lost among his companions he appeared even more insignificant than when he visited Villa Sirena.

Michael remained motionless, with his glance fixed on the group. "You are going to do something foolish," admonished a voice within him. And there passed through his memory the image of stern Saldaña, kindly and tolerant with the weak, like every one who is sure of his strength. He recalled one of his sayings which had never before crossed his mind: "A gentleman must be kind and never take unfair advantage of his strength." He was sure that his father had said that to him when he was a child. But immediately the duality of his inner being expressed itself through another voice which was stronger and more imperious, a woman's voice like that of the other counselor of his youth: "Spend; don't deny yourself anything, put yourself above everybody; always remember that you are a Lubimoff." And he saw the dead Princess, not the Mary Stuart with her theatrical mourning robes, but the dominating and still beautiful woman, the one who had overwhelmed her husband "the hero" with her rage, and turned the Paris residence upside down.

Suddenly he found himself near the group of officers, and again his eyes met those of Martinez. The latter came toward him with a smile of interrogation. Michael realized that he had beckoned to the soldier, without being aware of what he was doing, through an impulse of will which seemed entirely detached from his reason.

"So much the worse! Let's get through with the business!"

With a certain haste, he took the young man toward the vestibule of the Casino as though anxious to avoid the presence of the groups who were filling the anteroom.

"Lieutenant, I have something to say to you.... I must ... ask a favor of you."

He stammered, not knowing how to express the command which he himself felt was absurd.

This vacillation, together with the trembling in his voice, finally irritated him.

They stopped beside the glass door at the entrance. Martinez was no longer smiling, as he gazed in amazement at the hard look and the pallor of the Prince.

"In a word," the latter said resolutely; "what I have to ask you is that you pay fewer visits at the house of the Duchess de Delille. If you should refrain entirely from going to see her, it would be even better." And he paused, breathing with a certain freedom, after having expressed this demand.

An expression of amazement gradually took possession of Martinez' face. He hesitated for a moment, with his eyes fixed on Lubimoff's. No, it was not a jest: the hostile look of this man who had always treated him with amiable indifference, the sharpness of his tone, and a certain trembling of his right hand, indicated that he had expressed his real thoughts, and that behind these thoughts lay enormous depths of hatred against him.

His surprise caused him to talk with timidity. He visited the Duchess because the lady asked him to come and see her every day. He had often felt his assiduity might prove to be a nuisance, but every attempt he had made to break off his visits had been fruitless. He scarcely left her for a few hours but the good lady had him sent for. She was as kind to him as a mother. Suddenly his humble tone vanished. His eyes guessed in those of the man who had stopped him something that he himself had never imagined. The Lieutenant seemed transfigured, as though rising to the same level as the Prince. His eyes shone with the same wild splendor as the other man's; his body stiffened with the tension of a spring about to be released; his nostrils quivered nervously. The little clerk, with his timid bearing, recovered the air of gallant bravery of the fighting man. His voice sounded harsh, as he went on talking.

He would go wherever he was asked, wherever he felt like going, without recognizing the right of any man to interfere in his actions. The Duchess was the only one who could close her door to him. Why did the Prince interfere in that lady's affairs without consulting her first?

"I am related to her," said Michael, inwardly hesitating somewhat at making use of the relationship which he had often preferred to deny.

They both found themselves on the other side of the entry, on the platform above the steps of the Casino, in the open air, opposite the groves of the square and the groups of passersby who were walking about the "Camembert." They were obliged to stand aside, in order not to disturb those who were entering and coming out.

"Besides," continued the Prince, "it is my duty to shield her from gossip. I cannot permit that. Seeing you in there at all hours, they should suppose...."

He almost regretted these words on noticing the double effect that they had on the young man. First he became indignant. Had any one dared gossip about that great lady who had been such a saint in his eyes? But this protest was accompanied by a certain unconscious satisfaction, by childish pride, as though he were flattered, in spite of everything that his name should be connected in absurd conjecture with that of the Duchess. It seemed that Martinez had just been revealed to himself, giving substance and a name to the obscure sentiments that until then, in an embryonic stage, had pulsed unrecognized within him.

The jealous mind of the Prince guessed, with keen penetration, everything that the other man was thinking, and this added fuel to his wrath. What impudence in this little clerk to take up Alicia's defense? What a conceited show he was making of his love for her!

"If any one takes the liberty of talking about the Duchess," said the Lieutenant, "if anybody dares to gossip because she does me the honor of receiving me in her home—the greatest honor in my life!—I will take it on my shoulders to punish whoever invents such a lie, no matter how high up he may be, no matter how powerful he may think himself to be!"

Lubimoff listened impatiently. Now it was Martinez daring to attack him. Those last words had carried a threat for him.

Besides, the Prince felt irritated at his own clumsiness. His imprudent action had served merely to open this young man's eyes, and make him think of the possibilities of many things which he had never yet imagined, and which if he had imagined them, he would have cast aside immediately as foolish. And now no less than the Prince Lubimoff had elected to show this cheap Lieutenant that, in the opinion of gossips, such things were possible.

The tone in which the officer defended Alicia aroused his anger even more. He divined in it great pride, the vanity of a poor fellow who had known love adventures only in books, and who suddenly found himself in supposed relations with a Duchess, as the rival of a Prince. How glorious for an upstart!

"Boy ..." said Lubimoff, in a hard voice.

This simple word, which was the term in which waiters were addressed in the hotels, was followed by a haughty look of overwhelming superiority, which seemed to sweep away everything extraordinary which the war had given Martinez: his uniform, his decorations, and his glorious wounds. For the Prince the officer no longer existed: there only remained the poor vagabond of a few years before, wandering from one hemisphere to another in quest of bread. "Boy," he repeated in a tone that brought back all the class distinction and social gradations of dead centuries, so that the man whom he had accosted might realize the enormous separation between him and the man to whom he deigned to give advice—

"Boy, let's come to the point—. And if I were to order you not to return to that house? And if I demand that...?"

He was unable to finish the sentence. His threatening voice, harsh as a cry of command, roused the indignation of the man in uniform. To have faced death for three long years, among thousands of comrades who were now lying in the ground; to have learned to set little store on life, as something proved worthless at every moment on the battlefield; to have stripped himself forever, by dint of frightful adventures and awful wounds, of that fear which the instinct of self-preservation puts in all beings, only to the end that now, in a pleasure resort, at the door of the most luxurious of gambling houses, a man, rich and powerful, but who had never done anything useful in his whole life, should dare to threaten him!...

"You say that to me!" he said, stammering with rage. "You give orders to me!"

Michael felt a hand seize him by the lapel of his coat. It was like a bird, tremulous and aggressive, pausing for an instant in its blind impulse, before flying upward. He was aware of the blow that was coming, and raised his arm instinctively, both hands met as that of the young man whirled close to the face of the Prince. The latter, who was stronger, seized the ascending hand and held it motionless, in a firm grip, while at the same time he smiled in a gruesome fashion. His eyes contracted as his eyebrows arched in the smile. They became again the eyes of an Asiatic. His nostrils dilated as he breathed like a stallion. The remote ancestors of the Princess Lubimoff must have smiled thus in their moments of anger.

"Enough: I consider that I have received it," he said slowly, "Name two friends to confer with mine!"

And freeing that hand of Martinez, he turned his back on him, after making a deep bow. The movements of both men had been rapid. Only one of the doorkeepers, with his official cap, standing guard on the platform above the steps, had guessed that anything had happened; but his professional experience advised him to remain passive as long as there were no blows. He imagined that it was merely a dispute over some gambling affair. It would all be settled by an explanation, and forgotten after a winning! He had seen so many such things!

Prince Lubimoff reënters the Casino. He crosses the vestibule and the anteroom holding his head high, but without seeing any one, gazing straight ahead, with a faraway expression.

It seems to him that time has suddenly been reversed, causing him to return to the past with one bound. He is back in his youth. He walks arrogantly. He is surprised that the sound of his firm tread is not accompanied by the tinkling of spurs and the metallic scraping of a saber. At the same time he begins to see imaginary faces, faces of those who disappeared from the earth many years ago: the Cossack who had come from a distant garrison in Siberia to avenge his sister; a friend in the same regiment as the Prince, who died from a sword thrust in his breast after a tumultuous supper, while Lubimoff wept, suddenly awakening from his homicidal intoxication; the faces of others who had been present as mere witnesses, but who had died and were now resurrected in his memory, cold and insensible to remorse and vain regrets.

"The Colonel. Where in the devil is the Colonel!"

He crosses the gambling room, in quest of a gray head, with a straight part from the forehead to the back of the neck, dividing the glistening hair into two shining sections. He sees it finally rising above the back of a divan, between two women's hats, four eyes darkly bordered as though in mourning, and cheeks with wrinkles filled with white and rose-colored enamel. A terse sentence of the Prince interrupts the explanations of the war news with which the Colonel had been thrilling the two ladies.

"Colonel, an affair of honor. I intend to fight to-morrow. Look for another second."

Toledo seems disconcerted by this order. His first thought flies to Villa Sirena. He sees his black frock coat, the solemn vestment of honor ready to leave its prison. Then a cloud of doubt obscures this joyous thought. A duel! Would it be fitting now that men are fighting in masses of millions, giving their lives for something higher and more important than personal hatred? His training immediately smothers this scruple. "A gentleman should always be at the orders of another gentleman." Besides, it is his Prince. And ready to fulfill his mission, he asks the name of the adversary.

"Lieutenant Martinez."

Don Marcos thinks he had heard wrong; then he seems to totter and stands there looking at his "Highness" in a sort of stupor. Instinctively, without taking the pains to disentangle the confused thoughts that assail him, he sees in his imagination the Duchess de Delille. Why did the Prince ever give up his wise theories on the woman question! He recalls, like a happy past, the flourishing days of the "enemies of women"! Only four months had gone by, and it seems as though they were centuries. A duel right in war time—and with an officer! And that officer is Martinez, his hero!

He shrugs his shoulders, bows his head, and makes a gesture denying all responsibility as he always does when his Prince, with a hard look on his face which reminds Toledo of the dead Princess in her stormy days, gives absurd orders.

"Shall I look for Don Atilio? He has had several affairs of honor; he knows what it means, and may be able to help me."

The Prince is willing. In the bar of the private gambling rooms, he will wait for them both to talk over the conditions of the encounter.

He remains motionless in a deep armchair, opposite a window gilded by the light of the setting sun, on which the threads of shadows, projected by the moving branches of the trees, weave and unweave. Suddenly it seems to him that he is obliged to wait an unreasonable length of time. It occurs to him that Castro is not in the Casino and that Don Marcos is looking for him in vain. He scarcely remembers the past at all. The officer's figure is sunk into a gray mist which falls across his memory: it is no longer anything save a vague outline. The one thing that he can see, in sharp relief and as though looming close to his eyes, is a hand: a hand which is gripping his breast and rising toward his face, that no man ever yet had slapped. His indignation causes him to come out of his deep fit of distraction. To do that to him! Trying to slap Prince Lubimoff!

When he raises his eyes he sees Toledo approaching, but alone, with a certain embarrassment, fearing in advance the anger of the Prince. The latter, who feels kindly and tolerant since the scene of violence on the stairway, guesses what he is going to say to him. He has not found Castro and he absolves him with a benevolent smile.

The Colonel speaks:

"Marquis: Don Atilio refuses."

"What!" And at the questioning glance of Lubimoff, who cannot understand, and who does not want to understand what he hears, Toledo repeats, growing more and more embarrassed.

"He refuses to be your representative. He told me to find some one else. He has some ideas of his own that...."

And he hesitates to express these ideas. He stops, in order not to say anything which the Prince ought not to hear from his lips: and he accepts as a blessing the silence of amazement which comes between them; he is afraid to let the Prince recover from the astonishment with which this news has overwhelmed him.

As he starts to go away, he proposes something which seems to him a way out.

"Does your Highness want me to call Don Atilio? He will surely come. Perhaps the two of you talking together...."

And he goes away in search of Castro, while Michael Fedor once more becomes motionless in his seat, quite unable to comprehend the situation.

* * * *

The Prince saw Castro standing by the little table close to his chair, with a certain appearance of haste in his look and bearing, like a man who is facing a difficult situation, and anxious to get out of it as soon as possible.

The Prince invited him to take the nearest seat, but Castro consented only to sit down lightly on the arm of the chair, to indicate his desire that the interview be brief. Besides, he spoke first, bluntly expressing his thoughts, without any preamble.

"The Colonel has doubtless told you my reply. I can't. You know very well that I am your friend: you even do me the honor of recognizing me as a relative; I owe you a great deal; but what you ask me now ... no! It is a piece of foolishness, madness. It all had to end like this! There was no other way out of it. I had a presentiment of it some time ago. Perhaps you were right when you talked about women as you did, and about the necessity of being their enemies—if such a thing is possible. But it doesn't do any good to bring up the past: You are no longer the Lubimoff who said those incoherent things. As for me I am mad, I'll grant you that: but you are even more so than I: and for that reason I can't be with you."

Michael looked at him fixedly, without abandoning his silent immobility, waiting for him to go on.

"A duel right in war time! Is there any common sense to that? You are the gentleman who remains quietly in his home, with all the comforts that the present time can allow, without running any risk whatsoever, while half of humanity is weeping, starving, bleeding, or dying. And just because one fine day you happen to be in an ill-humor—perhaps you know why—you want to fight a poor boy who has survived almost by a miracle, and who is sick and weak from having done what you and I are not capable of doing. You ask me to represent you in such a piece of business?"

"He insulted me—he tried to strike me. I caught his hand close to my face," said the Prince in a low but rancorous voice from the depths of his chair.

This caused Castro to hesitate for a moment, as he had no idea of the importance of the clash between the two men. But his hesitation was brief.

"There is something that I don't understand and that you are keeping silent. The very seriousness of the insult indicates that there was something extraordinary on your part. For that poor, respectful, and timid boy to dare to strike, and strike a man like you!... What did you do to rouse him to such a pitch?"

Lubimoff did not deign to reply. Without abandoning his frowning reserve he asked briefly:

"Well, are you going to, or are you not?"

Castro, irritated by this attitude, replied without hesitating:

"It's all nonsense, and I refuse."

Lubimoff still remained motionless at this refusal, but Atilio was sure he guessed the Prince's thoughts in the hostile look fixed on him. He was accusing him of ingratitude. At the same time he was holding the "General" responsible: believing that the latter must have influenced his decision. That Lieutenant was so greatly admired by Doña Clorinda!

As though replying to these unexpressed ideas, Atilio went on:

"Do you think I am interested in that boy you are bent on fighting? He is quite indifferent to me; I even dislike him, because of the great extremes to which certain women go in their admiration of his heroism. That is always annoying to those who are not heroes. I think how insignificant he must have been only four years ago. If I had met him then, I would have found him, I dare say, a book-keeper in some hotel, or a clerk in my haberdasher's in Paris. Imagine what a friend! But the war has swept over us, turning everything upside down, making some emerge, and burying others in the deepest depths, without any certainty of rising again. This boy happens to be somebody now. He is of more consequence than you or I. He has been of some use; and for me he is sacred, in spite of the fact that he inspires envy in me rather than admiration."

The Prince finally made a gesture of protest. Then he shrugged his shoulders disdainfully, and sank once more into motionless silence. That little adventurer worth more than he, because they had punctured his skin in a fight or two!

"We would never come to an understanding, even if we talked all the afternoon," continued Castro. "I have changed considerably, and you are the same man you have always been. I believe that yesterday I came to my 'road to Damascus.' I feel to-day that I am a different man."

And, through a certain need of expressing his great inner turmoil, he went on talking, without paying any attention to whether or not the Prince was listening to him.

He had come to his "road of Damascus" near the Monte Carlo railway station, beside the tracks. He was with two ladies, in one of whom he was greatly interested. (Michael thought once more of Doña Clorinda.) A trainload of soldiers was returning from Italy; a somber train, without flags and without any branches of trees adorning the doors and windows. They were Frenchmen. They had been sent to Italy as reënforcements, after the disaster of Caporetto, and now they were being hurriedly recalled, to defend their own soil, which was again in danger.

"No songs and no wild merriment; they were all silent, tired and dirty, with an epic dirtiness. The cars were more like wild beasts' cages, with their pungent odors of the animal ring. The soldiers were young men but they looked old, with their bristling beards, spotted uniforms, and faces parched by the sun, hardened by the cold, and cracked and chapped by the wind. The heat had caused them to remove their blouses, and they were in flannel shirts of an undefinable color, drenched with the sweat of so many fatigues and so many emotions.

"One could guess that they were the battalion always predestined to arrive in time to sustain the hardest shocks; the one that punctually appeared in the places of greatest danger, with the heroic resignation of the strong, who allow themselves to be exploited, and who not only do their own work, but help out all the others who work less. Where had these men not fought? On their own soil, and on that of the Allies, and perhaps in the Orient, and now, they were returning again to the land of their first combats. Just when they were thinking they had accomplished everything, they had discovered they had as yet done nothing. In the weaving and unweaving of the web of war, it was necessary to begin all over again. Four years before, they imagined they had triumphed decisively on the banks of the Marne, and now they were returning once more to the Marne. Every winter, sunk in the mud, buried in the trenches, under the rain, they said to one another: 'This will be the last.' And another winter came, and another, and still another on the heels of the last, without any noticeable change. This was the reason for their fatalistic and resigned demeanor, the look of men who adapt themselves to everything and finally come to believe that their misery will be eternal, that human times of peace will never return."

Castro stopped talking a moment and paid no attention to the face of his friend, which seemed to be asking what all that story had to do with him. "We were standing on the edge of an embankment, leaning on the barriers, and our heads were on a level with the men huddled in the carriages. The long train, the head of which had already reached the station, was slowly advancing. The two ladies were waving their handkerchiefs, smiling at the soldiers, and calling words of greeting to them. Many of the latter remained unmoved, looking at them with eyes of sleepy wild beasts. They had been greeted with ovations for four years. They knew realities, the terrible realities that lie beyond ovations! Others, young or more ardent, aroused themselves at the sight of these two elegant women. Electrified by their smiles, they stood erect, passing a hand over their wrinkled flannels, and threw kisses, trying to recover their gentleness of the days when they were not soldiers. Suddenly, one of those who were passing, forgot the women and noticed me, also waving my hat to them, and shouting hurrah. He was a sort of red-haired, bitter devil."

Castro could still see him, as though his head were peering through one of the bar-room windows; perhaps he would be able to see, as long as he lived, the whitish parchment of the man's face, drawn across his prominent cheek-bones; his red beard hanging from his jaws, as though it were a piece of make-up, and above all, his insolent, sarcastic eyes, a muddy green color, like that of oysters. He was the soldier who criticizes, grumbles, and talks against the officers, while carrying out their orders. In civil life he must have been the disagreeable rebel who never approves of anything. As his eyes met those of Castro, the latter had a feeling of repulsion. He divined the man with whom one always clashes in the street, in the cars, and in the theater. And nevertheless, he would never forget his momentary meeting with that soldier who was passing and was disappearing in the distance, with only just enough time to say six words.

He gave the two women a scornful, ironic smile—then another at Castro, who was still waving his hat, and pointed to the end of the carriage, shouting to him:

"There's still room for one more!"

And that was all he said.

"He said enough, Michael. Since then I keep hearing his harsh voice: I shall always hear it, in my happiest moments, if I remain here. And the look in his eyes? I understood all the mute insults, the rapid comparisons that he made between his misery and my strong, well-groomed appearance. For him I was a coward gallivanting with women, when men are with men, giving their lives for something of importance."

"Bah! You are a foreigner," interrupted the Prince, who seemed wearied by his friend's words.

"I live here; and the land where I live cannot be foreign to me. This war is for something more than questions of land; it concerns all men. Look at the Americans, whom we all considered very practical and incapable of idealism; they know that they are not going to gain anything positive; and nevertheless they are entering the struggle with all their might. Besides, there is the spirit of the women. Would you imagine that the two that were with me laughed at the red-headed fellow's insult, considering it very apropos? And don't tell me that women are always attracted by the warrior, on every occasion. Perhaps by the warrior in peace times, shiny and beplumed. But these fellows now look so miserable! No; there is something very lofty in everything that surrounds us, something that you and I have not been able to see, because of our selfishness."

His listener once more shrugged his shoulders with a gesture of indifference.

"And when I think of my meeting yesterday, as I constantly am doing, and see the place that that damned redhead offered me jokingly, as though I were a woman, and as though I would never have the courage to take it, you propose that I arrange for a deadly combat with another of these men who consider themselves, not without reason, superior to us! No; now you know my answer: I won't accept."

He had left the arm of the chair and was standing, facing the Prince. The latter made a gesture of weariness. He was bored by Atilio's words, by that childlike story about the train, the red-haired soldier and his insolent invitation. That might move Doña Clorinda, but nobody else; he had more important things to think about just then. And since he refused to do him the favor, he could leave him alone.

"Good-by, Michael!" said Castro, with the conviction that this farewell was going to be something more than a momentary parting.

"Good-by," replied the Prince, without stirring.

When he had almost reached the door, Atilio turned back.

"I know what my refusal means, and what it is up to me to do. Good-by again. Remember that if you were to ask me anything else...."

But the Prince interrupted his words with another gesture of indifference, and Atilio went away, hiding his emotion.

Immediately Don Marcos entered the bar, as though he had been waiting on the other side of the curtain for Castro to come out. His "chamberlain" had never seemed to the Prince so active and intelligent.

"It is all arranged, Marquis."

As he had felt certain that Atilio would not allow himself to be persuaded, he had gone in search of another second. He thought for a moment of going to Monaco, to speak to Novoa. Then he remembered the professor's relations with Valeria. Such a visit would be equivalent to informing the Duchess of the entire affair. Besides, the scientist did not know anything about such matters, and was a fellow countryman of Martinez. It was quite enough that one Spaniard should figure in this affair.

"I have my second," he continued. "It will be Lord Lewis."

In the Colonel's eyes, Lewis was more of a Lord than ever. He was thankful for the promptness with which he had granted his request. The Englishman was winning money that afternoon, and was in an excellent humor. He even got up from his seat, leaving the gambling, to listen to the Colonel. He wanted to take him over to the bar, affirming that with a whiskey in front of a fellow he can talk better; and Toledo guessed from his breath that he had already taken several drinks to celebrate his good luck. Lewis was disposed to serve his friend Lubimoff. As far as fights were concerned, he was acquainted only with boxing; but he had absolute confidence in the Colonel's expert opinion and would support anything he might say. Immediately afterwards he had returned to his play.

Michael gave Toledo his instructions. It would be an encounter under rigorous conditions, like those which he had witnessed in Russia. It could be nothing else: he had received a blow. And he said this with a sullen voice, quite convinced of the absolute reality of the insult.

As night fell, he left the Casino, avoiding his acquaintances who were invading the bar, and obliging him to smile and keep up frivolous conversation, while his thoughts were far away.

In all his moments of profound anger, when unable to put his feelings into immediate and violent action, his nervous excitation was followed by a certain lassitude which caused his muscles and nerves to relax.

It was with a real pleasure that he entered Villa Sirena, finding an unwonted voluptuousness in all the details of its comforts. He spent the time he was waiting for the Colonel in reading. At nine o'clock he was obliged to eat alone. Then he returned to his book, but this time in his bedroom, finally lying down, book in hand. He smiled with a smile that was almost a grimace, as he thought that his nervous fatigue had caused him to stretch out in the same posture as the dead.

He went on turning the pages without losing a single line, and nevertheless he could not have told what he was reading. Suddenly, he concentrated his attention in an effort to remember. Something had happened; something was awaiting him. What was it? "Oh, yes!" And after reconstructing in his memory what had taken place that afternoon, and imagining what was to take place the following day, he returned to his meaningless reading.

The pages melted away like snowflakes; he felt his hand grow lighter; the book finally fell on the bed. Instinctively he sought the electric button to darken the room, and before completely losing all perception of the outer world, he could hear his own first regular breathing.

A light striking against his eyes made him sit up. He saw the Colonel beside his bed. The deep silence of the night, which seemed even more absolute when emphasized by the sound of the sea, was broken off by the panting of a motor-car.

The Prince rubbed his eyes. What time was it?

"One o'clock," said Don Marcos.

Everything was arranged. The meeting was to take place on the following day, at two o'clock in the afternoon. It could not be managed earlier! There were still a great many things left to be done. The place selected was Lewis' castle; an encounter in the principality of Monaco would be impossible. All the houses there were close together, without a single quiet spot where two men might face each other, pistol in hand.

Lubimoff almost jumped out of bed, so great was his surprise. The choice of arms was his, as the injured person, and he had mentioned to his representative the saber, the favorite weapon of his youthful duels. Toledo, for the first time faced the furious look of his Prince without a tremor.

"Marquis," he said with dignity. "It could not be anything else! You must remember that this poor young man is a convalescent, almost an invalid. I am astonished that he should have persuaded his seconds to allow even pistols. His representatives did not want to accept anything. They are among those who feel that this duel ought not to take place."

The Prince calmed himself. A sense of equity caused him to accept Toledo's decision. That sick fellow was not an enemy worthy of his saber; it was necessary to establish a certain equality between them, and the pistol would do that, being the only weapon that lends itself to surprises and whims of chance.

"At any event I shall kill him," thought Michael, remembering his skill as a marksman.

"I must tell your Highness," the Colonel went on, "that all weapons are the same to him. This young man and his two friends are well acquainted with everything that concerns warfare, but they haven't the slightest notion of duelling and the weapons that are used on such occasions."

Then he enumerated the conditions. The distance was to be fifteen meters; each one was to fire a single shot, but each might aim and fire while he, who was to direct the combat, was counting from one to three. With a marksman like the Prince, such conditions would be serious.

Exactly! The Prince found them acceptable.

"Good-night," he said, burying himself in the bed, and pulling the coverlet up to his eyes.

Once more sleep overwhelmed him, now that his curiosity was satisfied.

Toledo would have liked to do the same, but he was obliged to fulfill the sacred duties of his exalted position, and he went from room to room looking through every drawer and climbing on chairs to rummage around on the top shelves of the closets. He was looking for a box of duelling pistols, that had been given to him in Russia by one of the Generals who was a friend of the dead Marquis. When he finally found it, he was obliged to spend more than an hour in cleaning the luxurious weapons, which had lost their silvery brilliancy in the oblivion of their long confinement.

He felt tired, yet at the same time his feeling of importance warded off sleep. Was he not the soul of the drama which was being prepared for the following day, he alone? Without him, neither his Highness nor Martinez could fight. Lord Lewis and the two soldiers who represented the adversary were incapable of a single idea, and had to follow him as though they were his pupils.

Consciousness of this superiority caused him to recall from mid-afternoon to mid-night all his past negotiations and triumphs.

He had gone in quest of Martinez, with a certain hesitation. In spite of his old beliefs, he felt Atilio's protests were quite reasonable. Perhaps what he said was right, that this duel was a piece of foolishness, madness even, on the part of the Prince. But his traditional ideas revolted against such scruples.

"Honor is honor." And, hearing the Lieutenant accept reparation by arms, with joy, and with a certain haste, as though he were afraid that Toledo would repent and withdraw the proposal, the Colonel felt the satisfaction of a person who, after long hesitation, becomes convinced that he is in the right. Heroic youth, ready to maintain all points of honor! Don Marcos found it natural that he should act thus. Martinez was from the same land as himself!

For a moment his memory dwelt on the image of the Duchess. Perhaps she was the involuntary cause of this clash, and the boy was animated by a feeling of vanity. He was going to figure in a duel such as he had read about in the story books of his youth; he was going to be a chief actor in one of those dreams of high life that seemed to him to belong to another world. But the Colonel immediately put aside such speculations, which had been suggested by the frank rejoicing with which Martinez accepted the challenge, as though it were an invitation to a party.

From that moment on Toledo began to be more and more bewildered. The world had changed, changed completely, and he advanced from amazement to amazement.

To favor his compatriot, he wanted to know the arms for which the latter had a preference.

"I am acquainted with so many!" exclaimed Martinez.

In an attack he had wounded with the point of a saber a gigantic German who was threatening him with his bayonet. The thrust had met something hard that crunched, and spurted a shower of blood into his face. Then, on growing calm, he saw that he had driven the weapon through his adversary's mouth, breaking his spinal column. He was also acquainted with the revolver, but was not a marksman. He was more expert with other weapons: the hand grenade, which reminded him of youthful ball games; the machine gun, which he had handled as a mere aid; explosive hurled with a sling. He was even fairly skilled in artillery, but trench artillery, in loading short range mortars, used in firing torpedoes and asphyxiating projectiles into the neighboring trench!

He smiled scornfully when Don Marcos insisted on the fencing formalities to be employed with the saber. He had his own style of fencing; to go straight up to the enemy and strike first. But in hand to hand fighting he preferred the knife. With a revolver he had never bothered about aiming. He didn't fire until he found himself close to the enemy, and was sure of his shot.

"And the duelling pistol?" asked the Colonel.

"I am not acquainted with it at all. I should like to see one: it must be something curious."

Toledo's hesitating glance wandered over the officer's breast, as though taking an inventory of his decorations, pausing at the stars that dotted the striped ribbons of his War Cross. Each one of them symbolized a great deed.

When the Lieutenant presented his seconds, the bewilderment of Don Marcos was not relieved. They were two extremely young captains. Toledo guessed they were twenty-five or twenty-six years of age. Their uniforms fitting very tight about the waist, their kepis of the latest style, their neatness and elegance pleased the Colonel, who immediately took them to be professional soldiers. They must have come from the school of Saint-Cyr; his professional eye could not be mistaken; they were of a different stock from humble Martinez!

One of them had had his face burned on one side by German liquid fire: the other's face was burrowed with a network of scarlet threads, which were the remains of scars. They both limped; one of them, with an enormous foot covered with wrappings and shod with a felt shoe, was quite frankly leaning on a stick; while his companion, who had a stiff leg, wore a trim tiny shoe, displaying a certain vanity also in a slender rattan cane, which he really used for support.

Their first words were rather embarrassing for the Colonel and Lewis. What was the meaning of this, a civilian daring to insult a soldier who was recovering from his wounds? What was the idea in proposing a duel in the midst of war? Any one who wanted to die himself or kill someone else had only to go to the front, like the rest. But Martinez, who was still present, intervened, entering into a rapid discussion with them. Did they want to do him this favor he had asked them as comrades, or not? Yes, but they were giving their own opinion of the matter. In their judgment the logical thing would have been to put an end to the quarrel right there on the Casino steps: two good punches at that slacker who wasn't going to war and took the liberty of annoying those who were doing their duty! They talked like men thoroughly aware of the fragility of life, like men who know how easy it is to take another man's life, or to lose one's. They laughed instinctively at the importance, the ceremonies and the so-called "equities" with which in peace times a private encounter is surrounded. But in the end, since their comrade insisted on their representing him in this farce, they would do it to please him, even though their compliance might get them into the guard house.

Scarcely had Martinez withdrawn, when one of the Captains, the one with the elephantine foot in a felt shoe, confessed his lack of competence in such matters.

"I never saw a duel in Bordeaux. I have no idea what it's like. Before the war I was a traveling salesman in Mexico. Wine was my line. I sailed with all the Frenchmen who were living there, and by a miracle we were not captured by a *Boche* pirate. I started in as a second class private; but I did what I could. If it were a business matter I would give my opinion, but in a thing like this!... Perhaps my comrade here." Another Martinez! Don Marcos forgot the Captain with the felt shoe. He was the Lewis of the opposite side. He concentrated all his attention on the Captain with the shiny boots and the toy cane. The latter must be an adversary worthy of him. It was a shame that his clear eyes should have the ironical expression of a man who makes a joke of everything, and that under his red mustache, trimmed short, in the English fashion, there should flit a faint look of insolence!

He was born in Paris, as he proudly declared as soon as he started to speak; and when Don Marcos slyly sounded him to find out whether or not he was an expert in affairs of honor and had witnessed many duels, he said in a simple way:

"More than a hundred."

Toledo had not been mistaken. This was the man with whom he would have the struggle. Then he thought of the number, and compared it with the Captain's age. More than a hundred, and surely he was not over twenty-six! He had a presentiment that he was going to be up against some famous swordsman, whose glorious name has been momentarily obscured by the war.

The Captain and the Colonel were the only ones to do any talking. In the beginning the Captain had had an air of jesting, with a Parisian sense of humor, at the solemn, high-sounding terms in which Don Marcos treated questions of honor. But the Colonel's reserved and persistent grandiloquence finally got the better of the other's inclination to banter. The young Captain took the same tone as the Colonel, finally interested in the affair and recognizing its importance.

At certain moments, the Colonel felt doubtful on listening to the way in which his rival formulated amazing heresies, revealing absolute ignorance of the great authorities who have codified the laws of encounters between gentlemen. And this man had been present at more than a hundred duels! Later, Don Marcos was amazed at the promptness with which the texts he had cited himself were appropriated by the young man; at the ease with which his classics had been assimilated, somewhat inverted in meaning, to be sure, the better to sustain affirmations contrary to his own.

When the encounter was arranged for in its slightest details, the Captain summed up his impressions with a simplicity that made the blood of Don Marcos run cold.

"One or both perhaps will be wounded. There is nothing extraordinary about that. Who isn't wounded these days? Surgery has made great progress; it is quite different from what it was at the beginning of the war. If a man doesn't die on the spot, he is nearly always saved. Besides, they will put them to bed and they won't remain abandoned on the field for days and days, as happens in war."

But the placid expression with which he talked about wounds was clouded over, giving way to a grim look.

"I am assuming, of course," he continued, "that no one is killed. Because if, for example, my comrade, Martinez, who is as gentle as a lamb and of whom I am very fond, should die in this farce, I'll kill your Prince on the spot, without any rules whatsoever, the way we kill a *Boche* at the front."

The tone in which he said these words was so sincere, that the Colonel, deeply impressed by them, did not observe how strange they sounded in the mouth of an expert in the laws of honor.

The conversation became more intimate and cordial as always happens when a difficult matter has been settled. Toledo was obliged to tell them about his life as a soldier—at least the way he imagined it had been, after so many years—and both young men, who had witnessed the combats of millions of men, showed the same interest as children listening to a strange tale, as he related obscure encounters in the mountains, battles that did not even have a name and were remembered only in an exaggerated fashion by Don Marcos himself.

The Parisian Captain, elegant and charming, also talked about his past.

"As for me, before the war, I worked in the Box Office of the theaters on the Boulevard. I haven't any other position."

Don Marcos had to make an effort to conceal his surprise. Indeed, he had seen more than a hundred duels; but in plays on the stage, between actors, who draw out the preliminaries of the encounters with ceremonious deliberation, in order to prolong the suspense of the audience. He should have guessed it on hearing his nonsense! What a fool that boy had made of him!

But immediately his eyes fell on the coats of the two young men. The same as Martinez: The Legion of Honor, the Military Medal and the War Cross, with stars. That of the former ticket seller was even crossed by a golden palm.

Ah, indeed! The world had changed. Where were the days of Don Marcos? Then he thought of all he had done in his life to increase his own self esteem; by appearing in full ceremony at various duels where most often no blood was shed. He also thought of what these young men had done and seen in less than four years. Their obscure origin brought to his memory the various warriors of Napoleon, whose names were celebrated and whose origin had been even worse. Some of them had succeeded in becoming kings, while these poor Captains once the war was over, would have to return, laden with glory, to their former occupations, struggling day by day to earn their bread!

They separated, agreeing to meet after dinner, to sign the paper stating the conditions of the encounter. They were all four in accord, but on mentioning this number, Toledo noticed that there were only three. Lewis had witnessed the long preliminaries with a certain impatience, seated on a divan in the ante-room of the Casino.

"There's a friend waiting for me. I'll be back in a moment."

And he had entered the gambling rooms, which were forbidden to the officers.

The Colonel had no illusions as to the duration of that moment, about two hours having passed. After leaving the Captains, he found Lewis at a *trente et quarante* table, with a heap of thousand franc chips in front of him. Of course he did not understand what Toledo whispered in his ear. He had to make an effort to recall.

"Oh, yes, the matter of the duel! I have every confidence in you; do whatever you please, I shall sign what you give me, but I am not going to get up, even though they might tell me Lubimoff was dead. What a day this has been, my friends! If they were all like this!"

And he turned his back, to make the most of his time, before the flight of luck would change.

Don Marcos had dined in the Café de Paris, going over in his mind the various articles he should put in the dueling agreement. The consideration that they were all relying on his superior knowledge caused him to be very exacting with himself. He wanted something concise and brilliant which would inspire respect in those boys, who were covered with glory. And he spent more than an hour, with the dessert dishes in front of him on the table, scribbling over sheet after sheet of paper, tearing each one up and beginning all over again on another. It was futile work: both signed in the reading room of the Casino, hardly giving the eloquent text a glance. As for Lewis he was obliged to get him out of the private gambling rooms by every sort of trick, and entreaty. The Englishman had forgotten to dine, in order not to offend Madame Fortune by his absence, and that stubborn Colonel came and disturbed him with his damned affair of the duel!

He signed the document without looking at it; he gave his word to the officers that he would come and get them in an automobile to take them to his castle. Then he ran away immediately, not without first saying to Don Marcos in a gruff tone:

"Until four o'clock, no later! If it isn't all over at four, I'll let them kill each other alone and come back here. That's the hour that the fine deals commence. To-day's luck is going to continue."

And he fled, smiling with pity on people who were occupied with less important things.

On finding himself alone, the Colonel began to make preparations for the encounter. He needed a doctor. He would go next morning and find an old physician in Monte Carlo who visited the Prince from time to time. He needed powder and balls; he proposed to go in quest of them to-morrow also. He needed two cases of pistols, and he had only one!

The matter of the two cases he considered essential. The other man's seconds did not know where to get theirs. No matter; he would find them one. The indispensable thing was that there should be two, so that fate might decide which they should use. Without that, the conditions would not be equal. And he spent the time until about one o'clock in the morning, asking hotel employees, rousing people out of bed, going down to the rooms of the Sporting Club, until an American whom he knew gave him a note for a certain fellow-countryman, a gloomy, half crazy fellow, who lived in an isolated villa on Cap-Ferrat. He thought he would conclude this negotiation the following day; and to do so he had rented an automobile.

Owing to the lack of vehicles and gas, the cost of the car was enormous; but it was necessary owing to the importance of his functions.

But now he was in Villa Sirena, at two o'clock in the morning, slowly cleaning the pistols, as though they were fragile jewels.

In the silence of his bedroom, far from mankind, influenced by the lonely mystery of the small hours of the night, which puts a certain vagueness in things and ideas, he felt an enormous self-aggrandizement. No; his world had not changed as much as he thought. The proof was that he was there, cleaning weapons for a duel!

On waking up the next morning, the Prince could not find his "chamberlain". The rented auto had carried him off at seven o'clock, to complete his preparations.

Lubimoff wandered about the gardens, stopping in front of the cages, which sheltered various exotic birds. Then with an absentminded look, he followed the evolutions of various peacocks, spreading their tails, colored blue and golden, or a royal black, in the sunlight.

His old valet interrupted his promenade. Some men had come with a truck to get Señor Castro's baggage.

Michael showed no surprise; they might hand over everything to them that belonged to Don Atilio. But the servant added that the same men also wanted to take away the little that belonged to Señor Spadoni, news which amazed the Prince. He, too! What reason had Spadoni to desert him?

He glanced at the brief note written to the Colonel and signed by them both. In his flight, Castro was taking with him the dreamy pianist.

"All right," he thought; "let them all leave; let them leave me alone. If they think that by doing so they are going to make me refrain from carrying out my intention!..."

Then he resumed his walk.

Only a few hours remained before he would find himself facing that young man whom he so hated. He was going coldly to do away with him, so that he would not continue to be a nuisance. The conditions planned by the Colonel were sufficient for a marksman of his skill to bring down his adversary. He needed only a single shot.

For a moment he thought of going to the end of the gardens, where he sometimes passed the time shooting. It was a good idea that he should practise steadiness of hand—the pistol is full of surprises. Then he decided not to, as it seemed unworthy that he should add these preparations to his evident superiority. His mediocre adversary could not be practising at that time. He had no facilities for doing so in Monte Carlo where he had no other friends than his convalescent comrades and a few ladies. He, on the other hand!... he held out his muscular arm, keeping it rigid for a few seconds with his eye glued on his fist. There was not the slightest tremor! He would be able to place a ball wherever he wanted. Poor Martinez might consider himself a dead man. And not the slightest sign of remorse disturbed the Prince's infernal pride in his implacable strength.

His consciousness of superiority was so great and his certainty in the result so absolute, that he finally began to feel some doubt, that feeling of uneasiness which is inspired by the mystery of things still to be accomplished. Suddenly there came crowding into his memory stories of combats in which the weak unexpectedly triumphed over the strong, through an obscure mandate of inherent justice. He recalled many novels in which the reader draws a sigh of relief on seeing that the hero, modest and agreeable, placed in danger of death by the "villain," who is stronger and wickeder than he, not only saves his own life, but in addition kills his adversary, through some happy chance; all of which goes to show the existence of some superior and just power which on most occasions seems asleep, but at certain moments awakens, giving each person what he deserves. Since the time of David, the little barefoot shepherd, killing with a stone the huge giant clad in bronze, humanity has enjoyed such stories.

Pistols are capricious weapons, and lend themselves to the absurd determinations of fate. Might he not fall, with all his skill, at the poor Lieutenant's first shot?

He held out his arm again, as before, looking at his clenched first. Then he smiled, with the smile of his ancestors, which gave his features a Mongolian ugliness. Mere traditional fiction, inventions of story writers, to flatter the public in a sentimental love of equality! The strong are always the strong. Within a few hours he would sweep that nuisance out of the way, calmly and without remorse, the way superior men always act.

A roaring sound coming from the railway line drew him from his thoughts. It was a trainload of soldiers approaching, like all the others, with an ovation of shouts, acclamations and whistling. It was rolling along towards Italy, in the direction opposite to that of the numerous trains coming to the French front. The Prince walked over to a garden terrace, the stone flower-covered wall of which descended to the track. The cars seemed to pass of their own will before his eyes, showing him one side as they rounded the curve, and then the other as they reached another curve, where they were lost to view.

The uniform of these combatants puzzled the Prince for a moment, as an unexpected novelty. They were dressed in dark blue serge, with their blouses open at the neck, and sleeves rolled up. On their heads they wore white caps with the brims turned up all around, like the little paper boats that children make.

He finally recognized them: they were sailors from the United States, a battalion, sailors from the fleet, going to Italy so that the Stars and Stripes might represent the huge republic on the icy summits of the Alps and on the hot marshy plains of Venetia.

With the rapidity of mental visions, which reveal, one superimposed upon the other but nevertheless distinct, a great number of diverse images, the Prince recalled the harbors of North America which he had visited in his youth, aquatic beehives, gathering together all the work and riches of the earth; monstrous, interminable cities, with populations as large as nations, and in which liberty and well-being seemed to have reached their highest limits.... And these men were leaving the comforts of a scientifically organized existence, their productive business, their amply remunerative work, their immediate hopes of wealth, perhaps to die for an ideal in the Old World, merely for an ideal, since they were not seeking new strips of land nor indemnities for their country! And until then, the average person had considered this country as the most materialistic, the least poetic and idealist of all nations, calling it the land of the dollar!... It was true that unselfish ideals were something more than words, since millions of men were coming across the sea to give their blood for them!

The sailors, after passing through the city of Monte Carlo, where they were greeted with cheers and waving flags, were entering the open country, where their shouts faded away with no answering echoes. For this reason their attention was attracted by that flowering terrace and the man appearing above it. It was like a procession on review: the carriages, one by one, came to life as they passed the Prince. From all the car windows arms with sleeves rolled up projected, shaking white caps. On the car roofs, a few strapping lads were gesticulating, with arms and legs extended, while the wind rippled in the folds of their dark trousers, above the white leggings. More than a thousand throats greeted the solitary man on the terrace with gay whistling, hurrahs, or unintelligible cries, which gave vent to the exuberant feelings of those youths, hungry for danger and glory, full of joy and curiosity, as they passed through an Old World which to them was new.

Lubimoff remained motionless, with his elbows on the railing, and his chin in one hand, as though he did not see that pent-up river of men, gliding along below his feet. The gay sailors, as they passed, turned their heads, repeating their shouts and greetings, as though anxious to awaken that human figure, rigid and clinging to the balustrade as though forming a part of its decoration.

He had completely forgotten the thoughts and worries of a moment before. All he saw was that torrent of young men rushing to meet danger and death for certain ideals as simple and beautiful as their blossoming youth. They were coming from the other side of the earth with that naïve faith that accomplishes the great miracles of history; and in the meantime, Prince Lubimoff, who, by dint of seeking after superior ideas and exquisite sensations, had finally come to believe in nothing, was there at his garden rail, calculating the surest means of killing a man, a man who was useful, like those who were passing.

Castro's image arose in his mind. He, too, had witnessed two days before, the passing of a train. He recalled the impression so deep and powerful that had impelled him to leave Villa Sirena, and break with his relative. He could see, just as it had been described to him, the bitter look of that red-headed soldier insulting him with scorn.

"There's room here for one more!"

The American sailors continued their whistling, and their exuberantly youthful shouting; but it seemed to him that these voices and waving of hands said the same as the other man's words, inviting him with ironical politeness: "Come; there's a place here for you!" A little later, and the voices were dumb, but he could still hear them, deep in his soul, like the far-off booming of a bell. He had considered himself a brave man, who as a matter of distinction, of sophistication, of refined indifference, preferred to keep aloof from things which rouse enthusiasm in other mortals. But the far-off tolling of the bell protested, ringing in his ear, repeating a single word: "Coward! Coward!"

He walked about the garden in a pensive mood until Toledo arrived in the afternoon. They had lunch in a hurry, and the Colonel made several recommendations. His knowledge of dueling matters, which has as many branches as the tree of science, touched in one of its ramifications on cooking. The Prince should not take any wine; since he must keep his hand steady. And as the Colonel said this he was praying inside that the bullets would all go astray, since both contestants inspired an equal interest in him. Some soft boiled eggs, nothing more; and not much liquid. At the last moment he should remember to empty his bladder. A terrible thing a wound with internal leakage! Nothing escaped the Colonel—he thought of everything.

He went up to his room to put on the frock coat he wore at duels. The moment for officiating had arrived. He remained hesitating in front of the mirror, realizing the lack of harmony between this majestic garment and the derby that topped off his appearance. Oh, the war! He smiled at the absurd thought of presenting himself thus four years before—it seemed like four centuries—in those Paris duels, in which the seconds and adversaries felt that it was only decent to go to meet death with an elegant, shiny, high hat.

Having omitted this solemn touch, he felt that he might look somewhat ridiculous sitting in the automobile beside the Prince, with his long frock coat and the two pistol cases on his knees.

The carriage stopped in the Boulevard des Moulins, in front of the doctor's house. Wounded soldiers were passing, some with fixed stares, tapping the pavement in front of them with sticks, others tottering along out of weakness or owing to an amputation.

A woman's voice, smooth and sweet, greeted the Prince. It was the voice of an extremely slender nurse, who was walking arm and arm with two blind officers. Michael and Don Marcos recognized Lewis' niece. She smiled at them, showing them the two strapping Englishmen whom she was serving as a guide; two fair-haired Apollos, tanned by the sun, with Roman profiles, shining teeth, and lithe bodies, strong and symmetrical, but with vacant eyes—like fires that have gone out—and a tragic expression on their lips, an expression of despair and protest at finding themselves dead in the midst of life.

"They are my two 'crushes'. How do you like them?" She was jesting in order to cheer up her companions, with that joyousness and daring of a Virgin Dolorosa, passing through the world scattering pale rays of Northern sunlight in the ambulances and hospitals. She seemed to be made entirely of the same stuff as the sacramental Host, fragile, anæmic, white and transparent, like dim crystal. And she went away, guiding like children the two blind men, despairing and handsome, whose heads towered above her own. A slight pressure of their fingers would have been enough to crush that body, like an alabaster lamp, all light, of no more substance than was necessary to guard the inner flame and cause it to shine through.

"Good-by, Lady Lewis!" said the Prince.

Don Marcos started on hearing his voice; it was a solemn voice such as he had never heard, a tremulous voice like a sentimental song in the depths of which lay teardrops.

The doctor laid his surgical case on the frayed carpet in the auto. There were three such cases now. It was not until then that the Colonel decided to relieve himself of the two precious boxes, placing them on top of the doctor's.

The car started off up the mountain, by a road that rose in sharp zigzags. At the end of each angle, Monte Carlo was revealed, smaller and smaller, and more sunken, like a toy city built of blocks with its red roof and many ants threading its streets to gather together in the Square. On the other hand, the sea seemed to arch its back, constantly rising, devouring with its blue rectilinear jaws a portion of the sky at each turn in the climb.

On the crest of the hill a huge mass of masonry kept growing more and more gigantic; La Trophee, a name which had finally changed to La Turbie, the medieval name of the little gray, walled village, which huddled about the monument. Two slender columns of white marble flanking the rubble-work, and a piece of the cornice were all that remained of the proudest of Roman trophies—a tower 30 meters in height, with a gigantic statue of Augustus, on its summit, which marked on the Alps the boundary between the lands of the Empire and those of the conquered Gauls. The auto, leaving the hamlet of La Turbie behind, was now running along the ancient Roman road.

"I can see the Legions," Don Marcos gravely murmured.

It was a mania of his. He had never had sufficient imagination to be able to see the Legions for himself; but after witnessing in a moving picture film a procession of supers, with bare legs and short swords, following Julius Cæsar's horse, Roman military life had had no mysteries for him, and every time he went up to La Turbie he murmured the same words: "I can see the Legions."

A few minutes later he forgot his resurrection of the warlike past to point out various buildings, of such a bluish gray color that they blended with the hills behind them. It was Lewis' castle. Standing out from it, one could see solitary towers, joined to the square mass of the buildings by causeways; watch towers flanking the gates; sharp slate roofs, with double rows of tiny dormers; roofs that only had the wooden rafters, through which one could see, as though the interior had been gutted by a fire; walls half built, descending at a right angle like a stone carpenter's square riveted to the ground on its long edge.

From a distance the castle might have been taken for an abandoned ruin. Lewis, having lost hope of being able to finish it, declared in good faith that it was better thus, since it would save him the trouble of decorating it with artificial ruins. It looked like some legendary fortress, such as those his father, the historian, had described, made for gray skies, for moist green forests, and which seemed anxious to escape from the sun-baked landscape of scanty vegetation, and to shrink from contact with the olive trees, the cacti, and the woody thickets covered with coarse flowers.

They got out of the car on a smooth piece of ground, bordered on two sides by two buildings, meeting to form a right angle. It was the court of honor, the future parade ground of the castle. On the other two sides, some walls that rose only a meter above the soil, suggested what the courtyard might some day be, if Fortune would only cease being so intractable for the proprietor. At the open end of the flat ground was another hired car, and beside it the three soldiers.

Lewis came forward to greet the Prince. They had arrived a short time before, and as he was in a hurry, he went into conference with the Colonel at once.

Don Marcos was the oracle that he must consult in order not to lose any time. Might they end this business right here? Would it not be better to do it behind the castle, in an orchard surrounded by old olive trees? The Colonel, with a pistol case under each arm, was examining the terrain. The one thing that really concerned him at first was his own person. He felt, indeed, that he looked ridiculous. There were these three officers with their uniforms; the Prince, with his dark blue street suit; the doctor, dressed like an old man; Lewis, as usual, with the wide straw hat, without which he would never dream of taking a trip to the castle; and there he was himself wrapped in his large, solemn frock coat, which seemed to frighten the very doves, that had taken refuge in the gables and the ruined walls.

After taking a glance behind the castle, he decided on the court-yard, which was free from trees. He would place the two contestants so that their figures would not stand out as targets, against a wall in the background.

Lewis, in spite of his haste, felt it necessary to do the honors of the house.

"A glass of whiskey?" As they had not given him time to make preparations, and as he was now living at Monte Carlo, his cellar was exhausted. But he was sure that by looking around a little he could come across a good bottle. What respectable house could not produce a bottle of whiskey for friends?

"When we have finished, my Lord," said Don Marcos, scandalized at this invitation which was an infringement upon solemn regulations.

The four seconds and the doctor were in a room on the ground floor, adorned with ancient battle trophies. The two contestants had been forgotten in the courtyard, like actors waiting for their turn to appear.

Toledo opened the pistol cases, and gave the captains the one he had found that morning at Cap-Ferrat. Fate was to decide which of the two were to be used.

"It isn't necessary," said the Parisian. "Either one, it's all the same to us. Arrange it all to suit yourself."

Don Marcos protested against this irreverent desire to shorten the ceremonials. It was all quite necessary; they were there on very grave business.

A five-franc piece shone in his hand. What efforts it had cost him to obtain that piece of money. Of all the preparations of the morning, that had taken the most time and been the most difficult to arrange. Coins had disappeared with the coming of the war. One could find nothing but paper money, and a five-franc note was of no use in a matter of heads or tails! He had been obliged to ask one of the important officers in the Casino to hand over that precious disc.

"Heads or tails?"

And the Colonel felt a secret thrill of joy as luck favored his ancient pistols. He was beginning to triumph!

The doctor, in the meantime, was looking out of the drawing room door, with a certain air of amazement, not to say of indignation. His eyes were fixed on the Colonel. Finally, he called Don Marcos aside. Was that Lieutenant the man who was going to fight the Prince? He knew the boy; a friend of his, an army surgeon had talked to him about the Lieutenant's case as an astonishing instance of vitality. It was a disgusting piece of foolishness that was being planned: it amounted to murder. Why, that boy might fall stark dead before the first shot was fired! They had performed an amazingly delicate operation on his skull; it was a miracle that he had survived at all, and he might fall dead instantly at the slightest emotion.

Don Marcos found an heroic answer, worthy of himself.

"Doctor, for a man like that, fighting is not an emotion."

He then proceeded with slow solemnity to carry out the most delicate part of the proceedings: the loading of the pistols. The two captains followed with a look of curiosity this operation, which was quite strange for them, though they imagined they had seen a whole lot of military life. The Parisian almost laughed as he watched how Toledo handled the diminutive ivory spoon which contained the charge of powder, scrutinizing it carefully before pouring it into the barrel of the weapon, with a certain fear of having put a grain more in one than in the other. Toledo was sure the heroic jester was making fun of his scrupulous precautions. But the Captain would not dare deny his interest in the novelty of the ceremony.

Lewis went out to get the automobiles moved away as far as a nearby grove, much to the disgust of the chauffeurs. They obeyed reluctantly, intending to return, even though they might have to creep along the ground, to witness the spectacle.

Toledo left the two pistols on an ancient Venetian table. They were ready! No one was to touch them! They were something sacred. Then his eyes, falling on the wall in front of him, were lighted with a sudden gleam of inspiration; he hurriedly advanced and unhooked two rusty swords from a panoply and went out with them into the courtyard.

Deserted by their seconds, the contestants had begun to pace up and down, pretending they did not see each other, and each catching the other looking at him from the corner of his eye.

They both suddenly found themselves in the situation of the preceding afternoon. It was as though no time had passed, as though they were still on the top steps of the Casino.

All that the Prince had been thinking over in the last few hours and that had followed him until then in his thoughts, with a suggestion of remorse, immediately vanished. So this young gentleman was the man who had tried to strike him, Prince Lubimoff! He would soon find out what such daring was to cost him.

But his anger seemed less violent than on the preceding day, something more reasoned, more completely the product of his will; and this weakening finally made him angry at himself.

The other man was more instinctive in his rancor. As he looked at the Prince, he saw also the sweet image of that great lady, his benefactress. It was because the Prince was rich that he had tried to trample on him, treating him like one of his serfs, on his far-off estates in Russia. All the best things in life had been for this aristocrat, and now he was claiming possession of the few scattered crumbs, even of happiness that fall to the unfortunate! He did not know how to kill a man in these regulated combats; but he was going to kill, nevertheless, and felt the absolute confidence in himself that had animated him out there in the trenches in the cruelest days of danger and success.

The presence of Don Marcos with a sword in either hand disturbed their reflections and interrupted their walking back and forth. They both came to a standstill. The Colonel looked at the sky, then took several paces in different directions. He wanted to fix it so that neither of the contestants would have the sun in his eyes.

Finally he proudly thrust one of the swords into the ground. It seemed to him appropriate to the character of the place, to make use of these ancient weapons. They seemed to him more in harmony with Lewis' romantic castle, than two stakes or two cans. But his satisfaction this time was of short duration. On raising his eyes, he saw that Prince, and he saw Martinez....

Poor Colonel! Up to that moment he had proceeded like a priest intoxicated by his own ceremonious words and his own incense, without thinking of the person in whose interest they are offered up. He had prepared all these formalities with the blind fervor of a professional who resumes his functions after several years of inaction, and thinks only of his work, forgetting for whom it is being done. He had managed everything in accordance with the rites, so that two gentlemen might kill each other in compliance with the strictest conventions; but now, at the supreme moment, he realized for the first time that these two men were his Prince and his Martinez, his fellow countryman, his hero.

He was amazed to think that he had been able to go as far as he had gone up to that point. He felt the astonishment of a drunken man recovering his reason in the midst of objects broken by him in a fierce delirium. He recalled Castro's words and those of the doctor; why had *he* not seen that this duel was a piece of foolishness? Repentance seemed to rush upon him. There was a burning sensation in his eyes, which began to fill with tears. But now it was too late. He must go on, even though his serenity should fail him.

The one thing that he had forgotten in his minute preparations was the tape measure, and he saw in this omission an act of Providence. Starting from the sword planted in the ground he began to pace off the terrain. But they were not paces that he took; they were enormous strides. He fairly leaped. Now he was absolutely sure of the ridiculousness of his appearance, as his coattails flapped back and forth like wings, as they were thrust aside by the vigorous movements of his legs. "Fifteen paces." And he planted the second sword.

If he could have had his way, he would have gone to the farthest end of the open field; perhaps as far as the place where the automobiles were awaiting. Then he looked uneasily at the ground he had measured. It was surely over twenty meters; a betrayal! What cowardice! Might God and gentlemen forgive him!

Once more he brought out the five-franc piece. He had to decide again by chance the position of each contestant. The Parisian captain greeted this proposal with a bored air.

"But I told you before to do whatever you pleased!"

Lewis was muttering impatiently under his mustache.

When the coin had marked the position of each one, Don Marcos placed the Prince beside one sword.

"Marquis: your hat," he said in a low voice.

Lubimoff, understanding this suggestion, took off his hat, throwing it some distance away. His adversary could not fight with his *kepis* on his head. Its yellowish color and the emblem of the Legion embroidered on the brim of the cap made him conspicuous in an unfair manner. His uniform also worried Toledo, who tried to do away with all the visible details on it.

Assisted by one of the captains, he proceeded to strip Martinez of his decorations of honor, after placing him beside the other sword. It was like a ceremony of degradation. They took off his *kepis*, then his medals, the red ribbon that hung from his shoulder, and the dark tan strips across his breast and the belt of the same color around his waist. The Lieutenant seemed reduced in stature and dignity in his loose uniform, without his decorations. The Parisian, always in a merry mood, compared him to a plucked bird.

The Colonel felt that it was necessary to repeat aloud the conditions of the duel. The Prince knew them and was accustomed to such encounters. It was Martinez who needed his suggestions. After he, as the director of the combat, should give the word "Fire!" he would slowly count, "one, two, three." They might aim and fire in that space of time. "Be very careful, Lieutenant!" Don Marcos spoke with tragic solemnity.

"If you fire before the *one* or after the *three*, you will be declared a felon."

The matter of being declared a felon frightened the young man. He didn't know exactly what it was, but the Colonel's look as he said this terrible word, made a deep impression on him. He no longer thought so vehemently of killing his adversary. This desire retreated into the background. Nor did he think of the fact that he himself might be killed. His one preoccupation was to calculate the time properly and obey instructions without bothering about aiming; to fire before the terrible *three*; so that he should not be given that horrible mysterious name that made his hair stand on end.

Don Marcos entered the castle, and appeared again with the two loaded pistols. He gave one to the Prince. The latter did not need any lessons. He put the other in the Lieutenant's right hand, and told him how he should stand, with his arm bent, holding the weapon high, presenting only the narrow side of his body to his adversary. Once more he dwelt on his warning. He should be careful not to make a mistake! Now he knew! *One ... two ... three....*

He himself stood midway between the adversaries withdrawing only a few paces from the line of fire. At that moment he was willing to die, so they both might remain unharmed!

He took off his hat solemnly, and with a gesture of profound sadness.

"Gentlemen ..."

During the entire morning, as he walked from one place to another, making his preparations, he had not ceased to think of what he would say at that moment, working up a superb piece of oratory, brief and stirring. He had frequently spoken at duels, meriting the approval of the other seconds, retired Generals, and such experts, accustomed to formalities of the kind. But the short harangue of to-day was going to be his masterpiece.

"Gentlemen ..." he repeated. He hesitated, not knowing what to add, as it had all been blotted from his memory. With a stammering voice, he went on saying whatever occurred to him, with no attempt at order, and without remembering a single word of the phrases which he had so carefully polished some hours before.

"There was still time ... a little good will on their part; they were both men of courage who had proved their valor ... an explanation at the last moment was no dishonor!"

His words were lost in a tense silence. But this silence was not absolute. There was somebody behind the Colonel, kicking the ground. It was Lewis who was consulting his watch, with a scowl. It was after three o'clock; the good series in the Casino had already begun.

The Colonel decided to end his speech. Besides, he was frightened at the motionless and rigid figure of his Prince, with his pistol raised. He had never seen him so ugly. His face was an earthen color, there was a squint in his eyes, and his cheek bones protruded. His features had been changed in a moment, as though the savagery of his remote ancestors, awakened within, had risen to his face.

"Since there is no possible agreement ..."

At that moment the Colonel thought he had recalled the last part of his forgotten speech. But the tread of brilliant words escaped him again, and he was obliged to improvise, so he ended in a solemn fashion:

"Come, gentlemen! Honor ... is honor; and the laws of chivalry ... are the laws of chivalry."

He heard at his back the murmur of approval. It was the voice of the former ticket-seller. "Bravo! Wonderful!" But he did not care to hear what he said. You could never tell when that fellow was in earnest.

"Ready?"

The silence of the two adversaries gave the Colonel to understand that he might give the words of command.

"Fire!... One ..."

A shot rang out. Martinez, who was only thinking of the terrible three, had fired.

He saw the Prince standing in front of him. He looked much taller; he could see the black hole of his weapon, and above that hole an eye, with a look of cold ferocity, which was choosing a point on his antagonist's body to send the obedient bullet. And with unconscious arrogance, he turned on his heel, so as to present not his profile, but the whole breadth of his body.

The four seconds did not see this. Their eyes had focused on Lubimoff, the personification of death.

Time contracts and expands us, according to our emotions. Its measure and rhythm depend on the state of the human mind. Sometimes it gallops along at a dizzy rate, over the faces of clocks that seem to have gone mad; at other times, it collapses and refuses to proceed, and a thousandth of a second embraces more emotions than months and years of ordinary life. The four witnesses felt as though the hours had been paralyzed, and the sun were remaining motionless forever. Time did not exist.

"Two!" sighed Don Marcos, and it seemed to him that his lips would never cease uttering this word, as though it were composed of an infinite number of syllables.

Lewis had forgotten the existence of the Casino; he was conscious only of the present. The Captain from Bordeaux, bending forward, was leaning on his wounded foot, without feeling any pain; the other officer was swearing between his teeth, and shaking his rattan cane until it hummed. The doctor, with professional instinct, was stooping over the surgical case that lay at his feet.

Lubimoff was going to kill him! All four were sure that he was going to kill him. An implacable expression of security, and of ferocious coolness, radiated from that man, with arm upraised, so motionless, and pitiless. The expression on his Kalmuck face was of such deep fatality, his one eye tightly shut and the other open, that they could all see an imaginary line drawn from the mouth of the pistol to the breast of the man opposite, the road that the tiny sphere of lead was going to follow with inexorable accuracy.

Proud of his superiority, the Prince postponed the moment of dealing death, with a sort of savage playfulness. He had his enemy in his claws, and could toy with him during those three months, that were as long as centuries.

In the dizzy coincidence of image whirling through his brain, he could see the Princess, his mother, beautiful and arrogant, as she was when she recounted to him as a little boy, the greatness of the Lubimoffs. Then he saw his father, the General, somber and kindly, saying in a rough voice: "The strong man must be kind."

As he thought of his father, his pistol swerved slightly, but immediately he corrected his aim.

In his imagination a train was slowly passing. French soldiers. He saw Castro and the insolent red-haired fellow who was offering him a seat. Another train advanced in the opposite direction, an endless train that kept coming from the depths of the ocean. Hurrahs, whistling, dark blouses, blue collars, little caps that looked as though made of paper. "Good afternoon, Prince!" The luminous smile of a pale Virgin: Lady Lewis with her two blind men, handsome and tragic....

His pistol fell. Above it he could see the entire body of his adversary, that obscure soldier, condemned to die before long no doubt, from wounds received in a land that was not his own, for a cause which was that of all men.

"Three!" said the Colonel.

But before he could finish the word, a shot rang out. The grass stirred at intervals along the soil as the invisible bullet ricocheted into the distance.

The scythe-like stroke passed close to the legs of the Director of the combat; but Don Marcos was in no mood to notice such a thing. His child-like joy made him run hither and thither. His frock coat seemed to laugh as its tails flapped up and down.

He was so happy, that he almost embraced Martinez. The latter must shake hands with the Prince, a reconciliation was necessary.

The officer refused to take this advice. He had his doubts about the way the combat had ended. The Prince had fired at the ground, and he was not going to let him spare his life like that.

"Young man!" said Don Marcos, with an air of authority, "you are new in such affairs. Let yourself be guided by those who know more and give the Prince your hand."

Immediately he went in quest of Lubimoff.

He saw him standing on the same spot. He had thrown the pistol away and was covering his face with his hands.

The only one beside him was Lewis.

"Come, Prince! What's this? Be calm! Perhaps a good glass of whiskey." Toledo heard a sob of anguish, the choking of a stifled breast.

Respectfully he drew away one of the Prince's hands leaving his face uncovered. At present it was a dull brick red, shiny with sweat and tears.

Lubimoff was weeping.

The Colonel recalled the dead Princess in her days of stormy humor, when, after an explosion of wrath, she would wring her hands, and ask forgiveness, weeping hysterically.

As he gently took his hand, he felt that the Prince was following him, meekly without any will of his own. Martinez was waiting a few steps away.

"Shake hands. It's all over. Gentlemen are always ... gentlemen."

They shook hands.

And then something unexpected happened which produced a long silence of surprise and amazement.

Michael bent forward, knelt down, and raised to his lips the hand he was holding in his own, with the same humble gesture that the serfs of the Steppes had used in the presence of his powerful ancestors.

Then he kissed it, moistening it with his tears.

CHAPTER X

A WEEK passed, and Lubimoff had not once left Villa Sirena. In his conversations with the Colonel—his only companion in this solitary life—he had avoided making any allusion to what had occurred in Lewis' castle. Toledo, for his part, displayed absolute discretion, as though he had forgotten the duel and the strange ending which the Prince had given it; but the latter guessed that the Colonel's silence concealed many things that might have proved distasteful to himself.

The other seconds had probably told everything. What people must have been saying! And fearing the curiosity of society which was doubtless repeating his name on all occasions, Lubimoff remained in retirement, with the hope of being forgotten. Some one would lose or win an enormous sum in the Casino, and that would be enough to make the gossips stop talking about him.

His loneliness, however, began to weigh upon him like a fate. He was getting tired of walking about his garden all the time. It seemed to him narrow and monotonous. Besides, Lewis' niece, abusing her privilege, came every afternoon, with a constantly renewed escort of wounded Englishmen. She ran about with them through the Avenues, amid the cries of the exotic birds, weaving great garlands of flowers for her soldiers. Meanwhile he was obliged to hide in the upper stories of the villa to escape this child-like joy, which seemed to him to have something gloomy and funereal about it.

The nights seemed endless. He thought with wistful longing of the quiet evenings with the "enemies of women", when Spadoni used to sit at the piano or perform his infinite calculations, always doubling; when Novoa would indulge in his scientific paradoxes, and Castro relate the adventures of his grandfather "the red Don Quixote." Where were they now, those comrades of his dreamy happiness?

Atilio interested him particularly. He had asked Don Marcos about him twice, without the latter being very clear in his explanations. The Colonel never saw Castro any more in the Casino; he doubtless was keeping away out of fear of gambling. The Prince had a feeling that the Colonel knew something more, and was refusing to talk from motives of discretion.

One morning, the weariness of his imprisonment finally galvanized his stupefied will. Why should he not go in quest of those friends? Perhaps if he were to take the first step he would succeed in renewing relations with them, and re-establish his former life.

As he was going out, the Colonel stopped him to speak again about a matter that had occupied their attention the evening before. What reply should he give the Paris business agent? The *nouveau riche* who had bought the palace on the Monçeau Park, wanted to buy Villa Sirena also. The Prince's manager was transmitting a final offer; a million and a half. The man would not give any more, and it was necessary to reply in haste, before his caprice should turn toward some other acquisition.

Michael shrugged his shoulders, as though the matter were something of no interest to him.

"Tell him I don't want to sell. No—it would be better still not to reply at all. We shall see later on; I shall think it over."

On getting out of the street car in Monte Carlo he passed to the right of the Casino, and followed the upper Boulevards. First he was going in quest of Spadoni, who lived nearest. Besides, the latter would surely know better than Novoa where Atilio was staying. Perhaps they were living together.

He had a vague idea of the house, through Castro's joking. The pianist was "the guardian of the tomb" above the Sainte Dévote ravine.

From the summit of a bridge the Prince saw this ravine at his feet. Its sides were covered with gardens, luxurious villas and hotels, and at its outlet stretched the smiling harbor of La Condamine.

Sixty years before, the ravine had been a wild spot. It was visited only by religious processions coming from the walled City of Monaco to pay homage to Sainte Dévote in a little white church, which to-day seemed still more diminutive beside the arches of the railway bridge.

In the earliest times of Christianity, a bark without oars or sail, guided by the will of God, who had deigned to grant a patron saint to the inhabitants of "Hercules Harbor," had grounded keel on those shores.

The bark contained the miracle working body of a Corsican Christian martyrized by the Romans. Nobody knew her name, and popular devotion called her simply the Sainte Dévote. Once a year, at nightfall, on her feast day, a large crowd from the Casino left roulette and *trente et quarante* to watch the sailors of Monaco, to the sound of music, burn an old bark in front of the church, thus cutting off all means of retreat to the Holy Patroness.

The stony fields, once planted with prickly pear and olive trees, were now covered with palaces, as large as barracks. They supported a second lofty city, above, which stretched away along the slopes of the Alps, and united Monaco with Monte Carlo. The land here, now sold at fabulous prices, was a spot so neglected half a century before that any of its owners might arrange without interference to be buried on his own property.

An obscure officer in Napoleon's Army, born in Monaco, and who had succeeded in becoming a General in the days of Louis Philippe, had had his tomb built in an olive grove above the Sainte Dévote ravine. Later gambling had made Monte Carlo rise above the wild plateau of the Caverns; the elegant, new city was spreading out to join old Monaco, covering all the land of the principality with buildings, and the tomb of the unknown warrior was imprisoned by this wave of great hotels, palaces, and villas. The olive grove around the tomb was sold by the yard, making a fortune for the soldier's heirs. Between the sepulchre and the edge of the ravine there remained a level space, from which one could enjoy a view of the splendid panorama. A millionaire from Paris had been bold enough to construct over the spot a house in "artistic" style, with gardens descending in terraces. He had imagined it would be an easy matter to have the General transferred to the cemetery and the mortuary chapel demolished. But the dead man was on his own land, and could not come to life to cancel the arrangements he had made in his will with so little prescience of the extraordinary growth old Monaco was to make; as a result there was no power on earth that could demolish his last dwelling place.

From the harbor Michael had often, above the heights of the ravine, seen this pantheon which was to serve him now as a place for meeting Spadoni. It was a simple block of masonry, with white-washed walls, four pinnacles at the angles, and a cupola of black tile. From a distance it looked like a Mohammedan hermitage, the tomb of some saint of Islam, and the similarity was carried out by groups of palm trees in the neighboring gardens.

Castro had often made him laugh by telling him the story of the dead General and his wealthy neighbors. The owners of the villa could not sleep with a dead man on the other side of the wall, and moreover, it was a nameless dead man, which made it all the more creepy and mysterious.

Nobody could remember the name of this gentleman, who had commanded thousands of men, and was still exerting his will power on the living. The owners decided to rent the villa with all its elegant furnishings for a modest sum, and at first, the ladies who were gambling in the Casino, quarreled as to who should get it. How wonderful it would be to live in a little palace adorned by famous Parisian decorators, and with a magnificent view, all for five hundred francs a month! But the renters hastened to give up this bargain to others. Imagine having to pass the General's mausoleum at midnight, on returning from the Casino! And think of not being able to open one's window blinds without having to look that corpse in the face. Besides, the spiteful tongues of the women gave each successive tenant the nickname of: "The guardian of the tomb."

Then Spadoni appeared. Castro had a vague idea that the pianist had paid the first month's rent, but he was not sure. What he knew for certain was that he had not paid any more. The owners, living in Paris, had finally accepted the situation, considering the pianist an unpaid caretaker for that house, which had come to inspire them with terror.

The Prince descended the wide road between garden balustrades and walls of rock broken by tufts of flowers hanging from the crevices. On seeing the sepulchre at close hand, he understood why all the tenants had taken flight. The General had known how to do things. The pinnacles, as well as the iron cross which surmounted the cupola, were adorned with skulls and cross-bones; and these funereal symbols, by force of contrast, made a still deeper impression because of the green splendor of the adjoining gardens under the bright blue skies and the dazzling sunlight, with the smiling harbor in the background, and the ruffled surface of the violet sea. The gate of the nameless mausoleum had not been opened for many years, and the wind had heaped the dirt against the underpinnings. Between the iron gate and the walls a thick, wild growth of vegetation had appeared, a diminutive forest, in the dense growth of which insects made war and devoured one another after sending forth endless flying and creeping expeditions against all the neighboring houses.

Lubimoff passed close to the mausoleum in order to reach the entrance of the villa, a handsome building in the Tuscan style of architecture. The gate was a complicated piece of iron work; the windows had stained glass figures; the gray walls were encrusted with marble bas-reliefs, and ancient escutcheons.

He knocked in vain with the iron dragon that served as a knocker. Finally from an adjoining alley-way, between two walls, appeared a woman with dishevelled hair, holding an infant in her arms. It was a neighbor, who acted as a servant for Spadoni, when he stayed in the house. The arrival of a visitor was an event for her.

"Yes, he is in," she said, "don't you hear him?"

As a matter of fact, Michael had heard the sound of a piano, deadened by the thick walls.

The woman, convinced that the artist would never hear the blows of the knocker, disappeared around the corner. Shortly afterward, her head and the child she was carrying in her arms appeared above the edge of the wall.

"Maestro!" she shouted. "A gentleman to see you! A visitor!"

And she came back again, smoothing her skirts as though she had just descended a ladder.

The door groaned on its hinges, as it opened, and Spadoni appeared in the opening.

"Oh, your Highness!"

There was no expression of surprise in his smile. He greeted the Prince as though he had seen him the day before.

Then he guided him through corridors and drawing-rooms, which were sunk in deep multi-colored shadow, and smelled of dust and mold. It had been many months since the stained glass windows had been opened, or the curtains drawn. Spadoni lived his entire life in a single room. Lubimoff collided with furniture and curios, as he advanced, almost upsetting two huge Japanese vases, and nearly impaling himself on the numerous projections in the profuse decoration of a "romantic studio," which had been in style twenty-five years before.

They finally returned to the light, a dazzling light that entered by three open doors overlooking a terrace bordering the ravine. It was the "hall" of the villa, decorated with Hindustanee draperies and divans. The Prince saw that Spadoni had excellent quarters in his "tomb". A large grand-piano was the only piece of furniture kept clean in this dust-invaded room. On the music rack several albums of music in manuscript lay opened.

Seeing that Lubimoff noticed them, the pianist gave a look of despair.

His poverty was very great: he was forced to give concerts in order to live, and found himself obliged to study the new operas.

He spoke of this labor as though it represented the cruelest imposition of inexorable Reality, the greatest degradation in his life.

Various ladies who organized benefits for the soldiers had sought his aid. He played for nothing, "out of patriotism", but the good ladies always found a way of giving him a fair sum. His poverty was tremendous! He was going to the gambling rooms only at long intervals. He hadn't enough money to play even the roulette wheel, where the stakes were but five francs!

The Prince started to read the titles of the scores, but Spadoni covered them up in comic haste.

"Awful rot! You mustn't look at those, your Highness. Here on the Riviera, when the ladies are getting on in years, and do not find any one to fall in love with them any more, they devote themselves to writing love songs or dance music for great spectacles; and the Casino accepts their work in order not to offend them. It results that on certain days the Monte Carlo Theater becomes the Temple of Musical Imbecility. No; it would be better for you to see what we are giving this afternoon. It is the work of a millionairess who writes the whole thing, music and words."

And he read aloud the titles of various "picturesque scenes": *Dialogue between the Butterfly and the Rose, What the Palm Tree said to the Century Plant, Prayer of the Grasshopper to Our Father the Sun.*

"Fortunately, your Highness, this humiliating situation will not last. I have a way out of it—a way out of it!"

And forgetting the piano, the scores, and his musical degradation, Spadoni suddenly launched into the world of dreams. He knew the secret of the great man, the Greek, who was winning millions at the Sporting-Club. He had guessed it, with his own cunning, after worming certain data out of a man who accompanied the lofty personage. It was a simple combination, like all ideas of genius. For example....

And he reached for a pack of cards which was on the table, lying on a number of albums bound in red: The nine Symphonies of Beethoven.

"Oh no—if you please!" the Prince brusquely restrained him, to keep him from plunging into that mania for demonstrating.

"I hoped to meet Castro here," he said, in a quiet voice, a moment later.

Spadoni seemed to awaken.

"Castro?... Oh, yes! He lived with me for a few days, but he went away."

Still obsessed by his marvelous combination, he talked in an absent-minded manner without showing the slightest interest in what he was saying. Castro had expressed a desire to live with him; he had told him so, late one afternoon in the Casino, and Spadoni had left Villa Sirena to accompany him. It was the least a friend could do!

"But when did he go? Where is he?"

"He went day before yesterday, and must be in Paris. A fool trip! Imagine, your Highness, during the last few days he had an extraordinary run of luck, winning as high as twenty thousand francs. If he had only gone on! But he wouldn't! He was in a hurry. He gave me five hundred francs, and I lost them immediately; it was very little money for my combination. I think he was going to be a soldier; he kept talking to me about the Foreign Legion. You can expect almost any foolishness from him. A man who is winning and runs away!..."

Then, as though the disordered workings of his brain were functioning logically for a few seconds, he added, with a smile of cunning:

"Doña Clorinda also went to Paris. She left two days before him.... Oh, your Highness! How I think of what you told us at the lunch once about women! I know them, Prince: They are all enemies to be feared."

And he pointed spitefully to *What the Palm Tree said to the Century Plant*.

In vain the Prince kept questioning him. The pianist did not know anything more, and Castro's fate did not arouse his curiosity. He had gone to Paris, to be a soldier, and Spadoni had so many friends, already, who were soldiers!

The "General" being a woman, aroused more interest in him; she stimulated his love of gossip.

"I think," he said, with a smile that showed his hate for women, "that she went away out of jealousy, out of pique. The Duchess de Delille took that Lieutenant away from her, though the 'General' had been the one to introduce them. It seems even that this Lieutenant has had a duel...."

The pianist grew pale, looking at Lubimoff with an expression of terror. His look was like that of a person who is talking aloud when he imagines himself alone, and then suddenly notices that some one is listening to him. He sat there embarrassed and stammering:

"I don't know ... people tell so many lies!... Women's gossip!"

Lubimoff felt a like embarrassment on realizing that even Spadoni had taken up his adventure with delight.

He felt there was no use in continuing the conversation with an imbecile like that. He arose, and the pianist, still trembling at his own indiscretion, showed similar signs of haste to end the visit.

"And Novoa?" asked the Prince on reaching the outer door. "Has he also left?"

No; he was still in Monaco, working at the Museum, when he did not have any more urgent business. They met very seldom. How could they see each other if he, Spadoni, on account of his poverty, refrained from entering the gambling rooms?

"He goes on playing, your Highness; but very badly, with the timidity of a novice, and for that reason he loses. He isn't made of the same stuff that we are, we who are true gamblers."

And the pianist drew himself up to his full height as he said this, as though he had never lost and possessed all the secrets of chance.

"I sent him two tickets for this afternoon's concert: one for him and the other for that Señorita Valeria, the Duchess's companion. Poor man! Always doing something silly, like a young lover!"

But his smile, which was that of a superior person exempt from such humiliations, disappeared, as he realized that once more he was saying something offensive to the Prince.

The latter passed close to the tomb again, but without seeing it, or even remembering the unknown General. Castro had gone!... Castro wanted to become a soldier!...

After going down along the Monegetti road as far as the parade ground of La Condamine, he ascended once more the gently sloping avenue that leads up to Monaco. After his long seclusion, this walk aroused a certain pleasant tingling in his muscles.

Finding himself between the two turrets that mark the entrance to the gardens, the memory of Alicia flashed across his brain. There, a little farther on, they had gotten out of their carriage; behind the trees was a bench on which he first had told her of his love; below, at the edge of the rocks, lay the solitary path along which they had passed as though treading on air, wrapped in the twilight and with lips joined. Then, had come the tearing of her dress, the sweet comical difficulties in mending it, and the pearl pin of the Princess.... Only a few weeks had passed, and these happenings seemed to belong to another happier race of beings, to have taken place on a different planet, bathed in a light that was different from the light of earth.

He made an effort to forget. At present he was standing on an asphalt square, opposite the steps of the Museum of Oceanography. For the first time he noticed the architectural decorations of the white building. They had adopted as an ornamental motif the cluster of twisting arms of the octopus, the semi-circular striations of sea-shells, the trailing filmy umbrella form of the jelly-fish. He observed the sculptural groups symbolizing the powers of the Ocean, or the arts of the navigators, he read the names carved on the frieze of the edifice, and the titles of ships famous for scientific explorations.

He stood there motionless for a long time, seeking a pretext to justify his visit. Finally he went up the steps of the building, and found himself in a deep, cool shade like that of a Cathedral, but without the stale, musty odor of shut-in places, and with a whiff of salt air coming from the nearby sea. He knew the stately edifice: on one side was the vast hall for the lectures and scientific assemblies, like that of a parliament building, with lamp shades of frosted crystal affecting the different shapes of animals from the ocean depths; in the middle of the vestibule was the statue of Prince Albert, dressed as a sailor and leaning on the rail of the bridge of his yacht; on the opposite side and on the upper floors, were the collections gathered during the voyages of the famous scientific explorer: thousands of fishes and molluscs, gigantic skeletons of whales, some *kaiaks* and fishing implements from the polar seas. On the lower floors, under his feet, in that second palace which, clinging to the cliff, descended to the sea, were the aquaria, where the mysterious creatures of the depths continued their lives in crystal cages amid the silver bubbles of running water.

The gate-keeper in a long blue coat, and a *kepis* with red braid, started to offer him a ticket, but paused on seeing that he was stopping at the turn-stile, asking for Novoa.

"He went out a moment ago. Perhaps you may find him in the neighborhood of the palace. Almost every day, before lunch, he makes the rounds of 'the rock'."

"The Rock," for the inhabitants of Monaco, is the nickname of the high promontory on which Monaco is situated, and "to make the rounds" means to follow the circle of gardens and abandoned bulwarks, which, starting from the palace of the Princes, returns to it, after completely embracing the old city.

Lubimoff followed the outer line of the San Martino gardens. He did not dare enter them; he was afraid of coming across the bench where he and Alicia had been that afternoon. He entered the City streets, narrow, without sidewalks, and paved with wide stones, as in many towns in Italy.

The dwellings, which were old and lofty, recalled the time when ground was precious on a peninsula narrowly enclosed by its fortifications. Some of the houses were pierced by tunnels and at the end of the archway, one could see the sunlight and the whiteness of the next street. The largest buildings were convents, or religious schools. Above the roofs, the bells slowly tolled as in a Spanish village; in the streets there were many sacred images lighted by tiny lamps.

When the paving stones resounded with human footsteps, the shutters all opened half way. A carriage caused many heads to appear at the windows. The few passersby were often canons from the cathedral, Barefoot Brothers with a crown of hair about their shaven scalps, or nuns with huge starched butterflies on their heads.

Only a little door separated the old city from the other situated on the heights opposite, with its Casino, its hotels, its orchestras, and its wealthy pleasure-loving crowd. A short ride by street car was sufficient to give one the illusion of having suddenly slipped back two centuries. Lubimoff recalled the expressions of surprise awakened in people by several of these barefoot brothers crossing the Casino Square on their way down to Monte Carlo.

He passed under a covered archway that joined two houses. A large open space, like a plain, opened in front of him. It was the Palace Square. Opposite it rose the lordly dwelling of the Grimaldi, a jumble of buildings dating back to different periods, which recalled the palaces of certain sovereign princes in ancient Italy. It was of a dark rose color, cut by the Archway of the Loggias, and was flanked by towers of white stone surmounted by battlements. He knew this edifice likewise. It was a mere show-place, and quite uninhabited, since the Prince, during his short visits to his domains, preferred to live on board his yacht.

The first thing that attracted his attention was the guard. The soldiers of Monaco, old French gendarmes, had gone to the war, and a national militia was taking the place of the Prince's army. It was composed of actual citizens of the "Rock," where citizens must be descendants of at least four generations resident in Monaco. They alone could contribute to the ideal defense of the principality, since they enjoyed the advantages of belonging to a country, unique in the world, where all who were born there, had bread and work assured them, thanks to the Casino.

Lubimoff admired the warlike guard, an old man with a white mustache, and stooping, almost humped, shoulders, dressed in a dark tan overcoat and a derby hat. A red and white arm band was his entire uniform. On his shoulder he carried an ancient gun which because of its tremendously long bayonet seemed even more enormous and heavy than it was. He might have rested beside a sentry box, painted with the Monaco colors; but he preferred to pace incessantly up and down, like a squirrel in a cage, looking in every direction to see if any one were trying to enter the palace of the absent sovereign. Other men who were fathers and even grandfathers, dressed in their Sunday clothes, were patiently waiting on a bench for their turn to exercise the honorable function.

The most notable thing on this esplanade was the artillery, a collection of XVIII century cannon placed there as an ornament, like the panoplies of a drawing room. On both sides of the entrance to the palace six huge, magnificent cannon, cast in green statue bronze, and chiseled like museum pieces, were drawn up in a row. Around their mouths, the metal curved backward forming a leafy design like that of a capital on a column; the other end was surmounted by a Medusa's head. The barrels of these hollow columns were ornamented with the three *fleurs de lis* of the ancient French Monarchy; the handles on each cannon were two dolphins, and all the pieces displayed the pretentious motto: *Nec pluribus impar* of Louis XIV, with another more somber one: *Ultima ratio regum.*

The Prince smiled at the latter motto.

"These days, artillery," he said to himself, "is no longer 'the last argument of kings', but it is of peoples. We have progressed somewhat."

Each of these green cannon had its own name, just as a ship or a regiment. One was named *Nero*, another *Tiberius*; farther on *Robust* and the *Snorer* opened their round mouths.

On the parapets enclosing the large square on both sides, other more modest, but equally huge and ancient cannon, thrust their mouths out upon the harbor or the open sea. The solid balls of these cannon formed pyramids, and parasitical vegetation had crept in between these iron spheres.

Behind the palace, like the back-drop on a stage, rose the French Mountain of the *Tete du Chien*, with the windows in the barracks of the Blue Devils, the *Chasseurs Alpins*, gleaming on its rounded summit. The Monaco plateau was simply the lowest step in the great stairway which the Alps let fall to the sea. Above, clouds were caught amid the peaks, covering them momentarily with a shadow ominous of storm. Below, amid the rose-colored walls and the white towers of the Grimaldi, rose the tropical palms, the cocoanut and plantain trees, giving this Ligurian castle the luxurious aspect of Brazilian farm.

Lubimoff was seated between the cannon, on the parapet that overlooks the open sea, when he saw Novoa strolling along the bulwarks that rise above the harbor.

On recognizing the Prince, the professor hastened forward with outstretched hands.

How likable the Professor seemed! His frank manners had never been so attractive to Michael as they were then. Novoa was greatly pleased at this meeting, attributing it to chance, and the Prince did not see fit to mention his visit to the Museum, so that Novoa would now know that he had come in search of him.

Mechanically they began to promenade between the row of guns and the trees that cast a pallid shade on one side of the Square.

It was Lubimoff who began to talk, questioning Novoa, showing an interest in his affairs and greeting his laments with a kindly smile.

The Professor appeared unhappy. This place with its gay, pleasant life was fatal for study. To think that back in his own country, he had imagined himself making useful discoveries in the mysteries of the ocean! The Casino spread its influence in every direction, reaching even the Museum of Oceanography. Often, while he was studying the *plancton*, a new idea would occur to him as to how he might penetrate the mysterious workings of the *trente et quarante* series. Mornings he worked with his thoughts fixed on Monte Carlo; and no sooner did afternoon come, than he felt an irresistible desire to go there. It was useless for him to invent pretexts to remain there on the "Rock." He had lost sums that for him were enormous, and he needed to get them back. He was worried at the thought of the money he had received from home as an advance payment on the modest fortune inherited from his parents.

"Some days, common sense tells me that I ought to return to Spain, and I immediately want to act on that good advice. Unfortunately there are certain things that keep me here and shatter my will power."

"I know what you mean," said Michael smiling. "First of all, there is love."

Novoa blushed, and then accepted the words of the Prince with a comic look of embarrassment. Yes; there was something in that, but love had its disillusionments, the same as gambling.

Lubimoff suddenly saw in his eyes an expression like that of Spadoni's. He, too, knew what had happened, and in speaking of love immediately recalled that absurd duel. But Novoa was a different person, incapable of feeling the malign pleasure of gossips, who rejoice in other people's shortcomings. Besides, Michael felt that he was very frank, and was immediately convinced of this. Quietly, without thinking whether or not his words might annoy the other man, the Professor alluded to what had occurred at Lewis' castle. He lamented it as something illogical and untimely, but had not ceased to be interested in the affairs of the Prince on that account. If he had refrained from going to Villa Sirena, it was in order not to seem forward. He had often talked with the Colonel, asking him to take his best wishes to the Prince.

Then, as though repenting the severity with which he had judged the duel, he hastened to explain. The image of Castro passed through his mind, causing him to look at his comrade with brotherly tolerance.

"I can understand a great many things. I am not a fighting man like you, and nevertheless, I once felt a desire to fight. At present I laugh when I think of it; but, in similar circumstances, I would do the same again. What power women have over us! How they change us!"

The Prince did not protest on hearing that Novoa supposed him to be in love, attributing the duel to a woman's influence. And he continued to remain silent, while the Professor, through a logical association of ideas, began to talk about Alicia. The kindly simple savant showed a keen satisfaction in telling certain news which he thought would please Lubimoff.

He felt a similar interest in his compatriot, Martinez. He did not hate any one. He had even forgotten the disagreements with Castro, which had caused him to leave the comfort and plenty of Villa Sirena.

"That poor Lieutenant is less fortunate than you, Prince: this duel has been rather hard on him. I enjoy a certain intimacy with people who are close to the Duchess de Delille.... I do not need to say any more: you understand that I am in a position to know what is going on in the Villa Rosa. Well, then; since the duel, I don't know what has happened, but Martinez calls at that house less frequently. Whole days go by without his daring to ring at the door. Sometimes he goes there, and a person whom you know tells me that the Duchess refuses to see him. At present he is a mere visitor, a friend like any other. The Duchess is anxious to avoid their former intimacy; she continues to send him little gifts at the Officers' Hotel, and to look after his comfort. She sends the young lady who is a friend of mine to find out if he needs anything, but she receives him only at rare intervals. The lunches and dinners each day have come to an end, with that life in common, which would have been complete if he had slept in the house. And the poor boy seems sad, and full of despair at this change."

The Professor was encouraged in his confidences on noting the pleasure with which the Prince received them.

"A certain person," he continued, after some hesitation, "who has spent several nights in the street where the Duchess lives—the deuce, a certain person! Why shouldn't I tell the whole truth—I, who sometimes spend hours in the neighborhood of Villa Rosa, waiting for the young lady in question, have surprised Martinez near the house, slinking by close to the gate, looking at the windows. Poor boy! And they tell me that during the day time, when he is afraid that the Duchess won't receive him, he goes by there, just the same."

Lubimoff was stirred by a double feeling: one of rage, at the conviction that he had made no mistake: that little soldier boy was in love with Alicia; and one of delight on learning that he was not received in the house, as before, and was hovering about the neighborhood in vain. It was a negative sort of joy for him, but joy at any event, to see that youth in a situation like his own.

Novoa, being a man of simple tastes, could not understand love except under conventional circumstances, and between people of similar ages; and he laughed at this passion of the officer, as though it were something exceedingly amusing.

"How absurd! To fall in love like that with a woman old enough to be his mother!"

The Prince started on hearing this, looking fixedly at his companion. No; the Professor had discovered nothing. He was laughing at his own reflections, without any indirect insinuations. No one but Lubimoff himself could possibly know Alicia's real secret.

They walked back and forth several times between the cannon and the trees. Suddenly, the bells of the churches and convents in Monaco, began to ring, answering, through the luminous atmosphere, those of the Monte Carlo frontier.

Twelve o'clock! Novoa became restless. He was a man of fixed habits, and besides, the Monaco people at whose house he was living were absolutely punctual in their meal hours. To think that there was not a restaurant in Monaco, where for once he could be extravagant and invite the Prince! The latter proposed that he accompany him to the far-off Villa Sirena to lunch together. It was so pleasant to be in his company! He gave him such interesting news!

"Impossible!" the Professor hastened to say. "I must see some one in Monte Carlo as soon as I finish my lunch. They will wait for me."

And the Prince did not insist, guessing that the person referred to was Valeria.

A single carriage had taken refuge in the pale shade of the trees. It had remained there after bringing some tourists who, on coming out of the Museum, preferred to return on foot by the ancient path along the fortifications.

Michael got into it, and drove to Villa Sirena.

The rest of the day and a great part of the night passed very pleasantly for him. He was going over and over in his memory the news he had just heard. It had not been a bad day. He scarcely remembered Castro. Castro was in Paris; that was the one thing certain. On the other hand, the misfortune of Martinez made him hum gaily to himself, and this unusual good humor quite deceived the Colonel.

"All I say is, Your Highness ought to go out, and see people. I was sure that to-day's walk would do you a world of good."

The following day, the Prince had an even pleasanter surprise. He had finished his lunch, when his valet announced ceremoniously: "Dr. Novoa, the professor, to see you, sir."

Michael, having a presentiment that it meant something very interesting for him, received the Spaniard with extraordinary effusion, such as Toledo had never seen before. "Awfully good of you to come, Novoa! You don't mean to say you have had your lunch already? What a regular life you Monaco bachelors lead! Well, at least, you'll have coffee with me?"

And the Prince hastily finished his lunch and went into the *salon*, where coffee and liqueurs were waiting. The impatience of the visitor to talk with him privately was so obvious, that Lubimoff hastened to invent an excuse for Don Marcos to go away.

When they were alone, Novoa left his cup on the little table, took several puffs at his cigar, as though to summon all his strength of will, and finally said in a resolute voice:

"I have a message to give you: a certain person sent me here ... and I suspect that I am playing a rather cheap rôle. A man like myself doing such errands as this!... Besides, men ought to help one another. You who are a real gentleman, may perhaps consent to do something for me...."

And the good Professor talked as though he felt himself united with the Prince by a sort of professional comradeship, by being in the same condition.

Lubimoff, anxious to know the message, gave a look of acquiescence. Yes: it was true; he was capable of doing anything for him that he might ask. At that moment he felt the savant his best friend. But what was the message?

Novoa continued, with a certain hesitation. The day before, after his meeting with the Prince, he had seen that young lady ... that young lady who is a companion to the Duchess. He had told her everything; a bad habit he had, but lovers cannot always talk about themselves.

"We were together at a concert, and this morning she came to the Museum to tell me to see you immediately. I refused at first to take the message, but you know what women are. Besides, the young woman has a mind of her own. To make it short, here I am repeating what I was told."

He was silent for a moment, and after looking all around, he added, in a mysterious voice:

"This afternoon, at St. Charles."

On his way there Novoa had been worried by the obscurity of the message. What St. Charles was it? A hotel? A promenade? As a resident of Monaco, the Professor knew only the Casino in Monte Carlo. The one thing certain in his mind was that Valeria's message came from the Duchess.

Michael made an effort to hide the joy which these words gave him. Alicia was looking for him! In spite of his satisfaction he felt a need of asking for fresh details. Hadn't Novoa been told the time?

"No, Prince. 'This afternoon, at St. Charles'; not another word more. The young lady almost became angry because I asked her to make it clearer. I told you that when we are by ourselves she can be cross—like all the rest. She told me that you would understand the message at once."

Lubimoff nodded in affirmation; yes, he understood. What a nice fellow the scientist was! At that moment he wished him every sort of happiness that men can enjoy. If he had not known Novoa's scruples and his pride, he would have asked Don Marcos for all the money there was in the house, to hand it to him in handfuls. But since a material gift was quite out of the question, he expressed the hope that Valeria, whom he had always considered an ambitious climber, would bring happiness and beauty into the Professor's life. His satisfaction made him so optimistic that he even believed that he had been mistaken in regard to her, and he endowed the Duchess' companion with a great number of hidden virtues.

Toledo had returned, and the Prince, who wanted to please Novoa, talked to him about Oceanographic explorations, displaying a lively curiosity in his questions, though his thoughts were far away.

But this attempt at flattery was wasted. The Professor replied to his questions with hesitation. He was in a hurry; some one was waiting for him ... doubtless Valeria needed to know the result of his errand at once. And the Prince also displayed a certain haste in accompanying him to the gate, with the greatest possible show of friendliness. He must return often to Villa Sirena; he was his one real friend. What a pity he refused to live there, as he had formerly!

When Lubimoff found himself alone, he went upstairs to his rooms on the second floor. He was afraid the Colonel would guess the cause of his satisfaction. A sensation of pride and triumph mingled now with the joy of the first moment.

He thought of his situation, Don Marcos had remained silent since the duel, and he, himself, a prey to loneliness, had been in the depths of despair, imagining himself the laughing-stock of every one.

Now he could see things clearly, Alicia wanted to come back to him. She had fallen in love with him again. Everything showed that: the Lieutenant practically expelled from the house, which two weeks before he had considered as his own; and his former protectress avoiding him, so that his visits were becoming rare. Doubtless, on learning through Valeria that her former lover had voluntarily left his retirement in Villa Sirena, she was hastening to make an immediate appointment with him in haste to resume their former relations.

He congratulated himself on his unexplainable aggressiveness which had impelled him to offend Martinez. He, who, in the last few days had repented of that mad affair! What had weighed upon him like remorse, was perhaps the most sensible and opportune act of his life. Alicia, seeing that, mad with jealousy, he was doing something which many people considered absurd, fighting for her sake, doubtless felt flattered in her vanity, and was looking upon him now with new interest.

"Oh, these women!" thought Lubimoff. "You've got to know them. They have an instinctive admiration for the strong. There is nothing like an act of brutality at the right moment to conquer them. They take a certain joy in yielding to a man who impresses them by violence."

This had been his first happy moment in many, many days. Once more he was the Prince Lubimoff who had always had his way, triumphing on obstacles, sometimes with his money, but more often with his imperious pride.

Satisfied with his rough strength, he felt the need of making himself handsome before keeping the engagement. He was thinking of the males of the animal kingdom, who in addition to teeth, claws, and spurs, have combs, manes, and plumage to fall back on when it comes to inspire a sort of mystic slavish admiration in the females. It was the same among human beings. Education, laws, and traditions do nothing but disguise the barbaric foundations of human nature.

His thoughts were interrupted by something which worried him. At what time should he appear at the place indicated. It occurred to him, that as no hour was mentioned, it must be the same as that of the previous meeting at the door of St. Charles. But he finally was convinced that the Professor had forgotten something, and his uneasiness made him keep the engagement much earlier.

He spent more than three hours waiting anxiously, wandering about the streets in the neighborhood of the church, standing motionless at the corners, and changing from one place to another on noticing the curiosity of the passersby. He entered St. Charles several times, and was always greeted by the same sight: the multi-colored stained glass windows growing paler and paler, as the daylight waned, the clusters of flags, the altar pieces breaking the shadow with the dull splendor of their gold background, and women kneeling and motionless; women who seemed the same as on the other occasion, as though weeks had been minutes.

With the superstitious feeling of those who wait, he said to himself that Alicia surely would not appear until nightfall, and the day seemed endless to him.

As night came on he began to doubt.

"She won't come. She must have repented."

He was standing on the corner of a curved and sloping street adjoining the church. From there he could observe the steps leading to the little square with the sunken boulevard. No one climbed them; all the carriages passed without stopping.

Suddenly, he had a sensation that some one was approaching from behind. He heard a light step, and on turning his head, he saw a woman in mourning.

Suddenly recovering his triumphant joy, he forgot everything: his long wait, his doubts and the fatigue of standing there in endless expectation. He was so sure of the motive which had induced her to ask for this interview, that he went forward to meet her with chivalrous cordiality.

"Oh, Alicia!" he said, holding out both hands at once.

But his hands clutched unavailingly at empty space, without finding anything to take hold of, and finally dropped in dismay.

Lubimoff felt disconcerted at the expression on the woman's face. All the ideas that had been with him until that moment were so many illusions. They vanished in an instant, leaving him dismayed face to face with reality. Of that reality there could be no doubt. There was a look of hardness in the eyes that surveyed him fixedly.

Alicia spoke rapidly, as though she had come on a matter of business with a person rather distasteful to her and wanted to end it as soon as possible, and be rid of his presence.

There was a money matter between them which had to be settled. She had not written to him because, since certain recent happenings, she felt a letter was inadvisable. Besides, she could neither go to Villa Sirena, nor receive him at her home. For that reason, on hearing the day before that Michael, whom she imagined ill, had been seen taking a walk, she had boldly made an appointment with him there, so that they might see each other for a few moments. That was all.

"Let us talk like business men; business men who are in a hurry and do not waste words. I owe you some money and it is impossible for me to have any peace of mind until I return it to you: three hundred thousand francs which your mother gave me, and what you lent me in the Casino—perhaps something more. I have enough to pay you. If you don't care to take the matter up, send me Toledo."

Lubimoff stood there dumbfounded at these unexpected words. After making this proposal, she seemed anxious to get away. Now she had said all she had to say; it annoyed her to remain there with the Prince; she had nothing to add.

"No!" said Michael energetically.

So that was why she had called him? And that was all she had to say to him, after they had been separated for so long?

His refusal was so resolute, and his pained surprise was reflected in his features in such a manner, that Alicia felt it useless to insist.

"Very well; let's not say anything more. I know your character, and I know that we would stay here arguing for hours without any result. I shall try and find a way to return what belongs to you. Good-by, Michael!"

The Prince tried to stop her by gently taking one of her hands, but she withdrew it with a nervous gesture of repulsion.

"And you are going away!" he said in a tone of deep discouragement.

The humility in his voice seemed to irritate the Duchess, causing her to stop as she was turning away.

"What did you think?" she asked indignantly. "I am surprised at your self-absorption, your failure to think of other people. Michael! Michael! You'll always be the same; you don't consider any one but yourself: nothing counts but your own desires. You've hurt me so much! And now you say like a child: 'And you are going away, ...' What, pray, did you expect after your despicable conduct? I want you to realize it once for all: I despise you. Your presence is odious to me. I despise you!"

Poor Lubimoff saw his conduct once more as he had during his days of voluntary confinement. Alas! Where were the deceitful dreams that had cheered him until then? His sadness, and his repentance were so obvious that Alicia softened the tone of her words.

"Perhaps despise is not the word; but I am sure that you fill me with pity; pity much like that which I feel for myself. We are two poor, mad creatures, Michael: our misfortunes have followed us a long way."

Recalling their lives, Alicia thought of builders who make a serious mistake in putting in the foundation of a building, and go on raising it, imagining that their work is in a straight line, without observing that it is entirely out of plumb, owing to the defect in its base.

"We began wrong. If the world had gone on the same as before, perhaps we would have been able to keep on our feet and be triumphant. Our surroundings sustained us: we were like children."

But the Universal cataclysm had made them lose their balance forever. They were toppling over, with gaps that could never be brought together, ready to fall in a heap.

"We belong to another period, and no one can protect our frailty. I feel pity for you, Michael; and you must feel the same for me, for me, whom you have wronged so deeply!"

The Prince, in spite of his dejected humility, protested. He had been imprudent: that was sure. His aggression in the Casino and the miserable duel had caused a stupid scandal to be sure. But what irreparable harm did she mean, that caused her such profound sorrow? How could his madness, which injured him only, making him the object of comments and laughter, cause her such despair?

Alicia interrupted him with a gesture of impatience, as though she felt it impossible to make him understand her thoughts.

"Look," she said pointing to the church door. "Before, I could go in there. Remember the last time that we saw each other on this spot. I had just been praying, and talking with my son; it was an illusion perhaps; but illusions help us to live. And now it is impossible for me;

I feel remorse where before I found hope. And I have you to thank for this, you who took away the last consolation that I had invented for myself."

She no longer looked at the Prince with hostile gaze. Her trembling voice, and her moist eyes, were those of a poor woman making an effort to hide her emotion. Michael stammered in embarrassment, not knowing what to do or say. Had he really been able to do her such an evil turn? When? How?

Alicia, deaf to his questions, was thinking only of herself and her misfortune.

"I had a son, and I lost him," she went on saying. "He was my hope, my one reason for living. The suffering made me look for consolation. What would become of us if we did not have the power of deceiving ourselves by creating new illusions? And I had a second son, a son whom I invented, sad, condemned to die, but young like the other, unfortunate like the other, and lacking a mother to bring joy to his last days. I wanted to be that mother. I can feel only the sweet, protecting joy of maternity; my rôle as a woman is over: all I can see in a man is a son, and you take away this last consolation! You robbed me of my poor joy!"

Lubimoff began to understand. Alicia was talking about Martinez; and he felt once more the sting of jealousy.

"When we saw each other here the last time I had sought a quiet refuge within my sorrow. I was praying for my son in the church, talking with him, and telling him how he was a brother in misfortune to one who was still alive, but who perhaps would soon go to join him. Then, on returning home I found the other, and my illusion was so great, that I was able to fuse them into a single person, imagining that time and the war were all a dream, and that my son was still alive, and had returned from his captivity and was by my side. They do not look alike, I am sure, although I avoid looking at George's pictures—but they seem to me the same; it is the uniform, misfortune, and nearness to death. Besides, the poor boy was so good! He was so timid, satisfied with anything, looking at me with the sweet look of a gentle little creature: he who is so proud! He venerated me like a being descended from an upper world. I was his mother. His words and looks breathed a feeling of deep respect. I wasn't a woman to him: I was something like the angels. And you, with your crazy interference, have spoiled it all. He is no longer my son: my dream has ended. I am obliged to do without his presence, and it is only at rare intervals that he finds open to him a house which I had taught him to consider his home. Through your fault, this boy, in whom I saw a son, is now merely a man, and I, his mother, have become once more a woman."

Lubimoff's features became dark and gloomy with an earthly cast, as on the afternoon of the duel. He was beginning to understand.

"What did you do, Michael!" she continued in a tearful voice. "You aroused the poor boy by your madness. On fighting you, he imagined he was fighting for me, and that I was simply a woman. He saw me suddenly in a new light, as though he had been asleep until then. I might almost be his mother; for women of my class prolong their youth, preserve it artificially, and we are still desirable when women of the lower classes are already coming to old age. Besides, I understand the element of vanity in his admiration, that vanity which exists in all our sentiments. To him I am the unknown, the mysterious, a great lady, a Duchess, brought by these topsy-turvy days within his reach. Poor boy! A few weeks ago he used to laugh in my presence with childlike simplicity, and look at me placidly, without the shadow of an evil thought in his eyes. He was happy, and so was I; while now...!"

The Prince pictured Martinez pursuing Alicia with his amorous desires. "I'll kill him: I must kill him," he said to himself. But this homicidal anger lasted only an instant. The various scenes of the duel passed through his mind: a vision of himself kissing the officer's hand, in a sudden burst of unexplainable humility, which kept returning to torment him like remorse. What could he do now? After what had happened there was something sacred about the man. And once more he gave himself up to his despair, while Alicia went on talking.

"My dream is dead. My son has become my son once more, and Martinez is a man like any other. At present it is impossible for me to pray; I am ashamed to hold imaginary conversation with my real son. I am assailed by thoughts of what I told him; I am overwhelmed when I think that I go on talking with the other boy, in spite of what he has said to me, of what I read in his glances, and of what I know of his real desires. What a wrong you have done me! I lost one son, and can think of him only with remorse; I invented another, and you have taken him away from me."

Then, as though complaining of some superior force that had presided over her destiny, she added:

"What torture! Not to be able to know quiet friendship, and the tranquil days of maternity. Always to have love looming up in front of one! In my younger days I considered that the one aim of life was to inspire admiration and desire, and now I am punished for that indeed. I sought in you a sustaining friendship, and you immediately desired me. I tried to deceive my maternal longings by caring for an unfortunate boy who may die very soon, and this son of my affections talked to me of love. Is it true that women are never able to enjoy the peace and confidence that come to men quite naturally?"

The Prince expressed his wishes, with eagerness and hatred in his voice.

"Don't see him: break with him; close your door to him forever. In that way you will recover your peace of mind, and I ... I shall be your friend, I shall be anything you desire, it will be enough for me that I see you."

She greeted his last words with a look of incredulity. Men had promised her so often to be friends! Besides, she knew Michael very well, and did not take the trouble to reply. The one thing that interested her was his advice that she definitely reject the wounded man, and not see him any more. Once more her eyes grew moist.

"Imagine driving the poor boy away! There are certain things you can't understand; you try to order affections about in the same arrogant way that you formerly disposed of people. Do you think I can abandon him? I am his mother in spite of everything, and you know very well how a mother tolerates and forgives things. The poor boy is not to blame for his evil thoughts; it was you who suggested them to him. Besides, it won't last; I have hopes that his foolish desires will die out."

The idea of deserting the crippled soldier aroused her pity, giving an amorous tone to her words.

"What would become of him! He doesn't know any one: he is alone in the world; the other officers are living, in their native land, they have families. Before, he could go and see Clorinda; now 'the General' has gone away, and I am the only one who remains, the only one! And you want me to forget him? You don't know him very well; you are an enemy of his. It is such a delight for me to recall the period of his innocence. He was like my son; no; there was something more about him; a thankfulness, a capacity for veneration concentrated entirely on me, such as I had never known before. You forget how his life hangs on a thread. Nor does he realize it himself; he does not know the real situation he is in; he has illusions of healthy youth; he thinks he will live for many years. Poor fellow! How hard it is for me to pretend that I am angry, to reject him with indignation because of the desires he feels for me ... me, who only want to be his mother!"

This tone of sweet pity wounded her listener. Alicia seemed to feel the remorse of a death watch obliged to deny a condemned criminal the satisfaction of his last whim. She was lamenting like a nurse who cannot give a dying man what he asks for in his last gasps.

Michael felt that he guessed the secret of the last interviews between this pseudo-mother and her adopted son. Perhaps she talked to him about his health, momentarily refusing to flatter him in his illusions of health, revealing to him the danger to which his life was exposed; and he, in a suicidal ardor of passion, was perhaps entreating her like a child who has placed all his dreams in a toy: "once, just once."

He was convinced that this was the truth of the matter. He read it in her eyes, which in turn seemed to guess what the Prince was thinking, and she blushed slightly.

"What harm you have done me," she repeated. "I must send him away from me, and I can't bear to desert him. It would be a crime if I abandoned him to his fate. You don't know what this constant struggle means to me. At times I see him hovering around my house; hidden behind the window blinds, I look at him, and I can hardly repress my tears. He seems so sad! I remember my son, who also lived alone, even more friendless than he, and who perhaps became interested in some woman, anxiously desiring many things without succeeding in possessing them, and I feel a desire to call to him, to shout: 'Since that is your dream, my dear child, your last wish in life, take it! Take it, and be happy!' Yet I think of his health, I think of many other things, and I restrain my impulse, and weep, letting him wander about near my house, imagining himself forgotten, though I am thinking of him all the time. Alas! May God give me strength! May I not lose my self control! May I continue to resist my absurd charitableness! Sometimes I fear I won't."

"Oh, Alicia!"

The Prince uttered the words in a tone of desperation. His presentiment was becoming a reality; he could already see that dying youth possessing what he had not been able to obtain. There was a look of homicidal anger in his eyes.

This hostile expression annoyed Alicia, making another woman of her. The harsh look and the cutting tones which had accompanied her arrival appeared in her once more.

"Enough said. I came here to return your money. You refuse to take it? You refuse? Very well, I will find a way to make you. Good night, Michael!"

As a matter of fact, night had fallen, and the Prince saw her disappear in the shadows of the street whence she had come: a street dimly lighted by a single blue street lamp.

For a moment, he thought of heading her off, humble and entreating. He would never see her again: he was sure of that. But at the same time he perceived the uselessness of insisting. She wanted him to forget her; the interview had merely been to suppress all traces of the past still existing between them. And he allowed her to pass out of his sight.

From that day on, the life of the Prince lacked a purpose. Something had broken within him: his will had crumbled to dust, enveloping his senses in a sort of fog. What was to be done? Not even the narrowest of paths remained open to his initiative. Alicia hated him as though he were an enemy. It meant good-by for all time! There still remained the other man, but the Prince was invulnerable as far as Martinez was concerned.

It was enough for him to think of what had happened in Lewis' castle to lose all intention of violence. He cursed his Slavic sentimentality, so confused and incoherent, like his mother's, which prevented him from going to the end in malice, and causing him to fall, when he least expected it, into exaggerated submission. Alas, for his tears of repentance! Alas for that kiss on his adversary's hand! If he avoided returning to the Casino, it was in order not to meet Martinez and those two Captains who had witnessed the incomprehensible conclusion of the duel. He no longer had the energy to impose his will; his former harshness of character had melted with the catastrophe of his desires.

He shut himself up once again in Villa Sirena, in order not to see any one. He hated people, and at the same time he thought with a certain terror of the ill-concealed smiles that might greet his passing, and the remarks that might be exchanged behind his back.

Don Marcos was the one companion of his loneliness; and Lubimoff, who during the first few days exchanged but a few words with him, finally came to wish that he would hurry back from Monte Carlo, at nightfall, in order to hear the news, which in other days he would have considered insignificant. They entered into long conversations on what was going on in the Casino, or on the happenings of the world. It was the curiosity of a prisoner or an invalid, who takes an exaggerated interest in things, as he loses his sense of values, owing to his inability to move about in his confinement.

The Colonel was giving less and less importance to the events of daily life. All his attention had been focused on the Atlantic Coast and the opposite shores of the ocean.

"They keep on coming!" he said, after greeting the Prince. "The Americans keep on coming: a regular crusade. There are hundreds of thousands of them; there are millions. And to think that a lot of people considered the talk of sending armies from America mere bluff!"

He was really indignant at such ignorance, quite forgetting his skepticism of a few months before.

"A great country! And that fellow Wilson, what a man!"

At present he believed the American people capable of accomplishing anything they set out to do, no matter how extraordinary; but his old-fashioned ideas prevented him from feeling sustained enthusiasm for anything collective and abstract, without human physiognomy. The former partisan of absolute monarchy, preferred individuals: one man to think for the rest, and give them orders. And after a few words, his enthusiasm for the American democracy began to shrink in scope until it rested in concentrated form on the head of Wilson.

"The greatest man in the world!"

His eyes moistened with idolatrous fervor as he read the President's speeches; he exhausted all his vocabulary of superlatives in expressing his admiration for the personage who had made a great people unsheath their swords, disinterestedly, in defense of justice and liberty, and who prophesied at the same time a future of peace for mankind, with no greedy nations to menace the life of the humble and the weak.

One evening he found a new phrase to express his admiration.

"What a poet!" Lubimoff, in spite of his melancholy, began to laugh. President Wilson a poet!

Don Marcos, stammering at the laughter of his Prince, tried to explain himself. Perhaps "poet" was not just the word to express his thought accurately. But poet he would call him nevertheless, and with good reason. A poet for the Colonel was a seer, who says very beautiful things about the future of mankind; a prophet who dreams upon his heights, embracing with his glance all that the common crowd swarming below cannot see; a being who, on speaking, in whatever form he may choose, succeeds in making people who are listening blink their eyes with emotion, while a shiver runs down their spines.

His tongue became twisted as he said this but above his stammering, arose a firm unshakable conviction.

"After all, I know what I mean. For me, he is a poet: a man who has wings ... very long wings."

The Prince began to laugh again. Wilson with wings! He imagined the President with his high hat, his glasses, and his kindly smile, and growing out from each shoulder of his long coat two enormous feathery triangles like those of the angels in religious paintings. What an amusing fellow the Colonel was!

Then suddenly he became thoughtful, while his features took on an expression of great seriousness.

"You are right," he said. "I can see him with wings, wings that are too long perhaps. A great thing when it comes to flying, but when one is obliged to live among men, and has to walk along on the ground!... I am afraid he will drag his wings; I am afraid they will be stepped on some day, and that people will find them a great nuisance...."

And they dropped the subject.

The Prince wanted to break the confinement which he had voluntarily imposed upon himself. Why should he stay there at Villa Sirena, near certain people who constantly occupied his thoughts yet whom he did not wish to see? The best thing would be for him to return to Paris as soon as possible. The long range cannon was continuing to fire on the Capital; almost every week squads of German aeroplanes made night excursions about it, dropping explosives. Such a trip offered the inducement of danger and excitement to the lonely man, tormented in his perfect health by an inactive and monotonous life, which offered nothing more stimulating than the irritations to be derived from his recent experiences.

Every morning, when he got up, he formulated the same plan: "I am going to Paris." But the trip kept being put off from week to week. It was a case of abulia, the loss of will power of an invalid, who makes projects of active life, and no sooner attempts to carry them out, than he loses his strength again, and postpones them indefinitely.

The most insignificant details loomed gigantically before his diseased will. He had to go to Nice to make reservations at the Sleeping-car Office. He thought of sending Don Marcos; then refrained, considering it preferable to go himself. And days went by without his taking the short ride preliminary to his Paris trip. Both of them seemed equally long. He, who had thrice circumnavigated the globe, wearily shrunk at the thought of the slowness of travel due to the war. Just imagine sixteen hours on a train!

One afternoon, bored by his splendid gardens,—now so monotonous!—by the silence of his house,—now so deserted!—and by the increasing absent-mindedness of the Colonel, who was always having something to do either in Monte Carlo, or in the gardener's pavilion, Lubimoff started out on foot toward the City. And he met some one.

He had turned quite mechanically and without thinking in the direction of the upper boulevards, near the street in which Villa Rosa was situated. When he realized this, he decided to turn back. Just then he saw Lieutenant Martinez coming along on the opposite sidewalk, in the direction that he himself had been going a few moments before.

The soldier seemed to him taller, stronger, and as it were, surrounded by a halo of glory. His uniform was the same, frayed and old looking after some years of service; but to the Prince it seemed entirely new, even dazzling in its freshness. Everything about the Lieutenant looked magnificent and he seemed to illumine the objects about him by mere contact. His features perhaps were paler and more angular; but Michael imagined that he radiated a certain inner splendor, composed of pride and satisfaction. A sort of ethereal mask, enveloping him in astral light, made him appear handsome and gave him a new physiognomy, Apollo-like and triumphant.

They passed without speaking. The Lieutenant pretended not to see him, as Lubimoff's eyes followed him with a questioning glance. What was there that was new in this man? The Prince doubted that lack of sound health, that perilous condition which worried the doctors so much. It was all a lie made up to impress the ladies! He noticed the proud firmness of the soldier's step, the jaunty, boyish air with which he swung the rattan he used as a cane.

On losing him from sight, he could see him even more clearly. His imagination kept vividly recalling certain details over which his eyes had wandered carelessly. There was something that stood out in painful relief in his memory: a few roses, a little bunch of roses, which the soldier was wearing on his breast, between two buttons of his uniform. An officer with flowers seemed rather strange! That was what had shocked the Prince at the first glance, shocked him so violently that his whole vision had been deeply disturbed. Yes, those flowers!...

He spent the rest of the day thinking about them. As he stretched out in his bed that night, darkness clarified the maze of thoughts and doubts whirling in his brain. He could see it all in a cold clear light. "It has happened already!"

He jumped out of bed and turned on the light, pacing up and down his bedroom in a fury.

"It has happened already!"

He kept repeating the words with anguished obsession; he repented his generosity, as though it were a crime. "Why didn't I kill him?" Then in plaintive tones he would repeat his original affirmation, concluding that what had happened was irreparable. Then he put out the light again; and for a long time, in the darkness, which once more filled the bedroom, the curses of the Prince resounded, alternating with fierce exclamations of wounded pride and sobs of rage.

The following day his conviction still persisted. The childlike beauty of the morning, which always inspires optimism, meant nothing to him. How was he to know the truth about that thing which he had suspected and feared, but which he never imagined would really come to pass?

A desperate curiosity caused him to spend the entire day in Monte Carlo. He met Martinez again. The officer kept on walking, turning his glance away in order not to see him; but the Prince imagined he caught a fleeting look of generous pity in his eyes, an expression of compassion for an unfortunate and inoffensive rival. Again he was wearing flowers; doubtless different from those of the day before.

Lubimoff repeated to himself the laments of the previous night: "Yes, it had already happened." It was impossible to doubt it. But the thought of killing him did not recur, nor did he repent of his generosity. That was all so useless now! He merely thought with envy of people in the submerged classes of society, who feel the impulses of passion very simply, without any disturbing sense of honor and solemn promises. They were men who could act regardless of laws and customs. When they wanted to kill some one, they went and did so!

He saw that Martinez was thinner than ever, with a feverish look in his eyes. Oh, that indefinable something, that suggestion of youthful vanity, of triumph and satisfaction, which seemed to radiate from his features like a halo of glory!

That evening, Toledo found himself brusquely repelled by his Prince, when he tried to tell him about a letter which he had received from Paris. The Administrator of the Prince's estate was getting impatient; he was asking for a reply from his Highness in regard to the sale of Villa Sirena.

"I don't know; leave me alone. The best thing is for me to arrange the matter myself. I'll go to Nice to-morrow and see about my trip to Paris.... No, not to-morrow: day after to-morrow."

He could not explain to himself why he had conceded that additional day to his idleness: it was an instinctive postponement, without any motive whatsoever. The following day, after breakfast, he regretted it; but it was already too late to find the chauffeur he had gotten the afternoon of the duel, and whom Don Marcos had just promoted to the rank of "purveyor to his Highness."

Where could he go, and be sure of not coming across the persons present so bitterly in his thoughts? Toward the end of the afternoon he went to the Casino terraces. There was an open air concert which was attracting a huge crowd. It was improbable that Martinez and the woman should show themselves in such a gathering.

It seemed as though he were living in peace times; as though he had gone back to one of those rare winters which used to attract all the wealthy people of the globe to the Riviera. Both terraces were filled with well-dressed people. The bombardment of Paris and the attacks of the German *Gothas* were keeping a great many elegant ladies in Monte Carlo who formerly would have felt they were losing caste if they stayed on the warm coast when winter was over.

Chairs were lacking. A large part of the audience was seated on the balustrades and steps. Around the orchestra *kiosque* there was a mass of pleasant colors, formed by women's hats, spring dresses, and fluttering fans. Opposite the terraces the sea stretched away between the rose-colored promontories. The far-away sails reddened by the setting sun seemed like so many flames. Across the violet surface of the Mediterranean and the crystal opalescence of the evening sky the music fell voluptuously.

Nobody was thinking about the war: that was a calamity that belonged to another world, to other skies. Even the convalescent soldiers in uniform, who were living entirely in the present moment, breathing the salt air, listening to the wail of the violins, and surrounded by gayly dressed women, did not seem to remember it. Many eyes were following the progress, along the horizon line, of a string of ships strangely painted like fabulous monsters, and escorted by several torpedo boats. But the lulling music that rang in the ears of the idlers took all significance away from the fearful disguise of the boats, and from the cautious slowness with which they were gliding along off the Shores of Pleasure.

When, after seven o'clock, the concert was over, the terraces gradually emptied. On the benches only a few couples remaining, putting off the time of parting by conversing quietly in the silence of the blue twilight.

The Prince succeeded in walking from one end to the other of the lower promenade without once having to submit to contact with the crowd.

Suddenly he stopped, with a feeling of surprise and pain, as though he had just received a blow in the breast. Down the wide steps which joined the two terraces, a couple were descending. His instinct recognized them even before he could see them clearly. It was a soldier. It was Lieutenant Martinez ... and she!

Alicia was dressed in mourning, just as he had seen her near the church; but she was walking less resolutely, shrinking and timid, on finding herself on that spot which shortly before had been occupied by all her neighbors from the city.

They were talking as they slowly descended. Absorbed in the view out upon the sea, they did not turn their eyes toward the spot where Lubimoff was standing motionless. At the bottom of the stairs they chose to walk in the opposite direction, and the Prince was able to follow them.

He felt that some extraordinary power of divination was sharpening his faculties; a sort of second sight which was enabling him to see and study both their faces, in spite of the fact that their backs were turned toward him.

Alas, that walk! It was the desire for light and open air, which people feel after a sweet confinement. It was the insolent need lovers have of displaying their happiness in public, when the joyous hours, through monotonous repetition, begin to weigh on them. It was the desire of prolonging in the sight of every one the sweet intimacy enjoyed in secret and now spiced with the added incentive of being obliged to feign, and to hide all real feelings.

Michael considered his intuitions as beyond all question. Of course! It was the officer who had proposed that walk. How proud he would be to walk in a public place with a celebrated lady, and in full consciousness of the new rights he had acquired over her! It was no longer possible for him to question the visualization which had made him groan in the silence of the night.... It had taken place! It had taken place!

Alicia's appearance dispelled all doubts in advance. She was walking along with a certain dismay like a person obliged to go on in spite of herself. He could see her invisible features. They were sad, profoundly sad, with a melancholy look of the woman who has fallen and is conscious of her abasement, but considers it irremediable, the result of an irresistible destiny, of a cause beyond the radius of the will's action.

Her head kept bending down to one side toward her companion, for her eyes to gaze on him. It must have been the gaze of a willing prisoner anxious to forget the pangs of remorse and taking a sensuous satisfaction in her shameful slavery. While her soul shrank away at the memory, her body was bending under physical attraction to that other body, instinctively seeking the contact that was causing her youth to bloom again in a new spring-time; a sad spring-time, like all the surprises of fate, but sweeter far than the dull gray hours of solitude.

Hate, repugnance, and indignant jealousy caused the Prince to stop. Why should he follow them? They might turn their heads and see him. He was ashamed at the thought of meeting them. The wretches! There must be Some One above to punish such things!

And he left them, walking toward the other end of the promenade in order to descend to the harbor of La Condamine.

He was just leaving the terrace when something happened behind his back which brought him to a stop. The couples seated on the benches suddenly rose and ran shouting in the direction whence he had come. He could hear people calling to one another. Some news seemed to be circulating through both levels of the garden, bringing people forth from the walks, from the clusters of palm trees, and the walls of vegetation.

Lubimoff allowed himself to be carried along by this alarm, and retraced his steps. He saw in the distance a noisy mass of people ever increasing in size, a group which was being joined by the winding lines of curiosity seekers running down the steps. The garden, which a moment before had been deserted, was pouring forth people from every opening.

As he drew near the crowd, he could hear the comments of various detached onlookers, who were telling the news to the new arrivals.

"A convalescent officer.... He was taking a walk with a lady.... Suddenly he fell in a heap, as though struck by lightning. There he is."

Yes; there was Martinez, in the center of that human mass, a pitiful object, lying on the ground, with his body bent into the shape of a Z: his head made a right angle with his breast, and his legs were doubled, making another angle. Lubimoff came forward until he could look over the shoulders of the first row of stupefied onlookers. A constant sound of hard breathing, a rattle like that of some poor beast in the death agony kept coming from his foaming lips. In his motionless body, the only sign of life was that moan, repeated with clock-like regularity, with no change in the tone.

Officers were leaving their women companions to force their way into the center of the crowd. On recognizing Martinez, their surprise assumed a caressing brotherly expression.

"Antonio! Antonio!"

They bent over him to talk in his ear, as though he were asleep; but Antonio did not hear them. One of his eyes was hidden in the dirt of the walk; a small pebble was clinging to the eyelid of the other.

All one side of his uniform was white with dust. The terrible harsh breathing was the only reply to their words of endearment.

A military doctor stepped through the crowd. He took hold of Martinez's hands, and felt his pulse. A look of helplessness came over the doctor's face. The Lieutenant had had many attacks like this one. They could only hope that it was not to be his last....

Lubimoff could see Alicia kneeling on the ground, stunned by the shock, showing the sinuous curves of her back, under her mourning garments, oblivious of everything about her, with her eyes fixed on the man who a few minutes before had been walking at her side, talking and smiling, convinced that life is happiness, and who now lay stretched in the dust, convulsed and inert, a pitiable vessel slowly emptying itself in dying gasps.

Suddenly she stood up, with an instinctive sense of danger. She did not care to remain in that posture before everybody's gaze. Her large eyes, with a blank, frightened look, began to move about over the crowd, without however recognizing any one. For a moment they rested on Michael and her gaze met his with an expression of anguished entreaty. But the Prince, lowering his head, concealed himself behind the front row of onlookers, and her eyes went on in their search about the circle, with a look that became dull and gray again. She believed, doubtless, that it had been an hallucination.

As Alicia remained standing there, people began to point her out. That was the lady who was with the officer. Some of them recognized her, and repeated her name: "The Duchess de Delille." Through an instinctive feeling of repulsion, or a cowardly desire not to get mixed up in any "affair," no one spoke to her. She was left alone in the center of the crowd, with a look of stupefaction in her eyes, that seemed to ask for help, though without knowing just what help.

Willing souls began to take the initiative with an air of authority.

"Air! Give him air!" They began to shove the crowd back in order to increase the circle around the fallen man. But the people immediately pushed forward again with useless suggestions of aid; and once more the space was narrowed, until the feet of the nearest spectators grazed the panting lips of the dying man.

A young girl had run of her own accord to the bar at the entrance of the Casino and was coming back with a glass of water.

"Antonio! Antonio!" his kneeling comrades vainly called the Lieutenant, using all their strength to open his jaws and force him to drink. His lips repelled the liquid, and went on repeating the painful moans.

Ladies, attracted by the news, began to arrive from the gambling rooms. They all knew the Duchess; and looked at her with a certain hostility, after gazing at the dying man. The Prince heard fragments of their comment: "A poor fellow rescued from death by a miracle.... The slightest emotion.... That woman...."

Beyond the group, park policemen were running about giving orders. The stretcher bearers had arrived; the same ones who, according to public rumor, were passed by magic through the walls of the Casino to carry away the gamblers dying in the play-rooms.

This time the stretcher was absent. The onlookers were separating to open the way for an extraordinary novelty. A hired carriage was coming across the terraces, which were forbidden to vehicles.

Suddenly Lubimoff saw the Duchess rise above the heads of the crowd. She had just gotten into the carriage and was standing in it, with a dazed look and the inexpressive features of a person walking in her sleep. Perhaps she had done it without thinking; perhaps the military doctor had invited her to get in, thinking she was a relative of the patient. Several men in uniform lifted the inert body of the officer.

The harsh breathing that rent his chest continued.

And then, in the presence of the crowd, whose eyes were sightless with stupefaction, the Duchess proceeded as though she were alone. She had just dropped to the seat. She had them lay the corpse-like body across her knees, and she herself, as she held Martinez with one arm, laid his panting head against one of her shoulders.

The carriage slowly started off in the direction of the officers' hotel, followed by a large part of the crowd. The doctor went along on foot, telling the driver to go slowly.

Michael saw Alicia pass, upright and rigid in her seat, her eyes wide open, with terror, her mouth tense with grief, and holding the dying man on her knees. Her attitude reminded him of the Divine Mother at the foot of the cross; but there was something impure and shameful in Alicia's sorrow that made the comparison inadmissible.

"Oh, Venus Dolorosa."

The Prince was interrupted in his reflections. He felt himself rudely shoved aside by a woman in uniform. It was Mary Lewis, running, as fast as her legs could carry her, to overtake the carriage.

The Amazon of Good Deeds always arrived in time to catch up with suffering.

Lubimoff saw how the vehicle slowly drove away with its embroidery of people. Its journey as far as the hotel would be endless; all Monte Carlo would see it go by.

He felt sad, very, very sad. That officer was his enemy; but death!...

He was not so sorry for Alicia. He smiled a malicious smile as he looked for the last time at the carriage and its following, which was constantly increasing.

In the line of scandals there was nothing commonplace about this latest of the Duchess de Delille.

CHAPTER XI

TWO days later, in the morning, Lubimoff saw the Colonel go out dressed in black.

He was going to the funeral of Martinez. He and Novoa felt it was their duty, as Spaniards, to accompany the hero on his last earthly journey.

On his return he told his impressions, with painful conciseness, to the Prince. A few convalescent officers had followed the bier. The Professor and he were the only ones in civilian clothes present. In spite of his garb, those kindly heroic boys, seeing that he was a Colonel and a compatriot of the dead man, had obliged him to preside over the funeral services.

The Beausoleil Cemetery lay half way up the slope of the mountain on the crest of which La Turbie is situated. On account of the war, it had been necessary to enlarge it by several level plots of ground that formed a series of terraces. From these esplanades the eye embraced a magnificent view: Monte Carlo, Monaco, immediately below that, Cap-Martin advancing out over the waves, finally the infinite expanse of sea that rose and rose until it mingled with the sky. A monument with a rooster arrogant and victorious on its summit held the remains of the combatants who had died for France. Don Marcos was still much moved by the speech he had delivered, while all stood hushed, at the entrance to this common tomb, which was about to swallow up forever the body of Martinez.

"It was a speech for men," said Toledo, with pride, "for men who had been crippled in warfare. Nothing but heroes before me! There wasn't a single woman at the funeral."

This was the detail that interested the Prince most: "Not a single woman." And he asked himself again what could have become of Alicia.

Toward the end of the afternoon, as he was walking about his gardens, he saw Lady Lewis coming, preceded by the Colonel.

The Prince took refuge in his house. The nurse was undoubtedly arriving with a group of convalescent Englishmen, and wanted to run about among the trees and pick flowers. He did not feel he had the strength to listen to her chatter, which was like the twittering of a gay but wounded bird and was filled with a happiness that persisted tenaciously in the midst of grief, and continued even to the threshold of death.

The Prince was going up the stairway to retire to the upper rooms, when the Colonel overtook him; but before the latter could speak Lubimoff turned on him in a rage. He didn't want to see the nurse! Let her take her Englishmen over the gardens; she might go about in them as though they belonged to her; but as for himself, he wanted her to leave him alone.

"Marquis," said Toledo, "the noble woman has come alone and must talk with your Highness. She has something important to say to you."

The Prince and the nurse sat down in wicker chairs out of doors in a little open space surrounded by leafy trees. A fountain was laughing as great drops of water scattered from its lazy jet.

The greenish light reflected through the grove made Lady Lewis appear weaker and more anæmic. What was left of life seemed concentrated in her eyes, before taking flight and vanishing like some volatile fluid, into space. The Prince was beginning to forget his recent anger. Poor Lady Mary! Once more he had a feeling of tenderness and respect for her. Her physical wretchedness finally changed his pity into the kind of admiration that disinterested sacrifice always inspires.

Accustomed to living amid the deepest sorrows, to witnessing the greatest catastrophes, Lady Lewis paid little attention to the conventions prevailing in ordinary life and spoke at once, with a certain military abruptness, of the reason for her visit.

She was coming in behalf of the Duchess de Delille. She had spent the last two days at Villa Rosa, sleeping there in order not to leave the Duchess a single moment. First, Alicia's wild despair, followed later by a complete collapse, had frightened her. The lady had tried to kill herself.

"Poor woman!... She finally grew calm, seeing the true light, and realizing the path she must take. I feel satisfied that I've accomplished that much by my words."

Lubimoff's questioning glance remained fixed on the English woman. What light and what path was she talking about? But there was something that interested him more: the motive of her visit, the message that the Duchess had given her for him.

Lady Lewis read his thoughts.

"She asked me to see you, Prince; that is her last wish as she leaves the world. She begs you to forget her, never to seek her out, and above all to forgive her for the harm she has done you involuntarily. Forgiveness is what she most ardently yearns for. When I tell her that you don't hate her, it will restore the serenity she needs for her new life."

Michael had been absorbed in deep thought. Forgive her? Alicia had not done him any harm. From himself, from his own desires and disillusionments, his sufferings had come. If he had remained faithful to the principles he had announced some months before when he hated women, he would not have suffered the slightest change in the sensible life he had been leading. Besides, where was she? Could he not see her?

This flood of questions was interrupted by Lady Lewis. She continued to smile sweetly, but her voice revealed the firmness of an unalterable will.

"The Duchess is no longer living in Monte Carlo; I have arranged everything in regard to her trip. I am the only one who knows where she is, and I shall never tell. Do not look for her; let her go away in peace in her quest for truth; think of her as dead ... as others have died, as thousands of beings are dying and will continue to die in this period of ours, with each day's sun. Forgive and forget. Poor woman! She is so unhappy."

Lubimoff understood how futile all his questions would be. His curiosity, no matter how strong and subtle, would fail in contact with that impenetrable reserve. Alicia had disappeared forever ... forever!

He now felt sadder and lonelier than ever before. As he sat there beside this Amazon of human sorrow, he had a feeling of confidence similar to that which the Duchess must have felt during those last few days. It was a desire to make a confession to her, an instinctive impulse to bare his soul, as though from that woman who brought to death beds the light-hearted merriment of a bird, might come the supreme counsel of wisdom.

The Prince nodded his head, murmuring his assent: "Yes, I forgive her." He did not wish the other woman to bear the slightest burden of grief on his account. He would shoulder all that, himself. But immediately afterward he could not resist the impulse of that anguish to express itself. He was himself astonished at the words which, over-riding all restraint, escaped from his lips.

"I, too, Lady Lewis, am very unhappy."

The nurse did not show any surprise at such a burst of confidence. She simply continued to smile, and said laconically:

"I know."

Her smile was changing to a look of sweet pity, of beneficent compassion, as though the Prince were a child in need of her advice.

She had guessed his unhappiness long before the Duchess had talked to her in the hours of despairing confession. He believed he was unhappy through being crossed in love; but actually, this sorrow was only the outer shell of another which was deeper and more real, and which depended on himself alone.

He had tried to live apart from his fellow-beings, ignoring their troubles, selfishly withdrawing into a shell. He had wished, by loitering on the margin of humanity which was suffering the greatest crisis in all its history, to prolong the pleasures of peace into a time of war. One could understand such aloofness in a coward, dominated by the instinct of self-preservation; but *he* was a brave man. One could tolerate it in a man who was burdened with children, who constantly felt the imperious duty of supporting them, and was afraid on that account; but he was alone in the world.

"We are all unhappy, Prince. Who doesn't know grief and death these days?"

And she talked in monotonous tones of her own misfortune, as though she were reciting a prayer. Her smile, the smile that animated the anæmic homeliness of her features with a vaporous light of dawn, gradually faded.

Six of her brothers had been killed in one afternoon. They belonged to the same battalion and she had received the news of the six deaths at the same time. Thirty-two of her relatives were now beneath the ground and very few of them had been soldiers in the beginning. Before the war they had lived lives of pleasure. They enjoyed great wealth and titles: Life had been as sweet to them as to Prince Lubimoff.... But when they heard the call of duty!... "No one chooses the spot where he is born; no one can decide which his country shall be and what his lineage. We come into the world according to the whims of chance, in the upper or the lower stories of society, and we mold our lives according to the place designated by fate. Neither can any one choose the times he will live in. Happy they who are born in peace times, when humanity is wrapped in calm, and its prehistoric savagery is slumbering within the shell formed by civilization; happy also they who are born into a powerful family and find themselves exempted from the struggle of life."

"But when we are born into a period of madness," she continued, "we have to resign ourselves and adapt ourselves to it, without seeking to avoid the painful burden that falls on our shoulders. It is our duty to suffer so that others later on may be happy as our forefathers suffered for our sakes."

What grief she had felt on receiving at a single stroke the news of the death of all her brothers! She did not consider herself an extraordinary being; she was simply a woman like any other. She had wept. She had abandoned herself to her despair. Then, an idea kept drifting through her mind joyously refreshing her drooping spirits. Supposing men were immortal in this life! Then despair would be horrible indeed. If you considered that the dead might have saved their lives by keeping far from every danger! But no one was immortal.

"Whether you die from a bullet wound or from microbes, makes little difference. Only the external circumstances vary, and for many people there is a greater fascination in returning to dust in a lightning-like manner in the full intoxication of battle, with a generous idea in one's mind, than in slowly fading away in confinement between two sheets, defiled and degraded by the filth of a material nature beginning to disintegrate.

"It is a sort of holy fear necessary, for that matter, to the preservation of human life, and it troubles people and makes them hide from themselves the terrible truth that waits at the end of every life. Sensible people consider it madness to go out in quest of death. It is all very well if death is something motionless which sets hands only on those who draw near it of their own accord. But if man does not go forward to meet death, death, with its hundred-league boots, runs in search of man. Who can guess the moment of the meeting? The best thing, then, is to scorn it; and not pay it the tribute of constant thought which engenders anxiety and fear.

"Besides, death in bed is an unfruitful and sterile death. To whom could it be of use, except one's heirs? The other kind of death, death for an idea, even for an erroneous idea, means something positive. It is an act of energy and faith and the aggregate of such acts makes up the noblest history of humanity."

The Prince admired the simplicity with which this woman, who was almost in a dying condition, exalted the heroism of life and scorned death.

She had placed her ideal very high beyond the selfish desires which form the warp and woof of ordinary lives. If every one were to suit merely his own convenience, humanity as a whole would have no reason to consider itself superior to animals.

The noblewoman possessed an ideal: to sacrifice herself for her fellow beings; to serve them even at the cost of her own life. She was almost glad of the war, which had helped her to find her true path. In peace times she would have done the same as every woman, linking her lot with that of a man, bearing children and building up a family.

"Amorous affection reduces the world to two beings; a mother's love finds nothing of interest beyond her own progeny. Only when old age is reached and the illusory perspectives of life have faded away, is the great truth apparent that people must be interested in every living being, ready to sacrifice themselves for every living being. But the exalted sympathy of old age is unfruitful and brief."

Mary Lewis considered herself fortunate in having rushed forward in the right direction from the first moment, without the long evasions of other people, who are late in reaching the truth.

"I have had my romance, like every one else."

She said this simply, but at the same time what blood was left in her veins animated her features with a faint blush, as though she were confessing something extraordinary.

She had been loved by a scholarly man, a former secretary of her father, the Colonial Governor. Only once had they confessed their love. Afterwards their life continued as before, both of them keeping the secret, postponing the realization of their dreams to an indefinite future.... But the war came.

He had hastened, among the first, to enlist as a volunteer: "Mary, I am a soldier." And Mary had replied: "That is right." They wrote short letters to each other at long intervals. They had more important things to do. He did not have the handsome features and the strength of a hero, like Lady Lewis' brothers. He even suspected that his bearing was scarcely military because of the ungainliness that comes from a sedentary life, spent in bending over a writing table. But he did his duty, and more than once he had been cited for his cool audacity.

Their desires would now never be fulfilled. Even though she might succeed in surviving the war, she would continue her present existence in civilian hospitals, in far-off countries scourged by plagues. He perhaps would marry another, or perhaps would remain faithful to her memory, devoting himself for his part to relieving the pain and sorrows of his fellow beings. But they would live apart, going where duty called them, thinking constantly of each other, but without meeting, like the cultivated monks and passionate nuns of other centuries, who filled their lives with spiritual friendships maintained in widely separated monasteries and convents.

Once more Michael admired her abnegation. Lady Lewis belonged to that small group of the elect, who do not know what selfishness is and long to sacrifice themselves for what is good. She was one of that immortal line of saintly women who existed before the birth of religion and who will continue to flourish just the same when skepticism has finally ruined all our present beliefs.

"You are an angel," said the Prince.

"No," she protested; "I am a lover, a great lover."

Lubimoff smiled with a certain air of pity.

"You a lover?"

She went on talking as though her listener's surprise annoyed her. What was other women's love compared to hers? They fixed their tenderness, their desire for self-sacrifice, on one man only. Beyond him they found nothing worthy of interest. She loved all men, all of them, even the soldiers of the enemy whom she had often cared for in the ambulances at the front. They were mistaken, and if they really were guilty souls and wished to continue being so, all she could see in them was their physical condition as, threatened by death, they lay stretched out on their beds, with their flesh mangled. They were simply unfortunate beings, and this was enough to make her forget their nationality.

She wanted her own side to triumph because the other represented the exaltation of brute strength, the glorification of war, and it was her desire that there should be no more wars. She longed for the time when love would rule the whole world!... It was bad enough that men could not suppress with like facility, poverty, pain and death, the black divinities which seize us at our birth and with whom we struggle up to the last moment.

"I love everything that is alive: People, animals, and flowers. Beside such love, what is the affection between a man and a woman, which people consider the only love and is simply the selfishness of two beings setting themselves apart from their fellow beings, and living only for themselves? My love is likewise a kind of selfishness. I realize it; perhaps it is something worse: pride. If you only knew how gay I feel when I have saved from death one of my 'flirts,' one of those poor wounded men whom I shall never see again!... No, don't admire me, Prince, and don't feel sorry for me. I am merely a poor woman! by no means an angel! Moreover, I am very bad; I have my repentances, like every one else."

"You, Lady Mary!" the Prince exclaimed again with a look of incredulity. That he should have no doubts about it she hastened to relate the great sin of her life. Traveling through Andalusia she had seen some boys on a river bank who were trying to drown a stray dog, throwing stones at it. Mary fell upon them, mad with rage, striking them with her parasol. One of the little fellows wept, and blood spurted from his nostrils. This unhappy memory had often troubled her in the night. Now she could not see a child without caressing it with all the ardor occasioned by remorse.

Also she had had quarrels in various countries with drivers who were whipping their work animals and with hotel keepers who would not allow her to keep in her room lost dogs and cats she found in the streets.

Before the war, her pity had been entirely for animals. Humanity was able to defend itself. But now, the butchery of beings in uniforms had turned her sweet tenderness toward mankind. They needed love and protection more than the poor brutes.

The mention of her "flirts" suddenly brought her back to her duty. At that very moment they were tossing, covered with bandages, in their beds, and anxiously calling for her presence. Or else they were sitting on a bench with motionless eyes turned toward the sun, refusing to take a walk until they could feel the gentle support of her arm. "Good-by, Prince!" She must go! Her lovers were waiting for her.

As she stood up, she thought again of the reason for her visit and spoke once more in the tone that revealed the firmness of her will.

It was useless for him to seek the Duchess. The poor woman after entering so many blind alleys in her life, had finally found the true path, the one she herself, more fortunate, had discovered while still in her youth. The Virgin Dolorosa spoke in a simple, natural way of Alicia's past. She knew it all. In the silence of Villa Rosa, the other woman had confessed it in despair, without the nurse feeling either scandalized or amazed. What did the moral capacity of a mere individual mean, when at every moment the world was beholding the most unheard of crimes.

"She left this morning and is a long way off—a long way!" said the gentle woman. "It is possible that you will never see each other again. I will write her that you forgive her. That will afford her the peace of mind she needs in her new life."

The Prince was going with her as far as the entrance to his gardens. During the walk he began once more to lament his fate. He needed to relieve by articulation the despair in which he was left by the refusal of the English woman to tell him where Alicia was staying.

"I am very unhappy, Lady Mary."

"I know," she replied. "My misfortunes are greater than yours, but I rise above them better."

For Mary life was a sort of balance. In one pan of the scales suffering had perforce to fall. No one could free himself from that burden. But the spirit must re-establish the equilibrium by placing in the other pan something great, an ideal, a hope. She had found the necessary counterweight: love for everything alive, sacrifice for one's fellow beings, and consequent abnegation.

What did the Prince have to counter-balance the shocks of destiny?... Nothing. He went on living the same as in peace times, thinking only of himself. He was still just as the great mass of men had been, before the war drew them from their selfish individualism, making the virtues of solidarity and sacrifice flourish once more in their souls. For that reason all he needed to feel desperate was a mere obstacle to his desires, a disappointment in love, that should really be an affliction only in the life of a mere boy. Oh, if only he could get a high ideal! If only he could think less about himself and more about mankind!...

They shook hands beside the gate.

"Good-by, Lady Lewis!" said the Prince, bowing.

If Don Marcos had been present the Prince's voice at that moment would have sounded familiar to him. It was the same as on the afternoon of the duel, when he met the English woman with the two blind men; a beautifully solemn voice which wavered close to tears.

Toledo did not appear until a few moments later, coming out of the gardener's pavilion, to meet the Prince, who was returning pensively toward the villa.

Lubimoff spoke and gave an order in stern tones.

"I am leaving for Paris. I want to go to-morrow. Make all the necessary arrangements."

Then, as he gazed into the Colonel's eyes, he continued in a gentler voice:

"I think I shall never return here.... I am going to sell Villa Sirena."

CHAPTER XII

DON MARCOS is descending the slopes of the public gardens toward the Casino Square, in conversation with a soldier.

He is no longer the ceremonious Colonel who used to kiss the hands of the elderly and noble ladies in the gambling rooms, and was present as the inevitable guest at the luncheons of all the titled families stopping at the Hôtel de Paris. There is nothing about his person to recall the long velvet lined frock coats, the high white silk hats, and the other splendors of his eccentric elegance. He is soberly dressed in a dark suit, and there is something rustic about his appearance, which reveals the man who lives in the country, enjoys cultivating the soil, and feels constraint on returning to city life. He is wearing gloves, just as in the good old days; but now it is out of necessity. His hands remind him of a certain narrow garden around his diminutive villa, with five trees, twelve rose bushes, and some forty shrubs all of which he knows individually, by names he has given them. He has been caring for them so fondly, and caressing them so often, that his fingers have become calloused.

The soldier is also walking along like a country man, looking with curiosity in every direction. A stiff mustache covers his upper lip, one of those stiff and aggressive mustaches which come out after long periods of continual shaving. His uniform is old, faded by the sun and rain. The yellowish cloth has the neutral color of the soil. His right arm hangs inert from the shoulder and moves in rhythm with his step, like a dangling inanimate object. His hand is covered with a glove, the rigidity of which reveals the outline of something hard and mechanical. The other hand leans on a knotty cane, and smoke is curling from a pipe in his lips. On his sleeves, almost mingling with the color of the cloth, is the one narrow officer's stripe.

"It has been ten months and twenty days, since your Highness left here. How many things have happened!"

The soldier is Prince Lubimoff; but Lubimoff seems stronger, more serene and decided than the preceding year, in spite of his artificial arm. There are the same gray hairs, scattered here and there, on his head; but his mustache, on being allowed to grow, has come out almost white.

The Colonel's side whiskers are like his mustache. With the disappearance of his elegance, the touches of the toilet table have likewise ceased, and the modest gray, obtained by careful dying, has given place to the white of frank old age.

Don Marcos points to the Square toward which they are both going.

"If your Highness had only seen it the night of the Armistice!"

The news of the triumph made every one come running. They descended from Beausoleil, they came up from La Condamine, and they arrived from the rock of Monaco. For the first time in four years, the façades of the Casino, the hotels and cafés, were illuminated from top to bottom.

The Square was overflowing with people. They all seemed to blink as though dazzled by the light, after the long darkness in which the submarine menace had kept them plunged. Several brass instruments roared out the Marseillaise, and the crowd following the flags of the Allied countries and, unwilling to leave the Square, kept marching about the "Camembert," like moths about a flame.

Suddenly a long dancing line formed, a *farandole*, and it began to run and leap, growing at each twist and turn. Every one, in the contagion of enthusiasm, joined out; officers grasped hands with privates; solemn ladies kicked up their heels and lost their hats; timid girls shouted, with their hair flying; the faces of the women had the look of enthusiastic madness which is seen only in times of revolution. The lame hopped and skipped, the blind imagined they could see, and those who had lost their hands held on with their stumps to the serpentine line. The Marseillaise seemed like a miraculous hymn, giving every one new strength. Peace!... Peace!

In one of its evolutions, the head of the human snake climbed the steps of the Casino. The *farandole* was trying to enter the antechamber, and the gambling rooms, to wrap its coils about the crowd, the *croupiers*, and the tables. Every selfish activity should cease in that hour of generous joy.

"Alas, the gamblers! What a malady gambling is, Your Highness! On reaching the Square they took off their hats to the flags, and almost wept, as they sang a verse of the Marseillaise. 'Long live France! Long live the Allies!' And immediately they entered the Casino to bet their money on the same number as the celebrated date, or on other combinations suggested by peace."

The gate-keepers, with the air of old gendarmes, concentrated in a heroic body to keep off with their breasts, their bellies and their fists the turbulent snake dance which was trying to enter the sacred edifice. They seemed indignant. When had such extraordinary insolence ever been seen? Peace was a good thing, and people might well rejoice; but to come into the Casino like a dancing riot, to interrupt the functioning of an honorable industry!... And they had finally shoved the line of disheveled women down the steps, and the decorated soldiers who were suddenly forgetting their infirmities and their wounds were driven after it.

The Prince and Toledo arrive at the Square and turn to the left of the Casino, toward the Café de Paris.

Lubimoff sits down at a table, at a protruding angle of the sidewalk café which people nickname "The Promontory." The Colonel remains on his right. He has spent the afternoon with the Prince, and must return home. He is no longer so free as before; some one is living with him, and his new situation imposes unavoidable obligations.

In his mind's eye he can see, on the heights of Beausoleil, the little house he lives in, surrounded by its little garden. It is all his by registered public deed. But the fate of his property does not worry the Colonel; no one will carry off his walls and trees. What makes him nervous is a certain non-commissioned American officer, young and well built, who has a mania for walking about the dwelling; and certain bright eyes which from a window follow the soldier with a hungry look; and certain lips red as cherries, that smile at that American; and certain hands which Don Marcos thinks he has surprised from a distance throwing down a flower, though their owner shrieks at him in fury every day to convince him that he has been imagining things.

Don Marcos is married. A few weeks after the departure of the Prince, a great change came into his life. Villa Sirena already belonged to the nouveau-riche who was a maker of auto trucks and aeroplanes, and who had also bought the Paris residence. The Colonel on giving him possession, remembered only to praise the merits of the gardener and his family.

Lubimoff, before leaving for the front, had arranged for his "chamberlain's" future, assuring him a pension of ten thousand francs a year, and also sending him a certain sum with which to buy a house.

Since the Colonel had set his mind on dying in Monte Carlo, he ought to have a little Villa Sirena of his own.

After digging in the garden on his property for a short time, with an occasional glance down on the Casino Square, Toledo went in search of Novoa. The Professor was his best friend; besides, he was a Spaniard, and it was the latter's duty to be of service to him, in the most important event in his life. He needed a best man for his wedding. The Professor was dumbfounded on being informed that the Colonel was going to marry the gardener's daughter. She was young enough to be his grandchild! It was tempting fate for a man of his years to expose himself deliberately to such dangers.

"You, Don Marcos, as a Spaniard, must remember," said Novoa, "that the Saint whose name you bear has a bull with long horns for his emblem! Besides, youth has its rights."

"And old age its duties," replied the Colonel, with a kindly air, resigning himself to his future.

At present, standing beside the Prince, he stammers with timidity and embarrassment. He hates to confess that he must desert him.

"Mado is waiting for me: you see, the poor girl doesn't go out very much. She likes to have me take her to the afternoon concerts on the terraces. It is five o'clock."

And when the Prince assents, with a slight nod, Toledo rushes off precipitously. Then, farther on, he begins almost to run up the slope, panting, but without feeling his weariness. He wants to reach home as soon as possible, and yet is afraid of doing so. He is sure of Mado only when he is within range of her shrieks. He shudders when he thinks that he may be "imagining things" again.

As the Prince remains alone, the glass that is before his eyes gradually fades away and with it the adjoining tables, and the people seated around the "Camembert." His vision contracts, and buries itself deep within his mind to contemplate other images of memory.

He arrived in Monte Carlo that morning. Only a few hours have passed, and he has seen so much already!

He recalls certain remarks of his friend Lewis; and remarks, made during one of the luncheons at Villa Sirena: "Life is strange and uneven as it flows along. Time goes by without anything extraordinary arising, and then, all of a sudden, hours do the work of months, days are as eventful as years, and things happen in a few moments which, at other times, would take centuries." How many people have died in the relatively short space of time that has elapsed since he last left Monte Carlo!

Lubimoff recalls the brief and exciting period after his arrival in Paris: his enlistment in the Foreign Legion; the Commission of Second Lieutenant granted him in recognition of his former service as Captain in the Imperial Guards; his departure for the front, after distributing or investing the million and a half derived from the sale of Villa Sirena, his hard life in action, the battles and slaughter accompanying, with gruesome prodigality, the advances of the triumphant offensive. He recalls his meeting with a member of the Legion who suddenly called to him and whom he had some difficulty in recognizing: Atilio Castro! Castro had changed. His ironical smile had vanished. He looked on life with greater seriousness, and now seemed convinced of the worth of his actions. They belonged to different battalions, and they did not see each other again, till late one afternoon, after a fight, he came across him. The poor boy was lying stretched out on the ground, among other corpses. His forehead had been crushed in and his brain was showing under the wound! On that face the death grin was a smile of serenity. Poor Castro! What could have become of Doña Clorinda?

The Prince's mind wanders from that memory. Other lost friends claim his attention. He evokes finally a more recent vision: his arrival after a long convalescence in a hospital, in Monte Carlo. On getting out of the train, Toledo deeply moved, gazes at his artificial arm, which hides but imperfectly the amputation. He had suffered for several months from the consequences of a stupid, accidental wound, received ingloriously a few days before the armistice.

He ascends the slope to the delightful little home of Don Marcos, which will be his own while he remains here. Down below, projecting into the sea, the promontory of Villa Sirena meets his eye. It now belongs to another man, and he turns his glance away to keep certain memories from welling up. In doing so his eyes chance to meet the eyes of Mado, Toledo's *señora*; eyes which doubtless consider Prince Lubimoff more interesting, with his mustache, his elderly appearance, and his uniform, than when he was the elegant master of her parents. Poor Colonel! And Michael flees the tempting glance, and the full scarlet lips, which seem to challenge him to smile.

After lunch he follows a path which zigzags up the mountain; he sees a stone wall, passes through a door, and briefly contemplates a monument surmounted by a huge rooster.

Toledo bares his head. Peace to the heroes! Then he points to the entrance of the funereal structure.

"Poor Martinez is there."

They descend several steps to another part of the cemetery, lying in terraces on the mountain slope. On that level plot the tombs are leveled off even with the soil, with slabs of stone protected by low rectangular fences of chain, or simply bordered with flowers. An æsthetic instinct seems to explain the sparing use of ornaments here. From these mournful esplanades of death one can see a great expanse of green coast, dotted with the white of villas and towns; the rose-colored Alps, the capes of purple rock, the deep intense blue of the Mediterranean, and the soft limpid blue of a cloudless sky. And the graves seem to smile at all this splendor of Nature.

The Colonel searches among them, reading the names.

"Here, Marquis."

He points to a slab with a simple inscription: "Mary Lewis."

"Just like a bird, your Highness. One morning at dawn they found her poor little body dead on the hospital cot. She hadn't cried out, she hadn't complained; she departed as she had lived. The nurses say that the face was smiling. Her body was as light as a feather."

Around the tomb several wreaths were turning black, as though scorched by fire. Toledo seeks among these offerings of the dead woman's companions, until he points to a handful of fresh roses, which are beginning to decay.

"They must be from Lord Lewis," he goes on to say. "When things go badly in the Casino, he comes up to see his niece. Your Highness must know, of course, that with the death of Lady Lewis, he is now a Lord—really a Lord."

The Prince shrugs his shoulders. To think of human vanities in a place like this, which makes all earthly worries seem grotesque!

Don Marcos guesses his impatience, and as they descend two more terraces, he goes on explaining.

"The English woman died before the other; that is why they buried her farther up. So many people have died in the last few months!"

They reach the last terrace of the cemetery, the lowest one, a square field of reddish earth in which there are no slabs, no truncated columns, and no fences of chain. Little mounds of earth taking the form of a coffin indicate the location of the graves. Some of them have wooden crosses. From one of the latter hangs the picture of a young soldier in the center of a wreath laid there by his parents.

Two men show their heads and shoulders above the ground and disappear from sight again after emptying their shovels. They are opening a grave for some one who is soon to come. Michael notices floating up from the vibrant, luminous air, the mournful sound of a bell, tolling in an unseen church below.

The Colonel insists on explaining.

"It is a temporary grave, without any slab, without any name."

On account of the war, it was impossible to send the body to Paris. It will lie here the length of time the law demands, and then the young lady, who is her heir, will have her taken to the vault in the Passy Cemetery where her mother is buried. He hesitates somewhat as he examines the mounds, and finally stops in front of one of them, and takes off his hat.

"Here it is."

Lubimoff cannot hide his surprise. "Here?..." He sees a heap of earth, without anything to adorn it, without anything to differentiate it from the rest, and which inspires in him no emotion at all. He looks anxiously at his companion. Hasn't he made a mistake? Are they not standing beside the tomb of some poor soldier who died of his wounds?

The Colonel, somewhat offended by the question, repeats energetically: "Here it is." He remembers that he was the only man present at the funeral. Three nurses, Señorita Valeria, and he, followed the coffin to these heights; there was no one else.

Poor Duchess de Delille! Toledo is moved on remembering her unexpected death. Lady Lewis had sent her to the front. Having been born in the United States, it was fairly easy for her to be admitted to a hospital unit with the American Divisions that were fighting at Château-Thierry.

The Prince, listening to the explanations of Don Marcos, recalls a confession Alicia once made to him. Her hands were clumsy. Her spirit, anxious to do good, weakened at the moment of action through a lack of material training. Doubtless for that reason she had been sent back a few weeks later to the Riviera, to give her services in a quieter hospital than the ambulance stations at the front.

Toledo had not seen her. She was living in the neighborhood of Monte Carlo without his ever suspecting it. The first news he had had of her was that of her death; a death which leaves the Colonel pensive whenever he recalls it. She became infected by a surgical instrument which had just been used in an operation. Perhaps it was because of the clumsiness of her hands; perhaps ... who knows! Don Marcos believes that the Duchess was tired of life.

"A horrible death, Marquis. I did not see her: I am glad I didn't. They tell me she was black and swollen. Besides, for several hours she was in torture, lifting herself on her head and heels, arching above the bed, with the muscles of her body tense with the most atrocious suffering. Tetanus! How terrible for a great lady, so beautiful, so elegant to die like that! But in the midst of such pain she found the peace of mind to dictate her last testament. Señorita Valeria has inherited Villa Rosa, and several hundred thousand francs: all that she won that night at the Sporting Club. As for your Highness...."

The Prince interrupts him with a gesture. He has known for a long time, from the letters of Don Marcos, that Alicia remembered him in her last moments, leaving him heir to her silver mines in Mexico, all that she possessed on the other side of the ocean; nothing at the present moment, but in the future perhaps a fortune, almost as great as that which Lubimoff formerly held in Russia.

He remains with his eyes fixed on the grave. On it he sees some fine moss, a miniature forest, opening its branches at the breath of spring, and among the tiny leaves diminutive flowers are stirring. Several greenish black butterflies, spotted with red, are fluttering above this murmuring forest of budding life, much as the monstrous prehistoric birds fluttered above the first vegetation of the globe.

Michael sees a relation between these insects and the spirit that dwelt in the organism now disintegrating a few feet under the ground beneath his feet. The varied, clashing colors remind him of the dead woman's soul. In the same way a few minutes before, a white butterfly fluttering above the flowers brought by Lewis reminded him of the child-like and sublime soul of Lady Mary.

At present, sitting in the café, his emotions are greater than in the cemetery. He can see events through a veil of memory, spiritualized, and free from the sediment of reality.

Poor Alicia! Poor woman, disillusioned of life! The triumphant Venus, the Helen of the "old men on the wall," the beauty who was the center of the Universe, more eager for admiration than for love, is lying in this miserable cemetery, among the bodies of soldiers. Perhaps she voluntarily hastened her exit from a world in which she could not find her place, defeated by her own actions.

Our lives are nothing more than what we will them to be. We create life in our own image; it is useless for us to complain of fate: we are what we want to be. It was impossible for Alicia to end her days save in some extraordinary manner, in harmony with her previous career. He, too, has lived as most men do not live, and he will die a different death from them.

He feels neither grief nor resentment. He is surprised that he could have hated Martinez and desired this woman with such vehemence. At present he feels only melancholy and a deep sadness at the memory of those dreams that no longer exist and which are beginning to die a second death, in being forgotten by those who knew of them. They have no immortality save in the memory of the Prince, a poor memory destined to fade away in turn before many years.

In his imagination he attempts to pierce the mass of earth that covers the dead body; he makes an effort to penetrate with his vision into the densest of the shadows. Only a few months of decomposition have gone by: her personality has not yet wasted away completely. He sees her as she was in life and at the same time as she is now. Her flesh is disintegrating in little putrid rivulets that run down the folds of her clothes, blackened and eaten away. She is forced to smile at all times in the darkness: she no longer has any lips. Her eyes serve as a refuge for the prolific grave flies which engender millions and millions of destroyers. And this annihilation of something which existed, thought, and loved, is as yet only in its first stages.

After the devourers of the soft parts will come the irresistible artisans of the bones. Myriads of micro-scopical workers will plow the skeleton, cleaning away the last impurities clinging to the framework, undoing the marvelous articulations, scraping away the cement which holds the vertebræ together. Some day the lower jaw will loosen, falling toward the abdominal cavity, leaving the upper jaw bone, the teeth of which knew the splendor of smiles and the caress of kisses. Some other day, the skull, as the pivot on which it rests comes apart, will fall in turn and mingle with the dust of the ribs and the little bones of the feet which mark the rhythm of an undulating walk. Within a few centuries revolutions and wars will perhaps bring this skull to the surface. Why not? Lubimoff has just seen at the front numerous cemeteries swept away by gunfire, with the dead emerging from the earth, raised thus by the bursting shells. And when some one, in the future, with the eternal curiosity of the Shakespearean Prince takes Alicia's skull in his hand, he will not be able to tell whether it belonged to a lady or a servant, whether it belonged to a beauty or to a drab.

Michael recalls with ironical sadness all the illusions, all the desires, he had in the past, concentrated on this nothingness. He begins to feel the need of forgetting the corpse. His eyes, looking within, see the diminutive foliage, the gaudy butterfly, and all that nature has placed on a nameless tomb. This is what a life which considered itself superior to all others has left as the only trace of its existence. Perhaps in the corolla of one of the little flowers there is something of Alicia's soul, the butterflies sip it, and continue in an intoxicated flight above the tombs.

Springtime! The Prince lifts his thoughts above the sorrows of individuals. He recalls what he has seen in a corner of the world ruined by man's bestiality: cities in ruins; villages that raise their walls only a yard above the soil, like towns which have been excavated after a cataclysm; barns set on fire; endless fields made sterile, torn apart and turned topsy turvy by five years of bombardment; many graves—thousands of graves—millions of graves. Women, dressed in black, stagger along the roads through the ruins and the funnel-shaped chasms opened by the monstrous projectiles. They have lost their children, they have seen their husbands executed, and now they are exploring the soil in search of their homes that were....

But the Winter-time of war is over; and now the Spring of Peace is here. The same hand, touching all things with green, puts little flowers and butterflies on the nameless graves, hangs fragrant garlands on the fire-blackened walls, spreads a velvet carpet of emerald on the sides of the shell holes, makes the birds warble and the insects stir above the tombs, and guides the curling creepers over the black wood of the crosses, as though trying to change them into thyrsi.

Alas! The earth knows nothing of our sorrows.

The Prince comes out of his abstraction, and sees the Colonel greeting him from a distance.

Don Marcos is already back, and with him is *Madame* Toledo, whose head scarcely reaches his shoulder. On the way she looks back several times, with the hope of finding herself followed by the American soldier.

On recognizing the Prince in the café, however, she forgets the other man, and seems to be entreating him with her eyes to leave his seat and to go out with her to the terraces.

The Colonel and his minx disappear in the direction of the terraces, and again Michael plunges into meditation. He recalls his talk with Don Marcos, shortly before, as they were descending from the cemetery.

Toledo seems inconsolable. According to him the war has not ended properly. He appears scandalized at the absurd manner of its conclusion! What terrible times these are! The fugitive of Amerongen disconcerts and irritates him.

"And imagine me doing him the honor of comparing him to a Lieutenant! I considered him man enough at least to blow his brains out!

"For thirty years he has been frightening the world with the rattle of his saber, and with his boastful mustache; for thirty years he has been calling himself war lord, making whole races tremble at his frown, his heroic attitudinizing, and his melodramatic speeches; for thirty years he has been preparing millions of men for slaughter, obliging peoples of the world to live under arms in the midst of peace. And now, when misfortune seeks him for her own, when he considers his life in danger, he shamefully flees to a foreign country and deserts his supporters, like a merchant going into a fraudulent bankruptcy."

"It is the greatest lie humanity has ever known," the Colonel shouts indignantly. "The greatest swindle in history."

It does not prove anything to kill one's self; Don Marcos is well aware of that. But in this life there are so many things that do not prove anything and which nevertheless are beautiful and logical! The despair of those who commit suicide through love does not prove anything either, and yet it has inspired the greatest works of poetry and other arts. The sailor, who wrecks his ship, kills himself; every man of honor who considers his fault irreparable appeals to death, in order that when he falls, he may fall in a dignified manner.

"And that Emperor," Toledo continued, "who planned an organized slaughter of ten million men, wants to live to a ripe old age. It's the most shameless thing I ever heard of!

"Military honor, such as it had come to be understood through the various centuries, was unknown likewise to his generals. Those specialists in burning towns, those technicians in executing peasants, those artisans of terror, on seeing disaster coming, tranquilly returned to their castles, like office boys leaving their work.

"Of all these companions of the 'war lord,' the only one worthy of respect was a civilian, a manufacturer, a Jew, the munition maker Ballin, of Hamburg, who on seeing the Empire ruined, did not want to survive it and shot himself. In the meantime the Marshals of the strategy that failed, tranquilly begin to devote themselves to training their dogs, writing their memoirs, and looking after their health.

"Napoleon, in one of his last battles, stopped his horse over a lighted bomb; later he tried to poison himself at Fontainebleau. He courted death, and resigned himself to living, like a fatalist, only on becoming convinced that death would have nothing to do with him. The other Napoleon, the one of Sedan, may have taken refuge in Belgium, abandoning his troops much as the sad German Cæsar had done; but ill and fainting, on his horse, he nevertheless preferred to gallop along a high road swept by gun fire, hoping that a shell would tear him to pieces."

That is the way Toledo understands military honor. That is the way it has been accepted in all ages.

Against the Imperial generals, recreants, ready to run in the hour of danger, like comedians thinking only of their reputations, his anger is implacable. Hemmed in by the Allies, with their lines broken, they might have fallen nobly fighting until the last moment. But they preferred to beg for an armistice and hand over their weapons, in order that the imbeciles who had admired them so greatly might go on believing in their divine invincibility, and be sure that if they were retiring to their estates it was only out of consideration for internal politics.

"Sorry comedians, like their master, up to the very last moment!" And Don Marcos, thinking of the fear these men have made the whole world feel for thirty years, cries out in anger:

"Swindlers! Swindlers!"

Once more the Prince comes out of his reverie. Somebody has stopped in front of him, and he hears a well known voice.

"Your Highness, what a joy to see you! The Colonel has just told me of your arrival."

It is Spadoni: the same old Spadoni, as though but a few hours have gone by since his last interview with the Prince; as though it is only yesterday that he bellowed with indignation, as he studied at the piano *What the Palm Tree Said to the Century Plant*.

He doesn't want to sit down: he is in a hurry; he came just to shake hands with his Highness. He will make a point of seeing him later when he has more time, in the Casino. He takes it for granted that the Prince is going into the Casino. Where else could a decent person go in Monte Carlo?

He gives Lubimoff's uniform a rapid glance, and admires his rough soldierly appearance.

"I have heard of the great deeds of your Highness; I always used to ask the Colonel about you ... a hero!"

Lubimoff has scarcely time to shake his head at this praise. Spadoni starts to talk about something more interesting. The war, heroes, and all that, are nebulous, meaningless things. He is for reality, and begins to talk about a new personage whom he admires, a Portuguese who plays big stakes, and whose name, because of his winnings, during the last few days, has been filling the gambling rooms.

"I am studying him; besides, he is a friend of mine and I think I have his secret. Imagine, Prince...."

The Prince grows uneasy, guessing that he is going to describe in all its details the combination of the Portuguese, which he already considers his own. But the pianist looks towards the Casino, stammers, and finally interrupts his account. Some one is coming and he wants to share his secret only with the Prince. He takes his leave with the promise that some time he will reveal the precious combination.

Lubimoff thinks of his life during the last few months, his adventures as a soldier, of his wound, of all that has happened to him and to the entire world, while that musician has remained stationary in Monte Carlo, admitting nothing as real save the hovering flight of the Great Delusion.

His friend Lewis holds out his hand to the Prince. It is he who, by his approach, has stopped the pianist's flow of eloquence. Gamblers, out of professional rivalry, avoid telling one another their secrets. Time, which seems to have forgotten Spadoni, leaving him the same as when Michael last saw him in his "Villa of the Tomb," has laid its claws on Lewis, making him older, as though months for him have been years.

He is sad because of the losses he has been suffering, and because of his memories. That niece of his was all the family he had! Lubimoff knows through the Colonel that he has not inherited anything from her. The nurse spent her entire fortune on ambulances and hospitals. Her title is the one thing that has gone to Lewis. His prophecy has come true: he is now the third Lord Lewis, surnamed "the Worthless," the name he gave himself.

He gazes on the Prince for a long time, notices the rigid arm and then shakes his left hand effusively.

"You're a man, Lubimoff. You know how to do things."

And in these words there is a reproach for himself. Unable to tear himself away from Monte Carlo, he will live here and die here, doing the same things over and over.

Nevertheless, this is a great day for him. In the morning he received a visit from a friend who is coming to live with him, he does not know for how long, perhaps for two days, perhaps for two years; a great friend from whom he had had no news and whom he had often imagined dead; the Count, the famous Count.

He has come as far as the café with Lewis, who refuses to be separated from him; he has shaken hands with the Prince as though he had seen him the day before, without noticing his uniform or his mutilation. He sits silently in a chair, running his hand through his white, curly hair, fixing his round eyes, with a nocturnal fire, on the people who are walking about the "Camembert."

Lewis believes he ought to feel happy. What a day of surprise it has been! First the Count, and then the Colonel telling him of Lubimoff's arrival.

He avoids talking about his niece: he sinks his sadness in the sadness of all the rest.... Peace has surprised him: who could have imagined it would come so soon, following immediately on the most anxious phase of the war?

The Count comes to life at this query.

"Every one," says he. "The great soothsayers, the great ones, announced at the very beginning, that the war would end in the Fall of 1918. It was well known to everybody. I have always said so. You have heard me say so many times yourself, Lewis."

Lewis makes a gesture of surprise. But he cannot doubt the science of his learned friend, and prefers to admit that it is he who has forgotten. He has such a bad memory! Perhaps, even, he may have misunderstood. These guardians of a knowledge of the future never express their truths clearly: they refuse to talk like ordinary mortals.

The conversation begins to lag. The Englishman is thinking of the Casino. He was just going in when Don Marcos gave him the news of the Prince's arrival. He keeps the Count by his side. The Count has just returned from a mysterious trip and has the devil's rosary safe in a certain pocket of his trousers, constantly feeling in it with his right hand.

"Later on we shall see each other at the Casino. I suppose you'll come in for a moment. We'll see if luck treats me well to-day after such pleasant meetings."

And he goes off with the Count in the direction of the *Palace* where he is destined, as though in prison, to spend the rest of his life.

Lubimoff notices two Italian soldiers who are looking at him from the sidewalk around the "Camembert." They are a couple of *bersaglieri*, dressed in gray, with little round hats decked out in cock's plumes. Noticing that the Prince is looking at them they become embarrassed, turn their backs as though ashamed, and walk away, but not without smiling first and raising their hands to their much beplumed hats.

The Prince recalls what Don Marcos told him. Oh, yes! They are Estola and Pistola, changed into soldiers! They have come on leave to see their families. They are going up to the Colonel's house in the evening to pay their respects to their former "Lord." They seem taller, and more vigorous. A few months of war have been sufficient to transport them from adolescence into maturity. In every man there is a soldier!

Just as he is getting up to take a walk around the terraces, he sees hurrying toward the café a gentleman who is violently waving to him, and then has to stop to fasten his glasses more securely on his nose.

It takes some time for the Prince to recognize him. He guesses who it is more by the tone of his voice than by his features. Dear old Novoa! The months that have gone by have left a deeper imprint on him than on the rest. He is no longer the young man preoccupied with worldly pomp, who used to consult the Colonel about the merits of various tailors and hatters. He has returned to the slavery of baggy-kneed trousers and ready-made neckties. His beard is full grown and bushy. He is still as young as ever in his voice, his eyes, and his lively and clumsy gestures; but he is dressed, not to say disguised, as an old man.

The Professor is more effusive than the rest on seeing the Prince. He keeps blessing the happy chance, which brought Lubimoff to him, through his meeting with Don Marcos shortly before.

"If you had waited two days longer, Prince, I wouldn't have had the pleasure of seeing you. I am going back to my country day after to-morrow. I have had enough now of Monte Carlo. When I think of what I've lost here!... Money, dreams, everything."

Michael shows discretion. He suspects his friend has had some unexpected disillusionment, some deception, such as one must forget not to be continually tormented by it. He remembers Valeria, and sees nothing in the Professor's appearance to indicate the slightest trace of contact with that lady. He is a ruin, a dry dead tree; the bird that formerly sang in the branches must have flown away long since.

Novoa is equally discreet. He looks at the other man's uniform, and the sleeve with the artificial arm; but he speaks in a general way, with vague regrets, only of what has taken place during the last few months.

"What extraordinary things have taken place! How many friends of ours have died! Life has finally become one of those dramas in which one dies at the end of the last act."

The Prince guesses that Novoa is thinking of Alicia and in order not to give him pain, is refraining from mentioning her. As a matter of fact he is indeed thinking of the Duchess, but she is merely a point of departure before he comes to the other woman with whom his memory is constantly occupied.

At last he speaks, giving full rein to his melancholy. He can tell the Prince everything because he is the only man who knows his secret. (He has told the Colonel and even Spadoni the same thing, on lamenting his misfortune.) And he breaks into despairing recriminations against Valeria.

She has become a different woman. She is no longer interested in "lands of love," where women marry without dowries. Since the Duchess's death she has become a candidate for marriage. Her hand will bring with it more than three hundred thousand francs. The Professor has found himself jilted and forgotten. How he had grovelled before her when the truth was known; what shameful efforts he had made to remedy what he had considered at the outset a woman's passing whim! He hates to remember moments such as those.

"It is all ended, Prince. At present she is crazy about an American officer and will finally marry him. No one counts here except the Americans. Everything is for them: even love. The humblest little milliner considers herself disgraced if she hasn't a soldier from the United States to promenade with in the evening. Every afternoon she and the other man dance in the hotels of La Condamine, or right here in the Café de Paris."

He stops, as though some one had touched him on the shoulder. He does not see any one behind him, but his eyes, wandering over the groups sitting at the tables meet something which makes his voice tremble.

"It is she, Prince."

Michael would not have recognized her. He sees two ladies, escorted by two American officers, entering the Café. One of them is Valeria, dressed with gay and showy elegance, as though anxious to compensate in a moment for years of frugality and privation.

Against the soft twilight the café windows begin to gleam with a reddish glow. One after another, the large lamps within are lighted. To the Prince's ears come the voluptuous wailings of violins.

"Life has changed very greatly since you went away, Prince. Every one feels a desperate hunger for amusement. The first thing that peace brought back to life was the tango."

Then Novoa begins to think about himself:

"What can I do here? I am poor. Everything I possessed in my country I have dropped here in the Casino. I have studied the mysteries of the ocean enough. How dearly it has cost me! I have had my little dream, and now I am going to resume my ill-paid work back there as a day laborer in science."

He thinks once more of her.

"Did you notice?... The poor Duchess, who made her what she is now, is lying up there in her grave, and here she is dancing, only a few months after her death."

He feels the harsh indignation, the sense of outraged morality, that all who have been scorned experience.

His anger grows so strong that he gets up from his chair. He cannot remain there. The woman has seen him, and might think that he is pursuing her, that he is waiting for her to come out, in order to entreat her. Never; he has had enough of certain humiliations which he does not care to remember.

He hurriedly says good-by. They will see each other again soon. Don Marcos has invited him to dinner at the little house in Beausoleil. The Colonel was sure that his visit would please the Prince.

He grasps Lubimoff's hand and does not seem to notice it is the wooden one. His eyes and his thoughts are on the café windows, ablaze in mid afternoon. Through them the cadenced murmur of the violins is passing. As he walks away he still repeats his protest.

"The poor Duchess up there forgotten.... And the other woman. What a scandal! I am glad I'm going away soon, and will never see her again."

On remaining alone, the Prince leaves his table. Don Marcos is doubtless telling the news of his arrival to every one he meets, and Michael is afraid that other less interesting persons will appear.

As he walks along he notices something which he had not seen before when he was with the Colonel. The United States flag is floating above all the buildings. In the city streets there are as many signs in English as in French. There are American soldiers everywhere. Lubimoff's uniform and that of the other French fighters are lost in the great flood of men dressed in mustard color. The light automobiles of the American army pass incessantly. They are everywhere. One meets them in the streets, on the roads along the coast and climbing the slopes of the Alps like buzzing, snorting ants. Everything seems animated by a robust, gay, self-confident life, the life of a twenty-year-old boy. The concert on the terraces is being given by an American band. The people walking in the streets absentmindedly whistle dance tunes from across the ocean and marching songs of the soldiers from the States. People stop in the squares to admire the skill of the Americans in shirt sleeves throwing a ball and sending it back again after catching it in a kind of fencing glove.

Monaco seems to have been conquered by the troops of the Great Republic; a good-natured and kindly conquest, which makes the conquered smile. It is the same in Nice and everywhere on the Riviera. The Prince recalls his brief stay in Paris a few days before. There he saw Americans just as here. How many are they? What superhuman power has been able to create in a few months this army which though of recent birth, seems to fill all space?

A people has just risen above all the peoples of the earth. Never in history has such a rise been known. It dominates through friendliness, through its generous acts, and by the beneficent strength of its activities; not through terror, the base of all greatness in the past.

Lubimoff recalls his doubts of the year before. No one would have believed that a people without armies could improvise a military force equal to those of old Europe. And in only a few months the United States had organized and transported two million men to decide the outcome of the struggle, and the world's fate.

Arriving at the last moment, they had liberally given their share of dead. In five months of campaign a hundred and twenty thousand Americans had perished, a huge proportion compared to the losses of the other nations during five years of fighting.

Michael, in his silent enthusiasm, enumerates what has just been done for humanity by this great people, which shortly before was considered utilitarian and selfish, and which now reveals itself as the most romantic and generous.

Two great wars are the most striking incidents in its history: one within, for the suppression of slavery; the other, without, to prevent the glorification of war, the brutal hegemony of one people over all, the exaltation of a mystic imperialism.

For the first time in history, a democracy has intervened in the fate of a world through the centuries subjected to the rule of kings. The modern republics had until now lived an inner and retiring life. The wars of the French Revolution were defensive. The Republic of the Convention fought to exist, since all the monarchs wanted to suppress it. The American Republic had voluntarily entered the struggle, without being threatened by any immediate danger, because of a mandate of its conscience, indignant at German crimes, because of the responsibility developing upon its greatness, its democratic strength.

Before arming, before intervening in the European crash while living in patient neutrality, battles were being won for it. This war was different from others. Against Germany, ready through long years of preparation for the struggle, and with all its industrial and commercial strength mobilized for war purposes, the Allies fought during the first few months, as a brave but backward people fights against a modern nation. They showed much bravery, and great heroism, sometimes in vain, against the blind mechanical force of industrial invention applied to destruction.

If this inequality kept diminishing, it was thanks in large part to the Republic beyond the sea. Its money barons made enormous loans to the Allies; its captains of industry facilitated the manufacture of the gigantic equipment demanded by the demon-like progress of military science; its ships defying the submarine menace, brought bread which had grown scarce in Europe through the war.

And when, its patience finally exhausted, it directly intervened, what generosity it showed!

The American combatants fought for simple and robust ideals: the rights of the weak to live, the dignity and freedom of mankind, the elimination of wars, understanding between peoples, sovereign right ruling the life of nations; things which shortly before had made the Old World skeptics smile.

All the countries of Europe had frontiers to reëstablish, strips of land to claim. The United States of America was not asking for anything, it did not want anything.

Each one of the contestants, on thinking of victory, calculated the indemnities it should collect to compensate for its endeavors and sacrifices. The American Republic spent more than all the other nations. The maintenance of each of its soldiers cost it as much as seven soldiers from the other countries, and nevertheless, it entered the war and withdrew from the war without demanding any particular reimbursement.

Lubimoff admired its enormous strength in victory: Never had any Empire in the past reached such greatness; not even Rome.

It was the only country, at once both industrial and agricultural, on earth. It formed a world apart within the world. It might, without suffering, isolate itself from the rest of the Globe; but the world would feel a sensation of emptiness if the Great Republic were to turn its back upon the other nations.

Its armed citizens were retiring without boasting and without commotion, just as they had come, and without asking anything for their great endeavor. They would disappear like the fairies and enchanters in ancient legends who, after doing good, need to return to their mysterious domains.

Years would pass: history would speak of this endeavor, unique in its intensity and its generous character, and on the Riviera and in other places there would remain of this great world a memory disfigured by time. The boys of to-day, grown old, would remember how they learned to play baseball from the soldiers who had come from a land of marvels beyond the sea, the girls, becoming grandmothers, would yearningly recall the American lovers they once had.

The Prince calculates again the greatness of this people, the only one capable of still working the miracles, that religions sometimes work in the early period of their exaltation.

The Great Republic is the world's creditor. All the victorious nations owe it fabulous sums; England is its debtor by thousands of millions, and France the same. The smaller countries, Belgium, Serbia, and the rest, have been able to live, thanks to its enormous loans. It is not all known as yet, years must pass before the full extent of these generosities is brought to light. This country, which likes advertisement and loud propaganda in its commercial affairs, is modest and concise in speaking of its disinterested acts.

"To go on freely living after the cataclysm, humanity is going to need America's support, or America's benevolence," thinks the Prince. "The political center of the world has shifted. It is no longer in Paris, nor is it in London. It remained for a while, trembling unsteadily on its base, in Berlin; but now it has leaped across the ocean."

The man, as yet unknown, who in the future is to take his place in the White House for four years, professor, lawyer, merchant, or farmer, as he may be, will sway the destiny of the world more than all the rulers who fill history with the din of warlike glory. His power will be based on something more permanent and solid than the strength of armies. It will have behind it industry and wealth, which create armies; democratic power, which the power of public opinion creates.

The irresistible strength of this power is clearly seen by the Prince.

Germany, in spite of her continual military triumphs in the first few years of the war, has finally fallen in defeat. Public opinion was against her. The democratic spirit of the entire world rose against the spirit of Empire.

This triumph of democracy is beginning to be manifest everywhere.

"There is no longer a single emperor left in Europe," Michael goes on thinking. "The vanquished empires want to be republics. All the kings are forgetting their ancestors with their divine rights, and are trying to have their crowns forgiven them, that they may imitate the simple life of a president."

This unexpected attitude of the world gives it a new love of life.

He has realized, for the last few months—since he gave up Villa Sirena—that Prince Michael Fedor Lubimoff has become an unfashionable personage. Perhaps, with the lapse of years, others will be as he was. History repeats itself. Times of peace and plenty inevitably produce men such as he had been. But at present humanity has been restored by grief and sacrifice, humanity is anxious to live, and longs for something new, without knowing exactly what, and is working to secure it.

Michael looks on himself with pity. What is he going to do? What can men like himself do for their fellow men?

He recalls the luncheon in the little house of Don Marcos. He is still offended by the attentions the Colonel shows him at table, cutting his meat, looking after him like a child, trying to make up for the absence of his arm. It is something disgraceful!

Farewell to Prince Lubimoff!... Even if he still wanted to continue his selfish existence, entirely given up to pleasure, it would be impossible for him. He is a cripple; he considers himself quite old. No one but Mado, who doesn't really know what she wants, would ever notice him.

Besides, he feels poor. For the first time he recalls with a certain satisfaction the heritage left him by Alicia. It was not worth anything at that moment, but who knows but what some day...! He dreams that perhaps those Mexican mines may replace his lost fortune in Russia; and then...! He feels a strong desire to regain his wealth in order to do good; a longing which is something like remorse. He knows the inefficiency of individual effort in remedying human misery: a mere drop lost in the ocean, a grain of sand on the beach. But what difference does that make? He is satisfied in giving happiness to some fifty unfortunate beings, among the hundreds of millions who people the earth.

Then he thinks of his present situation. That very morning he determined on his mode of life. He will flee from the poor Colonel, because of Mado. Others may take it upon themselves to bring misfortune to Don Marcos, but not he! He will take up his residence in Nice, in a Russian *pension* run by an impoverished noblewoman. In the evenings they will talk of the days when she was rich, beautiful, and desired; of the dances at the Petersburg Court, in which they danced together so often. Lubimoff even has a suspicion that one of his duels was over this boarding-house keeper.

The remnants of his fortune will bring him a sufficient income to live in modest comfort. He will swell the number of wrecks retiring to the Riviera, to recall, under the palm trees, their forgotten triumphs. His old valet will accompany him in his dethronement.

He already has an occupation to fill his hours. He wants to be a contemplator of life. He is glad to have been born in the most interesting of periods.

Something is going to happen; something new in history.

The smoke has not yet cleared away from the battlefields. It is a mist in which people lose their way and which does not allow them to see the complete outline of things. The very actors in the recent drama are blind. Years will pass, before the mist rises and vanishes, leaving the new world visible.

Will it be the same stage setting as of yore, merely with a few lines changed? Will all these bloody efforts to suppress violence, selfishness, and pre-historic ferocity as the chief bases of society, turn out to have been in vain?

The Prince thinks bitterly of the possible disillusionment. How terrible to see primitive bestiality rise again unharmed after a cataclysm which has been accepted as a regeneration! How terrible to contemplate the failure of so many generous spirits, of so many noble minds, aspiring toward the triumph of good, anxious for peace among men, and the sweet association of people, working against war as medical societies labor to exterminate diseases!

Faith in the future suddenly animates him. The world cannot always be the same; great convulsions, when they have passed, never leave the soil the same as they found it. Will children always be annihilating each other just because their fathers and grandfathers did so? Must they look on each other with hostility because they were born on different sides of a mountain, a river, or a wood, which politics calls a frontier?

We all have two native lands! The place where we were born, and the State to which we belong. Why not generously broaden this conception to include a third country? Will not a blessed time come in which men will talk as fellow being to fellow being, without thinking whether or not History commands them to hate and kill each other? With deep love for one's land of birth, cannot they be at the same time citizens of the world?

The Prince is leaning on the balustrade, above the terraces and the harbor. His pensive walk has brought him thither, without his realizing it.

He turns his back on the sea and on the crowd which, after the concert, is beginning to thin out there below. The American musicians are passing close to him, followed by a swarm of small boys accompanying their retirement.

He looks at a gap on the horizon, between the Alps and the promontory of Monaco, where the sun has just gone down. Above the reddish expanse a star is shining with the brilliancy and luminous facets of a precious stone.

Lubimoff is thinking of the ancient fathers of poetry who sang about it three thousand years ago. Homer called it *Kalistos*. Sometimes the morning star and at other times the evening star, Lucifer, Vesperus, or the "Shepherds' Star," it finally received the name of Venus, because of its shining whiteness, like that of a diamond on a woman's breast.

The Prince feels the sweet caress in his eyes as he gazes on the soft glow of the planet. Its name symbolizes beauty and love. He imagines the people who inhabit that celestial point of light lost in space. They must be of a purer essence than ours, entirely free from a past of primitive animality—ethereal beings, like the angels of all religions.

Then he smiles bitterly.

There is another star shining in the sky, more beautiful and larger than that one. It is blue instead of white, a soft blue: the color of poetry and dreams. It sparkles, in the dark depths of space, with the mysterious glow of the enormous bluish diamonds which Oriental monarchs place in their tiaras. Those who contemplate it feel in their eyes the velvety dew of divine mystery. Perhaps the poets of other worlds sing of it as a chosen refuge and a place of eternal beauty, where only the souls of the pure and the elect may go to rest. Perhaps it has given rise to religions and is the object of cults, having its altars, as the sun had in former times.

And this blue diamond of space, this world of soft light, which the populations of other planets contemplate as a poetic star, and as one in which all creatures lead a purely spiritual life, is the Earth, our poor globe, where twelve millions of men have just died on the battlefield, where as many more millions died of the emotion and plagues, which are the consequence of war; and where six hundred thousand millions of francs have been consumed in smoke, fire, and bursting steel.

Lubimoff remembers his impressions, a few hours before, standing beside a tomb which was beginning to be changed at the first halting words of Spring. The Infinite does not know us, nor does the very earth which maintains us know us either.

We are alone in the infinite, without other support than that of our own lives, our own illusions, and our own hopes. Man can rely only on man.

And he repeats what he had said of the earth that morning.

The sky knows nothing of our sorrows.

He slowly turns toward the square.

From all the cafés, restaurants, and hotels, comes the musical rise and fall of the cadenced violins. Behind the great windows, reddened by an inner light, he see couples passing intertwined, following the rhythm of the music. They are dancing, dancing, dancing.

Youth does nothing else. Dancing is a sort of sacred rite, prohibited during the war; and people are all devoting themselves in dancing now, with the fervor of zealots finally celebrating the triumphs of their persecuted religion.

The Prince recalls his recent passage through Paris. He had never seen the women better dressed, with so manifest a hunger for pleasure and luxury. The tango of the violins on the Boulevard is answered like an echo by the tango of the violins all along the Riviera, and at the summer resorts which are beginning to open. Woman's dearest wish, at the moment, is to dance the latest dance with a fighter from the United States!

The nightmare of war has vanished; everything has been forgotten. For many people nothing remains to recall the conflict save the uniforms, more numerous than formerly in the *thés dansants*.

Michael confines his meditation to this coast, which was always the domain of the blessed! For four long years war has turned Monaco upside down and filled it with darkness.

His imagination runs up and down the gulfs and promontories. There is a cemetery on each. In Mentone thousands and thousands of negroes lie under the earth. The combatants from Africa, whose fathers knew only the lance and the breech-clout, have chanced to perish like gladiators on this shore of European millionaires. In Cap-Martin the English have left their dead; in Monaco, there are some of every nationality; in Cap-Ferrat, the Belgians sleep, under wreaths already old; in Nice, are the bodies of the Americans; and everywhere, from Esterel to the Italian frontier, there are Frenchmen, Frenchmen, Frenchmen.

The dead are innumerable. Were they all to rise together, those who come to prolong their lives under the palm tree and the olive on the shores of the Violet Sea, would flee aghast.

But the aim of life is to live. Life is an endless Springtime, and covers everything it touches with the eager moss of pleasure, with the swiftly creeping ivy of dreams.

The cemeteries, strikingly white, seem to take on a duller tone, and are lost in the smiling landscape, like an unessential note in a song. The softness of the skies and the surrounding country changes them to gardens. A body occupies so little space and the earth is so large!... The hotels which were hospitals, are regilding their signs, disinfecting their rooms and sending advertisements to the great newspapers of the world. Already people may come and dream between the walls which just now shook with cries of pain, or the rattle of death agonies. Music is beginning sweetly to moan along the happy coast, amid the murmur of the waves and the rustling of the orange trees, of epithalamial perfume. The old shepherd of the Alps, who, after sixty years, has not yet recovered from his amazement at the Monte Carlo which has arisen there below on the once deserted tableland, will see it grow with new palaces and new towers, further expanding its opulence like a city of dreams.

The passage of death has made love of life more keen. Every one, seeing the black banner of the Adversary vanish in the darkness, finds new zest in pleasure.

Lubimoff stops in the middle of the square. It is beginning to grow dark. With one ear he hears the musical swing of a dance invented by the negroes of North America for the enjoyment of the whites; and with the other he hears other negro music, the South American tango. In the adjoining streets new orchestras are playing wherever there is a public place, café, hotel, or restaurant—with a sign in English at the door, to attract the heroes of the hour: *Dancing*.

He gazes at the mountain which forms a background for the square and watches over the graves on its slopes. Then he looks on high....

The earth and the sky know nothing of our sorrows.

And neither does life.

THE END